FINDING EVER AFTER SERIES | BOOK TWO

THESE GRIMM FATES

K E BARDEN

Cover Design by Etheric Tales

Chapter Artwork by EthericTales

Map designed by AdrianoBezerra

Typography and Formatting by Turtle Publishing

Paperback ISBN 978-1-7635308-4-3

Hardcover ISBN 978-1-7635308-5-0

eBook ISBN 978-1-7635308-3-6

Distributed by K E Barden and Lightningsource Global

OTHER BOOKS BY K E BARDEN

The Gilded Mirror

To Bobby,

For believing I could reach the stars.

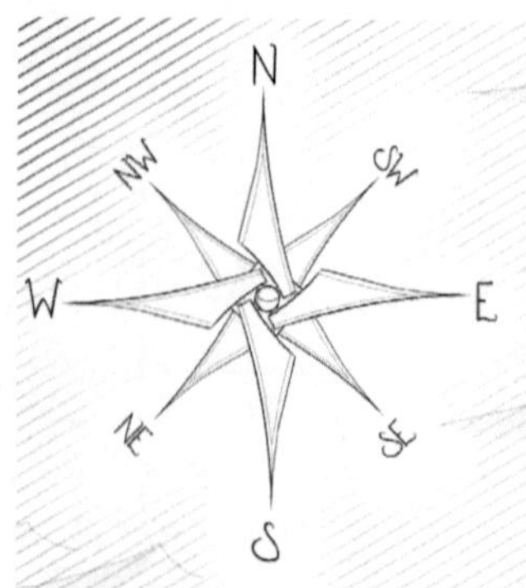

N
NW
NE
W
E
SW
SE
S

Beast Cove
CRULLFELD
ASHENFELL
Lake Moss
The Luna Lighthouse
The Tower and the Maze
Candor
XERSAILLES
ARDENBEAX
Mountains Le Bleu
The Lantern Lighthouse
Annice
Lake La Belle
Waters Keep
The Channel
WHITE BRIDGE
THE BLACK COVE
THE ISLAND OF MYORCAI
THE EVER AFTER
THE REALM

Isles
The Northern Lighthouse
8
AURELIA
The Realm of Dragons and Giants
The Coral Coast
ING'S KEEP
Butterpond
Blarney Forest
Hasleholme
Maelstrom
The Briar Rose
The Marshes
Mines of Parador
Ellendale
CARNELL
THE MOUNTAINS OF EYRIE
Peaks of Carfell
Eastborne
ADOW FOREST
Arrow's Den
Ivywood
The Crystal Lake
Bell's Peak
THE DARK FOREST
THE SILVER CITY
PERRIDORM
Roserock
Witches Hut
Dove Port
The Elysian Fields
The Skinny Piglet
BELLATORRE
Forest
LDRYN
Wolf's Den
The Queen's Mines
TEAL COVE
ATLAS
NYSA
THE ISLE OF NYSA
Lighthouse Luvon

*Once long ago, the kingdom of Aurelia glittered
in gold and thrived in trade, its very heart a
beating, living thing. Each year, to celebrate
their good fortune, the king would throw a grand
celebration, full of lights, feasts, and dancing.*

*The kingdom flourished, and with it,
its people flourished, too.*

Prologue

Princess Snowfall sat on her window ledge, staring into the sprawling gardens below, her fingers fiddling with a hem that had come loose from her blue dress. From here, she could see the top of the hedge maze, the way the gardeners looked like scattered shards of glass, sunlight glinting off their pruners as they cut back the blooms of yellow roses lining the path. Keeping it neat, controlled.

Snow pitied the flowers. They were meant to spread and grow, their roots digging deep and their stems rising tall. She scowled as the gardeners stripped back any inch of freedom they might have gained throughout the cooler weather.

Snow was like those flowers, she realised. Pretty, but wild; snipped and pruned to the size of a mere sapling by Myrenna at every chance. She was a princess, but she was also the Queen's pet. The thought made her twitch. She'd been lucky today: her stepmother was ensconced for most of the morning in front of her ghastly mirror again. It meant Snow could take advantage of her meagre freedom.

She leaned close to the window, her fingers grazing the glass, when Hansel stepped onto the path. A smile curved her lips as she took in his crisp black and mauve uniform, her heart fluttering at the sight.

Snow grabbed her shawl from her favourite button back chair and wrapped it around her shoulders before sneaking a glance in the mirror. Blue eyes stared back at her, brighter than usual with her excitement. She straightened her dark hair, tucking away the unruly strands between her fingers before lightly pinching her cheeks to bring forth a lovely rosy pink to match her porcelain skin.

She glanced towards the clock by the door and hurried towards the portrait of her parents hanging beside her wardrobe, the painting dripping with colour. Unlike the removal of the rest of the portraits in the castle, Snow had managed to keep this one safe. It was a minor act of rebellion, but one she treasured all the same.

With a wink to her dark-haired mother, Snow grabbed a fairy lantern and knocked on the glass case to wake the creature. It gnashed its teeth but glowed in compliance.

Ignoring the creature, Snow blew away the strands of hair tickling her nose and reached for the worn latch built into the portrait's frame where cold air greeted her. Cobwebs glinted under the fairylight as she orientated herself, letting her eyes adjust to the darkness.

Over the years, the secret tunnels had become somewhat of a home, a subtle fight against her imprisonment within the castle. Her fingers grazed a corner as she passed the frail chalk mark of a bird, each symbol a secret code to navigating the labyrinth within the walls.

Snow veered left and hurried down the stairs to the east wing. Her feet were light as she skipped down the next passage, her stomach grumbling in response. She'd made a point to skip breakfast to avoid Myrenna.

She pressed her ear against the stone wall before it popped open with a hiss behind a tapestry of the cold Queen looking every inch the regal monarch.

'Late as always,' Hansel said in greeting.

Snow whirled, her insides warming at the sight of his smile. His eyes crinkled and his hair was a mess, not yet breaking his habit of running his hands through it.

Her cheeks heated as he approached. 'You only just crossed the gardens. I'm right on time.'

Part of Hansel's charm lay in his inability to see his own good looks.

When Hansel had first come to the castle, he'd been lanky and unsure, his hair bigger than his head. Now his shoulders were broad, his height almost that of a troll. His jaw was defined, his eyes warm. It was strange how much the years affected a person without realising. At least his dimple remained, his cheeky grin unchanged. Snow had always admired how he could do that. How despite his past, he'd always tried with her, always smiled when others had not.

Snow grabbed his hand and tugged him towards the library. They both giggled like children, slipping past the watchful eyes of the castle staff as they entered the paper-filled room and weaved through the stacks. The second level was rarely visited, the books old and neglected. Snow loved the musty smell and the way the dust danced as they passed.

'I should have known you'd skip training for books,' Hansel teased.

Snow rolled her eyes. 'Not everything requires a sword, you know.'

She slowed as they reached a bookcase near the back, the weight of Hansel's gaze heavy. Biting her bottom lip, she turned to find him assessing the blue gown she wore. She'd picked it specifically to bring out the blue in her eyes. Plus, the lower cut didn't hurt, even if Hansel wasn't one to gawk at a woman showing a little skin.

'Would you do the honours?' Snow asked.

Hansel bowed. 'Anything for you, Princess.'

Though he jested, she couldn't help the flush of heat on her neck. With ease, Hansel pulled back the bookcase, a half-moon carved into the wooden floor from years of use.

Behind it was one of their usual hiding spots when the Queen was busy. The other was the castle gardens where Hansel and Malak taught Snow basics in training. Personally, she preferred the library.

Snow had come across this secret place when she'd discovered the tunnels running throughout the castle, craving any semblance of control while locked away. Fear was a powerful tool, and it was one the Queen utilised frequently. Staff were never to speak to Snow, let alone acknowledge or help her.

Whilst she had some freedom, she was still required to heed the Queen's call. It had become more frequent the older she grew, but it was a dance she knew like her own heartbeat. Each week, Myrenna would haul her in front of the mirror and wait for it to speak. Snow hated the mirror's voice, the way it clawed under her skin in that heavy, ancient tone.

But the answer was always the same: *Not yet.*

And just as it had been the day before, Snow would be left alone.

Her life had been spent within the castle walls.

'*For safety,*' the Queen would hiss.

She'd tried once, though. To leave. She'd taken a steed one afternoon out of desperation and made her way through the miles of gardens, only to hit an invisible wall on the border near the gates. When the Queen had found out, she'd been furious, locking Snow in the dungeon for three days as punishment. Dinners from that moment on had been stiff, Myrenna the ever-watchful eye as Snow attended her classes, her readings, her riding lessons, her music. The Queen owned Snow in all the little moments and the large ones.

'The realm is a wicked and vicious place,' Myrenna would coo. 'Nothing a princess should have to endure.'

Over the years, Snow had managed to piece together that the border spell imprisoned her when others could come and go as they pleased. Not that it mattered, anyway, when Myrenna could find her anywhere. Kill her if she wished. She had her murders of crows and other beastly animals scouting the land for any misdeeds or whispers of treason.

'You know, Princess,' Hansel said, his voice luring her out of her thoughts. 'These are my favourite moments.'

Snow watched the way his finger marked the book's page, noting it was one she'd recommended. She hugged a pillow nearby, snuggling her chin into the soft velvet. 'Too bad they're few and far between.'

Hansel sighed. 'I wish we could do it more.'

'Me too,' she replied. 'Maybe one day we could be like the heroes in the old stories. Travel across the grassy plains on horseback, perhaps save a princess from a dragon.'

Hansel's eyes darkened. 'Why rescue another princess when *you* still need to be rescued?'

Snow laughed. 'Bold statement when there's ears everywhere in this castle. Plus,' she added, 'there's no dragon here.'

He swallowed. 'No, but you're still a prisoner.'

She frowned. 'As are you.'

Hansel ran his fingers through his hair before he took a deep breath. 'I have something I need to tell you about the Queen.'

Snow dismissed his grim expression. He had a penchant to expect the worst sometimes, the trained soldier in him outweighing the young huntsman from the forest. She was about to reply when an enticing smell wafted through the air. It was cinnamon, sugar, and butter. Three of her favourite things.

'Snow,' he insisted, 'the Queen—'

Snow waved away his concerns. 'Will continue being the Queen.'

Hansel reached for her as she wandered towards the hall, sniffing the air as if in a trance. 'Wait.'

His hands were rough against hers. His touch was electrifying, gentle despite the blood they'd been coated in. She almost winced when he pulled her towards him.

Hansel grabbed a book and tore out a back page. He checked his pockets, panicking when they came up empty.

Snow laughed and delved into the satin pockets of her dress to pull out a smooth, silver pen. It had once been her mother's, elegant just as she had been.

'You're right about the ears being everywhere,' Hansel murmured. 'Best to be cautious.'

The Silver City's bells chimed across the stone walls, the clear sound echoing in the empty halls. She didn't care about the Queen's ears, especially not now. 'You have to go, don't you?' she asked.

He always had to leave. Always had to go for his *duty*. It made Snow want to scream, to bash against the castle walls, the time with him always too short, too fleeting.

Hansel was grim as he handed her the slip of paper and grasped her hand. 'Snow, you must be careful.'

The bells chimed again, and she shoved the paper into her pocket as they hurried out of the library. The scent of baking filled the castle, every hall and crevice like something from a dream. She swore she could taste the sugar on her tongue as she licked her lips, her mouth watering.

Snow ducked around a corner when the captain of the guard approached, his eyes honed on Hansel. 'Duty calls.'

'Yes, Sir.'

Snow ground her teeth at the sounds of their fading footsteps. She hit her fist against the statue beside her, the Queen draped in finery. Though made of stone, she was still beautiful. It was a painful reminder of the power she held.

Two staff rounded the corner and Snow ducked behind the statue, pressing herself against the cold stone of the Queen's dress.

'Ten years she hasn't used the kitchens, not since the King's death, and yet she waltzes right in and hijacks my kitchen as if she owns it.'

The other woman murmured, 'You shouldn't say such things. Technically she does own it.'

'I just mean—'

'It doesn't matter what you mean. Shut your mouth and keep moving.'

Snow frowned as they turned the corner. The possibility of the Queen in an apron was abhorrent. Snow stared at the Queen's statue, trying to envision it. But if the stories were true …

Without a second thought, Snow rushed to the nearest passage entrance, hidden behind a tapestry. But instead of turning left towards her rooms, she took the opposite staircase that led down to the kitchens.

Snow came to the grate in the wall near the stove. She held her breath as she peered through the gap, stilling at the sight of the Queen. Flour covered Myrenna from head to toe as she lifted out a freshly baked apple pie. The crust was golden, and steam coiled from the crafted edges.

Myrenna's dark hair was loose around her shoulders, wavy and shined to perfection. Despite the lack of makeup, she was still a beauty, her lips full, her cheekbones sharp. She was a sight in her royal finery, but here she looked younger somehow. Relaxed.

Despite the unsettling sight, Snow leaned in closer as the Queen untied her apron and hung it upon the wall.

Nobody baked an apple pie like her stepmother.

Myrenna had been a baker once, had won the heart of her father in their annual Yulemas baking competition. The king had taken one taste and fallen in love with her. At the time the people had called it romantic, a love story for the ages.

But that was before anyone knew about her magic. Nobody had even suspected.

When Myrenna had seen the castle for the first time, her eyes had been lit with awe. She had spent her time either by the King's side or playing with Snow. Snow had been ecstatic. Her father hadn't smiled since her mother had died. His happiness and his laugh had been like staring at the sun after living underground.

And then he'd become ill.

Myrenna had refused a healer, never leaving his side as she made pots of tea, creating cures of her own. Snow remembered coaxing him to drink, then swallow, then sleep. Myrenna would coo, tell them both she knew best, and yet he'd only deteriorated from there.

They'd mourned when he'd died. The Queen wore the finest black silks. But not two days after his death, she'd brought in that hideous mirror and hung it above the throne. She'd then torn down all the portraits of Snow's mother, burning any paintings of the previous rulers of Bellatorre.

That's when Myrenna no longer pretended to smile.

No longer played with Snow.

No longer baked.

Myrenna brought in new laws. Ones where treason meant long, painful, and public deaths. Ones where creatures were whipped, sold, or banished. Those that resembled humans hid for a while, like the witches and changelings with minor marks. But when poverty struck, people were cut from jobs, from homes, from society … they were left to either die, flee, or work in the hideous mines the Queen had built.

And amongst it all, Myrenna's magic continued to thrive.

As the years passed, Snow grew into herself, and one autumn afternoon, she was called upon for the first time. So it began, their tradition of a queen and a princess together looking into the mirror's depths. It was in those moments that Snow truly knew fear. The way it pressed on her chest and stifled her breath. The way she curled into herself and wished for it to be over.

Myrenna hummed as she left the pie to cool, her voice drifting down the hall. Heat rose off the golden pastry. Snow salivated.

She knew it was sorcery that had stolen her father's heart. Knew the Queen had craved his kingdom, but the question had always been: why? Why Bellatorre, when there were several other kingdoms in the realm? Why not Perridorm, or Carnell?

In a trance, Snow opened the door and stepped into the heated kitchen. The scent was overwhelming. She pressed a hand to her stomach, the hunger a desire that wouldn't let go. Somewhere in the back of Snow's mind a warning called, a voice screaming that something was wrong.

But she had never craved anything more in her entire life.

She dipped the fork into the pastry and brought it to her lips, its warm filling melting on her eager tongue. It tasted like autumn and home and spicy, sweet apple.

She moaned as it consumed her.

Tingles spread over her skin, and she blinked heavily. Dimly recalling Hansel's caution, Snow groped for the note in her pocket. Her fingers went numb as she tore it open.

The words blurred together, the warning clear but far too late.

She is coming for you.

Snow fell into darkness.

I

The Masked Villain

Eve's stomach grumbled audibly. She hoped it wasn't as loud as it felt. She was crouched behind a log in the forest, knife poised. Her eyes flicked to the brush on the other side of the glen as a small, twitching nose peeked through the leaves, followed by a furry, white body. Eve smiled, already basking in the victory at having beaten Hansel in his bet on who would capture dinner first. One rabbit wouldn't feed their whole group, but it was a start.

They were an odd group: a sneezing prince, a violent princess, a wise troll, a sassy fairy, a smartarse elf, and a hopeful huntsman. Not to mention whatever in the cauldron she was.

In all honesty, the last few days had been a blur. A mixture of sharpening knives, bickering, and negotiating what to do next.

But Eve knew what to do. She'd had priorities long before the huntsman had sent her world into a spiral. She was a girl cursed, forged into steel by revenge and death. The sisters Grimm were still out there, still haunting her dreams despite the detour she'd taken.

Eve's skin tingled. A shadow crested the earth. She turned. In a flash, her knife hit the tree, a hair's breadth from Hansel's ear.

Hansel raised his hands in surrender.

Eve scowled as the rabbit scrambled from its home, its ears flat. Flipping her other knife, Eve struck the blade straight between its beady eyes.

Hansel raised his brow. 'Impressive.'

Eve wiped her hands on her pants. 'I hate doing that.'

'Hate what?' Hansel asked, picking up the carcass. 'Hunting food for us to eat?'

'No.' Eve waved her arm towards it. 'Killing an animal that … *fluffy.*'

Hansel chuckled. 'Since when are you inclined towards small, fluffy animals?'

'Since the huntsman isn't hunting and I prefer to buy my meals in local towns.'

He smirked. 'Who said I wasn't hunting?'

Eve grimaced as he pulled open his satchel, revealing three rabbits. She almost wanted to punch him, but said instead, 'You set me up.'

He was playfully stricken, placing a hand on his heart as if she'd stabbed him. 'I would never dream of doing such a thing.'

Eve snorted, though it was half-hearted.

It had been easy between them in a way that only came with knowing someone over time. She'd learnt to listen for his even breathing at night; to smile when he made a joke, usually at her expense. She loved the way he encouraged others, how, no matter what, his faith in her never wavered, even when she didn't feel it herself.

But despite the newfound comfort, her feelings were unruly, ugly things. Self-doubt was a constant companion on her shoulder when it came to her grief, her guilt, and her relationships. Everyone she'd ever cared for was gone, cursed by whatever plagued her. Porchid had been the only stable companion in years, the fairy wearing her down over time. Eve had never trusted easily, never veered from her path. She was built for one thing and one thing only. To get her revenge on the Grimms.

She stared at Hansel now, wondering when everything had grown so complicated.

They hadn't touched since that fateful night under the stars, but the memory still tingled on her lips. Something about it – about *him* – had dug into her core, burrowing deep enough to scrape her bones.

For so long Eve had kept her walls, nobody but Porchid ever breaching them. Somehow, between Roserock and now, Hansel had snuck through her defences.

That was no small feat.

Eve's hands twitched at her sides as the urge to touch her lips took over. She curled them into fists. She couldn't be sure if it had been the same for him that night, but either way, it terrified her. She couldn't afford to let someone in, not when she still had so much to do. Not when it risked her life and anybody near her.

Braving the sisters Grimm? No problem. Facing the Evil Queen? Piece of pie. But trusting? Loving? She shook her head. Relying on somebody required faith, balance, vulnerability. All the things she liked to keep safely tucked away.

'I'll do the messy part, then,' Hansel offered, and Eve didn't argue.

On the walk back, he kept things light. He laughed about Pip complaining about the lack of tobacco; Malak's pining eyes for the princess; and how Snow was faring after waking.

Eve scowled at the mention of the Princess.

Princess Snow.

Fairest in the land.

And yet, a complete pain in Eve's backside.

It had been a miracle what Malak had done. He'd managed not only to survive the horrific attack but also break the Princess's curse.

The troll, the huntsman and the princess clearly had history. Even though Eve knew she couldn't fault any of them for it, she still felt the bite of envy as she watched Hansel and Snow together.

Snow was possessive. She gripped Hansel's arm in every conversation, laughed a little too loudly, emphasized her jokes to the point of being dreary, all while side-eyeing Eve like she was leftover vomit.

Eve had been stiff with the Princess since their violent introduction, possibly even rude. Eve was aware she was being petty, letting jealousy control her instead of being a grown up, but it was the eyes. The Princess's eyes might have been crystal blue but there was something hidden in them. Something malicious.

What pissed off Eve more was how Snow took the insults with grace and smiled that wide smile of hers, pearly white and almost … *unhinged.*

Eve cracked a knuckle to fend off her erratic thoughts.

'You're doing that thing again,' Hansel said, slowing his pace.

'What thing?'

'The thing where you retreat into yourself and nobody knows where you're at,' he replied. 'Is everything okay?'

Yes.

No.

'I'm fine,' she replied. 'What were you saying about Pip?'

He took the hint and shrugged, continuing his account of Pip's failed combat lesson. She knew she should listen, pay more attention. Considering she had minimal time alone with him these days, she wanted to make the most of it, but when her thoughts took over it was as if she wasn't there at all. Instead, she was a ghost standing on the sidelines, merely watching the scene as it moved forward in muted sounds.

Her father had once told her, *Jealousy is not your friend. Do not let it make a home inside your heart.*

But the words were easy to say and harder to fulfil. She shook off the memory and focused on Hansel. The world spun into colour as he smiled at her, arms moving with vitality at the funny story he was telling. Her lips tilted into a smile at the voices he put on to mimic the others.

It had only been a few days, but already the grotto felt small. She loved these moments, when it was Hansel and her, outside of them all and away from the troubles looming over them. When they were alone, it was simple. Free.

But her gift had been flaring, nibbling at her to leave. She could feel the pull of something bigger, tugging her back, deeper into the realm and its whispers. In her heart she knew this arrangement would end. Even though it was as new as a freshly planted seed, it didn't mean she couldn't mourn it. What could have been. That's what wishes and dreams were for, after all.

Hansel kept in step beside her. He smelt of oak and wood and smoke. She wanted to reach out, to touch him. But that nibbling feeling kept intruding, causing her to crawl back deep within herself. Block it out. She welcomed that comfort, the feeling of those petals folding in around her in that sheltered familiar wall.

The others had begun to fret about the dwarves; two of them, to be precise. Bonyx and Beetle had been taken by the Queen. But the others were still gone, too. The last they'd heard was that Bjorn, Bryn, and Rabbit had gone to their cousins in Carfell. Brufell and Bronson were travelling north.

Hansel dropped the rabbit on the ground and pulled out his knife to skin it. Snow spoke with Malak, who listened in his intense and silent way. It was an odd sight, a princess and a troll. Eve didn't quite know who to feel sorry for: Malak and his unrequited love, or her own tale of *what if* with Hansel.

Eve sat beside Hansel on the carved wooden log by the campfire. Florian was nearby, too, staring into the fire. They'd cleaned up the grotto, picking up the dust and debris to make the place as normal as possible again. Eve could have sworn the dust remained in her pores. The corpses of the grotto's fairies cracking in her ears each time she remembered holding their brittle forms.

Porchid had hidden in the cavern during it all and Eve couldn't fault her for it. They'd been her kin, and the grotto a potential home that had been ripped from her with sharp claws.

Eve blinked back the sting of tears as she reached for one of the rabbits, meeting Pip's glare as he lit his pipe. He raised his brow as she lifted her knife, a threat behind it.

Pip snorted but didn't speak.

The crafty elf knew her heart was fractured. It had been damaged the day her father disappeared. When Dante had fallen to sickness. When she'd found Porchid by the creek with broken wings.

Eve was the poster child for heartbreak. She'd survived the shattered pieces of her heart for years in the cottage, the circus, the realm, and the grotto. She wasn't the only one grieving, but it didn't mean it hurt any less.

'So, are we just going to sit around moping, or is this the part where someone takes charge?' Pip asked. He raised his eyebrow in challenge at the blank stares and scowls he received.

Eve smirked at the elf's lack of tact, her knife carving into the rabbit's hide. His question was valid though. The Queen still sat on the throne, still hunted for the Princess, and Eve, too. Especially after confronting them in the forest before they made it to Maelstrom.

Eve supposed Malak wouldn't leave the Princess's side, considering his oath. And Prince Florian couldn't return home, as he had nowhere else to go. Pip was following along out of pure boredom, and Hansel, well … Hansel wanted to save the world.

'You're still inside that head of yours,' Hansel said from her left, diverting her attention from whatever Malak's response to Pip was. 'You get this pinched line between your brows. It's kind of cute. In a grumpy way.'

'I do not,' she said, snapping a bone.

'You have it right now.'

Her nostrils flared. 'I just—'

Eve stopped herself before she said something reckless. Like how she was scared. How she was angry. How, no matter what she did, death always seemed to follow her.

Hansel leaned in closer, his smell intoxicating. 'You just what?'

'I don't want to talk about it.'

Cold air hit her skin as he leaned back, a frown peppering his brow. 'Why not? I thought we were past this.'

'Leave her to her secrets,' Snow said, that infuriating smile on her face. 'Let her sulk. It's all she ever does, anyway.'

'I don't sulk,' Eve snapped.

Snow shrugged. 'Forgive me, it's hard to tell with your constant grimace.'

Eve's hand hardened around the hilt of her knife, her knuckles going white.

Hansel spoke. 'It's been hard on all of us. We're all tired and lost and a little irritable.'

The words were meant to soothe, to deflect, but when Hansel went to lay his hand on Eve's shoulder, she snarled.

Pip coughed loudly, changing the subject. 'You can ignore my correct logic all you like, but the fact remains that we can't keep sitting around here like witless prey.' He paused. 'Or am I the only one concerned about the mass murder that we had to clean up?'

Hansel tensed.

'Truly poetic, Pip,' Eve drawled.

The elf went to speak when Snow stood with a sweep of her skirts. 'Why *are* we still here? It's been days. We've grieved. It's now time to move on.'

'Where exactly do you propose we go, Princess?' Eve responded. 'You don't exactly have a kingdom to return to.'

'At least I have a home,' she retorted. 'It's just been appropriated by a witch.'

Eve went rigid and stared at the Princess with cool eyes. 'Mine was also taken by witches and look where that got me.' She shifted, and a trace of her scars showed briefly beneath her shirt before she tugged her sleeve down.

'Eveline,' Malak warned. His eyes pierced hers with disapproval.

'I have people who are counting on me,' Snow said regally. 'A kingdom full of them. Something a ruffian like you would know nothing about.'

Eve bit her tongue to the point of tasting blood. They were on edge, everyone's emotions heightened. She took a deep breath. 'I suppose I wouldn't. I know nothing about crowns and kingdoms. I simply know how to survive.'

Hansel watched them both, his muscles taut. Eve held her knife firm. Snow pouted but thankfully retracted whatever argument she was about to ignite.

'I say we go to this rebellion,' Snow said to the elf. 'The one Hansel was talking about. Rally an army and take back my home.'

'It's not as easy as that,' Hansel said. 'Your army is small. Mostly farmers, welders, men of trade with women and children.'

Malak grasped Snow's hand. 'Compared to the Queen's combined forces from Carnell, her creatures, and the Queen's Guard, we have little chance.'

'Don't forget about her magic,' Eve said pointedly. 'Myrenna's powerful alone too.'

'Eve is right,' Hansel said. 'We need something bigger than what we have. Magic, or actual soldiers.'

Pip took a drag of his pipe. 'Small or not, I say meeting with the resistance is a good start, even if it is only common people. They would never hurt the Princess, and she can help it flourish from within. Maybe inspire some new recruits?'

Prince Florian, who had been quiet up until this point, said, 'Why don't you reach out to other kingdoms? Try and sway them to you just as the Queen did with Carnell?'

Eve smirked as Porchid purposefully threw dust, causing Florian to sneeze.

'Excuse me,' he sputtered.

Porchid glowed pink as she giggled.

'How do we know they aren't already working with Myrenna?' Malak argued.

Florian rubbed his nose, brightening it more. His blond hair had a dark hue to it from the ash, making him look older. 'Because she's invading the borders of Perridorm. It was common gossip when I was still in Maelstrom. I overheard my brother bragging about it. Saying that the royalty there was weak but denied Myrenna's request anyway.'

'Stupid,' said Pip.

'But brave,' Hansel replied.

'It's possible to be both,' Pip huffed.

'I think finding people who want to keep the Princess safe is a priority,' said Malak. 'She's who the Queen wants most.'

The Princess took Malak's hand in solidarity and gave him a demure smile.

Eve tried not to gag.

Hansel turned the skinned rabbit over the fire, roasting it slowly for dinner. 'The first place we'll need to visit, then, is the Skinny Piglet near Roserock.'

Snow frowned. 'Is that where the resistance is hiding?'

Eve scoffed. 'More like where stolen goods are hidden.'

'No, Princess,' replied Hansel, ignoring Eve's jibe. 'But the owner there knows where to find them.'

Pip raised his brow. 'So, you don't actually know where the rebellion is?'

Hansel's cheeks went pink. 'Well, no. They don't just let the Queen's soldiers in.' He ran a hand through his hair. 'There are enough rumours in the kingdom for me to follow a light trail. I'd managed to uncover the code before the Queen sent me to find Snow. I couldn't trust anyone else with the code or information, but I did manage to find out the owner of the Skinny Piglet – Marcellus – has ties.'

'Interesting,' Pip mused.

The conversation continued from there, but the words were lost to Eve as Hansel leaned closer. 'You've been awfully quiet for someone with strong opinions. I know it's not ideal, but what do you think?'

She met his golden-brown eyes, her skin tingling again with the remnants of his kiss.

Silly, stupid girl.

'Does it matter what I think?' she asked quietly.

His eyes shone. 'Of course it does. We could save a lot of people. Bring back the kingdom. Win this war.'

'I don't know, Hansel,' she started. 'I think there's a lot of room for people to die. Your so-called resistance is not what I'd call a terrifying force.'

'It's not now, but it could be.' The tone in his voice was whimsical, a hint of hope lacing the words.

Eve took a deep breath. She hated to be the one to crush his spirits, hated being the one to remind him that reality was not the same as an ideal or dream. Every facet needed to be considered, and a small army of common folk was not going to win wars anytime soon.

Hansel assessed her.

She turned towards him, her rabbit forgotten on the ground. 'Not everybody can be saved, Hansel. Think of the blood that will be spilled. Not just human, but all creatures.'

Hansel swallowed, his eyes stubbornly shining despite her scepticism. 'Everyone in the Realm is in danger, Eve.

Creatures are dying every day – have you not seen what's happening in the mines?'

She considered her words before continuing. 'I have. But you have this … this hero complex, and you think that everybody can be saved. You have this great big heart and even though only eighteen inches separates the heart and head, I wonder if you can't divide the two.'

His eyes bored into her as the words sunk in, the gold dimming. She had done that – hurt him – and she hated herself for it. But the realm was hard. She knew that firsthand.

'I think we can win,' he said, his tone hard. 'I think everybody deserves a second chance. A chance at hope.'

Hope was a fickle thing left for dreamers.

'You're not thinking about the consequences,' she replied.

'I'm a grown man, Eveline. I've seen more heartbreak and horror than you know. Of course I've thought about the consequences. But what's the price of freedom? Or happiness? Have you considered that maybe you think about consequences too much? Not everything is about revenge, or one girl losing her father.'

The words pierced her heart, creating a sharp ache in her chest.

'There are other families,' he whispered, more fervently. 'Others who have lost *everything*. Their homes, their children, their lives, their freedom. The list goes on. It's bigger than you. Bigger than *us*.'

'I lost everything, too, Hansel. Don't forget that.'

Eve was nauseous, she was treading into unknown territory. She watched his throat bob. The silence was as encompassing as the mist they'd seen at the Briar Rose.

Hansel ran his hand through his hair and swore under his breath. 'I know you did, and I'm sorry for your loss. If I could take it for you, I would. But who are you to judge which life stands above another?'

He leaned forward and laced his fingers together. Her anxiety grew as she watched them longingly, remembering what those hands felt like intertwined with hers. She swallowed and quickly averted her gaze.

'We are the only ones controlling our fate, Eve. Who are we to decide who fights and who doesn't? Don't they deserve a chance to hope for something better? A world far happier than the one we are dragging ourselves through now. We are not gods, nor are we the Fairy Godmother. How would you feel if somebody else decided your fate?'

Her gut curdled. Had Nona not mentioned that her own fate had already been decided? Had it not already been written in the stars that she was to be the saviour even though all she'd ever wanted was the one thing she couldn't find?

Her father.

He was most likely dead. Eaten and consumed by the sisters Grimm. There was no way he would have survived the forest with them. Anyone with half a brain would know his fate hadn't ended well. But it was more than that. Eve still craved some semblance of his life force, even if it lied in revenge. He'd sacrificed everything for her, his little girl, his princess.

Her father had always valued truth. Had valued inner strength and the ability to find something good, even when nobody else saw it. He'd held a spark of defiance. Of hope.

Sometimes she wondered if this was what her father had planned for her, or whether she had walked the path of revenge for so long she didn't know right from wrong. Was her own heart the masked villain?

Hansel had this unwavering belief in people. Despite his sister. Despite the witch's deceit. Despite the Queen.

Eve swallowed and blinked back her tears.

A small cough came from Pip sitting nearby.

Subtle.

Eve's voice came out smaller than intended. 'My fate has already been decided.' She headed for the forest, leaving the group stunned.

She didn't want to be with people. Didn't want to answer questions. She had so many already, and she was so tired.

For now, she wanted to be alone, and she wondered if she would ever want otherwise.

II

The Hunter and the Prey

Every time Hansel thought he knew Eve, he was reminded he didn't.

Eve's spirit was bright like a shooting star one moment, then quietened like the night sky the next. She was a smouldering fire in some ways and then she was as cool as dormant coals the next morning.

He'd come to learn her temper and her fears, the shy vulnerability she allowed only him to see sometimes. The kiss they'd shared had gripped his heart like no other had. He could still feel the warmth of her head nestled against his shoulder, letting him in. The way the silky strands of her hair tickled his skin and how her eyes had fluttered closed as she leaned into him.

Snow's head tilted in his direction, her assessing eyes asking him a question. *Is she worth it?*

Hansel avoided her gaze.

Eve had been cold since Snow's curse had broken, the tension smothering the air. He'd tried to diffuse the tension and brewing tempers as best he could, but even his patience had its limits. He wanted to be there for Eve, after all she'd been through. But she was not the only one that had suffered in this realm. What right did she have to decide the fate of the many for her own vengeance?

Thousands still dwelled in the Queen's mines, the country riddled with fear that their children would be taken. Used and abused. Broken and spat out by the Queen's ruthless rule before they'd even had a chance to live. Hundreds still starved as crops failed to grow, and even more lived in terror of retribution because they were simply different to humans.

He thought Eve understood their goal. Understood why the Princess was so crucial in all of this. Instead, he'd been met with resistance at every turn. With anybody else he would have moved on, forged forward. So why couldn't he do it with her?

Snow lifted her blue skirts and sat down next to him. 'I don't suppose you'll just let her go?'

He snorted and met her blue eyes. 'I don't suppose you'll ever stop having an opinion on my love life?'

She laughed. 'Only when you start to choose better. First Myrenna, and now *her*? Honestly, I'm surprised at you. I would have thought after everything, you'd want a calm girl. One who you could live a quiet life with.'

'It would be simpler,' he mused.

She dusted her skirt. 'But we don't do simple, do we?'

'No. We don't.' He closed his eyes, breathing in the air tinged with the scent of moss and flowers. Even with the stench of ash, there was life here still. Old magic that thrived against all odds. 'What would you do?'

She stayed silent for a moment before she spoke. 'I wouldn't let one girl – person – make me forget the bigger picture. You walk with enough burdens already, Hansel. There is much to be done for this realm, without the outbursts of someone with her own agenda. There's a rebellion to find and I know you want to save our kingdom. You've come so far – you came here to save me. And I'm with you. Can you say the same of her?'

Her words rang true, but his logic and emotions were muddy water when it came to Eve. He didn't know if it was his gut or heart that insisted Eve was important. Were his feelings clouding his judgment? Was she the key in this war, or simply the key to his heart?

Hansel clenched his fists. Despite Snow's misgivings, Eve did not get to run away because she was uncomfortable. She did not get to walk away because of self-doubt or pity. He was not her plaything; he'd been that before. This was bigger than them. This involved them all.

And that included her, whether she liked it or not.

Snow was wrong. Eve was not selfish. She was simply misguided.

Hansel threw the last rabbit to Pip, who jumped and blinked at him in confusion. 'Skin this. I'll be back.'

'I – what?'

Hansel didn't hear the rest of Pip's response as he huffed into the forest after Eve.

Snow seethed as Hansel sought out the Seeker.

She didn't understand why he seemed to care about the cold fish of a woman.

The Princess had hated her from the moment she'd stepped into that cavern. She was rude and abrasive, her scowl horrible and her demeanour worse. There was quite literally nothing to like about her.

Except her combat skills. A little voice inside her head said.

Snow loathed the admission. Sure, she was handy with her knives, but she was worse with her words, and it was clear to Snow that Eve had her own agenda, regardless of Hansel and his heart on his sleeve. In that way, she may as well be like Myrenna, for how keenly Hansel seemed to follow the Seeker, despite her not caring for his wants. Had he truly learned nothing from his bedding of the warped queen?

Snow scowled. She refused to let him fall into old, destructive patterns. She was his friend and sometimes friendship meant doing the hard things.

She picked up the rabbit beside Pip, who stared at the carcass with disdain, his wonky pipe dangling from his half-open mouth. She'd never skinned a rabbit before, but she'd seen Hansel do it enough times that she was fairly confident she could do it, too.

Eve and Hansel were a disaster in the making, and Snow didn't approve.

There was too much at stake. Too much to lose. Too many lives at risk. Could Hansel not see that? Had he lost his mind so completely over this reckless girl that he was forgetting the cause?

Enough was enough.

If Hansel could not see it himself, then she would help him see it. She would save him, just as he'd saved her.

Eve's heart ached at the choice she struggled to make. Did Hansel realise how much he affected her? And if he did, was it some sick game to recruit her to the cause?

She paused at the edge of the forest, the wind sweeping her loose braid and dusting the treetops.

Or did his heart pull in two directions just as hers did?

She shook her head and smacked the bark of a nearby tree. While most people lived having never met a royal, Eve now had the privilege of two wanting to kill her. Lucky her. A dry, hollow laugh escaped her at the irony.

The snap of a twig let Eve know that Hansel had followed her. As a huntsman he had an unnerving knack to be silent and deadly, so she should at least thank him for warning her of his presence.

She spun behind a tree, hiding amongst the thick expanse of its old wise trunk, and peered around the edge. Hansel's shoulders were hunched, his fists clenched at his sides. Eve knew he'd seen her, but her stomach was leaden, a sense of dread snaking over her skin.

'Why?' he asked. His voice was a low rumble in his chest, and she blinked, cautiously stepping out from her hiding spot.

Her eyes darted to his tight shoulders, to the ripped muscles of his arms, and his stern, piercing eyes that followed her all the same.

'Why do you behave the way you do? What was done to you that made you this way?'

She swallowed, unsure on how to stand, how to act. How to feel.

'I know about your quest for revenge, but even when I think I know your motivations, I'm always proved wrong. So why is that, Eve?'

Eve wasn't sure she had an answer. She'd only ever had one goal. One target. One destination.

The sisters Grimm.

What right did he have to question her choices? Weren't they hers to make? She was tired of prophecies and fanatics and royals. She wasn't a puppet, or a lackey, or a hero.

'Not everything is about saving your princess and this realm,' Eve replied, crossing her arms. 'Some of us carry the kind of scars that can't be undone by making peace. There are parts of this kingdom, people, who don't deserve saving.'

Hansel stalked closer, near enough to look Eve in the eye but not to touch her. Righteous anger sparked his gaze. 'You truly think this is just about Snow?' He shook his head. 'You're smarter than this, Eve. You're not the only one that carries scars. Some remain hidden, trapped on the inside. It doesn't mean they don't matter. In fact, it's more of a reason to fight, to find hope, especially when people need it most.'

She halted, a retort stinging her tongue. Was it just about the Princess, or something deeper? Eve had lived for so long trusting only her gut and her instincts that she didn't know how to let go of it. She wasn't sure if she even could.

As for scars, she knew about them, too. She was familiar with the kind that never left. The kind that lingered long after being healed. But it wasn't a topic she wanted to discuss, so she opted for the safer response. 'Snow certainly doesn't make it easier.'

Hansel stepped forward and grasped her hand, his voice cracking as he said, 'She's one piece in a larger puzzle. I'm not asking you to be her friend, and I'm not asking you to be a hero.'

Warmth coated her skin at his touch, and she loosed a breath. There was a sting behind her eyes as she took him in. 'Aren't you?'

Hansel squeezed her hand. 'I'm not asking you to be anything but you. Don't you see, Eve? With a queen like

Myrenna, it won't stop, it will *never* stop. She enslaves species for her mines, she kills whoever steps in her way, and manipulates those around her who she finds useful. She's evil. She's stepping outside of Bellatorre now. We're all that's left between her and the safety of the realm.'

The thing was, Eve didn't want to save the realm. It had never been kind to her. It had tricked her and beat her and changed her. The realm could go to the cauldron for all she cared, but when she looked at his trusting, golden-brown eyes, she couldn't form the refusal that sat on the edge of her lips. Would she be saying yes to saving the realm, or would she be saying yes to him?

'I don't know,' she breathed.

Not a refusal, but not acceptance either.

He smiled, his fingers softly grazing her skin. She wanted to close her eyes, wanted to hold him and breathe in his scent. To let him wrap his arms around her and shelter her. He was the hearth of a home in winter, a haven when she'd been exposed to the open for so long.

She blinked, heart thundering in her chest.

He was a breath away, his scent of pine and wood intoxicating in a way that made Eve tremble.

Hansel touched her cheek. 'I know the realm hasn't been kind to you, but that doesn't mean it deserves ruin. I know you carry your own scars. I'm not asking you to be the saviour of the realm. I'm asking if you will stand with me, help me. Your goal is revenge, right?'

Eve nodded and he swallowed. Her skin tingled with his touch, the way his fingers burned her skin and set her core on fire.

'I may not be able to offer you those medallions due to the Queen wanting to kill us and all, but what I can offer you is revenge. Dethroning Myrenna is the rebellion's goal, and finding the sisters Grimm for your father is yours.'

His voice was husky, but there was excitement, too. There was an eagerness to him that she loved. The way he saw the best in the others. The brighter future he painted was intoxicating.

When his lips lightly touched hers, Eve melted into it. She'd missed this. Missed *him.*

Her body was pliant under his hands, bending towards him in a way that left her full and heady. One brush, then two. She groaned as his tongue laced hers.

She didn't know how long they kissed, nor how long they stood there, but when Hansel finally pulled back it was as if she stood on the precipice of something, but she didn't know what.

He rested his forehead against hers. 'Eve.'

She loved the way he said her name. Reverent and husky and *hers.*

'Eve,' he said again. His intimate tone caused her to shiver. 'The Queen knows how to find the sisters Grimm.'

That was when she froze, the bubble of lust gone.

'I've heard her speak of them before, and Snow has seen her converse with the mirror,' Hansel continued. 'If we can capture Myrenna and bring her to justice, not only can she answer for her crimes, but she may have answers for you. Why is it she can locate them, but you can't?'

The words were a slap. A reminder of how fickle her gift was, of how she'd failed.

Eve stepped back and ignored the absence of him, the cold air nipping her skin in a painful reminder.

'What?' she asked, too confused to form any other words.

'The Queen is the answer,' he urged. 'She's the answer to saving the realm, the answer to you finding your revenge and giving Porchid the chance at hers.'

Porchid's revenge.

The loyal fairy had followed Eve through job after job and she hadn't even considered Porchid's wishes, her choice in this conflict. Porchid would want revenge for the grotto, for the monsters who'd hurt her.

Perhaps Eve didn't have to say yes to saving the realm, she just had to say yes to destroying the Queen. It was a suicide mission, but if Porchid got her revenge and Eve got her answers, then was it not worth it?

Hansel took her hands again, but he didn't kiss her this time. Eve let him, the guilt about Porchid choking her response.

Hansel rubbed her knuckles, a wayward strand of hair ticking his forehead. 'Come with me,' he whispered.

The words tugged at her heart, but there was something else, too. A deeper call, or perhaps a natural born defence that made her mind shout, stop, stop, *stop.*

Come with me.

Eve wasn't floating anymore. She was sinking. Sinking deep into that pit inside herself. The one where she'd built a wall to guard her feelings. A thick wall of comfort that guided her, loved her, coaxed her.

'I've been selfish,' Eve said, the words freeing themselves from a cage deep inside her. 'Porchid is all I have, and here I am solely focusing on my own end. She deserves a happy ending, too, and if that means finding the Queen … then that's where I'll go.'

He waited for her to continue, and when she didn't, he slowly stepped away. The relief she'd expected from him never came. The sparkle she'd seen moments ago vanished.

'I see,' he murmured.

She shivered, but not from the chill of the wind. He was cold, indifferent. Something so foreign to the man she'd known that her heart stuttered painfully.

Quietly, he released her hand and stepped back. She watched painfully as he stroked his hand through his hair and set his shoulders. He opened his mouth, but then closed it again, as if he wasn't sure what to say.

The air was thick with disappointment, drowning Eve in a way she wasn't familiar with. She'd never been close enough to someone to disappoint them.

She took a step forward, only for Hansel to turn and leave.

Eve watched him go as she stood beside the old oak tree, her mouth pinched as she held back tears. Her hands were numb, and she rubbed them on her jacket.

She'd agreed to go with him, but he'd walked away still.

Come with me.

He hadn't asked her to join the cause. Not really.

He'd asked her to join *him.*

Part of her wondered if she'd just missed out on the most important question she'd ever been asked.

She should shout his name and call him back. Her brain screamed at her to move, but her body couldn't bring itself to follow.

When she was truly alone, Eve spun on her heels, grabbed one of her knives, and hurled it towards one of the trees. The hit caused the old oak to groan.

A choked sob crawled up her throat. She went for her second blade when she paused. There was a stillness to the air, the heavy tang of magic cloaking her senses. Eve eyed the forest, her hand poised over her second knife.

'Hansel,' she croaked, her mouth fumbling over the words.

Her muscles went taut as she realised just how alone she was. When she tried to take a step, her movements were sluggish. There was a thickness to the world as if she was wading through mud.

A hushed whisper echoed through the trees. *She comes.*

Raised hairs lined her body as her mouth went dry with the acrid taste of magic. Icy fear trickled down Eve's spine. She couldn't move, couldn't scream. Even her knives wouldn't help her now. Nothing could help her now. Magic was in every pore of the realm and what she'd avoided for so long had now come for her.

A deep hissing echoed through the forest.

She comes.

She prayed then. To the cauldron. To the Fairy Godmother. To the stars. To anybody who would listen. The forest shifted around her and then the ground shuddered. She tried to steady herself, her heart thundering in her chest but it was no use. Before she could try to scream again, it ceased.

The trees stopped their murmurs, the leaves as still as the sleeping princess had been in her coffin. Not the chime of a bird or the crunch of a boot.

Then the magic snapped.

Eve grabbed her knife and ran. She may have been stupid with Hansel, but she knew when to run.

Dante's voice reverberated through her.

'You will feel it,' he'd said one night.

They had been sitting on the sand of the circus arena after practice. Where they should have been packing up, they instead were taking a break from duties to rest a while and stare at the stars that were gleaming down on them through the hole of the big tent.

The circus had stopped in a small town as opposed to a large city, leaving Eve to revel in the starlit sky where her father's tales came to life with each constellation. Queen Rose after the War of Thorns. Syrenna, the little matchbox girl who set a village on fire during Yulemas. The giant, Atticus, who stole enchanted glass to make a bridge from the island of Myorcai to the mainland.

Dante had gone sombre as he sometimes did, choosing the moment to give Eve some needed advice. Usually, she would laugh at his serious face, and he would he mess up her hair in that brotherly way of his. Other times he would take her by surprise, as if somehow, she knew it was time to listen. Time to learn.

'I will feel what?' Eve had asked.

Her head had been in his lap, his fingers plaiting her hair.

'Magic,' Dante had replied. 'You will feel it, even before you smell or taste it.'

'Lady Nona says magic is in everything,' Eve said, matter-of-factly.

Even though the Seer unsettled her, the old woman spoke only truth.

'Lady Nona is wise,' Dante said, lifting his calloused fingers and placing a bit of her hair behind her ear. She leaned into it.

Even in this cruel world with Madame Viper and strange magic, she'd had Dante. Her light, her brother, her guardian. She'd smiled at the thought.

'Do you think magic is in the stars, too?' she had asked, twisting her head to look up at him.

He'd chuckled. 'I believe it is.'

Her grin had grown wide as she'd turned her attention back to the glittering sky. She'd lifted her hand up, attempting a pathetic reach towards the open sky. Her tiny hand had been pale against the blackness of myths and tales of heroes, of tricks and curses and wicked villains.

The stars had felt like magic.

As she'd closed her hand, Dante had reached towards the stars with her. His eyes had gleamed.

She'd remembered a tale of a witch. Another old story her father had once told. The witch had been jealous of a princess born of starlight, and in her envy had cursed her to dance until her feet bled and she collapsed. By the time the prince had come, he had been too late, and the witch had laughed in glee before retreating to her hut in the woods. Eve had never particularly liked the tale, but something inside her stirred at the unfairness of it.

'Dante?' she'd asked.

'Yes?'

'Is magic good or bad?'

His smile had lessened. 'It is neither and both, all at the same time.'

She'd frowned. 'That's confusing.'

He'd laughed. 'It is and isn't. What have you just learnt?'

She'd pondered a moment before sitting up and staring into his dark eyes. His hair had been tied back in a bun with small strays escaping. He'd had bags under his eyes, and where he had normally sported strong, bronzed skin, he'd paled. Significantly.

'That I will feel it?' she had asked, hesitant in her answer.

He had nodded. 'You will feel it, and when you do, you will know. In those moments when it is unnatural or unusual, you must listen to your body'—he had paused—'What was your first lesson when I taught you the ropes and when you learnt to throw your knives?'

She'd bitten her bottom lip. 'To trust my instincts?'

'Trust your instincts,' he'd repeated, a curve to his lips. 'If I leave you with anything in this world, it is to trust your own body and your heart.'

Eve leapt over a branch, the forest floor a blur as her feet pounded the earth. A branch snapped across her shoulder, eliciting a hiss of pain.

A wash of deep blue smoke tumbled through the trees, the stench of magic so strong she had to breathe through her mouth. She pivoted left, searching for a gap in the trees.

Whoever, whatever, this was, it was powerful.

Eve had to warn the others. To warn *him.*

She dived over brambles and sticks and roots until she reached the bottom of a cliff, its black, metallic edge smoothed with time. A thin waterfall trickled down its surface, the rocks slick with condensation. Eve swore under her breath. She was cornered. In any other circumstance it would have been beautiful, but with the blue smoke unfurling at her back, she had to keep moving.

Despite the sweat building on the palms of her hands, she swallowed her fear and did the only thing she could.

She began to climb.

The rock was slick under her fingers, tiny green sprouts growing through the stone. She let her instincts take over, hating the way she shook with every movement.

Crevice by crevice, one-foot hold at a time, Eve climbed up. Her muscles groaned against the unnatural movement. Her heart thrummed inside her chest.

Don't look down.

A pink tower flashed in her mind, the caws of the Queen's crows. The tilt of her body made her dizzy. She grazed her palm on the sharp rock and swore as blood broke through her skin. She held her grip, her fingers screaming in protest, and braved a look below.

It was a mistake.

The ground no longer existed, replaced by a giant, yawning chasm. The blue smoke resembled outstretched hands, grasping at her heels.

Frantic, Eve aimed for a ledge to her right. The top wasn't far off, she could still make it. She just had to avoid looking down.

Channelling her fear, Eve squatted against the rock, aiming to gain some momentum, but she slipped. She cried out as the tang of smoke filled her nostrils, her hands grasping for the wall again and finding a ledge. At the sudden stillness of her fall, she grunted. Her knees were scraped, her breathing heavy as she settled herself against the rock.

You can do this. It's not far.

But the vertigo in her body reminded her otherwise. With another breath, Eve tried again. Her fingers went white, the bite in her cheek bleeding as she used her legs to launch herself into the air.

For one impossible moment, Eve flew, her hair curling around her as she stretched her arms towards the ledge. She screamed as the tips of her fingers scraped the edge – and missed.

Terror seized her as she fell.

The smoke swallowed her whole.

III
The Fallen Hero

Pip's tobacco smoke whirled in front of his nose. The odd stirring of the wind caused the hairs on his neck to rise.

Not a good sign, he thought. *Not a good sign at all.*

He took in Snow's tapping foot with irritation. Malak dozed nearby. Florian kicked a helpless pebble and rubbed irritably at a rash blazing up on his neck. Only the fairy noticed the change in the air. Her pointed ears twitched and her colour paled as she fluttered into the air beside him.

Pip doused his pipe abruptly and stood, nose scrunching at the thick, rotten stench of magic seeping into the grotto.

'We have to leave. Now,' Pip said, raising his voice over the sudden wind that swept through with its bitter tang. 'There's strange magic nearby.'

Snow's brow creased with the change in atmosphere. 'But Hansel—'

The ground rumbled, halting whatever she was about to say. Florian squeaked. Malak jolted from his slumber, eyes bleary.

'Did you not hear the part where I said magic is here?' Pip snapped, losing his footing on the shifting soil.

The scent of metal permeated the air. The trees groaned and the grotto rocked with a tremor. Pip stumbled forward, Porchid barely clinging to his shoulder, and Hansel broke through the brush, shouting a warning Pip couldn't hear.

A *crack* stole all sound as the grotto tore in two, the blow reverberating through Pip's bones. A tree crashed into the earth, the splintering wood flying. Pip's mouth went dry as Hansel twisted back towards the forest.

He wouldn't—

Pip shook his head vehemently, pleading. Surely the boy wasn't that stupid. Surely, he wouldn't run towards the magic causing this when they should be fleeing.

Pip cursed as Eve's name formed on the huntsman's lips before he spun and sprinted into the wild forest.

Porchid shrieked in Pip's ear and dived after the huntsman, her light so pale it might've reflected the moon.

'Fools,' Pip muttered as he turned back. Hansel and the fairy might want to save the Seeker, but Pip didn't give a flying flute if she lived or died. If Pip had cared less for his own life, he might have followed. He'd only joined this farce of a quest out of boredom. And survival. Because when it came down to it, Pip would survive. First, last, always.

Snow screamed at the metallic wind, her hands thrashing against Malak as he gripped her firmly. His heavy fingers fumbled where she fought him, but she didn't relent.

Another crack shuddered through the trees, a deep chasm yawning open between Snow's shattered coffin and their campsite.

The grotto came apart before his eyes. Near the trees he made out a path, and his short legs ran towards it before he could shout. He dodged a hole in the ground, his flute slapping against his chest as he continued toward the path.

He ran until the tremors lessened, until the stench of magic cleared. And then he ran some more.

It wasn't until he reached a clearing that he slowed, his old legs quaking beneath him. The trees murmured in the wind, as if awake and alive. At least the smell was gone, the threat far away.

Panting, Pip turned, and found he'd been followed. He thanked the Godmother that some of his companions had some brains – though Snow didn't count. She sobbed into Malak's shoulder, but the troll seemed fine, not even winded. His grip was firm beneath her legs, his eyes serious as he assessed for further threats.

Nearby, Florian wheezed from the exertion, his skin red. Pip knew of a tea he could make the boy for his allergies. But he'd save that for when the boy had earned it, or when he wasn't in mortal danger.

'What was that?' Florian wheezed.

'Magic,' Pip muttered, glaring at the ground as if he could threaten the quake away.

'But who would do that?'

'I don't know, but it was too old for Myrenna's stench.'

Snow's voice was raw as she spoke. 'Why would he do that? Run like that after … *her?*'

Pip eyed the princess and decided that she was, in fact, stupid.

'Because love has no reason – when it is true.' Pip darted his gaze briefly to Malak but locked eyes with Snow. 'Even the sanest of us can be driven wild by it.'

'Love can go to the cauldron!' she screeched.

Malak gripped her tighter as her shoulders shook, the four of them watching as the rumble of the earth suddenly went silent.

Snow beat her fists on Malak's back. 'Put me down!'

Malak eyed the clearing, then sighed. 'Will you promise not to punch me if I do?'

'I could do more than punch you,' she replied. 'I'm a princess, I could—'

'Have my head?' Malak said, a tilt to his lips.

The Princess huffed before twisting towards him. 'I could, you know.'

'You could, but you won't.'

The ground thundered again, unsettling them, but it was smaller this time, distant, as if the last of the quake had ended.

'What do we do?' Florian winced, bracing himself on his knees.

'We could start by avoiding *that*,' Pip said, pointing towards a blue fog sifting through the trees.

'By the Godmother,' Florian breathed.

By the Godmother, indeed.

Hansel fled through the trees, the ground thundering beneath him. His heart was beating too fast, and his breaths were sharp. He knew that Malak was with Snow, and he had to trust that Porchid had stayed with Pip. The elf wasn't the friendliest, but he did seem to protect those that were different from the rest, even with his smartass quips.

But the thought of his companions was minor compared to the panic in his chest. Eveline was still out here.

Hansel knew magic when he smelt it. Had smelt it for years under the Queen's service. Hers tasted metallic, like blood and salt. This one was still metallic but had the smoky hue of incense. His only relief was that it wasn't Myrenna coming. But if it wasn't her, then who?

The ground shook as he ran towards where he and Eve had fought. He eyed the nick on the tree where her knife had lodged, the mossy log where she'd paused.

He should have been elated when she'd said yes. He should have taken her hand and kissed her again. Instead, he'd been so angry. She'd agreed to the cause for Porchid's sake, but not for him.

He should have never left her alone. Never have picked a fight when he was the one being greedy and selfish. He was stupid to think he could have persuaded her otherwise, because he knew deep down that Eve didn't need that, didn't want it. And he loved her for that.

The ground paused in its anger, and he quickened his pace, his feet nimble. Magic seared his nostrils, thick and musky but it didn't deter him. Hansel tracked a trail of broken branches and blood, hoping Eve was alive. His breath hitched as panic gripped his chest, his hands already freeing the axes from his back.

Hansel hacked his way through the trees, ignoring the burn on his skin or his sweat-soaked back. He had no idea how long he had, how long the magic would linger. Eventually, the path opened to a looming cliff, the rock sharp and jagged and black. But it was the distant body high upon the wall that halted him: the shaking form of Eve as she climbed.

Thick, blue smog covered the terrain, reaching up towards her as the ground cracked open. Clammy sweat beaded his brow as she steadied her legs, ready to jump. Hansel wanted to be proud: despite her fear of heights, she kept climbing.

Terror gripped him as he pushed forward, the ground uneven. He shouted her name. Desperation sunk its claws into his skin when she didn't respond.

She can't hear me.

The beat of his heart drowned his ears. From here he could do nothing but pray to the cauldron.

Hansel shouted her name again as she gained momentum, her body flinging from the wall. She flew, her arms outstretched for a ledge he couldn't see. Her fingers grazed the rock, touching for a second before she screamed.

Then *fell.*

Hansel shouted, his throat burning with desperation as he kept running, hoping. Eve dropped into the fog below, and the world burst into a bright light. The blowback slammed him into a tree, his axes flying from his hands. He felt his back crack, and pain shot through his spine. His skin burned, vicious cuts lining his body from hacking his way through the forest. He blinked as his vision blurred, the ringing in his ears too loud as he struggled to get up.

Gnarled roots dug into his knees as Porchid flickered before him, her dark eyes wide. She pulled on his collar, desperation in her eyes.

Get up.

'Please,' he panted. His arm was bent in the wrong direction, leaving him to lean against a tree for support. He groaned as a sharp pain jolted through his side, but his legs were steady enough.

Porchid pulled again, her twinkle too fast to decipher, her light a terrifying white.

'Please,' he repeated. 'Not her.'

It was a prayer, an appeal, a wish for anybody who would listen.

He cleared the line of trees and stared at the chasm. The wind was gentle against his ripped skin, too soft against the threat of magic.

But there was no sign of her.

Porchid squealed, her light blinding. He understood her fear, felt it just as keenly. But he felt something else too, a call coming from the deep. It was a whisper on his skin, urging him forward. Before he knew what he was doing, Hansel faced the fading blue smoke.

There was little time. Hansel took a steadying breath and ran. He ignored the pain in his body, ignored the fear and the regret and the uncertainty. And when he reached the edge, the smoke already fading, he dived.

IV

The Hunger of Hearts

The Queen's pale hands clutched the windowsill, grasping for her waning strength. Her yellow nails were illuminated by the dawn as she panted, struggling to lift herself.

The magic was taking its toll.

How many hearts would she need to recover her strength this time? Ten? Twelve?

Myrenna longed for the days where a single maiden's heart had replenished her for years. Now, she was sweeping through them like a plague, cutting them out and devouring them like a pauper starved.

Youth was harder to catch, harder to keep. She'd ordered her guards to fetch her more maidens, those that were preferably lost and easily taken. Street urchins and innocent misses that she could keep confined to her dungeons, never far when she hungered for them. But the longer her guards took, the more her patience waned. Her body was slowly caving and decaying. Her knobbly white knuckles were stark against the billowing black of her cape. Her nails were chipped and raw.

She peered through the window, where the wind kissed her skin. The Crystal Lake shone against the rising sun, the city below just starting to wake with the day. Myrenna took in every detail: the loud smack of stores turning their wooden signs to 'open'; the rattling of the baker's cart as it was pushed down Main Avenue, the old wheels as they bounced across cobbled stone; a weathered woman hanging her washing out; and the mere shadow of a little boy scampering down a narrow alley.

But as she watched her city, jealousy laced her veins.

It was easy for them. Simple.

Myrenna's old knees buckled, and she swore as she clawed her hand deeper into the windowsill. 'Where are my incompetent guards?'

The parchment on her desk shifted in the breeze, her eyes darting to its worn brown page. The scrolls had been a curse and a gift.

She'd believed the spell to be a wish come true. The treasure she'd uncovered under this castle a blessing from the Fairy Godmother.

Bellatorre had always been the goal. Myrenna had begun her journey, made her choices, knowing precisely where they'd lead: to a kingdom renowned for hiding the last remaining powerful grimoires and scrolls etched in spells, long lost to the realm. To make her next move, she needed the ancient script.

It had been easy to woo the king of Bellatorre in the beginning, to claim his heart through her apple pie. Accessing those scrolls, however, had been the real challenge.

For years she'd sifted through them. Deciphering what she could. Waiting for some answer or clue on how to relieve herself from the web she'd woven.

The sisters Grimm either had no idea what truly lay beneath this castle, or they simply didn't care. Sooner or later, the crones would come for her, and she didn't have infinite hearts. The only solution had been Snow, and the little wretch lay elsewhere, hiding away with those filthy dwarves.

Myrenna's beautiful black birds had flown far and wide, returning with nothing but excuses, her magic proving useless against whatever protected her enemies.

So far, her fog dragon had been the only entity able to locate Snow. Even then, Myrenna had failed to retrieve the Princess's heart. Was the cost of the dragon's control worth it?

The layers of silk she wore felt heavy, the bodice too tight, too suffocating. It wasn't enough that she'd clawed her way into her position and used the mirror for power; now she had to suffer this, too.

The knock at the door couldn't have come sooner. 'Come in,' Myrenna called, her irritation barely hidden.

Her guards entered, towing in eight young girls. They ranged from twelve to twenty, each the fairest of their villages. Not yet broken or beaten, their innocence was like a wide-eyed doe about to take the arrow from the hunter.

Her favourite kind.

The Queen smiled widely, though it hurt her paper-thin skin. Their fear tasted like sugar.

My little does.

Myrenna readied her talons. Their deaths would be swift, their hearts torn and eaten for her power.

The Queen dismissed the guards and licked her lips. A brunette girl in a pale pink dress watched in horror as the door clicked. Her smooth cheek quivered, and a single tear fell slowly down her cheek, captured by her shuddering mouth.

All the girls knew what was coming. They knew their fate.

The beat of a heart, the intake of a breath, and Myrenna pounced.

The *drip* from the broken tap rebounded across the damp stone walls. Screams echoed along the prison, muffled by the hard, solid stone.

Bonyx shivered in his cell, his arms wrapped around his knobbly knees in a pathetic attempt for warmth. No matter what he did, it was always damp, always cold. There was a constant chill seeping into his frail skin and crawling between his bones, setting up camp between his shallow breaths.

The walls arched high above him, the shadows thickening near the ceiling. He whispered a prayer to the Fairy Godmother.

Bonyx's legs were shaky as he shuffled on the hay. His cane had been taken away from him, making movement hard, so the only time he ever stood was if he needed to use the bucket in the corner, or to peer out the iron bars to see down the hall.

He didn't know how long he'd been here, or what day it was. Time had become meaningless in the dark.

He'd tried a couple of times to contact Lady Nona. She was a seer, and a constant friend in an ever-changing scenery just as the Seven had been.

No. Not seven.

Six now.

It pained him to think of Beetle, twisted and bloody on the floor of the throne room. He blinked at the memory, his eyes burning.

Bonyx would be lying if he said he regretted his decision, even with the heartache and heaviness that came with it. For all he knew, the others were already dead, too. The best he could have done was keep Beetle close, but sometimes his best just wasn't enough. He'd learnt that the hard way when his own king had fallen in the War of Thorns.

When he wasn't dreaming of Beetle, he dreamed of the Queen. Her smirk was burned into his memory. A smirk that matched the face in the mirror in the throne room.

The gilded mirror was the key.

Bonyx's only hope was to get a message to Lady Nona, no matter how futile or desperate.

He closed his eyes, feeling for the thread of Lady Nona. But no matter how many times he tried, he kept falling through the shifting sands of memories, there and gone, grasped and lost in his wandering mind. Sometimes, he could smell the incense, see the gold and red hues of her tent—

And then he would be back in his dank cell.

He blinked again.

No light existed in this place except for the darting glimpse of light offered by the roaming guards and their torches. Even the grey flicker from the small, grated window did little to illuminate the stone. In his unknown time in the dark, Bonyx had learnt every crevice and touch of his cell, his bent fingers tracing the sorrows dug into stone, messages left by the fallen and the damned.

How many maidens had been kept in the dark? How many hearts had the Queen consumed?

He was distracted when metal slammed against stone, the door to his neighbour's cell opening. A whimper echoed as the guards snickered. Bonyx could hear a scuffle, then the throaty spit of saliva as the door banged shut. He held his breath, waiting for the dripping tap to steal back any sound.

When the guards were gone, Bonyx braved a step towards the bars.

A familiar voice came from the other side. A broken, rough sound. 'Hope is a lie.'

Fear sluiced through the old dwarf, but he remained calm. It was a sentence that came from his neighbour's lips regularly.

'What happened?' Bonyx urged. 'What did they do to you?'

Bonyx had not yet been released since that fateful day in the throne room. He'd begun to hope the Queen had forgotten about him.

A cough echoed back. 'He tries to take her apart. To break her. To see how she ticks.' His neighbour chuckled darkly. 'But she won't without me. She won't work without me.'

Bonyx had been trying to figure out the extent of this man's insanity since his capture. He seemed coherent some of the time and as silent as a corpse in others. Sometimes, Bonyx heard the man's whispers in the night, the scraping of nails, the screams.

Every time the prisoner was returned, he would be a little more broken – a wall that had been chipped at for so long that it was barely holding itself upright. One poke in the right place and the whole thing would crumble.

Bonyx chose his next words with care. 'She will not be corrupted, for she has you. There is still hope.'

His neighbour laughed, the sound cracked and dry. 'I feel your hope through the stones, you know. But hope is a disease. A lie. There is nothing for you now.'

Bonyx hugged himself in the dark, contemplating the words. In every story there was a moment where everything seemed lost. When the heroes had been pushed and prodded and torn apart so much there seemed like there was no hope. But there was always an ending, a moment of truth or bravery. Hope was neither a disease nor a lie, it was a gift.

Bonyx still had his kin to think about, but in here, he had his stories. And they were enough to give him courage.

'Do not forget, friend. There is always hope. You are hers as she is yours.'

The dwarf didn't know who 'she' was, but the stranger echoed the words enough that it had begun to provide some comfort. Every time he asked what it meant, he never received a straight answer. From what he could gather, 'she' was important to the stranger somehow. Maybe a daughter? Or a lover?

'I am hers as she is mine,' his neighbour whispered.

Bonyx heard the scratch of fingernails against the stone near him, and then the shuffle of hay from what he assumed was his neighbour's bed. He'd done his part to calm his companion today. Tomorrow he would try again.

Bonyx closed his eyes. He was exhausted; the effort to contact Nona was draining, and possibly a fool's errand. He would keep trying, though. Giving up wasn't an option. Bonyx curled into the meagre hay in the corner, knowing he needed to sleep to find any shred of his strength in his dank cage.

His neighbour's voice broke through the quiet, the sound surpassing the drip of the tap ringing through the cold halls. Though the words weren't meant for Bonyx, he listened anyway.

'I am hers as she is mine.'

V

The Heartbreak of Hope

Hansel's head throbbed. He wondered why he'd been stupid enough to dive into a pit of magic.

He squeezed the soft surface beneath him, disorientated, and groggily lifted his head. Porchid's tiny hand rested on his arm, her skin glowing a warm yellow. She was a sight for sore eyes, alive and well at least.

He groaned as he sat up, every muscle aching from the forest. His injuries were still there, his arm still bent in the wrong direction. He avoided using it as he shuffled, noticing the array of embroidered pillows surrounding him. They were gaudy, dressed in tassels and sequins.

Where am I?

Blinking, he took in the narrow room where he'd ended up. The decor was mottled with reds and golds. A fragrant oil lamp sat on the table next to him, eliciting a heavy scent of sage. A small kitchen lay near the back, a set of chairs surrounding another table in the centre where a glass ball glowed.

From what he could gather, it was a home, though it was small.

He saw nobody present but Porchid and himself, the fairy shifting and changing colours with her mood.

Where was Eve?

He'd followed her after all, had jumped into the chasm to find her.

He stretched out his good arm to reach for one of his axes, only to find them both gone. 'Fairy Godmother, help me,' he groaned as he tried to stand.

Porchid squeaked at him when a curtain was thrust open and a haughty, thin woman entered. She escorted an older woman, her pale complexion a stark contrast to the steely-gazed woman guarding her. 'The Fairy Godmother can't help you, but we might be able to.'

Hansel frowned at the intrusion.

It was the older woman who had spoken. She wore a long, cobalt dress draped with silks in violet and gold. Though she looked frail, there was a strength about her that Hansel couldn't pin. Her skin reminded him of parchment, papery and yellowed with time. He took in her murky, grey eyes, suspecting she was blind but somehow knowing that she saw far more than most.

The younger woman beside her stood three pixies higher, her sharp cheekbones adding to the harshness of her straight black hair. She stared down at him, her mouth turned downwards, as she helped the older woman sit. A rope draped her waist with an array of knives, hitched upon her red and gold buttoned jacket. She whispered to the old woman, and was waved away. Her bright eyes met Hansel's as she paused in the doorway. Her glare a deadly warning.

Hansel shuffled on the seat, eager to get away, when he winced. He was sure his arm was broken.

The woman smiled warmly. 'Let's fix that first.'

She reached into a box beside her, lifted out some herbs, and mixed a few ingredients, filling the room with a potent metallic smell. 'Come sit with me, young huntsman. My old bones don't move as they once did.'

Hansel didn't move. There was something about her that raised the hair on his arms, elicited a wariness inside him that he hadn't felt since Myrenna. When Porchid flew forward he almost shouted but could only gape as she inspected the woman. Porchid tugged on her hair, took a sniff and twinkled something the woman seemed to understand. When only a few words had been spoken, Porchid glowed in golden light.

Porchid returned, and she smiled at him before nodding to the woman.

'I don't trust her,' he said. The words harder than intended. But he was afraid.

Eve was still missing. There had been magic involved, and he didn't know this woman. He had to leave, to seek out the others. To figure out where he was.

He tried again to stand but was halted by the tug of his sleeve. Porchid was staring up at him. When he shook his head, she huffed out a breath and pouted. It was the same look she'd use to get extra berries at dinner. A look she knew he couldn't resist.

His eyes darted between the fairy and woman.

'I only aim to fix what is broken,' the woman said, nodding towards his arm.

Hansel glanced at Porchid one more time before he reluctantly gave in. His body groaned as he slowly dragged himself forward.

The old woman smiled in an odd, kind way. His nerves tingled as he tasted the magic in the air, and his back went rigid. He was sure she was the source of it. But when her weathered hands touched his arm and she began to chant, Hansel couldn't think past the pain.

By the time the stars had come out, Pip deemed it safe to return to the grotto.

Snow huffed the entire time, chastising Malak for taking her hostage. Florian walked by his side with the occasional sniffle, fiddling with the withered feather on his hat.

Pip ground his teeth together as Snow's high-pitched whining broke the quiet air, yet again.

Godmother, help us all.

Giants were one thing, but a snivelling prince, an outspoken princess, and a soft troll was not what he'd foreseen in his future. Back in his prime he was piping for Rumpelstiltskin, bringing in money and lovers and whatever else his elfish heart desired. The kingdoms hadn't been so torn then. Myrenna hadn't yet taken Bellatorre, and Rumple's underground network had run far and wide. The 'veins of the realm', they used to call it.

Pip wondered about Rumple, remembering the encounter Eve had told him about. Rumple would never have had his spindle stolen, let alone send someone else to retrieve it. He had many spies, many hiding holes, and many enemies. Fifty years with the giants had really dragged Pip into a new world, and even though he wasn't quite sure where he fit, he oddly felt like this was where was he supposed to be.

Not that it was a smart decision. It had all the warnings of being a terrible idea. He had doubts, more than he cared to admit, each one piling onto each other like pebbles on a beach.

The path they walked was narrow but easy to follow. Pip found it strange to believe that life had existed here mere weeks ago, but he'd seen it before, the cost of magic and its ability to bring things to life and then destroy it ruthlessly. To take meant giving something in return, an exchange of pure essence. Nothing was freely given in this realm, least of all power. To make an exchange without knowing what you gave up could mean losing your soul. Magic came from everything, but it could be amplified. Magical objects, blood, promises … they were all bargains that mattered, depending on who you dealt with. Whoever had wrought that earthquake would be facing those consequences now. It was not small magic, but something ancient and heavy and not easily wielded.

It made this quest all the more fraught.

Pip and the others made their way to the gap that Hansel had vanished through, Florian showing surprising skill in tracking. The path wound through brush, the largest trees so wide they must have lived lifetimes. Pip avoided their touch.

Snow gasped, dashing towards something on the ground ahead, and Pip slowed.

There was a murmur before Snow picked up an axe, the red hilt covered in dirt. A choked sob escaped her lips as she clutched it to her chest. 'Hansel would never leave this behind.'

'He had two,' Malak replied, his voice thoughtful. 'It's possible this one just dropped when he was running to help Eve?'

Whilst his point sounded reasonable, even Pip could hear the weakness to it. They'd all felt the earthquake and seen the blue fog.

'Eve,' Snow whispered, stroking the markings on the side. A twitch of pain crossed her delicate features. 'If he dies because of her …'

'Then he is still dead,' Pip drawled.

He held back a smile. *Oh, if looks could kill.*

He didn't mean to be cruel, but he was a realist. After fifty years as a slave, he'd learnt to look at life with a hardened gaze – not that he'd been much different prior to his imprisonment. Some people wielded weapons, others magic, some words.

Pip preferred the latter. 'Come now, Princess,' he said. 'You know Hansel is a sucker for a damsel in distress.'

His words were lost when Malak stepped forward, his jaw tight.

Pip followed his gaze to where Hansel's second axe lay, mere metres from the edge of a great chasm.

'Well,' Pip mused, 'there goes your theory, troll.'

Snow's vision honed onto the second axe. Voices buzzed around her like small insects as she stared at the blood. Hansel's blood.

Too much blood.

She heaved a breath, the air slicing into her chest as something else shifted inside her, a burning pile of coal roaring to life in her stomach. But her fire didn't burn hot, no, it was a cold, biting thing. Frost to match that of her steely heart.

Florian touched the bright red stains on the tree to her right, rubbing it between his fingers. 'It's fresh.'

Snow was breathless, her sense of control spiralling beneath her skin. Suddenly, her feet were moving, following the blood trail with fervour. She could feel Malak on her tail, his breathing as rough as her own, but even he couldn't soothe the ache building in her chest. The spool of fear.

She halted just before the edge of the chasm, the gaping hole at the base of a sheer black cliff. Malak held Hansel's second axe. He swept the area with panicked eyes as Pip and the prince caught up.

Snow sniffed the air, and the faint remnants of magic stung her nose.

Florian followed the blood trail until it ended at the edge of the chasm.

'Do you think a drop like that could justify survival?' Malak asked, his voice cracking despite how carefully he spoke.

Snow didn't want to think about what a fall like that could do. Didn't want to consider what that darkness meant.

The group was silent, leaving Snow to think through every worst-case scenario. He could have been killed by the magic. Been taken or injured. The blood wasn't a good sign and, as much as she tried to fight it off, a sense of hopelessness fell over her.

The silence was broken when Malak dropped to his knees. There was a look to him that unsettled her, one of grief and sorrow.

Snow wanted to reach for him. Wanted to tell him Florian was wrong, that it wasn't possible. She felt like a thread being untethered, the fall too far for her to climb back from.

And then Malak broke.

His scream echoed through the forest, cutting through the wind with such pain that Snow collapsed.

'No,' she said to nobody in particular. '*No.*'

She tried to focus on her breathing, on each inhale and exhale. But the beast kept scratching. Tearing. Itching to break free.

She was trapped. She was frozen. But she was also *angry*.

Hansel was gone.

All for that worthless Seeker. For that selfish little *bitch*.

Her shivering hand wiped at the hot tears streaking down her cheeks, the wet drops soaking her dirty fingers.

'You let this happen,' she whispered. Snow swallowed her fear and leaned into the icy anger that pinched beneath her skin. She threw herself at Pip, screaming. 'YOU DID THIS!'

Pip barely evaded her swipe, quicker than she anticipated as she landed in the dirt. Pain shuddered through her elbows as she stopped her roll. She twisted towards him, teeth and nails braced against her hurt and her fury.

'I didn't cause this, Princess,' Pip replied in that annoying, dry tone of his. 'I doubt Hansel did, either. He was simply following her.'

Her.

Eveline.

Something in her mind whispered, seething with heartbreak. Snow thought she knew pain. Understood what sorrow felt like. But she knew nothing.

She glared at Pip's grimace, the way his eyes held pity. But she didn't need pity. She needed Hansel.

Gone. He's gone.

'No,' she said again, but it came out as a broken whisper.

Hansel was the driving force, the haven and trusted tether to everything. He was her confidant. Her saviour.

Soulmate, her mind whispered. It was a voice she didn't recognise.

Pip awkwardly coughed, and stepped forward. 'I know this is a bad time, but we must move.'

Snow shook her head. 'No. He isn't gone. He can't be. It's magic. Magic makes *everything* possible.'

Pip mumbled a response, but she was too far gone to care. Snow stared at the stained grass, a memory of her training in the castle with Hansel and Malak surfacing. One where Hansel smiled as she finally got her posture right. Another where they played games in the library. Of words, spoken in shadow.

'I'll always be your friend.'

Magic had been here. It wasn't death. It was magic.

Magic was in *everything*. It was life. Death. Air. Wind.

'We have to get to the Skinny Piglet,' Pip said to Florian.

'But that was Hansel's contact,' Florian replied.

'And Malak's,' Pip replied.

'Hansel might be alive.'

'He isn't,' Pip snapped. 'You cannot follow the dead.'

Snow shook, a shadow crawling under her skin. 'He's alive,' she murmured, though she wasn't sure if the others heard. 'I feel it.'

Alive, the voice whispered.

'You can mourn on the road,' Pip said gently. 'There is no body for us to bury.'

'Us?' Malak hissed. 'You barely knew him.'

Snow didn't want to hear this. Didn't want the *lies.*

Her arms shook as she stood, her chin lifting proudly 'He. Is. *Alive.*'

Pip merely blinked. 'You might think I'm a monster right now, but I'm also trying to save you. He is gone.'

'STOP SAYING THAT,' Snow spat.

Even Pip had the sense to step back, his eyes stern but wary.

Snow's muscles seized, a choke escaping her lips, as she tried to refocus. In small movements, she found Malak and grasped his arm. 'He's alive,' she whispered. 'I don't know how. But focus. *Think.*'

Malak's cheeks were damp as his grip tightened around Hansel's axe. When his dark eyes finally met hers, her heart cracked again. Though there was doubt in his gaze, she saw his truth. He believed her.

Snow could have choked on her joy.

'Alive or not,' Malak said, 'we can't follow him down there.'

She focused on him, ignoring the searing pain in her chest as she swallowed. Pip may be wrong about Hansel's demise, but he was right about one thing. Wherever Hansel had gone, they couldn't follow.

Malak pressed his forehead against hers, offering a small piece of comfort. His hair smelt of moss and damp soil. Snow breathed him in, attempting a smile.

Alive.

Pip gruffed something to Florian from the shadows about false hope, but Snow ignored him, resting under the warmth of Malak's arm. He pulled her closer and she revelled in the familiar feel of him.

And as they stumbled through the trees, Snow took one last look at Hansel's bloody trail.

Hansel was alive. She knew it.

This time, it was up to her to find him.

Hansel screamed as his arm was snapped back into place.

Dull pain throbbed down his body, and his hazy vision was slowly clearing. The woman smiled at her work. The scent of peppermint lingered in the air as she applied a paste to his arm. The relief was almost instant, letting him loose the breath he'd been holding.

Once done, the woman handed him a goblet and urged him to drink. Hansel took a sip, trying not to choke on the tangy concoction.

'Eveline—' he croaked.

'Is fine,' the old woman said firmly, placing the salve back on the shelves. 'You must rest now. Your bones need to stitch back together. They'll only heal if you rest.'

Her smile was tired as she urged him to drink more. Hansel complied, but whatever it was made of, it worked fast. Hansel's eyes drooped and he swayed. Lifting the cup, his gaze narrowed at the worn indents near the rim, and he frowned.

He fought against the elixir's pull, glowering before he said, 'Rest? But Eve is …'

'Alive,' the old woman finished before a wave of exhaustion hit him. 'She is alive.'

He envisioned Eve's soft hair, the smirk of satisfaction she gave when she was proven right, and as he fell back into the cushions, the last thing he remembered was Eve's head resting perfectly on his shoulder as they watched the stars.

Hansel woke to the delicious smell of fried eggs, his mouth salivating. The rabbits in the glen felt like cycles ago. His stomach grumbled, reminding him that it'd been empty for far too long.

The ceiling above him curved, splattered in colours of the rainbow. To his left was a circular window, letting him know it was daytime. The glass was filled with a mosaic of animals and riders. It reminded him of living stories, the way each picture told a tale, engraved in memory.

He was lost in a depiction of a cauldron in the forest when a grunt distracted him. Hansel turned to see the dark-haired woman in red with the gold buttons. She was standing in front of a stove. Her brow furrowed as she lifted a pan, her hand in a thick mitten decorated with cats.

'Well, look at that,' she said. 'He's awake.'

She scooped the eggs onto a plate, served it up with some bread and butter, and slammed it onto the small table.

'Porchid?' he asked, looking at the food as if it held dark magic.

'No. That's eggs,' she said.

Hansel stared at her steely gaze.

'That was a joke,' she responded. When Hansel gave her a blank stare she sighed and pointed out the window. 'The fairy is with Nona. Talking in some fairy language that makes no sense to me. You need to eat. I didn't cook that just to watch you stare at it.'

He took his first bite, and a groan escaped. Whatever was in this tasted like home. Without another word, Hansel shoved the eggs into mouth. When he noticed the silence, he looked up.

The woman sighed and handed him a napkin. 'I know I shouldn't be surprised that a man your size was starving, but for cauldron's sake keep some semblance of courtesy when eating. It goes in your mouth, not down your chin.'

Normally he would have flushed, but he was too tired, too broken, too hungry to care. The woman scoffed as he accepted the cloth.

He shifted uncomfortably as a button dug into his backside from the banquet of cushions he sat upon. Once finished, he rolled his shoulder and stretched out his arm. Surprisingly, there was no pain, just a sense that it hadn't been used.

'Where am I?' Hansel asked.

She muttered under her breath about how nobody ever thanked her before she turned. 'You're in a vargo. A wagon of sorts. And my home. So, don't go saying anything nasty. I can see you thinking about it.' She stepped forward, though everything about her was stiff. 'I'm Viper. But Madame Viper to you.'

The name ricocheted through his body, his eyes wide as he took in the woman again. 'As in, Viper from the Cirque Magique?'

Viper preened at the comment. 'The very one.'

He'd heard of the circus, of course – they roamed the whole realm. But it wasn't that fact that had Hansel frowning. It was a piece of Eve's past. She'd shared as much at the Briar Rose. But when Viper nodded towards the window, he deflated.

There were no tents, no aerobics, no stage.

It was just a clearing, with the old woman and Porchid by the flowers.

'Before you ask,' Viper said, 'the circus is gone. The Evil Queen made sure of that. Sent most of my employees to the mines. Nona and I managed to escape, but'—she bit her cheek—'it's still gone.'

She pointed towards the older woman. 'That's Lady Nona. Why she called you, we're yet to find out, but she doesn't call unless it's important. That portal took a lot. Magic that big takes its toll.'

Nona gathered a bouquet of flowers, tying together the hydrangeas and snapdragons. The small fairy had picked some baby's breath, heaving it in her tiny hands, and placed it upon the top, her light glowing in joy.

Hansel swivelled back to Madame Viper. 'I'm looking for a woman.'

'Aren't all young men looking for a woman?' she said flatly.

'No. This one is different,' he said, ignoring her icy tone. 'You … you know her.'

Viper raised her brow.

'Her name is Eve. Eveline Rafter.'

The woman's eyes were cold, but he saw it, the flinch when he mentioned her name.

'Do you know where she is?' he urged.

Viper scowled, carefully turning the spatula over. With blank carefulness, she replied, 'I don't know anyone by that name.'

A truth for a truth.

Eve had told him about her time in the Cirque Magique. Had told him about Dante and the woman who ran it. She had no reason to lie, not then. Which meant Viper was lying.

'I have to find her.'

A gentle tap on the door interrupted them. Madame Viper shuffled past him and opened it, the topic of Eve drifting away like a breeze.

'Thank the cauldron,' Viper said. 'I don't know how long I could have stayed in here with this moping heap of a man.'

'I'm sure you've been a wonderful host, Tabitha,' Nona said with a smile as she entered. 'Now, help me up so I can talk to our guest.'

Madame Viper – Tabitha – gently helped the old woman into the vargo, making sure she sat comfortably next to Hansel. Porchid flew in behind her, zooming straight for Hansel's chest, where she nuzzled his shirt.

Nona was panting by the time she sat down, the shallow stairs into the vargo proving harder than anticipated.

Madame Viper frowned. 'Can this not wait, Nona? You need to lie down and take your medicine.'

Hansel heard the hitch in the woman's voice. Viper's tone had been softer, her eyes wary.

But the old woman waved her hand, her silver bangles jingling on her wrist. 'You know it must be now.'

'I don't see why we can't just wait until you're feeling better. The amount of magic you used—'

'I know exactly what toll that kind of magic takes.'

Viper's lips thinned at Nona's tone.

Lifting her paper-thin hands, Nona placed them calmly into Viper's, subtly winking at Hansel. 'However, more medicine would be good, please.'

Viper sighed, but obliged, leaving the vargo with one last glare at Hansel on her way out.

As soon as she was gone, Nona pulled out a pipe that smelt of apples and cinnamon.

'You know that stuff is bad for you,' Hansel said.

Nona chuckled. 'So are lots of things. Can't an old woman keep her pleasantries before she dies?'

Hansel frowned. 'It'll kill you.'

'Ah,' she mused, 'but I am already dying.'

Porchid winced, flying to Nona's lap.

The old woman smiled kindly down at the small fairy. 'Some things are inevitable, my little Riverbell,' Nona said, running her finger over Porchid's blue hair. 'Just as magic lives and breathes, so too shall we die. It's part of the adventure, is it not?'

'I suppose.' Hansel replied, his nose wrinkling at the scent of tobacco. 'Look,' he started, 'I'm grateful for the food and the help, but I'm looking for someone.'

'Eveline,' Nona confirmed, taking a puff of her pipe. It tinged the air, disappearing into the depictions on the roof. 'You're right. We don't have time for pleasantries. I'll admit, you were not my intended visitor when I opened that portal.' Nona leaned back, the smoke turning her eyes blood red. 'Eveline is alive – last time I checked, she was still breathing.'

'Is she safe?'

'Mostly,' she replied, her grey eyes darkening.

Hansel couldn't help the stone that fell into his stomach. Her words didn't soothe, nor were they alarming. He was more confused about why he'd ended up here and Eve somewhere else.

'What do you mean … 'mostly'?'

Nona took a deep inhale of smoke. Her eyes drooped, then returned to him. Despite the grey, there was something depthless about them, something sad and lonely.

'I don't have much time, so we will need to be quick,' she started. 'Like Viper, I'm an old acquaintance of Eveline's. What has she told you of me, of our travelling family?'

'She told me of a circus once. Of someone named Dante,' he said quietly. 'Otherwise, that's all I know.'

'She's a secretive little thing,' Nona replied with affection. 'Never been overly forthright with me, either. And she was stubborn. So much so that even fate couldn't deter her.'

'Fate?' he asked.

'Has Eve told you she is chosen?' Nona asked. 'If she's told you of Dante, then has she told you about his death? Has she spoken of her revenge and the prophecy?'

'I know about her quest to avenge her father's death, if that's what you mean?'

'And?' Nona pressed.

'And that she's after the Grimms.'

Nona smiled sadly at the mention of the sisters Grimm, her face contemplative somehow.

When she didn't respond right away, Hansel's thoughts spiralled. Eve might have given him a truth for a truth, but it was apparent to Hansel that he knew very little.

It wasn't a surprise Eve had held secrets from him, but he'd thought them to be little. The no-nonsense white lies that people keep to themselves. A stolen punnet of strawberries, an old broken heart.

'She was only little when she came here,' Nona said. 'She was terrified, and rightly so. Tabitha can be … strict. But Eve's path has always been forged, and I'm afraid it must be done alone. You may be looking for her, but do you think she is truly looking for you?'

He thought back to the forest, the glen and her words.

Come with me.

A truth for a truth.

It seemed that, whilst he was dragged along giving his truths, crumbling his own walls, she had kept hers.

It hurt more than he cared to admit.

'Perhaps,' Nona said, 'we should start from the beginning.'

VI

The Grimms Grimoire

'I am hers and she is mine.'

Bonyx woke to the grating sound of metal against stone. His lips were cracked and raw. Dirt and grime formed a thick layer on his body.

'You've been summoned,' a guard's voice echoed through the grate. 'Get up.'

Bonyx twisted his head, his old bones cracking as two rough hands hauled him through the cell doors. He blinked past hooded eyes, the glare of a fairy lantern blinding him momentarily.

Was this what death felt like? The slow and steady creak of bones, the groggy head, the weak muscles? Or did death come swiftly, like a ruthless blade cleaved through your neck?

'He's heavier than he looks.' The guard grunted to the others on duty.

Bonyx was led down the hall, towards a staircase. His nostrils itched from the sudden dryness of the stairwell, his body used to the dank cell below. He was taken through the lavish halls, the light streaming from the windows too bright for his sensitive eyes. His toes stretched into soft carpet as they stopped before a set of doors, and Bonyx wondered if this was where his story ended.

When a voice echoed, the guards shoved open the hard, heavy doors to reveal the throne room. The last time he'd been here he'd seen Beetle's heart torn out. Had watched as his cousin bled all over the floor. Bonyx steeled himself as he crossed the chequered tiles, following the same worn carpet to the familiar sight of Myrenna.

Her Majesty.

The Evil Queen.

Wrapped in red and purple, she smiled cruelly at him.

His eyes flicked towards the gilded mirror behind her, and Lady Nona once again came to mind.

The Queen stood, her ruby heels gleaming against the light of the chandeliers, and strode towards him. 'Hello, dwarf.'

Bonyx stared into the depths of her bright amethyst eyes and a shiver rolled through his body.

Myrenna only smiled wider. 'It's time for us to play.'

Myrenna was running out of time, and the mirror knew it.

It cackled in her dreams, its gilded frame shining through the haze of sleep. She saw it in the crinkle beside her eyes. The way her nightmares had begun to seep into her waking hours.

She was weary.

Bonyx had screamed in the throne room for hours, leaving her hollow with it all.

She still felt the magic on her fingertips from his torture, like a current cascading through her hands. She knew the thrum of his heartbeat. The scent of his blood. The sight of his muscles and veins.

And she'd felt each bone as it had snapped.

But the old dwarf hadn't given in.

His cries had echoed across the castle courtyards but it hadn't been enough. *She* hadn't been enough. She'd only stopped when a headache had begun to throb behind her eyes.

Another wasted day.

She raised her hand to her puffy skin and sighed. No matter the number of maidens, no matter the amount of magic, she was doomed without Snow's heart or the weapon in her mines.

If she lost either of them, then everything she had worked for, everything she had done to get here, would be for naught. To top it all off, she now had to kill the Seeker, the little wretch weaving her way into the destruction of all her plans. She was a problem. Another one to add to the pile.

Myrenna's building panic left a sour taste in her mouth. There was blood under her nails, the dried flakes curling around the edges of her cuticles.

'One problem at a time,' she muttered to herself. 'The dwarf is only one piece of the puzzle. Filthy creatures.'

She'd never dealt with dwarves prior to coming to Bellatorre. They weren't a common species up north. Her old village had the problem of trolls, and even then, she preferred trolls to the people who lived there. Humans were a selfish, destructive species.

Dwarves had been a new challenge. She'd imagined short, hairy things with little brain mass and a penchant for jewels. But what she'd found was vastly different. Short they were, but not necessarily hairy. They were miners, yes, but they were also scientists, magic wielders, writers, warriors.

Trolls were driven by gold, power, and their fanatical ways. They were easy to manipulate, easy to sway – especially when you could link it with their religious beliefs. Even if it was a sword into the skull of a brother or sister or lover. But dwarves held firm, protecting their kin even when all was lost.

It was infuriating.

Now she sat on her throne, staring at the blood coating the hideous carpet, as the sun fell below the horizon.

The mirror hissed behind her, seeming to follow her thoughts. *Age may have withered his body, but not his soul. The dwarf will fight you for the life you stole.*

'Shut up,' she snapped.

She didn't want to hear it, not when her own thoughts spiralled already. She swore she could feel its eyes boring into her back.

The mirror was a cruel reminder of what she had to lose should she fail.

She loathed the mirror and loved it the same. For, without its power, she wouldn't have become who she was. What she was.

With smooth movements, Myrenna let down her hair, the waves falling loosely around her shoulders.

Her spies were everywhere, yet the Princess and her party of followers couldn't be found. She knew they were being shielded by magic; it was the only explanation. It wasn't a matter of asking *how* they were being hidden, but by *whom?*

Next to the sisters Grimm, she was the most powerful sorceress in the realm. All Rumple had to do was give her power over the spindle. Just one teensy spindle. Just a few little dreams. That was all she asked.

But when the spindle had cracked, so had Rumple. It enraged her to no end. She'd even gone so far as smashing the vials inside her Tinker's tower. He'd merely bowed, his hunching spine, pathetic against her snarled threats. What good was the foul creature when he couldn't accomplish one small task?

Yet again, she was stuck between the sisters Grimm and a pouty princess.

The key was the dwarf. Despite his denials or silent temper or still demeanour, she knew he would break.

Myrenna barely looked up as her Captain of the Guard entered, his worn face dark against the low flames. 'Bring me Rumple,' she ordered.

Myrenna could feel the mirror's watchful eyes, its whispering power behind her.

She refused to look at it, to acknowledge her failures.

The only solace was that she'd not lost yet.

And she didn't plan to.

Bonyx shuffled onto his left side, his right arm going numb. His droopy eyes slid open to the sound of soft whimpers from the cell beside him.

He hadn't been able to reach Nona. Again. He'd waded through that pool of dreams sinking further and further, but the more he tried, the more he failed.

Violet eyes flashed before his vision, and he shook violently. Bonyx could feel it. The closeness of death. Age and resilience of the body did not go hand in hand, and the less he moved, the closer death crept. But he wouldn't tell her about the Princess. Not when Snow was so vulnerable. Not when he'd already lived and she had so much life to give.

He'd attempted a few more times to gather more information from his neighbour about Myrenna's plans but failed in that too. It seemed, that with each passing day the hopelessness grew closer.

The silence was suffocating.

VII

The Shadows of Madness

Eve's eyes flew open, her fingers gripping the hilt of her knife. She *hated* portal jumping, especially when it was against her will. Pain shot through her skull as she leaned against a stone wall, a cold sweat on her skin.

Eve blinked past her bleary gaze, taking in her surroundings with a shudder. Pale pink walls covered in ivy. A narrow window with a velvet-covered bed opposite a kitchenette in a circular room. A bookcase next to a blue chair.

A very familiar blue chair.

Her clammy hands slipped as she clutched her knife, her heart racing the longer she looked at the room. A room she'd seen a thousand times. A room in which she'd spent a thousand hours. With a girl whose shadows clouded not only her skin but also her mind.

On Eve's left stood a silver mirror. Etched into its frame were flowers and thorns, each petal carved into a distinct shape. Some bloomed like watchful eyes. Others closed themselves as if keeping a secret.

She jolted as a familiar face came into view, blond curls and bright eyes beaming at her.

'Welcome home,' the girl said, before Eve's nose was covered in cloth, a sickly smell knocking her into darkness.

Myrenna waited in her tower for her crows – her murders.

Her manicured fingers flipped through the pages of several ageing, decaying scrolls. A thousand times she'd shifted through these scrolls, and each time they'd proved useless.

'Useless again,' she muttered, frustration clear in her voice. 'What good is a kingdom if it doesn't bend to my will? What good is commanding armies if they can't follow basic instructions?'

There'd been so much sacrifice and yet, so little return.

The mirror had been annoyingly ineffective, its chastising voice a reminder of the toll Myrenna was taking. *Power comes at a heavy price my queen. Perhaps these humans are more than they seem?'*

Myrenna seethed at the response, the urge to scream rippling under her skin the more it spoke in riddles. The mirror always played by its own rules.

Her fingers clutched tightly at the edge of parchment, wrath tingeing her gaze red when she thought about her fruitless night, the old dwarf proving useless with no sugar or a scrap of blood to draw from in his brittle bones. She couldn't tempt him, couldn't bend him and she'd failed at breaking him.

She had followed the mirror's suggestion when she'd thrown the stubborn dwarf in the cell next to poor, broken Rumple. She hadn't liked the idea, preferring to isolate both prisoners to break their minds, but she'd obliged.

Annoyingly, the mirror had been right.

Rumple had been the perfect little spy without even realising it. The last time she'd yanked him from his cell, she'd brought his spindle. Her Tinker also attended. He hadn't just experimented on Rumple but on other prized prisoners, too. The Tinker had become obsessed with the bond between the spindle and Rumple, going so far as to manipulate the spindle as a tool to control Rumple's mind. To eat away at his sanity like a final meal.

Except Rumple only ever responded in the same way.

I am hers and she is mine.

To the mirror's endless amusement, impatience had gotten the better of the Queen. Before the night was through, Myrenna's screams had split the air, echoing with the vicious slice of her nails through Rumple's chest, where she'd felt torn flesh and scraping bone. It was only then, with a twist of her wrist, that she had finally broken the spindle's magic and in turn, Rumple.

The creature had shuddered before whispering one, simple word.

Nona.

Everything had gone into motion then. The healer was called – Rumple was no good dead – and Myrenna had fled for the stairs.

There was only one woman by the name of Nona. A seer. It was a rare, powerful gift.

Myrenna didn't think it possible, but a memory from long ago scratched at the surface of her mind.

There were travellers, those who journeyed the realm, who claimed to be seers, fortune tellers reaping the rich benefits of such claims. But they were usually fake. She'd dismantled enough troupes to know.

So, how was it possible this seer – Nona – had slipped through the cracks?

Myrenna's skirts whispered along the stone floor as she walked, aiming for her tower. She took the stairs quickly and threw open the doors to her study. She shoved aside some of the spell scrolls as she sat in the high-backed chair in front of her desk, then dipped the lone quill into the silky black ink and scratched a note onto parchment.

A large crow landed on the windowsill and bowed. Myrenna gave him the note, and he flew away. She tasted her own fear – an old emotion she refused to acknowledge.

Time was moving too fast.

She needed the artefact buried deep within her mines. She needed more recruits. More hands. Without the item, she was doomed. It was only a whisper, a forgotten thing, and even with her mines filling to its rim with new recruits, the artifact had not yet been found. She'd tried every avenue, every spell, but it was not something that could be called or commanded. It was a thing only found by the rarest of gifts.

A gift only one person held.

Eveline Rafter.

Had her biggest thorn now become her saving grace?

'No,' she hissed under her breath, turning towards the window with an impatient ripple of her gown. All she needed was her journals. They would be confirmation enough.

Two days later, when a crow cawed in the distance, his wings spread wide against the darkened sky, Myrenna finally smiled. He dropped a small scroll into her hand, his red eyes weary.

Her heart thrummed inside her chest as she tore at the ribbon and then read the words hungrily.

It remains untouched.

She smirked and twisted towards the crow. 'Stay hidden and stand guard. I'll be going out for a while.'

The crow nodded, spread his wings, and cawed over the castle. A collective call answered amongst the winds.

Myrenna had learnt long ago to never rely on someone else to bring you something when you could get it yourself. First, she had to visit the grave of a man she despised.

The day Eve's father died, her whole life had changed.

Within the span of one night, she had lost her only family, her home, and everything that had ever been familiar to her. Stumbling upon a pale pink tower after wandering alone, starving and delirious, had been like an illusion made real. Finding a girl close to her age with a roof, plenty of food and a warm bed was even better.

Eve had been welcomed into the pink tower without questions. Rapunzel had fawned over her with a thick blanket and fresh clothes. The girl had told stories, tucked her into bed, and somehow broke through the cold she'd been unable to shake since her father's disappearance. Impossibly, Eve had found a sister with whom she could mourn her loss. A sister who'd catered to her needs and made her feel safe when the whole realm was against her.

It had been good for a time. The two of them had swapped tales, shared recipes and experimented with games. But more than anything, in the moments when Eve had stared blankly at nothing, lost to the depths of her grief, the girl had sat with her and held her. The simple gesture had been enough to make Eve forget for a while.

They had never spoken of the shadows that lived and crawled under the girl's skin, smoky tendrils that had slithered beneath her bright smile and big eyes. She was a girl of contradictions. Erratic, and kind. Chaotic, and oddly still at times – like she had been listening to the writhing beneath her skin.

As someone with her own scars, Eve had never judged. But she regretted how blind she'd been. If only she had looked deeper. Paid more attention.

'Wakey, wakey, I've made us some food.'

Eve was sprawled on a blue chair near the bookcase, groggy and half conscious. The sting in her palm reminded her of the cliff, the blue smoke nipping at her heels before it had swallowed her whole.

She snapped her eyes open. She had fallen.

'You're awake,' a feminine voice said, and giggled.

Eve took in the room, and she was suddenly filled with dread.

But when she tried to move, the only thing she could manage was a tilt of her head.

Bad sign.

Her feet and hands were unbound.

Good sign.

Rapunzel grinned from the kitchen, the heat from the stove weaving its way through the room. She wore a laced gown, its green threads glowing dimly in the gaps of light that fought its way into the pastel tower.

'No need to speak, little Eve. Not that you can,' she said with a pout. She moved around the tiny kitchen, her quick hands grabbing and mixing ingredients. 'As long as you continue to behave, we'll get along so nicely.'

Eve could only watch, limp and defenceless, horrified as Rapunzel poured porridge into a brightly striped bowl. Her heart was a fist punching behind her ribs, her breathing jagged.

Rapunzel dragged a stool before Eve. She cocked her head like an innocent child, smiling wide, her eyes bright and unhinged. The woman's shadows writhed just beneath her skin, listlessly stretching above the demure neckline of her dress.

Eve had forgotten how *alive* they were. She swallowed against her heavy tongue. *What in the cauldron have I been drugged with?*

'Now, I know what you're thinking,' Rapunzel said, delicately laying a napkin across her lap. 'You think I'm being highly unfair. It's no matter, because in time you'll see we missed you. That we care for you.' She waited with a patient smile. Her lip twitched when she was only met with silence.

'Fine,' she said through gritted teeth. She spooned honey into the bowl and mixed it with precision, a hum seeping from her lips.

Eve avoided her gaze, taking in her surroundings instead. The room was the same as when she'd left, deceptively cosy yet clean. It was well lived in, objects displayed and cherished like a collector's favourite toys. As a child, it had seemed safe. But grown, it reminded Eve more of a dollhouse, a prison for unsuspecting toys, with no way out. The one solace was that it wasn't large, meaning her weapons wouldn't be far away.

Rapunzel continued. 'However, we do have the little teensy issue of your punishment before we can start the reunion.'

Eve's eyes darted back to Rapunzel, sweat coating her back at the word *punishment.*

'Don't look so worried!' Rapunzel said. 'We are sisters, remember?'

Rapunzel leaned forward and stroked Eve's leg. If the touch was meant to be comforting it had the opposite effect. It felt like a brand marking her for slaughter. Eve's body shrivelled away from the contact, the memories of what those hands could do rearing behind her eyelids. She tasted bile in her throat, phantom pains burning across her skin; scars well hidden by the leather she clad herself in.

'I will guide you. I know the true path we must walk, together.' Moving back, Rapunzel lifted a spoonful of food, the warped shadows crawling underneath her thin skin. 'Eat up. Mistress will be so pleased you are home.'

Eve tilted her head back and slammed her mouth shut. The click of Rapunzel's tongue was the only sign of her disappointment before she clasped Eve's jaw firmly. The grip tight enough to bruise.

'Eat up, sister.' Rapunzel cooed, squeezing Eve's mouth open. The spoon was warm as it was pushed between her lips, the metal grinding on her teeth.

Rapunzel's eyes glittered as she waited for Eve to swallow.

The porridge tasted like ash.

Rapunzel hummed in glee when Eve complied. 'Eveline and Rapunzel forever.'

Eve winced. Sweat beaded on her brow as she tried to force her body to move, to flinch, *anything*. Warmth burned at her side, the stone in her pocket pulsing like a beating heart. It called to her with a sting on her hip.

At least she felt something.

Pouting, Rapunzel placed the bowl down and closed her hands across her lap. The lace on her low neckline blew slightly from the breeze from the open window.

The same window Eve had once leapt from.

'Now, I know that I shouldn't have to,' Rapunzel said sadly, 'but that's the key word here, isn't it? *Shouldn't*. But I will anyway, just so we can tick our boxes.' Her smile widened, her teeth the colour of pearl, harsh against the dark shadows thrashing under her skin. 'Mistress always says, "punishment is the righteous hand that brings us back to humanity." Do you remember?'

Eve didn't have the capacity to agree.

'Do you remember when we used to giggle and I would comfort you? You told me you would never leave me …' She paused, her eyes glistening with glassy tears. 'And yet you did. You messed up everything!'

Rapunzel's shadows moved rapidly, pooling together like oil and water.

Eve managed to twitch her finger. The stone in her pocket was a steady reminder of what she had to lose.

'I don't want to punish you, Eveline. But your actions have left me no choice. You see why you need to be punished, don't you? The pain you caused when you left me. Actions have consequences. You ruined it, Eveline. You *ruined* everything.'

Her tone reached a fever pitch, the shadows swirling faster under her skin. She reminded Eve of a bruised corpse, the way a body decayed and became discoloured after death.

Rapunzel was delicate, had always been delicate. She was a storm of emotion set off by the slightest of winds. Eve had learnt to tame it over the years, catering to the girl's demands in that spoilt brat kind of way. Now, where Eve should have felt rage – the same rage she held for the Grimms – she only felt heartache.

Eve had lost her home, but she'd never lost her mind.

She twitched her fingers forward, pushing them closer to Rapunzel. The girl's eyes widened, and she dived for Eve's hand, sobbing. The shadows slowed. 'Oh, Eveline! My dear sister. I knew you would come back to me.

'Mistress said I was crazy, that it was a dream. She was certain you had abandoned me, but I knew better. I knew you would return. Mistress won't be pleased, though. We must placate her. You must never leave again. Promise me, Eveline. You must promise to never leave again.'

Eve's heart thundered. A promise was no small thing in this realm. Its very words were etched into that magical fabric of the realm. All Eve could do was twitch her fingers.

Rapunzel's eyes glittered. 'What fun we shall have. Mistress must be told immediately.' Rapunzel nodded to herself and whirled towards the kitchen. There, halting, her tone grew harder. 'Despite this happy reunion, I must admit, we cannot condone such behaviour, even upon your return.'

The words stilled Eve's heart. The echoes of her scars cried out, remembering. *Remembering.*

Rapunzel's arms turned inky black, her shadows heavy like soup, as she briskly tied her golden curls up with a bright green ribbon. 'Punishment is the righteous hand that brings us back to humanity.'

Bile rose up Eve's throat.

Rapunzel reached towards the bookcase, pulled out an old leather pouch, and unfolded it on the floor. 'I forgive you, my dear sister, but I fear Mistress may not if you do not pay for your betrayal.'

Sweat beaded down Eve's back. She looked towards the silver mirror standing against the wall where her reflection displayed terrified eyes, pale skin, matted hair. She tried desperately to reach for happy thoughts. Ones where Hansel had tried to outdrink her at a camping site. Hansel helping to calm her when her fear of heights had finally won. Hansel, who had kissed her under a starlit sky.

Hansel.

Who had fought by her side with the giants, and rushed to her aid, saving her and lighting up with relief when he burst into the inn's room and saw her smile.

A tear streaked down her cheek as Rapunzel came into view, a thin blade in her hand. 'Mistress must see the punishment. She must agree. And then, my dear sister, everything will be as it should be.'

Rapunzel's mouth quirked at the side as she lifted the blade.

Then began her first incision.

VIII
The Cauldron's Keep

The clouds veered across the sky, casting gentle shadows over the small band of dwarves. Bryn kept Rabbit close as they followed Bjorn up the sharp incline of a hill, all three of them puffing. The wind was cool, and the fading sun kissed their flushed cheeks.

Rabbit stumbled on a loose rock as they crested the hill and Bryn grabbed his arm to keep him steady. Rabbit awkwardly smiled at him, his teeth a green hue from some spiked leaves he'd been chewing throughout the journey.

Bryn's face creased with concern the more he observed Rabbit's anxious habit of constantly chewing on the mysterious leaves. 'What are you—'

'Storm's coming,' Bjorn said, sniffing the air.

Bryn looked towards the sky. Remnants of winter lingered in the chilly air, the snowcapped mountains gradually giving way to the beginning of spring the further south they travelled. When they'd left the grotto, they'd taken the twisting tunnels that honeycombed through the quieter, darker part of the mines. They travelled in secrecy, avoiding the main roads of the realm – particularly the road where Princess Snow had been found – and the Queen's Guard or unwanted eyes.

The journey had been hard – not just physically, but emotionally, too. The tunnels had been suffocating and seemingly endless. And when they'd stumbled upon the bones of a long-dead dwarf, Bryn had thought it a bad omen. He'd been proven right when they finally arrived at their cousins' home, only to find it abandoned. The hollowness of the desolate place still lingered with him.

Bryn tried to shake off the eerie feeling that kept creeping into his veins, focusing on not tripping over the rocky path. Bjorn was particularly quiet, his natural gruffness more prominent after what they had witnessed. Bryn put it down to the strange happenings long before the Seven had found the Princess. The Queen had laid siege to Perridorm, her armies doing their best to overwhelm its defiant borders. She was allied with the north, her power ever reaching. She was everywhere, the stain of her magic seeping from her gloomy mines. With the arrival of the Seeker, it was as though the world had shifted.

Hunting the trail of those that attacked their kin, they reached the edge of the Silver City. Bryn frowned at the pristine streets, feeling oddly offended by the brightly coloured buildings and shining cobblestones, so at odds with his dreary mood. To the west, the Crystal Lake glittered against the rocky mountains and sweeping plains, changing colours with the dying sun.

Rabbit kept swivelling his head back and forth, unable to keep still, his pupils unnaturally wide. When he stumbled again, worry began to creep under Bryn's skin.

'Bjorn, do you think …' His question fizzled out when he realised Bjorn wasn't listening. Despite their predicament, Bjorn was staring at the Queen's castle with such loathing Bryn was surprised it hadn't exploded already.

Bryn could only shake his head. 'Come on, let's go.'

Even with the sleet of rain slowly drenching them, the Silver City was beautiful. Its decorated buildings still shone despite the three defeated dwarves trekking up its cobblestone streets. Bryn couldn't help but compare it to the Queen: a shiny facade on the outside but rotted with wickedness deep within.

Bryn stayed close to Rabbit. They were muddy, wet, and miserable, but that didn't hinder Bjorn. The older dwarf trudged up the streets as if he owned them. Bryn kept his footsteps slow, attempting to blend in as best as possible as they rounded a corner near a canal. It was getting dark, and despite Bjorn's fervour to storm the castle, they all needed rest.

Bryn tucked Rabbit under his arm as they stumbled along the bridge, the rain dribbling into Bryn's now damp and heavy cloak. As they neared the corner of a run-down building, Bryn inhaled the melting pot of rich spices and the nearby market, his stomach aching and grumbling. If he could just rest and eat a decent meal, he wouldn't be so grumpy, he was sure of it.

Rabbit smacked his lips, the sound of his own stomach speaking for him. Their food had run dry days ago, their sacks no better than a featherlight presence at their backs. The dwarves walked sluggishly through the Silver City, their minds vague and trying to focus, a difficult task.

Bjorn was the one with a quick temper and a ready fist, bolstered by the flask of whisky he kept at his hip, knowing this realm was already on its way to doom. Rabbit was the mediator, the gentle soul, always willing to jump between conflict and be the calm he knew his kin didn't find easily. Bryn was a builder, a thinker and a dreamer, who took pleasure and pride in crafting things that mattered. The crystal coffin he'd built was a testament to that.

Bryn released Rabbit and placed a hand on Bjorn's shoulder, steering his attention back to his surroundings before he could tread off again. 'Why we don't stop here for the night?' he said, nodding towards a small sign just above a dimly lit fairy lantern.

The sign hung crookedly, attached by one thick chain as it swung against the lashing rain. Bryn squinted against the dark; the carved words nearly impossible to read.

THE CAULDRON'S KEEP

Music swelled behind the shut door, the scent of cooked lamb lingering in the air. Despite the dusk turning to night, Bryn could clearly see the makeshift posters that slapped against the rain-soaked buildings. Faces and names carved with words like 'treason', 'murder', and 'thief', a stark lineup of betrayal and bloodthirsty criminals. He scowled at the familiar faces before turning back to the establishment.

Bjorn glared at the tavern, his hand itching for his flask. His tone was blunt. 'It may be a warm dwelling in a storm, but we don't know what thorns it houses. Look at the signs. They clearly only welcome humans here.'

The capital had limited spaces for species other than human. Despite the Queen's mines, it wasn't openly illegal to be a dwarf, but it did cause concern. Nobody human trusted anyone *other*, and with the Queen's mines filled to the brim, everyone was looking for a quick medallion. But the dwarves' coin was as good as any other.

'There's no signage to say it doesn't accept dwarves,' Bryn said, shivering in the cold. His socks had long been soaked. His feet began to itch. 'We'll just have to be on our best behaviour. Right, Bjorn?'

But his cousin wasn't listening. Bjorn stared at the castle again, his eyes darker than normal, his face grave.

Bryn was used to Bjorn's grumpy ways, but where he would normally placate his cousin, honestly, he was too cold to do so now. 'Put your hate and distrust aside for tonight,' Bryn said, nodding towards the tavern. 'We just need to gather our bearings. Form a plan before thinking about storming a fortress of a castle.'

Before Bjorn could respond, Bryn pushed the peeling black door open and entered. A bell tingled on arrival, and a server met them at the door, taking their cloaks before guiding them to a booth towards the back. The tavern's interior was worn and damp, with old furniture and cushions that stank of mould. A tapestry hung from the wall: a faded forest, with an army approaching from the south, a great king steering his spear in a call of victory.

By the looks of the place, it was clear they weren't the only ones who sought safety from the storm. It was bustling. Bryn could see the keen eyes and handshakes of secret business deals, and the coin purse swaps for betting rings. In one corner, women sat on men's legs, giggling at whatever joke had been shared.

It took seconds for Bryn to see that they were the only 'creatures' mixed in a pub full of ordinary people. Maybe Bjorn had been right, they should have found a warehouse somewhere, or a safer haven closer to the slums. He clenched his fists as he took a seat in the booth, hoping nobody did anything untoward.

After ordering enough brew for twelve dwarves, Bryn finally relaxed. Rabbit sipped at his cup with care whilst Bjorn downed his in seconds. His cousin's face was wan, harsher than before, his usually trimmed beard longer, and Bryn wondered if he looked the same. Rabbit sniffled, Bryn noting the grey pallor rising underneath his skin. Rabbit inched his shaking fingers into the pouch at his side, already gripping the odd leaves he couldn't stop chewing.

Bryn snatched the pouch, frowning at its meagre contents. 'What have you been munching on?'

Rabbit didn't bother to look Bryn in the eye, his jaw working and his hands itching at his sides, taking in everything else except Bryn's question. Before Bryn could query further, the rowdy room broke into a bawdy song, stealing Bryn's attention. He couldn't stop taking in every detail, like his fingers wished to create everything he saw, even the rough edges of the scenery he sat amongst. The tavern was well spaced, the velvet curtains and bar dark and moody. The wooden beams lining the roof were carved to perfection, giving the feel of stories told over a fire. There were fairies and trees, wood nymphs and goblins. The windows were wide, meaning light would brighten the space during the day, providing pretty views of the canals.

Bryn took in the healthy gulps Bjorn swallowed of his tankard. The wild gaze of Rabbit, and the wary gazes that filled the tavern every time they stared at their little group. Bryn saw so much, and he grieved for the dwarven colony.

The once-boisterous community had been full of dwarves. Bryn faintly remembered how the children had run through caves and tunnels leading to pools of water. The way he was immersed in every crafting stall on market days. And how, whenever he felt too lonely, he could always wander the halls where the markings of old stories would keep him company.

But those weren't the memories he'd been greeted with when they'd arrived. The gates had been ajar, and silence reached them from as far as the road. Whipping posts had been left bloody and wretched from the sins that had been committed against folk who couldn't fight back, covering the courtyard in an array of pain and despair.

Bryn, Bjorn, and Rabbit had come for answers, and for help. Instead, they'd only found death.

Rabbit sniffled hard, yanking Bryn back to the present. There was sweat on his brow, his light hair sticking to his skin. Bryn touched the young dwarf's forehead, only to frown. It burned.

'Bjorn,' he said quietly, 'we need somewhere to rest for the night. Rabbit is unwell.'

Bjorn downed his third drink. 'I'll see if they have any rooms available. This place is as good as any, even if the brew is weak.'

Whilst Bjorn beckoned for service, Bryn noticed a group of soldiers that kept staring, their discontent ripe in the closed air. They wore the Queen's emblem: a bright red apple framed by gold. They wore their uniforms with vicious arrogance, the purple and red colours obnoxiously bright against the dull tones of the tavern.

Bryn's eyes darted past them and met a stranger's gaze from across the room. His uniform was unlike the others. Still pristine; ironed in a crisp fashion, with gold buttons. His hair was jet black, slicked back, with a set of piercing green eyes. He lingered just outside of his companions, with them but not quite. His eyes bore into Bryn's, challenging before he quickly winked and turned away.

Bryn jumped as Bjorn dropped a few coins into the server's hands.

'Maybe we should find elsewhere?' Bryn said, his skin prickling at the soldier's gazes. 'I don't think we should stay here. There are too many soldiers, and too few of our kind.'

'I disagree,' Bjorn grumbled. 'Everywhere is a soldier's domain in this city. It would be too suspicious to leave now.'

'But the posters outside—'

'Do not have our faces,' Bjorn said as he leaned across the table. 'If anybody asks, we'll state we're reporting for duty.'

Bryn frowned. 'Reporting for duty?'

'For her Majesty's mines.'

Before Bryn could reply, Bjorn raised his hand. 'I know you think I'm not thinking clearly. That I'm blinded by grief.' He scoffed. 'You can think whatever you like. I'm well-aware of our predicament. But this is how we get to them.'

Them. Their cousins.

Bryn's eyes flicked back to the stranger. His sharp eyes never left them, keen and predatory like a cat smirking at the wayward bird he stalked from afar.

'Okay,' Bryn conceded, 'but we need a healer.' He nodded at Rabbit, who was nearly laying his head upon the sticky table.

The server came, and Bjorn whispered in her ear, dropping a shard of a tiny gem in her hand. She choked in surprise but pulled herself together quickly. With a curt nod she turned and hurried for the owner. 'A good night's sleep, a meal, and planning out a murder should do our little Rabbit some good.'

'We are not murderers,' Bryn snapped under his breath.

Bjorn laughed. 'Of course not. But, considering our circumstances, dear cousin, we have little choice.'

Bryn's stomach churned. If they had kin alive, then the Queen's mines would be where they were kept. A project the Queen had started years ago.

Nobody knew exactly what she was mining, but it was something the Queen had extensively 'recruited' for. It was a place for those with no home, no hearth. It was a place for lost chances and lost hope, where death was a welcome friend.

Bryn sipped his brew, but it sat like a muddy puddle in his gut.

Murder, Bjorn had said.

But all Bryn could wonder was, what they would become before all this was over?

IX

The Fourth Grimm

Myrenna was not a fan of shapeshifting. The pain wasn't the kind from a small crack of a shoulder or paper cut; it was the kind that felt like a whip tearing through flesh, the kind that stole your breath and stopped your heart.

It was all she could think about as she panted before the mirror and changed. Her collar bone protruded first, cracking abruptly and shifting until her skin became fine as paper, barely covering her bones. Her teeth turned black, and sunspots speckled her gnarled hands. The only part of her not laced in pain was her scalp, where her hair transformed from raven locks to bone, threadbare tendrils.

Myrenna stared at her handiwork, holding back the shiver threatening to crawl up her spine. She hated herself this way. Frail. Old. Ugly. But with power, there was always a price.

Myrenna draped her cloak over her shoulders. It was heavy on her weak bones as she collected a basket full of fruit. The apples were ripe and red, just like Snow's lips.

It reminded her of blood.

The sky crackled. Flashes of white speared the night sky, the scent of rain pressing against the heavy air. Even nature knew something was coming.

Her mind flashed back to Rumple, beaten and bloody, as he'd wheezed out his confessions.

Nona.

One whispered word, and the Queen knew what she needed to do.

Satisfied with her disguise, she stood on the parapet and took a deep breath. The rain fell in sheets, soaking into her clothes. Nobody would see her fly. Nobody would suspect her. Nobody who did still lived.

She hesitated, ever so slightly, at the caw from one of her crows, then she twisted her wrist and broke into a wind made of ash, flying north into the dark rolling clouds.

The tavern had rooms for rent in a small building out the back, just past the stables. Covered in mud, Bryn managed to wrangle both dwarves into the room, one sick and one obnoxiously drunk.

The room was as Bryn expected: tiny and bare. But at least they were clean. Rabbit shuddered as Bryn filled a tub and helped the shaky dwarf out of his loose shirt and boots.

Bjorn was already snoring. The sound grated Bryn's ears. He picked up a bar of soap and soaked it in the bath's warm water. Rabbit coughed, his phlegm sickly and green. The server had advised them that a healer would come but couldn't promise anything until morning.

Bryn held Rabbit upright in the bath, ensuring the dwarf didn't drown. With the calming scent of the rich soap and a hum loosing from Rabbit's lips, Bryn's mind wandered. What was to become of them all after this? They couldn't just sail into the castle and attack like a pack of wolves. They needed allies, and to think logically.

But Bryn wasn't a strategist. He left that to Bonyx and Brufell. All he'd ever been good at was dreaming and creating.

Bryn tried to calm his spiralling thoughts as he lathered the soap and scrubbed Rabbit's scalp. When the dwarf was finally clean, he eased Rabbit out of the water, and put him to bed.

Bjorn had passed out on the floor, leaving the large bed free. Bryn stared at it dreamily. With the long journey, his full belly, and a brew, he climbed beneath the clean sheets and sighed. Despite the harrowing few days, and Rabbit's worrisome wheezing, exhaustion settled over his bones. Sleep lulled him with ease.

He dreamt of the colony, of the princess locked away in a crystal coffin, and just as he dreamed of Parador, he was startled awake by a figure in the dark.

Dawn had not yet broken when a hand clasped firmly over Bryn's mouth.

A stranger leaned over him, draped in black, with a bow covering their back. But it was the large, curved blade in their right hand that he truly feared. He squirmed, and the stranger's lithe form shifted. They raised their gloved finger to their lips.

Stay quiet.

Bryn's eyes widened as the jingle of keys echoed on the other side of the door. When the lock turned with a resounding *click*, the stranger silently moved off the bed and positioned themselves by the door.

Bryn knew he should run, but a part of him refused to move. The door handle rattled, and his sleep was long gone.

The door burst open and the Queen's Guard crowded the cramped room, blades ready.

Before he could scream, a sword sliced near his head. Bryn rolled from the bed, gasping as the guard swung again. Feathers fluttered the air, and a shout followed. The blade cut through the air but missed him by a hair's breadth. Bryn scrambled across the floor, the soldier pursuing at an alarming pace.

'Get behind me!' Bjorn yelled, axe in hand. Bryn yelped as his cousin stood on his finger before charging the soldier. There were screams, and the twang of metal rebounding off metal, soaking the room in sweat and blood.

Bryn barely had a moment to glance at Rabbit when a soldier charged him, knocking him over the table. He scrambled to his feet, barely avoiding the soldier's blade when the black-clad stranger emerged from nowhere to cut him down.

An axe was shoved into his hand, Bjorn shouting something he couldn't hear. He didn't get a chance to respond before another soldier was on them and Bryn raised his weapon. The metal clashed, ringing down his arm. The soldier pressed forward and Bryn barely held on.

There was the distinct sound of metal meeting skin, then a gurgle. Bryn was suddenly aware he had no armour, no protection. Desperate, he opted to shove his opponent with clumsy force. The soldier fell with a wet yell on a curved blade.

Bryn staggered back. The stranger ripped free her blade and winked at him from behind her black layers, then charged towards her next victim.

She moved faster than the night wind. Bodies fell beneath the slick cut of her blade, one after the other. Bryn stood in stunned silence as the stranger sliced and hacked and slashed. Though it had felt like hours, it was only moments until a sea of purple and red uniforms lay still on the carpet.

Bryn wanted to swallow but choked. So many corpses, so quickly carved up like pieces of meat by only two curved blades. He barely recognised Bjorn's tight grip on his arm as he raised his axe at the black-clad stranger.

Stepping casually over the bodies, she wiped her weapons on her pants and pulled down her mask to reveal a silver-skinned face. 'We need to move.'

Bryn sucked in a startled breath.

Her long hair was bright silver, her ears pointed at the end. He had never seen one of her kind before – they usually died at a young age.

'Changeling,' Bjorn grumbled.

'Hello, *dwarf*,' she replied, rolling her eyes. 'Now that we've established our species, could we please leave? Gather your belongings. More will come.'

The air had the metallic tang of blood, and with so many dead bodies, his stomach twisted on itself.

Bjorn braced his arms, ready for an argument as always. 'Why should we—'

'Get your belongings, Bjorn.' Bryn ordered, bile in his throat. Bryn ignored Bjorn's stunned gaze as he pulled on his boots.

'We don't know who she is,' Bjorn started.

Bryn pulled back Rabbit's blanket and tried to wake him. 'She saved our lives. If she wanted us dead, we would be.'

'But …'

'But nothing, Bjorn. Would you like to face down more soldiers, or her? Rabbit is sick. The healer isn't coming.'

The changeling checked the corridor. 'There will be medicine where we're going.'

Bjorn stared daggers at Bryn, but helped him get Rabbit to his feet, stumbling and weak. The changeling waited by the door, patient as the dwarves collected their belongings. Bjorn heaved Rabbit over his shoulder as Bryn adjusted the packs across his back and chest. The changeling peeked out the door, and nodded at them when it was safe to move.

The axe in Bryn's hand was heavy as he stepped over the corpses, his stomach queasy.

Murder, Bjorn had said.

Had he become what he feared already? Though her blade had been one to kill, he'd been the one to shove his assailant into it. The blood was still warm on his shaking hands.

As they followed the stranger through the halls, Bryn began to doubt his choice. Had he gone mad?

They piled out onto the empty cobblestone streets. Bjorn held Rabbit close as the changeling hushed them. Their feet sloshed through puddles from the rain. Rabbit panted, his pallor a sickly grey. Peering round a corner, the changeling waved them forward. Their short legs took two steps for every one of hers.

Bryn's eyes darted around, looking for the familiar purple and red. No matter how hard he tried, he couldn't calm his beating heart. It roared so loudly in his ears he was surprised it didn't leap up his throat.

Ahead, the changeling unsheathed her blades as two more soldiers turned the corner. They'd had no time to blink before her blades sliced them. The wet thump of their bodies hit the cold cobblestones.

The changeling ushered them forward. 'Quickly.'

The road wound up a small hill. The dank canal water stunk as they passed. Bryn noted the posters plastered across poles and bridges, clashing with the colourful walls of the establishments.

RECRUITS WANTED:
For her majesty's mines.
Species of any kind welcome.
Non-human preferred.
Large reward.

Bryn's skin prickled. What the posters failed to mention was that recruits received nothing until their contract was fulfilled, most of them not surviving long enough to claim its bounty.

The group rounded another corner, the road narrowing into a thin street as the changeling took another sharp turn into an alley. The wall on Bryn's left displayed more posters. Wanted signs for specific people. A thief here, a traitor there. But it was the freshly painted ones that caught his eye. For there, in a beautiful sketch, stood Eveline Rafter. And beside her, Malak and Hansel.

WANTED:
Traitors against the crown.

Bjorn's shout pulled him away, and he stumbled down the alleyway. The changeling stopped in front of a wooden cellar door built into the ground. She knocked twice, paused, then rapped thrice more.

The door opened with a nudge, and a man's head appeared. No, not a man — another changeling. He was broad in the shoulders, and the edges of the door creaked against his width. His skin was made of what appeared to be stone. He eyed the stranger first, recognition flashing in his eyes before they fell on the group. 'What is this?' he asked.

'Recruits,' she replied.

Bryn's body turned to ice. Had they run from one enemy into the arms of another? Bjorn grasped Rabbit tightly, shoulders ready for an attack. The comatose dwarf's condition had become considerably worse since they'd left the tavern.

'We need them,' the changeling insisted. 'They're strong – I've seen them fight. They'll be valuable to the cause.'

The cause.

Bryn's ears burned at the words.

'I told you this wasn't a good idea,' Bjorn whispered.

The changeling leaned forward, whipping her knife out and holding it at the man's throat. 'Let us in, Darquin,' she hissed. 'The guards are not far behind, and I outrank you.'

'You know I can't,' he stammered. 'Not without the code.'

She gritted her teeth but conceded. 'Skin as white as snow, lips as red as blood, and hair as black as ebony.'

'Fairest of them all, may she reign true,' Bryn interjected.

Darquin eyed them with renewed interest as Bryn finished the code. 'Okay,' he said, and turned to the silver changeling. 'Will the Commander be okay with this? You know, when he gets back.'

'You let me handle the Commander,' she said, motioning the dwarves into the cellar.

Resentment shone in Bjorn's eyes as they carefully lowered Rabbit into the stairwell. It was a tight fit, but the bottom opened into a deceptively large cellar. Rows and rows of casks mounted the walls, spreading into the dark.

The stone changeling grunted at them as they passed, and handed the silver assassin a flamed torch. She nodded her thanks before moving through the stalls into the darkness, not hesitating as the dwarves huddled after her.

Shouts rang above them as the man flipped back the wooden slate.

'Go on, then,' Darquin said, waving them away.

That was a close call.

Bryn blinked, his eyes adjusting to the dark. This was where dwarves felt most at home. Their eyesight far better than humans. The ground was made of sand, their steps silent as the flame flickered against the casks of wine.

'You know the code?' the changeling asked, though it wasn't a question.

'Seems we're on the same side,' Bryn said, cautious.

Beside him, Bjorn scoffed.

They reached a second door. The changeling pushed against it, revealing a much larger room, with pillars of ivory and high ceilings. And where the cellar had been devoid of life, this room was filled with the cacophony of voices.

Bryn looked to the walls, where tapestries of old were spread in all shapes and sizes. Some of gardens, and others of battle, raging over the hall like a living, breathing memory.

Fairies flew near the ceiling, their wings shining against the torch light. Trolls settled themselves in the back corner, sharpening their weapons. Mingling and sharing meals were dwarves, sea nymphs, pixies, and witches.

'What *is* this place?' Bryn gasped.

'The Sanctuary,' the changeling replied, with a soft smile. 'Our temporary home.'

Rabbit moaned.

The changeling flicked her eyes to Rabbit, concern lining her brow. 'I'll answer everything soon. Let me take your friend to Doc first.'

The dwarves followed her to a door near the back. The changeling lifted the curtains to reveal another room filled with narrow cots and a busy elf.

He turned in surprise at their arrival, almost falling off his stool.

'This is Doc,' the changeling said. 'He's the best there is. He'll fix your friend right up.'

Doc wore round spectacles perched on his slight nose, his hands careful and delicate with how quickly his narrow fingers moved. He was jittery. His hair thinned over his wrinkly scalp, and his clothes were roughly spun cotton. None of these traits instilled confidence in Bryn as they laid Rabbit onto a cot with care.

'Mmm,' Doc mumbled. 'F-fever. Yellow nails. Black veins.'

The elf took some notes, nodding to himself, before turning to the group. 'C-can you p-precisely tell me when your friend began eating vox leaf.'

'Vox leaf?' Bjorn repeated blankly.

'Y-Yes,' Doc replied. 'A small green leaf usually l-located in the lower p-parts of the mountain regions. H-highly addictive and unfortunately p-poisonous.'

'Could it have been the leaves he was chewing as we entered the city?' Bryn asked Bjorn.

'What leaves?'

'By the cauldron, Bjorn.' Bryn replied. 'What do you mean, "what leaves"? The ones he was chewing as we travelled.'

Bjorn only frowned.

'You can be insufferable sometimes,' Bryn hissed. He turned to Doc. 'Can he be cured?'

'If he's a recent user, then I m-might have s-some s-success,' he replied. 'I'm low on s-stock but we s-should have enough to s-sustain him for now.'

'How much is enough?' Bryn asked.

'Enough to cover the withdrawals until the scouting party return,' the changeling said.

Bryn nodded his understanding as he watched Doc put together a makeshift medicine. Rabbit calmed as soon as the tonic was placed onto his lips. The sight released the knot in Bryn's stomach.

The changeling touched his arm. 'For now, we'll find you somewhere to sleep.'

She farewelled Doc and led the two dwarves into the main foyer. Bjorn and Bryn stayed close, their eyes darting between the crowds. Bjorn yelled out a name and his pace quickened towards a dwarf Bryn didn't recognise in the crowd.

Bryn stood alone as Bjorn and the new dwarf embraced, both of them laughing. The dwarf was older, his trimmed, dark beard was stark against the white of his long hair.

'Bjorn, what in the cauldron are you doing here?'

'Looking for you,' Bjorn said, grasping his arm. 'We came across the colony, and it was …'

'Gone.'

The changeling lightly touched Bryn's arm and he flinched. Still, she didn't let go.

'The dwarves will have a bed for you,' she said. 'I'll come find you tomorrow. However, should you need me before that time, simply ask for Piccadilly.'

Bryn thanked her before she melted into the crowd.

Bjorn shouted and waved him over. 'Bryn, it's Zacariah!'

Bryn turned his head to his own kind. There was a warmth in knowing some of his kin had survived, but there was also a sense of dread. He let Zacariah embrace him as he joined the group, and accepted the food that was given. But even in this place filled with hope, Bryn couldn't help but stare towards Doc's door. Where Rabbit was possibly dying.

The onslaught of rain was a blessing.

It shielded Myrenna's tracks as she stood drenched before a burnt bakery in the town of Butterpond. Signs had been nailed in, worn but still legible.

Cursed, they read. *No entry.*

She shouldn't be surprised. She'd left this place in scandal, hated and plagued before she'd ever set a foot wrong.

She despised Butterpond.

The bakery was the only piece of this forsaken town that she'd truly loved, discovering and moulding her craft, creating her famed apple pie.

Myrenna shook off the memory as she veered down the rough dirt path, bypassing the old tavern where music danced against the misted windows.

Myrenna gripped her basket of fruit and quickened her pace, her old knees cracking in response. Even in disguise, she was loathe to run into anyone that might know her past life.

The path led her out of town towards the paddocks, where she spotted a familiar wooden temple, its lanterns swinging against the howling wind.

The walk was longer than she remembered, and more dire as she trekked up the small hill. The shapeshifting had depleted her more than she cared to admit. Her guards had been short on maidens, and though they were the most potent, they weren't her only option. She'd found that most hearts would do what she required.

The door creaked behind her as she entered the temple's old archway, her boots tapping against the marble floor as she marched towards the altar. On her left, a glow of yellow light stretched across the floor from a thin doorway.

Just as she'd remembered.

Taking one of the lit candles, she held her cape and made her way into the twisted, dark, the stairs transforming from marble to worn stone. Below the temple it was damp, cool, and she sensed the familiar tug that had pulled her down here all these years ago, calling like an old friend.

It opened into an intimate cavern. One wall was littered with wine casks, the other a library of scrolls. A reading area with a desk was situated in the middle, placed over an old, decaying rug.

Myrenna's nose twitched from the subtle coating of magic in the room. She would need to move with caution.

Lifting her candle, she placed the basket onto the table and rounded towards the back. There she found a pile of old tapestries rolled up and hidden away exactly where she knew they would be. Chains were draped over the shelves, but with a few muttered words she had unlocked them.

With fervour, Myrenna dug into the pile and unrolled them one by one. When the last one was left, she noted the decaying edges. Myrenna heaved it towards the larger part of the room, lay it down and carefully unravelled it along the floor. Its black ink was prominent against the long-faded reds and gold, but that wasn't what Myrenna was staring at.

A spark of fear coursed through her.

For in the middle of the tapestry lay a large cauldron, its clawed feet sharp with bone nails. And surrounding it was not three figures draped in cloaks, but four.

Myrenna had been naïve enough to hope it was only a dream. A small blip in this long lifespan of hers, but staring down at the tapestry, she *knew*.

'Can I help you, ma'am?'

Her head snapped up to see an elderly man in his sleeping clothes.

'The temple is closed, and this cellar is off limits.'

She plastered on her best smile. 'Forgive me. I got lost with the storm. I was trying to find a safe place to shelter in.' The lie rolled off her tongue with ease.

'Oh,' he said, startled. 'Of course. All are welcome to shelter from the elements. There are spare rooms in the upper levels. I can show you to a warm bed? I know how much the storms hurt brittle bones.'

Her heart trilled. 'I only just arrived. Perhaps I could sit a while, maybe eat something?' Myrenna nodded towards the table where her basket sat.

The man hesitated and looked up the stairs, then back to her. 'Yes, of course,' he replied. 'Did you pick all this fruit yourself?'

She smiled at him sweetly. 'From my very own garden. I'd hoped to stop by the bakery and sell it to them, but I was dismayed to find it burnt. And then I got caught in the rain on the way home.'

'I'm afraid the bakery has been shut for years. The villagers usually head to the city for speciality items these days.'

Myrenna coaxed some of her magic forth, using it to lull him into a sense of security. 'Yes. I heard it was cursed.'

He nodded sternly. 'Cursed is correct. There is an interesting tale surrounding it, actually.'

'I love a good story,' Myrenna replied. 'Come – share a meal with me, and you can tell me the tale?'

'Thank you, but I couldn't. My daughter is upstairs, and she wouldn't approve of me eating snacks in the middle of the night.'

'Oh, nonsense. What is old age but an excuse to do what we please?'

He chuckled again. 'Alright, then. But be sure to not tell her.'

'It'll be our little secret,' she purred, as she handed him the ripe apple sitting on top.

He took a large bite, moaning at its sweetness. 'This is divine. If our bakery was still open, I'm sure you'd make a killing.'

Myrenna smirked. 'Oh, you have no idea.'

'You are too kind,' he said, taking another bite. 'The baker was a good sort. He always helped with the market days and the Coronation of Cakes festival.'

Myrenna tried not to flinch at his words, urging him to eat.

'The poor fellow was widowed. He only had one daughter, but she was a plain thing, and very odd. The villagers didn't take to her too well.'

Myrenna gritted her teeth.

He continued. 'She kept to herself, but she showed promise. Her baked goods were impressive, but she was a jealous little thing. During a wedding between two of the village's sweethearts, she poisoned the cake and …' his fingers started to shake. 'I'm sorry. I'm not sure what's come over me.'

'Keep going,' Myrenna urged, a twitch in her lip giving way as he took another bite. When he swallowed, his old hands grasped the table.

'Tell me more about the girl,' Myrenna ordered. 'Plain girls amount to plain things, after all.'

The man began to choke, his face pale, as the apple slid from his palm.

Myrenna's smile broadened. 'Plain girls amount to plain lives.'

His eyes widened in horror. Black veins crept from his pupils, and his mouth foamed. Myrenna stood and watched him clutch his throat, satisfaction lining the cruel smile playing on her lips. 'Now, where is the grave registry information?'

His eyes bulged, his body teetering on the edge of the chair. Myrenna rolled her eyes. 'All you need to do is point to it.'

He sputtered blood upon the table, his body convulsing.

Myrenna sighed deeply. 'Fine. I'll find it myself.'

Clicking her tongue, she turned to the scrolls against the wall.

'Papa?'

Myrenna's head whirled towards the staircase. She swore under her breath before conjuring a tiny bit more magic. She recalled the old man's voice, its huskiness and its kind tone. With a cough, Myrenna mimicked it perfectly. 'Down here, my sweet.'

'Why are you in the cellar?' she called.

There was a shuffle of feet on the stone steps.

'We have a guest, my dear,' Myrenna cooed back.

'A guest?' she asked.

The light of the candle reached the bottom step, its glow fading as Myrenna stepped forward. 'Yes, dear. A *queen*.'

Myrenna's nails shot forth, piercing through the girl's young flesh. Her high-pitched scream echoed through the chasm as Myrenna gripped the throbbing heart within her chest.

'A queen who needs to feed.'

Myrenna tore the heart free, warm blood oozing down her hand.

The girl's body had not yet hit the ground before Myrenna tore into the heart with her sharp teeth.

X

The Blood of Sisterhood

Hansel couldn't settle. There were too many questions still lingering, too many variables and what ifs. The tension in his shoulders brought an ache, but part of that could have been his broken heart, too. A heart that was slowly withering the longer Eve was missing.

Nona smiled kindly at his unease. She reminded Hansel of a parent tucking in a child and reassuring them that monsters weren't real. But he knew better.

'The tale of the cauldron and the sisters Grimm is well known,' Nona began. 'But it's a tale that has warped over time.'

Nona sucked on her pipe, the scent of cinnamon filling the vargo in a fragrant haze. Porchid shifted until she was sufficiently comfortable, her wings nestled on a soft cushion, watching intently as she listened for Nona's story.

'I believe the best place to start is where all good stories begin,' Nona said. 'Once upon a time, when the stars ruled this land and when the realm was but a gap of dust between what began and what became, there lived only fairies.'

Porchid squeaked in excitement and Nona chuckled. 'Not the type of fairies we know today, little one, but ones who dabbled in tricks and games. Fairies who had pointed ears and were five pixies tall.'

Hansel rubbed his eyes irritably. Eve was somewhere out there, and he was listening to a fairy tale. He clenched his fist on his twitching knee.

Nona's grey eyes watched him carefully, but she didn't comment. 'These fairies were born by starlight, from a petal, only once a year. Upon one summer eve, when the dusk covered this realm, one fairy set out to find this flower. But when he came upon it, the petals were withered and without child.

'In his sadness, the fairy turned towards the stars. In those days, the stars held more power than any being in the realm. They would give, but they could also take.

'The fairy asked for a child, one made of his own blood and not from the petals of a flower. In their kindness, the stars agreed to grant his wish. But there was a condition. The child may share his blood, but would learn from the village, knowing what it was to be kind and selfless.

'The fairy was delighted and promised the stars it would be done. It was then the stars created a great gift of power. A fat-bellied onyx cauldron. The fairy in his glee took this gift and promised the stars they would share this bounty and build a realm full of kin and happiness.

'But the fairy's joy was not long lived. When the fairy approached his kind, they scolded him for his bargain. It was too much responsibility, too large a task, and they sent the fairy away. With a sad heart, he hid away within the darkest part of the forest, taking the cauldron with him.'

'I don't understand the point—' Hansel started.

'Of course you don't,' Nona said sharply. The air in the room tightened somehow, the swirling smoke almost coming to a halt as her eyes pierced his. 'You understand nothing until you understand history.'

His mouth was a tight line.

She continued. 'Years passed, but the fairy did not forget. He became a twisted, foul thing. Something dark and vengeful. Alone in that forest, his resentment festered. But the stars had given him hope. Despite his village banishing him, the fairy had created his children, four of them to be exact. But they were *other*; a breed unknown.'

Nona coughed, her hand shaking with the pipe.

'Are you alright?' Hansel asked, reaching out to catch her trembling hand.

'Yes, yes. Tabitha will bring my herbs in no time,' she replied. 'Please, don't distract me, I need to cover everything.'

Hansel blinked in concern. 'Go on.'

'After a time, the four children grew. Human form they took, and yet, not human at all. They held great power, but their minds were dark. They were cruel. Selfish. Nothing at all like the fairy had promised. Tell me, huntsman, do you pray to the Fairy Godmother?'

He had, once. It had been a belief ingrained in him since childhood. A power that ruled over fate and destiny.

Nona's eyes sparkled at his hesitation before waving her hand. 'Do not be worried. You are a creature of this realm. As we all are.'

'What happened next?' Hansel asked.

She smiled sadly. 'The four would play tricks, practicing their magic on other fairies they found in the forest. Taking pleasure in pain. But one day, when an unknown fairy from the village arrived, everything changed.

'The village fairy had come to find the Fairy Godmother, begging him to return. The other fairies now wished for the same dream and admitted to their error. A vision of smallings, raised by a village in peace.' Nona took a long breath. 'However, hate is a powerful thing. The Fairy Godmother lashed out, and they argued. Words turned to swords, and upon its end, the Fairy Godmother was killed.'

Porchid gasped, but Hansel could only frown. This was not the tale he knew from his childhood. In the version he knew, the Fairy Godmother had won and, as such, watched over the realm.

Nona took another puff of her pipe. 'In their revenge, the four children used the cauldron's power in an act of war. And in so doing, created four mirrors that gave them immortality. Silver for one, and gold for another; black for the third, and the final in ivory bone.

'Using this new power, the four siblings crafted new creatures. Green beasts who were huge in size. Fairies sly enough to snoop. Pixies with sharp teeth, and creatures that could live on both land and sea.

'In their hatred, the four siblings wiped out the village fairies, and let their made creatures build a home. But in their haste, they did not predict what would happen next. A future where those same creatures could create their own kind. Creatures who did not rely on flowers to bloom once a year, but creatures of love and hope and dreams.

'As time passed, the siblings' resentment grew. Once again isolated, they called themselves the sisters Grimm and ruled upon these lands. Authors of the realm. Keepers of the cauldron.' She waved her hand. 'And other names I'm sure you've heard of.'

Nona coughed again, this time a hefty thing, spraying blood on her palm.

Hansel pulled out a handkerchief and handed it to her. 'We can take a break.'

Her weathered hands shook. 'No.'

Hansel frowned as Nona gripped the table, sweat beading her brow. 'Four sisters there were, yet you know them as three. For the last sister watched their creatures grow, her heart twisting at the creation of love and hope and family. Whilst her sisters grew more isolated, focusing on their hate, the fourth sister grew weary.

'She had power and immortality, but without love she could not see a future. So, one day she vanished, leaving her sisters in their misery. Though not without a price.'

Nona looked up. 'You see, Hansel, the mirrors have long been hidden. They are the key to the Grimms' undoing. Upon the fourth's betrayal, her mirror of silver was damaged, leaving her with a long yet mortal life.'

'Did the other sisters not come for her?' he asked.

Nona snorted. 'They did. For a time. She scattered what mirrors she could, made them difficult to find. She suppressed her powers by eating the petals of a nightkiss flower. For years, she lived an ordinary life. Walking among the creatures, welcoming humans as they sailed to this great land and made it their home. Even on occasion, falling in love – only to watch them die of old age. But whilst she lives a mortal life, she still lives a full one.'

'She still lives?' Hansel asked, his interest piquing. The tales had only ever been of three Grimm sisters; to know there was a fourth, someone who might fight with them—

It changed everything.

'She lives,' Nona confirmed. 'She breathes today as she has done since the beginning of the realm.'

'Where is she now?' Hansel asked, almost afraid of the answer.

'She found her way to a circus.'

Blood and rain stained Myrenna's hands as she clawed into the ground of an unnamed grave. She could still taste the young girl's heart on her lips. Rich and pure.

She gritted her teeth as the sky shook with lightning, her violet eyes flashing in the dark. Dirt packed under her nails the more she dug and heaved away the thick mud, pushing deeper into the ground with fervour. She swallowed down the vile hatred she felt for its occupant.

The grave stood apart from the others. Its tombstone was blank, apart from a carved 'X'. Her nails cracked and bled, snapping as they hit the hardened wood of the coffin. Wiping the last remnants of mud away, Myrenna grinned in victory.

She'd coated this grave with hefty magic when she'd buried its occupant. A test of her power of sorts. A way of ensuring that only she could dig up its contents. And though she knew it had been protected, her paranoia had won out. Every year since that fateful day, she'd sent one of her murders to check on it, and every year they'd come back with the same answer.

It remains untouched.

The lid creaked as she pulled, her brittle bones fighting against the closed lid. It fought back, wanting to keep its contents hidden. She screamed in frustration as it finally cracked. She panted, throwing the wood to the side, and stared at its rotted interior.

The bones of a man lay inside, holding a bottle of rum. She snarled at it, then dived for a small chest in the corner. It was plain wood, carved simply, with a flimsy padlock.

She remembered a time when that padlock was secure, safe. A place where her dreams remained protected by a trivial key. She chastised the girl who had locked them away.

Myrenna pulled the box out of the grave and clutched it to her chest.

She stared at the night sky as the rain fell in harsh waves, lashing at her and the open coffin. The temple's lamp still swung in the dark. She thought back to the old man and his daughter.

Sacrifices had to be made. She'd known this from the very moment she'd stepped away from her old life.

'They had to die,' she whispered to herself.

She kneeled on the grass and snapped the small lock, opening it to see three leather-bound journals. Grinning wickedly, she ran back to the church, falling to the floor of the foyer and tearing through the fragile pages. Her handwriting was a blunt reminder that every memory, every emotion, had been a living, breathing thing. A tear slid down her face, mixing with rain, as old memories cut at her.

She hated it.

Hated them.

Hated herself.

The weeping, whining, pathetic little girl who'd written these passages. The girl who'd let weakness overtake her.

Her broken nails whipped through each page, dampening them with blood and water. She didn't want the beginning of the journals; she wanted what came after. The part where her life had truly begun. The part where she'd left that plain girl and turned her into something glorious.

She flipped through her lost journals and found a page with a tiny cauldron sketched into the top right corner and a prophecy.

Today Papa told me about a witch in the forest. He threatened that she would hurt me if I didn't do what I was told. But instead of running away, I went straight into the forest and met her.

She was old, and laughed at my Papa. She told me the old man knew nothing. She said she wasn't who I should fear, for she was not a witch at all. Just a lonely, old woman.

I remember being so angry that he had lied. Angry that this woman laughed at me just as the others do. But as I went to leave, she stopped me, and told me of the sisters Grimm. The sisters who live deep within the enchanted forest. The sisters who hold the cauldron itself. Witches who created this very realm, their power an untamed, unimaginable thing. How could Papa not know about such creatures? Such gods living amongst us just like the Fairy Godmother.

I didn't believe her. If Papa didn't know of them, then how could they be real? But Papa had also thought she was a witch. So instead, I listened as she pulled a book from her shelf and offered me tea.

'Witches four,' she read, 'at the dawn of days. A cauldron of onyx and the power to raze. A realm created and creatures grown, but power corrupts, turning hearts to stone. Witches four, but three remain, one's heart not twisted with darkness and pain. The sisters Grimm, ageless and dark, yet a sister lest forgotten with hope a spark. Witches three, who bargain and steal, whilst the fourth remains hidden with the power to heal. Witches three, with grimoires of gold, whilst the fourth will age, wither, and fold.'

She told me that they could see things. Things that have happened. Things that will come. A seer is a rare thing. The woman stated that, whilst three live in the forest, there remains only one true seer in the realm.

Someone named Lady Nona.

Myrenna screamed into the temple, the book skittering along the ground.

A fourth Grimm.

Her knees slammed into the floor. How could she have forgotten? How could she have not remembered?

The journals stared back at her mockingly, confirming all her fears.

Nona was protecting them. Protecting Snow. Protecting Hansel. Protecting the Seeker.

The fourth Grimm lived.

And she'd been in plain sight the whole time.

XI

The Prophecy of Mirrors

Hansel's palms were sweaty. The weight of the realm's history heavy on his shoulders. 'What does this have to do with Eve?'

'Eveline knows,' Nona said with a sigh, wiping blood from her lips. 'There is a prophecy one the Grimms have held since the creation of the mirrors. One Eveline is very familiar with.'

'What prophecy?' he whispered.

'I'll admit, I was surprised when she ended up with the circus after her father's death,' Nona said, ignoring his question. 'The girl, living and breathing and right here. I thanked the Fairy Godmother for her. She is the end of a great tragedy.'

'What prophecy?' Hansel insisted, louder.

Nona's smile was sad. 'The one that will either save us or doom us.'

She took a breath before she began. 'Mirrors four, of black and bone, of silver and gold, and night blue stone. At the dawn of light, with powers three, a soul will tear, and hearts will see.

'A gift for giving at the aftermath, or a land in ruin of pain and wrath. When one will stray, another shall gain, and in blood and loss they will be slain.

'When betrayal and love finally mix, hearts will shatter as seven become six. Wood from a tree that's existed an age, and mirrors of glass in a watery cage.

'The theft of a gem and its keepers' revenge, an obsidian cauldron and the price to avenge. Shadows of memory, death will reap, but an act of love will wake her from sleep.'

The silence encompassed Hansel, and he found it difficult to breathe. The more answers he discovered, the more questions arose.

Eve *knew.*

Everything that was happening, everything that would happen, was linked to her. No wonder she remained shut off. Careful. Protected. No wonder she remained alone and isolated, hesitating to help the rebellion. When one held that kind of weight, how did they cope?

His heart ached for Eve and for what had been done to her before she'd had a chance at freedom. She was a girl who chose her path, who fought for her choices and dreams, yet was dragged into a fate that she had no control over: to save a kingdom that had done nothing but give her pain and disappointment.

'Where is she now?' Hansel demanded, even though a thousand more questions pressed on his lips.

Nona fought a cough that wouldn't let go. 'She is where she needs to be. She understands her responsibility. She knew what choice to make, all the more for knowing you.'

'You backed her into a corner,' Hansel accused, jumping to his feet.

'She must do this alone, Hansel. It is her destiny.'

He kicked the chair. 'I can't accept that. She deserves better. She deserves to make her own choices, to have *freedom*.'

'You cannot help her now.'

'Tell me where she is. *Please*,' he begged.

Before Nona could argue, she coughed roughly, her form crumbling over the table. The door was almost torn off its hinges as Madame Viper rushed in, her hands filled with vials of medication. 'Nona!' she shrieked. 'What's happened?'

Nona collapsed onto the floor in a coughing fit. Madame Viper dropped the vials to catch Nona's head before it smashed into the ground. She lowered the woman with a softness Hansel didn't recognise. Then she whirled on him.

'What have you done?' Viper screeched.

He couldn't move. 'I …'

Nona locked eyes with him as Viper collected a vial. 'You must find the Seven and help them,' Nona coughed. 'Leave Eve to her destiny and she will find you.'

Viper dabbed the blood trickling down Nona's chin. 'Please, Lady, take your medicine.'

Nona swiped at it, the vial's contents smashing onto the wooden floor. 'It is her fate. As yours is to the rebellion. To free *him*.'

'Him?' Hansel prodded. His eyes widened as Nona's body convulsed.

'*Find her at the end*,' Nona gasped. And went deathly still.

Viper's scream pierced Hansel's ears and his thudding heart. He stepped back, confused and rattled. Porchid clung to his shirt with tears as Nona's dead eyes stared towards the ceiling, her body transforming before his eyes.

Viper stepped back, her long nails digging into his arm as she tugged him towards the door. 'We have to leave. NOW.'

But despite Viper's warning, all he could do was watch.

Nona's body shimmered.

The air grew taut, as if it were trapped in a bubble. Pain shot through Hansel's skull as the light around Nona bloomed.

The ground shook. And just as Viper screamed, everything exploded.

Hansel was thrown back as a wave of energy crashed into him. The vargo shattered. Hansel flew through the air, pulsing with light and screams and magic. The earth scorched his skin as he rolled into the tree line. He reached for a root, holding on tight, just as the world exploded.

He covered his face, the trees bowing to whatever force rippled outwards. Wind punched Hansel's skin in wild bursts. Debris sliced his skin. The ground shuddered. He blinked, and the clouds split, the ground crumbling as if nothing had ever stood before. The only thing he could do was grit his teeth against it all.

And then there was silence.

Hansel groaned deeply, his ringing in ears louder than his thoughts. He blinked, taking in the scorched earth. There was a burning sensation on his back, cuts and bruises no doubt lacing every inch of his skin. The ground was desiccated, but in the distance, swelling through the air, was a power rippling like a tidal wave across the realm.

Viper sobbed nearby, wailing as she sat in the destruction of her old home. Porchid winced beside him, blood mattered in her hair. Scooping her up, he assessed where she was hurt, but beside a cut on her brow she was okay.

The fourth Grimm was dead, Hansel still had no inkling where Eve was, and he was more confused than ever.

Find her at the end.

Nona's last words echoed through him like the blast of power. His destiny lay in the rebellion. In saving whoever 'he' was. And whilst his heart had completely shattered like the glass of a mirror, he knew what he had to do.

'May the Ever After hold you close,' he whispered into the wind.

Myrenna was flipping through the pages of her old scrolls when she scented magic on the wind. It smelt of dust and sage, with a hint of tobacco.

She was already standing when the screams in the city shattered the air. Through her tower window, the fairy lanterns dotting the streets blinked out. Wind swept with fury, pulling her hair free as the stench grew.

And far in the distance, the forest groaned.

'What in the cauldron is happening?' she muttered.

A knock banged on her door, angry and urgent. She'd only just turned when the air shuddered. She barely had time to brace herself before the magic hit, sweeping through her tower in a violent rage. She was thrown back. There was a *crack* as she hit the wall, and blood bloomed in her mouth.

The door burst open, her Tinker panting as he took her in. 'My Queen, I tried to warn you. The scouts saw it coming, but there wasn't enough time.'

Gritting her teeth, Myrenna steeled herself as she stood, scrambling towards the window. She ignored her Tinker as he followed. Ignored the way he wheezed.

'There was only one being with enough magic to release that kind of power,' she said, more to herself than him. 'A Grimm.'

The Tinker followed her gaze towards the sky where the magic left a trail of destruction in its wake. 'But even a Grimm isn't immune to the consequences of magic,' he said.

Her gaze snapped towards him, her mind turning it over. He was right. Magic had consequences, severe consequences depending on what the spell was. For something that large, that destructive, it could only mean one thing.

Death.

Myrenna cackled at her sheer luck. Maybe fate was on her side. Already, she thought of the possibilities, the potential.

A Grimm had died.

One down. Three to go. Myrenna eyed the gathering skies, latching onto the north star. 'I need a carriage. The finest we have.'

East it would travel. To Maelstrom. Where it would receive a royal welcome without her.

Myrenna could barely contain her excitement. 'If I move quickly, I can find the source.'

With the gilded mirror and a Grimm's grimoire at her disposal she would be one step closer to her goal.

'Is it prudent to go alone?' her Tinker asked.

She shot him a warning glare. 'You have your instructions, why are you still here?'

'Forgive me,' he said, and scuttled off.

Myrenna rubbed her temples. The mines were going strong, each day closer to the power she craved. Even with the princess gone, this presented a rare opportunity. A chance.

The grimoire would hold exactly what she needed. An answer to what she'd been searching for. The instructions on how to kill a Grimm.

For once, things were finally going her way.

The blade hovered over Eve's arm.

Punishment.

Rapunzel's delicate hands were slight but steady. Eve's mind crashed into a blazing sea of memories as the blade lowered. She shut her eyes tightly and thought of the days before her father had been taken. When she'd worn flower crowns and he'd sung her to sleep. The day she'd found Porchid – her first true friend. The day she'd laughed by a campfire with Hansel. She thought of Dante as he weaved stories about the stars, of how he held her elbow steady as she hit her first target with a knife.

Eve swam in her visions, preparing, waiting for the sharp sting of the blade. Her scars ached across her back and legs, heavy reminders of where she'd been punished before. The whip for theft. The small nicks for lying. The beatings for speaking back.

She pushed down those vile memories and swallowed bile. She'd survived this tower before. Had managed Rapunzel's emotions. But she had also leapt recklessly for her freedom, knowing what she risked. She wouldn't change any of her choices.

The hairs on her arms raised. There were vibrations first, then the scent of incense and tobacco and lilac.

Dante's voice echoed through her like a well-oiled bell: *You will feel it first.*

The stones rattled, and the air became thick with the taste of magic. Then a *crack* rang through the realm.

Power pulsed through the air, throwing Rapunzel into the bookcase with a heavy crunch and tumbling Eve's chair. Eve's head smacked into the stone floor, and her ears started ringing. Blood bloomed from her forearm where Rapunzel's blade had nicked her skin. Her hip went cold as the blue stone flew from her pocket and started glowing deeply. Her hand twitched. She gasped at the pain in her shoulder and smiled. Her body was sluggish, but she was moving.

Eve stretched out her arm, her hand inching closer and closer to the stone. She thought of Hansel, his open and honest heart urging her to take it. A tear snaked down her cheek as she stretched her arm to breaking point.

She had lost so much already. Her father. Her mother. Dante.

But she hadn't lost Hansel and Porchid. Not yet.

The stone was her home. Her way out. Her heart. Her last connection to Hansel. She would not lose it too.

She kept reaching, the pain in her shoulder from her fall like a blade as her breath hitched. Inch by inch she stretched, until finally, *finally,* her hand clasped the stone.

The stone's power jolted through her as if gold filled her veins. The power was a palpable, living thing. Gone were the pains, the bruises, the screams, and aches.

Rapunzel started moving in the corner, regaining consciousness. Eve lurched upright and stumbled for the bed. She knew all Rapunzel's hiding spots – Eve had even helped her build a place safe from her *Mistress.*

The clock on the wall chimed, the figurine of a princess twirling through its wooden doors, as Eve pulled up the mattress. Beneath the mattress was an incision. She tore into the material, her nails screaming, down feathers falling like snow.

Rapunzel cackled as Eve bolted to the stairs and yanked desperately at the planks, finding the loose ones, but—

Nothing.

Eve's ears pricked with silence. She whirled towards the bookcase, her fists raised and teeth bared. But all that lay before her was books and torn papers strewn across the floor.

Rapunzel's voice echoed against the stone walls, everywhere and nowhere. 'Mistress told me, you know,' she hiccupped. 'She told me you left on purpose. That you didn't love me. That you were a *liar*.'

Eve strode towards the bookcase, but Rapunzel wasn't there.

'I didn't believe her,' Rapunzel continued. 'I knew you would always return.'

Eve whirled around the room, tasting panic on her tongue.

Think. Think.

'You … you said you would never leave me. You *promised!*'

Eve's heart thrummed. She had no time, no memories of specific moments in the tower – most of them had been blanked out, pushed far down into the abyss of her mind. There was no point correcting the girl. Rapunzel believed what Rapunzel wanted; always had.

The Seeker grabbed one of the loose planks she'd found earlier and held it at the ready. Inside her, a spark of hope bloomed to life as she remembered the wardrobe. She stepped carefully as she moved towards the cupboard where a small compartment lay hidden in the floor. She remembered two little girls giggling as they built it. Placing a lid carefully over the handwritten letters to each other, full of promises and secrets.

Rapunzel's voice whispered darkly near her ear. 'My Eveline. *My sister.*'

Eve spun around to find nobody there. The destruction in the room reminded her of an abandoned house. She thrust open the cupboard door and peered inside. Her hands were shaky, her body a rush of adrenaline, as she smashed through the cupboard floor.

But even the letters were long gone.

'My little liar,' Rapunzel echoed.

Despair gripped Eve's core. After all this time, after all her training, she was still laid bare. No weapons and no indication of how the girl had vanished. She felt eight again. Lost in a tower with a friend and foe. A girl she loved and hated at the same time.

She dropped the plank. It was no good against an invisible enemy, anyway. She blinked as tears streaked down her cheeks, silent in her fear.

Eve raised her arms in surrender. 'Rapunzel, you can come out.' She said, carefully stepping around the debris as she neared the bookcase. 'I won't hurt you.'

Rapunzel cackled. 'Mistress will not be happy with you. Mistress will not let you live. Mistress will take you away.'

'Let me speak to Mistress. I'll make her understand.'

Rapunzel hissed. 'Mistress will only speak to me.'

Eve flinched, though she'd expected nothing less. The first time Rapunzel had flipped on Eve was the day she'd asked too many questions about Mistress. Despite living here for several months, Eve had never seen Mistress.

There had been shattering glass. Then Rapunzel's shadows as they'd snaked up her arms, transforming her eyes into an inky black.

That had been the day Eve received her first punishment.

The Seeker now stood inside the tower, her feet moving slowly through the broken furniture, and halted in front of the tall, silver mirror. She tilted her head.

Everything within the tower had shattered. But the mirror remained intact.

'Mistress does not forgive,' Rapunzel echoed. 'Mistress does not forget. Mistress will have your head.'

'Better than my heart,' Eve whispered back.

Eve stared at her reflection, not recognising the woman before her. She was strong, but her cheeks were hollow, and her eyes sharper. She had no soft lines, no delicate features.

'When trust is broken, sister, it can never be fully repaired,' Rapunzel echoed.

Eve reached towards the mirror, her hand moving of its own accord.

Eve's reflection flickered, smiling at her though Eve kept frowning. Her fingers twitched as she touched the glass, the surface becoming translucent, watery.

Her reflection whispered to her. *Come closer.*

'What magic is this?' Eve whispered to herself.

'This will be your final punishment,' Rapunzel promised, her voice steady and calm.

Eve felt heavy. She leaned closer, peering to see what made this mirror special, when a blast of heat shot up her side from the stone. Eve hissed and stepped back just as Rapunzel's round face appeared underneath the mirror's surface.

The girl's irises were pitch black against her pale skin, her golden hair limp.

Eve cried out as the stone burned her again. She yanked it from her pocket, almost dropping it. It was hot, searing. And it glowed like a pulsing heart.

Rapunzel calmly stepped through the mirror's surface, the thick shadows roiling under her skin. She lifted two familiar golden blades and aimed them at Eve. The weapons looked wrong in her dark and delicate hands.

'You were always a liar,' Rapunzel murmured. The shadows pooled, turning her milky skin into tar. 'Let's see how you lie without a tongue, *sister.*'

Eve twisted smoothly as Rapunzel dived, her blade aimed for Eve. Eve dodged, gasping as the blade nicked the skin of her ear.

Rapunzel's hunched form charged towards Eve for a second strike.

Eve ducked, and the blade whizzed past her cheek. She spun, barely avoiding each thrust as Rapunzel closed the space between them, unnaturally fast. Eve blocked with her forearm as she was backed towards a wall. When Rapunzel lunged again, she used her weight to thrust Rapunzel back.

Eve hurled her body towards the bookcase, ignoring the burning in her arm.

'You betrayed me,' Rapunzel growled. The sound reverberated through Eve's bones.

'*Please,*' Eve begged, 'we can stop th—'

Rapunzel dived, her arm extended. It left her right side exposed. Despite the guilt, Eve moved with precision and took her shot. Both rolled across the floor, limbs and bones and teeth.

Somewhere along the way, Rapunzel had lost a blade, but it didn't hinder her as she threw her arm out to attack.

Eve grasped a hardcover book and thrust it at Rapunzel before the blade aimed at her neck could connect. It sunk deep into the book's pages, the knife's tip poking through the other side.

Eve swore under her breath, re-evaluating her habit for consistently sharpening those blades. Pages of parchment and ink rained as Rapunzel yanked the knife free and swung towards Eve's face.

The Seeker rolled, her elbow screaming as the knife slashed her skin. Warm blood ran down Eve's side as she picked up the lost knife and spun, meeting Rapunzel's with a clash.

Rapunzel's nostrils flared. 'You are a spiteful, hateful, *lying* little girl.' She pushed Eve back, but the Seeker held her ground. 'You are no sister of mine. You are no daughter. You are *nobody.*'

The words hit Eve harder than any blade, and she faltered. Rapunzel's black eyes pierced hers, and Eve recognised nothing behind them.

'You are forsaken,' Rapunzel said, seething, 'Doomed by the cauldron to be alone.' Rapunzel's hands shook as she smiled, a wicked, quiet thing. 'You won't escape the prophecy no matter how far you run.'

Rapunzel tackled Eve and knocked the breath out of her, both crashing into the mirror. The glass creaked under their weight.

Eve grasped at Rapunzel's wrist, attempting to twist it, but failed. Rapunzel began to laugh, the sound maniacal and unhinged. They wrestled, and Eve's side burned with the stone's magic.

Rapunzel gained the upper hand, her grip locking onto Eve's neck. Her hot breath pressed against Eve's cheek as she squeezed. 'Mistress always knew you weren't worthy. Too weak to fulfil what needs to be done. Especially now that a Grimm has died. You are useless. *Pathetic.*'

Eve choked, tears stinging her eyes.

'Nona was weak. Already forgotten. Just as you shall be.'

Eve's cheeks heated at the pressure of blood, her eyes bulging with the lack of air. The room seemed smaller, the mention of death reminding her just how fragile mortality was.

Nona.

Nona was dead.

Eve's mind screamed as she gasped for air, her voice failing her. There was nothing she could do but stare at Rapunzel and unleash every emotion she could. Her grief for the Seer who had tutored her. Her pain for the loss of so many friends. Her fear from her moments in this tower. And her anger for the manipulations and broken promises of two little girls.

Rapunzel gripped harder as if she could see the threat in the Seeker's eyes. Could hear the violent thoughts seeping through. Her voice sounded hurt but hard when she said, 'Today, you will die.'

Rapunzel sunk her teeth into Eve's shoulder. Pain rippled through her. She tried to push Rapunzel off, but her muscles were already weakening. Black spots coated her vision.

She thought of Nona. Of a tale told to her again and again inside a small tent. A tale about a girl whose destiny had already been decided, and how compassion can change history.

The right choice was not always the easiest. Eve knew that now, more than she ever had.

Even though Rapunzel's skin burned black, the blood thick at her throat, she was still Eve's sister. A small piece of her that had helped her heal after her father's demise. And though there was only one way to end this; it didn't hurt any less.

Rapunzel tore free from her shoulder, blood coating her lips.

'I'm sorry,' Eve croaked.

Rapunzel only tilted her head in confusion. Her grip never faltered.

Eve didn't know how, or why, but that feeling she had when her gut pulled her towards finding something, it pulled at her now.

And she trusted it.

Her eyes were wet with the friendship she'd lost, and for the life she was about to steal. 'Mirrors four, of black and bone, of silver and gold, and night blue stone.'

Rapunzel's eyes widened. 'Eveline.'

Eve choked again, but the words had already registered. Rapunzel twitched, her eyes pleading. 'Eveline, no. I'll tell you what you need to know. About the ancient one and the other mirrors. Where they are. Please, Eveline. *Please.*'

Nona's death meant Eve's journey had begun. She was now in a series of unfortunate events that would eventually collide.

Eve reached towards her pocket. She gripped the stone like a weapon even as it seared her skin, its silver veins flowing with life.

Rapunzel screamed in fury and lunged for the stone. But Eve was too quick. She kicked Rapunzel off her, rolling to the side as she lifted the stone. A weight covered her soul.

She lunged towards the mirror, shoving back any hesitation, any regret, and using every ounce of strength she had left.

Rapunzel screamed.

The mirror cracked. A fissure in a rock. A web in a spider's nest.

Time stopped and started anew. A burst of light exploded at the first crack in its perfect glass, then spread, shattering along its surface.

Rapunzel sobbed violently, then attacked. She threw Eve to the floor, and straddled her, her fists aimed to strike. Pain ricocheted through Eve's skull, each punch of Rapunzel's knuckles just as powerful as the first blow. Eve could only lay helplessly, her body swollen and numb. She tasted blood and bile, Rapunzel's screams ringing all around her.

The cracked mirror glowed as magic seeped into the room, crawling along the floors like shadows. There was a hiss in the air. Then a shudder.

The mirror shattered.

Eve didn't feel the weight of her chest loosen. Didn't hear the scream of her old friend as she was swallowed by light.

Eve watched in horror, the tower shuddering. She latched onto the bookcase and prayed for survival.

But as Rapunzel screamed, her voice trembling the air, Eve understood that everything had changed. The realm had been forever altered.

When the world finally silenced, Eve rolled to her side, barely registering the bites of the glass strewn along the tower. She tasted blood and spat it onto the floor.

The tower lay in pieces. Glass amongst paper, paper against wood, wood against blood.

With shaking limbs, Eve crawled through the debris to her dead friend. Tears streaked silently down her cheeks as she took in Rapunzel's small frame and milky white skin. Gone were the shadows and the black eyes.

The mirror was destroyed, the only semblance of its existence etched inside the blue stone. Eve hesitated before picking it up, noting how cold it was against her skin and choked back a sob. One mirror gone, three more to go.

She had fought it, pushed against it, denied it, but the prophecy had now begun.

Fate sunk into her skin. She couldn't escape it now. The worst part of it all, was that she had more to lose now than ever before.

XII

The Breaking of Bargains

'The Sanctuary has been around longer than many know,' Cousin Zacariah said between bites of stringy chicken. 'I just thank the Godmother it existed when we needed it.'

Bryn sat quietly, observing the clash of personalities in the vast, underground hall. Bjorn sat beside him, taking a healthy gulp from his flask. The axe-happy cynic was never without his own supply of booze, and Bryn almost felt like he should have some too.

The last few hours had been a whirl of back slaps and hard hugs, their cousins' hospitality strong even in the face of hardship. Bryn and Bjorn had been allocated a bed, handed food, and given brew – much to Bjorn's glee. The dwarves remained hearty, but underneath the reunion, there was the blemish of hurt and festering anger. Bryn could see it in the wary gazes and the way people were slower to be free with their words. It's what the echo of scars could do to a person.

Zacariah had gathered the dwarves, distracting and entertaining them with grand tales and stories long past. Bryn steadily ate his dinner, noticing the embellishments the older dwarf liked to sink into his storytelling.

When asked about the gutted colonies, Zacariah turned solemn. He waited until the others were deep in conversation before turning to Bryn and Bjorn.

'There are some stories that can only be told in private,' he said. 'Follow me.'

He led them down a candlelit corridor, ending in a closed-off room. Once the trio were settled around a small table, their brew fresh and Zacariah's expression suddenly dark, he said softly, 'A story for a story. Tell me what drove you to the Sanctuary, and I'll tell you the tale of the colonies.'

Bjorn drunk deep, gesturing for Bryn to do what he couldn't. Where Bjorn was made for drinking, fighting, and bossing others about, Bryn was the one who could see past the smaller picture. Whilst his heart ached for what was lost – had been taken from them all – he knew that there was power in telling the truth.

Bryn sipped his water and ignored the clammy sweat on his palms. 'Well,' he started, 'it begins with an unconscious princess.'

Zacariah was quiet throughout Bryn's tale, nodding when it was appropriate and asking questions for clarification. His heavy eyes assessed their story, his hands interlocked.

Bryn exchanged a glance with Bjorn, noting his gruff pride, and sat a little straighter for the story he'd told. He hoped he hadn't missed anything. Stories weren't just tales passed between lips; for them, it mattered what was said and how it was told. The way of Dwarven tales was another kind of magic.

Their stories were what made legends.

Zacariah rubbed his chin before taking another sip from his cup. 'So, the little one – Rabbit – is with Doc?'

Bryn didn't know what he expected, but it certainly wasn't the pivot in conversation.

'Yes,' Bryn said. 'He's eaten some kind of strange leaf.'

'And what of the others?' Zacariah asked. 'The ones spread across the realm. Two in this glen of yours and the others marching to an unknown fate to Trolls Keep.'

'We've heard little since walking our own journey,' Bryn replied.

Zacariah's gaze was sharper than the gems they scavenged. 'Interesting that the Seven would ever separate, despite your vows. Is the Princess worth such a sacrifice?'

The air in the room was charged as Bjorn leaned forward in challenge, his tankard empty. 'Is Snow not the reason you're also here, cousin? This is the sanctuary of the rebellion, after all.'

Zacariah snorted. 'I haven't agreed to take up their cause just yet. Not when my own kin still require help.'

'Speaking of our kin,' Bjorn interjected, 'tell us your version of events. You've heard ours.'

'Indeed,' Zacariah responded, sipping on his drink. 'But perhaps another night.'

When the old dwarf stood, Bjorn blocked his way with a puff of his chest, his eyes lit with cold rage. 'You promised a story for a story. We've told ours.' he growled. 'I thought there was honour between dwarves and that we could speak freely, without favours owed. Has your honour changed so much?'

'Death marks us all differently, cousin,' Zacariah said, quietly.

'This is not your first time seeing death.'

'I see you're still a stubborn brute.'

'And you're still a secretive old fool.'

The two of them growled at each other, but Bryn saw the lines etched into Zacariah's face, the weight of his dead kin evident in his defeated shoulders.

Bryn reached for the jug as Zacariah took his seat with a huff and refilled their cups.

'Our ears are open,' Bjorn said, waiting.

'As are our hearts,' Bryn finished for him.

Zacariah nodded solemnly, his large hands clasping a mug. 'Since you seek the gory details, perhaps for your own conscience, I'll give you the answers.'

'Dodge the dramatics,' Bjorn snapped.

Zacariah's mouth was a tight line, but he didn't bite back this time. 'Things were changing in the colony before your arrival. By then, the Queen had begun recruiting and there was discord among the younger dwarves.'

'What kind of discord?' Bjorn asked.

'A lot of the youth wishing to break free and create their own clan. Just as the seven of you had done.' Zacariah's jaw tightened, a thread of anger seeping into his blunt tone. 'At first, we were hesitant. We are a traditional people, after all. And whilst we welcome you each year as kin, I cannot deny that some of us resented you for being the cause of this unrest.

'It was slow at first. Some young ones went off to explore the realm, others signed up for the Queen's army, and some even left to find you lot, deep within Parador.

'As the dark times set in, we shut off trade and hid away in our tunnels, living in the dark until … until the Queen came and offered us a reprieve.'

Bjorn nearly interjected, but Zacariah stopped him with his raised hand.

'We were desperate,' Zacariah continued. 'With the discord and with no trade, we were low on food and supplies. Gems are pretty things, but they do not feed a colony, nor do they keep us warm at night. We had weapons, but what good are they against a mist you cannot pierce?'

Bjorn's face turned a deep purple, his anger nearly palpable. Bryn placed his hand on his cousin's arm, giving it a small squeeze before nodding to Zacariah to continue.

'We struck a deal with the Queen that, should we work in her mines, she would protect us. We put it to a vote'—he paused—'We advised the Queen that some of our people would be willing to work if the rewards they earned would be given to those left behind – food, water, and anything else they required.' Zacariah swallowed the last of his drink. 'The Queen complied. For a time. When we hadn't heard from the others nor received our bounty, we sent word to her.'

Bjorn leaned forward, his thick forearms twitching in agitation.

'It wasn't a list, or a demand,' Zacariah said. 'We kindly requested an audience and reminded her of our bargain. She came back, instead, with another bargain.

'We had nothing, we were starving and desperate. We had to watch as our kin succumbed to sickness, helpless and angry. Those that voted against the Queen became hostile and turned to the rebellion. They sought out the schemers and secret fighters. Some chose to hide, seeking safety in obscurity, and others were more reckless, spreading public propaganda against the mines.'

Bryn recalled the vivid banners and water-stained posters plastered throughout the Silver City.

'It only got worse from there. When we couldn't meet her demands, she was enraged. I explained our circumstances and, in what she called her "kindness", she responded with violence. A few days later, her army came. She swept from her carriage dressed for death like one of those shaith creatures of hers, ready to meet the oncoming carnage. And she smiled. *Actually* smiled.

'That's when her dragon appeared, made of smoke and fog and reeking of death. We were defeated before we could fight back. Then came the whipping posts. She had carved away any wisp of courage that might've sparked. Those who fought back were whipped, or burnt, or taken away. Those who tried to flee were slaughtered.'

Bryn bowed his head, tears burning his gaze, his hands so still where he placed them on the table. Grief and rage and hurt filled the spaces where words couldn't. Bjorn gripped his drink with a tight fist, downed it in one gulp, and held the empty tankard like he couldn't put it down. His fingers trembled, and then he threw it, shards of clay hitting the stone floor. Roaring, he grabbed the empty pitcher next, and hurled it at the wall, his eyes raw with rage.

Zacariah didn't flinch at the outburst. His shoulders were weary, and his eyes were far older than they should be. This was a dwarf that had survived his own kind of wounds. 'We were broken, the heart of our colony destroyed in a blink of power. She took some that survived and forced them to work in her mines. Those whom she considered to be too weak to survive the night, she ordered to be killed. Another kindness. All for the sake of searching for something she deemed essential. We were blinded and conscripted in the same breath. Those of us that escaped were lucky to keep our necks.

'My group was part of a transportation party that crossed through the mountains on the way south. The guard was attacked by raiders. They set us free and pointed us here. And so, this is where we are now, at the beck and call of humans again, waiting to make another vote on whether we join the rebellion or not.'

'I can't see many of the colony trusting another group after that,' Bryn said.

Zacariah nodded. 'We may take sanctuary, but we are hesitant to make any more deals. More than half of our people have been taken, killed, or are missing. It is not an easy choice.'

'Nonetheless, it's a choice that must be made,' Bjorn said.

Bryn laid his hand upon Bjorn's arm. The quiet gesture was enough that his cousin sat back and let him speak. 'What are the conditions of your choice?'

'The Sanctuary has promised us revenge, provided us food, and water, and a place to lay our heads.'

'And what have they requested in return?' Bryn asked.

'They've asked for our swords and loyalty. With the promise of our blades and unyielding support, they swear they will fight alongside us to regain our home and save our kin.'

'And?' Bjorn prompted. 'What is it you are considering? Are we not warriors?'

Bryn remembered Bjorn at the colony, the burning hate and despair behind his eyes as the warrior came forth crying for revenge, their cousins' corpses strewn out before them.

Bryn cringed.

Murder.

'We *were* warriors,' Zacariah replied, though he sounded defeated. 'But that was an age ago. We have been slain already. Most of our kin are dying as we speak. What would you do?'

'I would free them,' Bjorn said.

'Ha!' Zacariah retorted. 'What was it you said? Pretty words.'

'We cannot do anything to save our people without support,' Bjorn said, eyes narrowing. 'I know your pride won't allow you to admit it, but we need this rebellion just as much as they need us.'

Piccadilly leaned against the balcony, taking in the bustling Sanctuary below. She checked the weapons strapped to her body, and tucked a lock of hair behind her ear.

It was dark, the room dimly lit as she watched her people sleep below. The trio of dwarves crept down to the secluded room at the back. She could only hope they had made the right choice.

Creatures were just as fickle as humans. An array of personalities and experiences that could tear them apart or bring them together. She'd been tasked to build an army. A rebellion. She'd found a mix of the human and others across the land and offered their broken hearts hope and glory. She had thought the dwarves would be an easy group to recruit, considering the Queen's brutality. But once they'd settled, they'd been reluctant, almost docile, the echoes of their fear showing in their jarred movements and their careful gazes.

The Commander wouldn't be happy.

The refugees were draining the pocket of the rebellion and without a resounding 'yes' to taking up the cause. She was scraping the bottom of the cauldron.

Once the dwarves had settled in, she'd taken a solitary moment to clean her blades, washing away every drop of blood, wiping the steel until it shone once more. It was sticky in her gear, and after a long hot bath, she'd changed into her favoured dark pants and a green top that draped over her shoulders. Her hair tickled her nose again, and with thin fingers she pulled it behind her pointed ears.

She heard the familiar stride of Flynn from behind her and turned. His slicked hair remained styled to perfection, black as a raven. He still wore his uniform, the gold buttons and purple tunic with red lining. The Queen's insignia was clear on his chest, shining in the light of the candles. She held back a scowl. There were only so many times she could scold him for wearing it within the rebellion's ranks.

His gaze followed hers towards the dwarves below. 'It's the aggressive one I don't like,' he said by way of greeting. 'He's unpredictable.'

Piccadilly smirked. 'Did you not think the same of me when we met?'

'Yes, but only because I didn't believe something as beautiful as you could exist.'

She scoffed. 'Have you heard anything yet?'

'Nothing. Not even a whisper. I've reached out to my contacts, but the trail remains cold. I also think I'm being followed.'

Piccadilly's shoulders tightened. 'Is it Dread?'

'Could be.'

She closed her eyes, feeling the exhaustion settle over her shoulders. 'But you lost them?'

Flynn raised his brow. 'I always lose them.'

It was late, but sleep was a luxury these days. Piccadilly was lucky if she got a few hours, let alone a whole night, and even when she did find the time, her thoughts were haunted. Her failures wreaked havoc inside her mind should one decision go awry. Each missing recruit was a burden upon her bones, each death another drop of blood on her hands.

'What about the gathering parties?' she asked.

'One should be due to return tomorrow eve, but the others are still silent. Each one is slowly dropping away without a trace. I can't tell if they're dead or just cut off as a precaution.'

Piccadilly sighed. 'Perhaps we need to start assuming the worst.'

'That's the first rational thing I've heard you say this week.'

'Your faith in me is overwhelming,' Piccadilly drawled.

He smirked, and turned her towards him, rubbing her arms. 'My faith in you remains the same, Piccadilly. It hasn't wavered since the day we met. But your weakness is your trust in people. I don't believe those scouting parties are coming back. I don't believe the Commander is coming back. And I don't think you should hold off any longer. The rebellion needs action, it needs a plan. This sitting around is doing nothing for their faith in the cause, or in the Princess, or the Commander.'

'I'm not the Commander.'

'Yes,' he replied, 'you are. Whether you chose it or not. He's been gone too long now for you to be anything else. Without you, we're all doomed. It will fail before it even begins.'

She knew he was right. He was the realist in an army of dreamers. But what if the Commander lived, only to find she'd slipped into his place?

Whilst the Commander was aloof, he was quick with his steel, and quicker with his mind. Piccadilly always had to tread carefully around him, her words as sharp as her crescent swords. She'd managed to work her way up, becoming his second despite the distrustful eyes of the rebellion. Even in a room of her own people she was still the dirt under their shoes.

Changelings would always be other.

After all, the Commander had been the only one to give her a chance to prove herself.

Flynn's eyes shone in the dark and Piccadilly shivered. She felt his hand grip her tighter, a tether but also a noose. She didn't pull away, because she needed him. Just as the Commander had needed him. He was a link to the Queen. The snake in the proverbial garden.

Despite the prickles that coated her skin whenever he was near, he was the closest thing she had to a friend. He hadn't failed her yet. He had kept her secrets. And if it did come to war, he could very well be the reason for their victory should fate smile upon them.

She stepped back and gave him a soft smile. 'I'll continue to play pretend about the Commander returning, but this remains a secret. We cannot afford a mutiny when the Queen finally makes a move. She knows we exist. She knows we crawl in the shadows. She's remained patient, but she will come for us. I pray the Fairy Godmother has kept the Commander alive, but for now we'll have to decide what to do next.'

'You already know what I think.'

'The cost of lives isn't worth it,' she said.

'Death isn't the worst thing that could happen to you,' he said, his dark eyes resting on hers.

She snorted. 'Ever the optimist.'

He chuckled at that, then paused, as if he was unsure on how to broach the next topic. 'I may not have good news, but I did have an interesting encounter.' She looked up as he gave her a smug smile. 'I met Princess Snow.'

Piccadilly crossed her arms. 'Fairy shit.'

He shrugged. 'That's what I thought at first, but she fit the profile. Knew things only the Princess would know. And I'm inclined to believe her.'

Piccadilly narrowed her eyes, 'If you're telling the truth, then why in the cauldron is she not here with her people?'

'Because I told her that if she was who she said she was, then we needed a leader.'

Piccadilly watched in silence as she waited for him to continue.

'I told her to gather an army.'

'We *are* her army,' Piccadilly said, exasperated. 'What in the Godmother's name were you thinking?'

'I was thinking rationally. We need a real army, with trained soldiers and combat skills. And no matter what you say, we need allies.'

'How do you expect a young girl to accomplish all that?' Piccadilly asked.

'By charming Perridorm,' Flynn replied, his green eyes sparkling.

Piccadilly groaned. 'I want to take you seriously, but you make it difficult at times.' She rubbed her temples. 'Get some sleep, Flynn, we have a lot to do.'

'Not as much as the Princess,' he remarked as she began to leave.

She didn't bother to respond. He would always be lingering there, watching her as he watched everything. And as her boots clicked against the tiled floors, she could feel his eyes on her back, a bird monitoring the worm.

XIII

The Nightkiss and Shadows

Eve clambered down pale pink walls, the sunlight bright and blinding. Her rope was old and frayed, which only heightened her fears.

Just one foot at a time, she reminded herself, trying to forget the terror of jumping out of the tower last time. Twice she'd escaped this tower: once with the intention of dying, the other to survive. Still, it didn't stop the shaking or the laboured breath from how high she was.

She wondered if the Mistress would come for her, or if the Mistress had ever existed at all.

Rapunzel had never been stable, but she'd also never been a liar.

Keep breathing.

Eve gritted her teeth, trying to focus on the tower's exterior instead of the drop below. She distracted herself with thoughts about what to do next but kept revisiting the prophecy.

Despite the acceptance of her fate, she also resented it. Wasn't having a choice the very thing that made your life your own?

Yes, she wanted to find the Grimms. Yes, she wanted revenge for her father. But why couldn't she have been able to do it on her terms? Why was she the one who had to save a kingdom when there was a brat called Snow to do it instead?

Princess Snow.

Eve's mind whirled to the grotto, where Hansel and Snow had intimately laughed together. Snow, with her perfect skin and perfect hair and perfect voice.

But even the thought of Snow couldn't hide the wound of Hansel and Eve's last conversation. They had started with a bargain and become so much more. She tried to be angry about it, but she couldn't be. Eve missed Hansel too much. Missed his smell of smoke and wood. Missed those sure hands and encouraging smile.

She winced as the rope burnt her palms. Her foot slipped as it missed a stone, and she spun from the wall in a cry. The rope slipped, her grip too unruly, and she fell.

Only to crash to the ground.

Her back took the brunt of the fall, adding to her already aching body. Cuts lined her arms from the mirror's shattered glass, the wounds sharp on her skin. She could already feel the swelling from Rapunzel's beating morphing her face into something unrecognisable.

She needed to deal with her wounds – hopefully find a healer – before she could begin searching for the next mirror. She suspected it lay in the south, though the tug of her gift was pulling in the opposite direction. Deeper into the forest. Bloody and torn, Eve knelt in the dirt and glared at the traitor of a rope. Luckily, she'd only been metres from the ground.

She eyed her surroundings. Whilst Lady Nona had spoken to her of the quest as a child, the Seer hadn't provided exact locations. All Eve had was a confusing prophecy and the knowledge of the mirrors' existence.

The stone in her pocket remained cool. She could feel the slightly ridged surface where the new, twisted, silver veins blended with blue.

Mirrors four, of black and bone,

Of silver and gold, and night blue stone.

Somehow, the stone was a key. It had soaked up the mirror's magic like the Queen did with hearts. Magic worked in weird ways, but even now, it terrified her. If the mirrors could hold the Grimm's magic, immortal beings of such power and might, then what kind of power did this stone hold?

And what right did Eve have to wield it?

The theft of a gem, and its keeper's revenge.

Getting the stone hadn't been an accident. A gift from Hansel, given deep within Parador. It seemed, no matter the choices she made, fate would always find her. Two rhymes, one meaning.

One mirror down. Three to go.

Eve groaned at the thought as she pulled herself upright, her body cracking with the sudden movement. The forest lay before her, the trees whispering in the wind.

This part of the forest cascaded throughout the middle of the land, hiding beasties and other vile creatures that made her shiver. It was a perfect playground for things best left alone.

Her gift flared, tugging her onwards and Eve swallowed. From memory, Rapunzel's tower wasn't far from her home village, Cawdor.

Gathering herself, she peered past the tower. There was nothing but weeds, and an old doorway sealed from within, its iron blackened and rusted with age.

She wouldn't miss this place.

Giving herself a pep talk, Eve started limping towards the horizon, heading for a place she'd never expected to return to.

Hansel, Porchid, and Viper entered the gates of the Silver City in a crowded wagon. Hansel sat at the back, choosing to ignore the whinging moans of Viper as she hissed at the pigs they were travelling with.

Porchid wasn't much better. She clutched Hansel's shirt with pale fingers, her glow changing with her shifting moods, and refused to leave his side.

Hansel calmly petted the backside of a pig with a brown spot near its tail. He decided to call it Jerry.

When Hansel had bribed the driver and the exchange went easier than usual, Viper had whispered, 'Nothing is that easy.' And as they rode along the main road, he couldn't help but think she was right.

The wagon halted, and Porchid dived into Hansel's pocket. He felt naked without his axes, more so now that half his coin had been drained by the pig farmer.

The driver yanked open the wagon's doors with a clang, leering with blackened teeth as he ushered them onto the street. 'I had to bribe them not to check the back, so I'm out ten medallions,' he said, lifting his hand. 'Hand it over.'

Viper sneered. 'We'll have nothing left after this thief takes it all.'

The man looked her up and down. 'There's other ways to pay than just coin.'

'Huntsman,' Viper seethed, 'pay the man.'

Hansel reached for his pouch, eager to leave the man behind, and handed over the last of his coins. He was loathe to let them go, and shot Viper a dirty look as they dropped into the driver's palm.

'That'll do,' the man said, dropping them into his pouch.

Hansel gritted his teeth. The man was an extortionist, but he'd hoped the fee would outweigh his desire to report to the Queen's army.

'We're near the market square,' the man said, pointing. 'The Crystal Lake is that way, and over there is the castle. The canal lies in that direction. Unless you're on official business, which the hay in your hair suggests otherwise, you best seek out the Commander. Though you didn't hear it from me.'

'The Commander?' Hansel asked.

The man leaned closer to whisper, leaving Hansel's nostrils burning with the harsh smell of chewing tobacco. 'The Commander is the head of the rebellion. Hides here in these parts, but not sure where. If you're looking to join the cause, then he's where you need to go. That's all I got for ya, or it'll be another ten medallions.'

The pigs squealed as the man slammed shut the back of the wagon. 'Try the laneway by the canal.'

'Thank you,' Hansel said.

Viper went to speak when Hansel grabbed her elbow. 'Walk, don't talk.'

Scowling at him, she followed.

'The only thing about that man we can trust is his greedy pockets. Now he's done his duty, what's to stop him from doubling his medallions and ratting us out to the Queen's army?'

Viper dislodged her arm with a hiss. 'I know what people are like. I don't need you educating me on the world.' She looked towards a street ahead. 'We'll lose him at the market.'

They made their way down the cobblestone street and veered left at an intersection. Hansel frowned, already confused at the tangle of streets. A procession rolled into view. They got off the road and squeezed behind an old couple. The elderly man grabbed his wife's hand and shielded her from the crowd. Hansel's stomach twisted in longing at the sight.

Horns blared, the procession marching down the Main Boulevard. The clipping of the horses' hooves echoed against the stones, the horn ringing out as a regal man shouted, 'Make way for the Queen!'

Myrenna.

Hansel's neck broke out in a cold sweat, and he gripped Viper's elbow, whispering harshly, 'We have to go. Now.'

Viper pulled free from his grip. 'We are surrounded by people. The sun is almost set. She won't even see us.'

The crowd tightened around them, and Hansel's panic grew as the procession gained momentum. The Queen's carriage was towards the middle, led by guards in their finery. It was coal black, trimmed with purple and gold filigree, and pulled along by four dark horses. The crowd gasped as it rounded the corner. Hansel ducked towards Madame Viper, who scowled at him.

'Why are you so close?' she whispered.

'To blend in.'

'Well, knock it off,' she snapped.

The couple in front of them shuffled forward, the crowd shoving from the back.

'Do you think there will be a wedding?' the woman whispered to her husband.

'I suppose so,' the man replied. 'She's still young.'

'How exciting,' the woman said, oblivious to Hansel's turmoil. 'The King in Maelstrom has twelve sons. The oldest one is visiting soon, so we'll have another royal in the capital!'

'How exciting a royal wedding would be,' he agreed.

'And just think,' the woman continued, 'if the Princess hadn't been poisoned, we might've had two royal weddings. Not to mention the summer ball.' She sighed, and the man squeezed her fingers. 'Perhaps we'll have some good things to look forward to.'

Hansel's heart ached at the mention of Snow. He'd been a terrible friend. He hadn't thought of her since the ground had split wide and sent him to Nona. Guilt smeared him like oil. He grabbed Viper's arm again and directed her as the crowd dispersed.

He'd started his journey seeking the Princess and promising to serve her. But when it came down to it, his choice was no question. It was Eve. He chose Eve.

What kind of soldier was he if he couldn't keep his honour to his Princess? His honour was his word, but he couldn't help his pull to Eve, or the way his heart skittered whenever he thought of her.

Nona had been stern in her warning, pushing him towards the rebellion. Perhaps Snow would find him. Perhaps Eve would too. And perhaps, he might never see them again.

Following the crowd, Hansel and Viper rounded a corner of the building and entered a large courtyard beside the canal. Hansel took a breath, revelling in the fact he was no longer surrounded.

The markets were a riot of colours, the thin canvas of the stalls billowing in the light breeze, shining with hues of ruby and orange. Stalls lingered at the courtyard's edge cluttered with everything from jewellery to clothing to plants. Smoke filtered from the middle where a temporary seating area had been set, complete with a roasting pig and puppet show.

A group of children ran past them playing tag, laughing as they zipped through the crowd. Hansel was jolted as a girl knocked into him. The girl paused for a moment when she noticed Porchid's head peeking out of Hansel's pocket. Porchid blushed and waved her little hand. The girl giggled in response before being pulled away by a small blond boy.

'Stay hidden,' Hansel warned Porchid, earning a pout from her.

Soldiers gathered near a cart overflowing with vegetables. A petite girl in pink blushed prettily when one leaned in close to tuck a stray curl behind her ear. A lone soldier lazed against the cart, biting into a crisp red apple. Despite his casual pose, his keen eyes took in every detail, watching the crowds of people.

Hansel blended into the shadows, ducking his head and weaving between stalls. He stopped by a stand of gaudy and eccentric hats. The woman behind the counter looked him up and down before nodding. 'I know exactly what you need, love.'

Hansel reached into his pouch, only to be reminded it was empty.

Viper smirked as she lifted out her purse and handed him some coins. 'Make sure mine is pretty.'

Hansel eyed the medallions before looking at her through narrowed eyes. 'You said you had no money.'

She batted her eyes, a picture of innocence. 'I never said anything of the sort.'

'You lied to me—'

He was silenced as the merchant appeared and placed an array of hats down on the counter. Hansel chose the ugliest hat he could find for Viper, one with a wide brim the colour of mud. She winced as he handed it over, then he chose another for himself.

Linking his arm with Viper, he veered her away from the stand before she could complain and strolled through the market at a leisurely pace. He wasn't prepared to stand out and he wasn't prepared to get arrested. If they were to find this commander, they had to blend in.

Eventually, they reached the edge of the stalls. The quiet whisper of the canal's water was close by. He could scent the mould in the air, the dampness of the stone which could never quite dry. The area was quieter, soot ridden, and dark. It raised the hairs on his arm, especially because he recognised nothing nearby. When voices echoed from the adjacent street, Hansel pulled Viper into a small alcove.

'She was definitely my kind of girl!' one of the voices bragged. 'Sweet and small and innocent.'

'Innocent?' his friend scoffed. 'A ripe little thing like that is begging to be swept away by a man in uniform. Even the Queen wouldn't deny me that.'

'Hush,' another said, his voice flat, gravelly. 'Don't speak about Her Majesty. She'll do as she pleases.'

'Cauldron help us, Flynn. Do you ever just have a laugh?'

'Not when there's a war coming,' Flynn said. 'And you make jokes about Her Majesty. You need to pick which side you're on.'

'What are you trying to say? I'm in the Queen's Guard!'

'I'm saying you need to watch your mouth, or it won't just be my sword going into your gut.'

The other man scoffed as their footsteps faded away. 'You're as dreary as a corpse, Flynn.'

Music echoed across the square as the three soldiers opened the door to a nearby tavern. Hansel peeked around the corner, watching as they entered the rowdy establishment. Though, one stopped, staring into the shadows that slunk down the nearby alley before he turned away.

A sinking feeling grew in Hansel's gut as he took in the tavern's name.

THE TINDER BOX

Hansel faced Viper and ran a shaky hand through his hair. He didn't need a map, or directions from a local; he *was* a local. He might not have recognised it before, but by the cauldron he did now. They were in the slums. His old place wasn't far from here, just a few blocks.

His head spun. Did Myrenna suspect he dwelled in her city once more? Could she feel his resentment? His mouth tasted like ash when he thought of all that he'd lost in this city.

Hansel held Porchid gently as he passed her to Viper, rubbing her wing reassuringly.

She glowed white with worry.

'I know where we are,' Hansel assured her. 'We need to tread carefully.'

Viper crossed her arms. 'As opposed to the seamless journey we had to get here?'

Hansel pointed to the tavern, his voice barely holding back his anger. 'You see that tavern over there? That's the Tinder Box. A known haunt of the Queen's Guard.'

When her eyes glittered with malice, Hansel sighed in frustration. 'Pay attention, Viper. Do you see any women around? There's a reason girls stay away. Most don't survive the night, and if they do, they wish they hadn't. This area is designated for debauchery. For selling and buying, including skin. Anyone with a conscience avoids this area. It's unsavoury. And dangerous.'

Viper scoffed. 'Don't speak to me as if I was raised in a temple, *Huntsman*. I ran a circus with unsavoury customers for an age. I bred creatures who were freaks, trained stars to take the tightrope. By the cauldron!' she said, raising her arms. 'I coached knife throwers. You know one of them quite well.'

Viper might have built her own little empire demanding order with strict direction, but fighting in a battle was different. He had no way of knowing how skilled she was with her knives in a fight.

Viper was no Eve. Ringleader or not.

'You have done nothing but complain since we started this journey,' Hansel said, seething. 'You've not lifted a finger nor offered anything helpful. I know this city. And a hat won't hide us now – not when Porchid and I could be recognised in an instant.'

'Was the fairy in the Queen's Guard too?' she quipped.

'Non-human creatures are not welcome here unless they're useful,' he replied. 'Porchid's wings will either be cut off, or she'll be indentured, trapped in a lantern as a living light.'

Hansel sighed, holding back his frustration. 'Not many people travel in this quarter, unless they work for the Queen, a brothel, or the black market.'

Viper raised her brow.

He continued. 'I have an idea, but we'll have to be subtle. Otherwise, it might be the Queen we'll be facing and not just her lackeys. How are your acting skills?'

She dusted off invisible lint from her jacket. 'I was almost famous once. I'm exceptional.'

Hansel held back his snort, the start of a smile tugging at the corners.

'What?' she snapped. 'It's true.'

'I don't doubt it,' Hansel replied. 'Let's see what you've got.'

Myrenna licked blood off her fingers as the Tinker moved about the room in precise movements. He studied the corpses of the maidens strewn about the floor as night began to set across the city.

Myrenna's tongue slipped under the curve of her sharpened nail, and she moaned.

It was almost time. With the fourth Grimm dead she would need to be crafty. Careful. Invisible. It was the only way she'd snatch the grimoire without interference.

It was why she'd watched the carriage procession wind its way down the narrow streets of the Silver City from her balcony in the throne room. Why she'd listened to the bellows and cheers from her people as the crowd closed in around it. Some had applauded their dark queen, whilst others had hidden in the eaves of roofs throwing food and curses.

But they didn't know it was empty.

She never travelled in the carriage if she could avoid it. It was used more as a tool, a way to calm and seduce those who feared the unknown or feared power. A carriage was a perfectly normal way to travel. Flying however, was not.

She turned towards the throne, its red and purple cushions soft against the gilded mirror hanging loftily behind it. The mirror's hum rippled across her skin as she stepped onto the dais.

'Mirror, Mirror, on the wall, I seek your guidance above them all.'

The mirror's watery surface melted, and a face of black with hollow eyes grimly stared back. The power behind the glass simmered, drawing her closer to its surface.

'The Queen, the Seeker, and the Princess Snow, an army, six dwarves, and a hunter's bow. The grimoire remains hidden and unseen, but you won't be the only one seeking it, my queen.'

'Where is the grimoire?' she cooed.

'You'll find it stowed beneath the Ancient One, bound in leather, hidden from the sun.'

When she didn't respond, the Tinker clicked his tongue. She turned as the Tinker walked towards the dais, footsteps eerily silent. 'Forgive me for eavesdropping, my queen,' he said, and bowed. 'But I believe the mirror speaks of a tree.'

'A tree?' she replied flatly.

He swallowed, bowing lower, his gapless grin wide beneath his hood. Myrenna waited to taste his fear, to smell it. But she never could with her Tinker. He was different, twisted. He was a pure curiosity. And it was precisely why she kept him.

She motioned him forward. 'Explain. Or it'll be you who becomes one of your little experiments.'

His eyes twinkled at the threat. 'I've heard tales, Your Majesty, from when I was a boy. The Ancient One is a tree that grows deep within the Shadow Forest. Its roots are as old as the realm itself. They say it is older than the cauldron.'

Myrenna side-eyed the mirror, whose depthless eyes told her that the Tinker spoke true. She smirked at the hunched man. 'You continue to prove your usefulness.'

'I am here to serve, Your Majesty.'

'And serve you have.'

He bowed again, lower this time.

Vibrations of power rippled against Myrenna's skin as the mirror spoke. *'Heed my warning, my dearest queen: ride on steed in the dark unseen. To remain hidden from spying eyes, you must be mortal to claim your prize. Power will be a beacon to them, for magic calls magic, like the Seeker's gem.'*

Magic calls magic. A warning as old as time. If she was to remain unseen, a shadow in the night, she would have to forgo her magic. The thought made her chest feel tight, her skin pinched and itchy. To be mortal was to be nothing.

'Tinker,' Myrenna said, her voice calm despite the thrum of her heart. 'I will need a few things. The petal of a nightkiss flower, a black steed faster than the shadows, and you are to tell no one of your tasks, not even my Crows. You have until the next toll to bring them to me. My guards can take care of the bodies.'

He nodded hastily and ran from the room. Slowly, Myrenna faced the mirror again. 'If you have doomed me, Mirror, then I will doom you.'

The mirror smiled, but it was a cold thing. *'My queen, you forget, we are one, you and I. Doom you, I would not. We are eye for an eye.'*

Myrenna twitched, the searing flame of her cold rage burning inside her. There was always more sacrifice. Always more to give. But, for the grimoire … being a mortal temporarily was a small price to pay.

The wind slithered across Myrenna's skin, her cape billowing behind her. The cold air was sharp with the bleak and empty night. It lashed against her face like tiny whips scratching her pale cheeks. The forest's edge urged her closer and she pushed her steed forward, digging her heels into its side as it panted underneath her.

Her Tinker had been ready for her as soon as she'd donned her travelling clothes. She'd hung knives at her legs, the black leather she wore contouring across the curves of her body.

Myrenna had held the petal in the palm of her hand, its deep purple a dark hue against her light skin. She could still feel its taunting presence as if it laughed at her, knowing what it would take. She could still taste the sour sting of it on her tongue as it suffocated her magic, numbing the well inside her.

Despite the trickle of doubt now coating her veins, Myrenna had to remind herself it was only temporary. Just long enough for her to sneak through the night, hidden from those nearby and from the Ancient One.

Her steed sped up, his hooves thudding against the dirt road like the beat of a drum. And Myrenna smiled.

This time she would succeed. This time there would be no room for error.

XIV
The Road to Home

Eve stumbled, her feet dragging across the road. Sunset grazed the treetops, leaving the world aglow. It would have been beautiful if she wasn't in agony.

Somehow against the odds, she was still alive.

Eve wondered if it would always be this way. One death to avenge another. She never wanted this, never wanted to kill, or steal, or lie. And yet here she was, staggering down a dusty, familiar road towards her old, broken home.

Her pocket thrummed, and she pulled out the stone. Its blue hue remained the same, the silver veins pulsing like a heart. Alive and stagnant at the same time. She peered closer, running her finger over the indents, and furrowed her brow. Part of her wondered how it would manipulate over time.

The sky darkened, reminding her she needed to find shelter quickly. She looked across the fields, her heart aching at what she'd already lost and the long road she still had to travel. She pocketed the stone and heaved herself over a wooden fence and down the other side. She was close to home. Or the shattered remains of what was left.

She felt eight years old again. A little girl cowering within the burrow of a tree, hidden by a man who would never return. No matter how time passed, how far she had come, all it took was the scent of the lilac-drenched fields to feel small and defenceless.

A single inhale and she was alone again.

She wiped at the sting in her eyes, battling back the threat of tears. Tears would do her no good. She needed to focus. She needed to survive.

She halted at the edge of the trees that surrounded her old house. Would it look the same? Or would it be changed like her? Had someone rebuilt there? Another family with another daughter?

She pulled out her messy braid, coated in dirt and dried blood, her fingers itching to do anything against the urge to run. Would it hurt to see someone else living where she once dreamt and explored, weaving stories the way her father weaved flower crowns? She never thought she would return, never cared to. She wasn't here to tend the home or watch the gardens flourish or decay.

Would it even be a home without her father? Her little kingdom. His little princess.

She smiled sadly at the thought. It wasn't the cottage that had been home. It was her father. Even when he left the glen on another merchant's adventure, she would run after him. She remembered the cart being pulled down this very road, his sing song voice raising high above the trees as she giggled behind, rioting with glee.

Feeling at home. Feeling safe.

She blinked, the memory fading away. 'Stop feeling sorry for yourself. No more carts, Eve. Only mirrors.' She gulped. 'And a kingdom.'

Hooves clomped down the road behind her, and she jumped, then paused on the side of the road as a man on horseback approached.

He slowed down when he spotted her, his keen eyes roving over her figure. 'It's getting dark. Are you lost?'

He wore farmer's clothes, and a frown almost hidden by large eyebrows. His skin was weathered, the years of toiling in the sun evident across his wrinkled skin.

Without thinking, Eve stepped back, some warning inkling under her skin. 'I'm unsure.'

'Unsure?' he asked. 'Are you aware that you're trespassing? Do you need directions? I live at the farmhouse across the creek. I know these parts well.'

As do I.

The man gave her a narrowed look and she swallowed with apprehension. She could only guess at her appearance – the dirty hair, the bloodstained clothes, the bruises.

Eve looked up to the man and blinked through hazy eyes. The sun became a distant memory as darkness blanketed her vision. She remembered a yelp, the sound of feet hitting the ground as the world tilted.

Then she collapsed into utter darkness.

Piccadilly watched from the shadows of the temple's roof as the three soldiers entered the Tinder Box. They clapped each other on the back in triumph as a cheer rang across the square at their arrival. It was always this way when the Queen left, as if the blanket had been lifted ever so slightly and the city took a breath.

The night was cool, the breeze rippling across her skin like a light kiss as she crouched in the dark. The pig farmer had come straight to her after entering the city, claiming he had new recruits. He was good for information, but bad at negotiating a fair price. Sometimes the price was worth it, finding valued warriors and some of her best spies.

This time though, he'd claimed to have found a huntsman and a circus ringleader.

The question Piccadilly had though, was he *the* huntsman? Because if he wasn't, she'd slice apart the pig farmer so quick, his corpse would look like the bacon he sold.

Her meeting with Flynn hadn't gone well. He questioned her at every turn, and if his faith had begun to lack, then it would ripple across the rebellion, too. She needed a win, something to put fire into the bellies of the army. To bring hope. She wondered what the Commander would do, what path he would have laid out for her should he have stayed behind.

When she had met him for the first time, she'd only been young. His blue eyes had been almost grey as she made herself stand tall to prove she was useful. He had smiled at her, then tossed a sword at her feet.

'You look like walking starlight,' he'd said, amused. 'But can you fight?'

She'd picked up the blade and he'd swung at her. She'd met the strike, metal clashing against metal. She remembered the quivering feeling of her arms, and the white of his grin as he swung again. Her body had moved on instinct, her jabs sloppy and her parries weak. But she didn't fall, and she didn't back down, sinking back onto her heels and slicing her sword with grit and determination.

She may have had no experience, but she knew how to survive. With every twist and parry, every smack of steel that she accomplished, she felt the thrill of the fight in her blood.

With a simple nod of approval from the Commander, Piccadilly had found a purpose. The possibility of becoming a piece of history, to be a creator of change.

After that day, she'd been entrusted to find resources and recruits. She hid amongst locals as a bartender, or a shop assistant. She was a chameleon, becoming a butcher, a baker, a farmer. Since joining the rebellion's ranks, she'd held many faces.

But it was different now.

The Commander hadn't returned from his most recent mission, hadn't sent a whisper of a word. With him gone, Piccadilly was in charge. It had been weeks now, and the rebellion was struggling. They were low on food, allies, warriors, and gold. Despite the poor odds, she believed the dwarves held value. If she could convince them to join the cause, not only would they have warriors, they would have miners, bakers, blacksmiths, fighters – an army of resources.

Maybe she was lucky the Commander hadn't returned. Her decisions were optimistic to say the least. But she knew the Commander did not see the potential, he only saw the cost. And what he saw in gold, she saw in lives.

And what was a life without happiness? Without freedom? Without choice? They were living in a cage. A kingdom of repression, where anything non-human was a disgrace. Where the Queen enslaved thousands. Where she committed genocide, and bigotry reigned free.

A queen was supposed to love her kingdom. To help it prosper. Myrenna was no queen.

But perhaps Snow was.

Snow was the realm's last hope. Hope in a young woman who had never left her castle walls, a woman nobody had seen since childhood. But while she survived, so did the rebellion.

Piccadilly's sharp eyes monitored the streets. Her legs were starting to ache; though, she didn't move from her crouch. She remained still as the shadows, the ends of her long braid fluttering in the spring breeze. She was a flicker of moonlight in the night.

Two bumbling drunks zigzagged across the square, catching her attention. Where the man was broad, the woman was tall and narrow, her thin frame struggling to hold up his slouched weight.

'Ale!' he yelled. 'Hail the Queen and'—he hiccupped—'the Queen and her brew!' He cackled as the woman grunted, both almost tripping on a cobblestone.

Piccadilly raised her brow.

The door of the tavern swung wide, and a group of rowdy soldiers left the bar. One of them chuckled, his own steps uneven. 'Looks like you got yourself a handful.'

'He does this all the time,' the woman howled. 'I just want a good man at home who'll love me.'

'I meant him,' the guard quipped, making his comrades snicker.

'I'm a delicate woman,' she winced, her lip wobbling. 'How am I to carry him with these weak, brittle bones?'

A soldier shuffled on his feet, clearly uncomfortable with the display. He turned to his comrades who backed off, leaving him alone to placate her. 'Look, lady. It's going to be fine.'

The woman wailed.

'Your husband looks perfectly merry to me,' another soldier replied, smacking him on the shoulder.

Swiftly, the drunken man grabbed the soldier by the collar and hurled him across the square like a javelin. One of the soldiers cried out, the sound of metal being unsheathed echoing across the stone plaza.

With a swift spin, the man ducked under the soldier's sword and slammed his fist into the soldier's gut.

Piccadilly snorted. Another soldier shot forth, sword raised. The large man ducked again, his movements graceful despite his size. She smiled amongst the shadows, admiring the swiftness of his punches and the ease with which he pivoted on his feet as he slammed his fist into the soldier's jaw. Marking the soldiers off one by one. Music bounced against the worn-down walls of the Tinder Box as if an orchestra played and he was centre stage.

When only the drunken man and woman remained, he pointed at the bodies before pushing the smaller woman forward. They bickered, the woman screeching like a puffed up shaith. He snapped at her to hush. Piccadilly watched in amusement as they hauled one of the bodies near the canal.

Piccadilly heard footsteps below and bent to check her perimeter. A group of soldiers were veering down the lane. She swore under her breath and readied her curved swords. The two reckless idiots would be ambushed. They were too slow, too distracted.

So much for not interfering.

She rolled her shoulders, took a deep breath, and launched herself off the roof's edge, landing smoothly onto the cobblestones below. The group of soldiers halted mid step, the one in the front eyeing her from head to toe.

He sneered when he noticed the sheen of her bright silver skin.

Piccadilly tilted her head, the corner of her lip curling. 'Hello, handsome.'

He spat.

Piccadilly unleashed her blades on them all.

Hansel and Viper were panting after hauling the three soldiers behind the lower wall near the canal, propping them against the mossy stone. Porchid flittered around and poked at their uniforms, glowing purple with curiosity.

Hansel wiped his bloody hands on his pants.

'You ever thought about joining the circus?' Viper asked. 'Because that was impressive.'

Hansel ignored her. 'How are you an entertainer when you were wailing like that?'

She shrugged. 'Dramatic effect. Works like a charm with crowds.'

He rolled his eyes. 'This is not the circus, Viper. This is life and death.'

She bristled at his comment before asking, 'How did you learn to move like that? Most guards can't even lift their swords. I'd pay you a lot of medallions to teach that to some rookies once I get started up again.'

'You have no medallions to give right now, let alone a job,' he retorted. 'Oh, wait, you do.'

'Not this again,' she muttered, taking a stand by the wall. 'I never said I didn't have coin. You just never asked.' When he didn't reply, she sighed, defeated. 'That circus was my home.'

Hansel ran a hand through his hair, guilt making his head ache. 'I know.'

A pebble stirred the water, and Hansel froze. His eyes searched the dark, where he heard the almost silent shuffle of feet, the whisper of a breath.

Hansel tore a sword free from the unconscious guard and held it high. Viper flinched as a female's voice drifted from above, silky and cast in steel. 'She's right, you know. Most of the Queen's army don't have the finesse you do.'

Hansel swallowed, his muscles taut. Viper remained still and met his eyes with caution. He could see nothing in the dark.

'Lower your sword, Huntsman. I'm not here to fight,' the voice said.

Hansel stepped back as a lithe body descended smoothly, her feet soundless when they landed on stone. Her hair was the colour of liquid stars, tied back in a neat braid. Her ears were slightly pointed, complimenting her sharp cheekbones. The swords at her side curved, long and sharp, just like the smile she greeted him with.

'Hello again.' Hansel blinked as a memory crept through the cracks of his mind. One of a tavern, with a pretty bartender and a scowling Seeker.

'Who are you?' Viper demanded.

'You're the changeling from the tavern in Roserock,' Hansel said to the stranger, surprised at how calm he sounded, though he didn't lower his blade. 'Aren't you supposed to be serving drinks?'

Porchid hissed from his shoulder, her glow an angry red. The changeling chuckled, then winked at the fairy and raised her palms in placation. 'Whilst I do pour the perfect brew, I'm better at serving the realm, I promise. I'm not here for a fight. I simply wish to speak with you.'

'Then why are you here?' Viper hissed.

'I'm here,' the changeling said carefully, 'for him.'

Eve woke to the smoky scent of a warm hearth and the rich smell of freshly cooked stew. Her stomach grumbled, pinching at her sides. Everything ached. Her head pounded in sync with the small movement of removing her blankets. Candlelight speared her eyes, making her groan anew.

Slowly, she grabbed her shoulder, searching for the open wounds that had carved apart her skin and made her blood burn with fever. Instead, a tight, clean bandage had been wrapped around her injuries.

Pushing her dishevelled hair out of her eyes she looked around the room. It was a tiny cottage, with a large fireplace and a wooden dining table situated in the middle. She lay in one of the twin single beds, covered with dark sheets. The home was scarcely decorated; either it was newly lived in, or the owner was not fond of material things.

Eve sat up, her arms shaking under the weight, and scanned the thick green cream across her arms, gleaming against the glow.

Somebody had tried to mend her.

Her legs shook like a newborn calf as she stumbled to the bubbling cauldron. It smelt of garlic, herbed chicken, and roasted vegetables, cooking nicely as she inhaled its delicious aroma.

Her solitude broke as the front door was flung open, a girl backing in with a large bucket of water. Eve grabbed for her knives, but found herself weaponless, and realised she was clad in a linen shift that brushed the tops of her knees.

'Oh my!' the woman squealed. 'I didn't think you'd be awake. You gave me a fright.'

Eve backed against the wall, looking for a weapon – a butter knife, a blunt pan – to defend herself with. When she found nothing within reach, she steeled her voice. 'Who are you?'

'I hate to be a bother, but could you help me?' the girl asked, water sloshing over the bucket's rim. 'It's for you, after all.'

Eve blinked. 'What's for me?'

The girl rolled her eyes. 'The water, of course. I just need you to shut the door, or help grab the bucket. If you're able to be up and growling at others, I figure you could help out.'

Eve blinked again before she made her way slowly across the room and reached out to lift the other side of the bucket. Together, they carried it to a large basin half-filled with steaming water. They poured the contents in, and the girl sighed, wiped her hands on her dress, then reached out her hand in greeting.

Eve could only stare at it.

'I'm Gabby,' the girl said. Her eyes were bright, her cheeks full. 'What's your name?'

'Eveline,' the Seeker replied carefully.

'Pleasure to make your acquaintance, Eveline,' Gabby said, before lowering her arm awkwardly. 'Papa said he found you on the side of the road before you passed out. Said you were lost, so he brought you back here to me. You must have had a real tough run of it to have collapsed like that. I mean, you were covered in blood and bruises and cuts. I couldn't fathom how you'd still been standing when

Papa found you. It's a miracle. The Fairy Godmother must favour you indeed.'

Gabby spoke so fast it made Eve's head spin. Each word tumbled over the other and Eve wondered if the girl had taken a proper breath.

Eve watched as the girl pottered around, prepping the bath with care and concern. A towel was folded to the side.

When she was done, Gabby turned to Eve with a kind smile. 'You're a skinny little thing. Papa always says to eat and get strong and big. Can't do what needs to be done when there's no meat on your bones.'

With surety, she grabbed for Eve's shift. Eve's arm shot out and snapped tight around the girl's neck.

'What in the Cauldron!' Gabby screamed, grasping at Eve's hold. Her face paled, but Eve couldn't seem to let go. She squeezed, her panic a slithering thing inside her. It wasn't until Gabby kicked out, almost hitting Eve's knee, that she blinked.

Panting with effort, Eve released Gabby's neck and stepped back. 'I … I'm so sorry.'

Gabby could only wheeze, staring at Eve in a whole new light.

'I don't like people touching me,' Eve whispered.

Gabby coughed. 'Noted.'

Eve shrunk into herself. Whilst she couldn't find her father, she sure had a gift for pissing people off.

Gabby surprised her. 'I probably should have asked.' She rubbed her throat as she stood, the skin red and raw. 'I'm just so used to doing everything. If I had known you'd knock me flat like that, I probably would have asked first. I'm sorry.'

Eve hugged herself, her arms a small protection against the hurt. 'No, I'm sorry. You didn't know and were just trying to help.'

Gabby's eyes softened. 'Well, Papa has stepped out for our privacy. So, if you don't wish to be helped getting undressed, I'll leave you to it. The water is hot, and I'm nearby if you need help with … anything.'

Eve said, 'Thank you,' and noted the slight trembling in the girl's fingers.

'I won't touch you if that's what you wish, but you are injured, and your wounds need cleaning if they're to heal.' Gabby bit her lip. 'Papa was worried you'd be dead or done for. He entrusted me with your care, but he doesn't like to wait, and whilst he can be kind, he can also be unforgiving.'

The scars on Eve's body tingled with the words. Rapunzel had also been unforgiving.

Slowly, Eve lifted her arms. Her fingers twitched at the pull of her shirt, her teeth grinding against the pain. Swallowing her pride, she turned to Gabby. 'Would you …'

'Will you put me in a headlock?' Gabby asked.

Eve held back a smile before shaking her head.

Sighing, Gabby stepped forward and helped her undress. Eve had cut people for less. For being this close. For letting her feel so weak, so small. Perhaps Gabby was lucky she didn't have her knives, or perhaps Eve needed to learn manners again from being alone for far too long.

Gabby's voice filled the silence. 'To find a lost woman in Cawdor of all places. What will the girls say? They'll be thrilled, of course, wanting to know everything about you – but don't worry, I'll not say anything you don't approve of. You must have been through a fright.'

Eve's clothes peeled off her like a second skin, hardened from the dirt and dust and blood. Eve didn't respond, instead seeking comfort in the steaming, soapy water, letting it coat her skin like warm velvet.

Gabby calmly reached for Eve's arms. She was gentle as she unravelled the bandages and began to wipe off the green goo. Her smile was cautious as she checked them, ensuring they were clean.

Gabby's hands were firm but soothing. Her voice washed over Eve as she spoke, Eve keenly listening as she was filled in about who had married whom and who'd been in trouble. She spoke of the village, her friends and occasionally her Papa, always ending in a less than endearing quality. Gabby spoke about the temple and about her father's duties and about the market on Sundays where they sold their goods. She explained market day with fervour, her voice hitting an excited pitch that caused Eve to open her eyes. Gabby's cheeks were flushed, almost as if she were shy about the joy it brought her.

But Eve knew that look. She had worn it herself, amongst the rays of light that came through the roof of the forest; had felt it when Hansel had looked at her – *really* looked at her – and loved her anyway. The words escaped before she could stop them, 'I'd bet you have a boy.'

Gabby's cheeks flushed deeper. 'It's not what you think.'

Eve gave her a knowing smile and sunk deeper into the water.

'I – you – we can't,' Gabby stammered. 'Papa cannot know. He would shun me and kill me and leave me out to dry.'

Eve furrowed her brows. 'Why in the cauldron would your papa worry about a crush on a boy?'

'That's the thing,' Gabby said. 'It's not a boy.'

'A beast then?' Eve joked.

But Gabby didn't laugh.

'A woman?'

'To my Papa, a beast all the same.'

Shock coursed through Eve at Gabby's admission, but it was the tears glinting in the girl's eyes that halted her from speaking.

'This is nice, isn't it?' Gabby sniffled, moving her hands to gently sponge Eve's back. 'I don't get much girl time, and when I do, it's always Tricia saying this is this and that is that. It's impossible to get two words in. Could you imagine?'

Eve kept quiet as Gabby veered away from the conversation. Fear was evident in the cautious way she moved, as if her secrets would unravel with only a breath.

'And what of you?' Gabby asked. 'A boy, maybe? Or a girl? Perhaps a troll?'

Gabby held out a towel for Eve to step into.

Water dripped down Eve's body as she stepped out of the tub. 'No, not a troll,' she replied, quietly. 'A huntsman.'

Gabby beamed. 'And what a catch he got with you. You're a great listener.' She paused. 'Do you headlock him, too?'

Eve smirked. 'Only sometimes.'

Gabby laughed, then grabbed Eve's filthy shift and pointed her towards a pile of neatly folded clothing. Carefully, Eve ran her fingers over the silver stitching of a teal shirt, where a sparrow had been artfully sewn. It was paired with fitted dark pants, and her boots, newly shined.

'I had no more dresses for you, and you didn't seem like a dress girl, anyway,' Gabby said softly from the doorway. 'So, I pulled that out of the trunk. It was my mother's. You can borrow them until I get yours cleaned, if that suits?'

'It suits just fine,' Eve replied, mouth dry.

The tunic was made of silk, soft on her skin, and smelt like daisies. She slipped it over her head and reached for her gift, finding it dormant. With a grimace, Eve picked up the comb on the bedside table and started untangling her wet hair.

'I told Papa he was okay to return now,' Gabby said, returning to the room. 'He's just up the way chopping wood. Got back from the village not too long ago. How hungry are you? I'll serve it up quick smart. You want a little? A lot? Perhaps I'll just give you some for now, and if you want more you can help yourself? I'll braid your hair for you soon, too. I've just got to serve dinner, or Papa will be furious. He gets angry when he's hungry, so it's got to be just right.'

Eve followed Gabby towards the kitchen, where she opened a window, letting some of the steam out. Feeling out of place, Eve stepped towards the dining table, pulling out the chair closest to her.

'Don't sit there,' Gabby snapped as she held a steaming pot. 'That's Papa's chair. He's awfully fond of it.'

Eve didn't miss the hint of fear in the girl's voice, or the way her eyes widened as Eve had lowered herself. Carefully, Eve stood and pushed the chair back in, then touched the seat opposite it.

Gabby nodded and looked towards the window. 'He's coming now.'

She set out eating mats and cutlery before taking a seat beside Eve and straightening her skirt.

'Papa is kind,' she said under breath.

Eve frowned, wondering if she was speaking to her or to herself.

Gabby bit her bottom lip before looking up, a warning in her eyes. 'He's just set in his ways. He can be superstitious, and sometimes a little … overbearing. But he means well. Trust me.'

Eve wondered at the wording, when Gabby straightened her back. The front door swung open.

'Hello, Papa,' Gabby chirped as the same man from the road entered the cottage. He was shorter than Eve remembered, his salt hair stark against the brown it still held onto. He hung up his jacket, his eyes curious as he took in Eve.

'Our guest is awake,' he said as he moved to his preferred seat. 'Good.' He stared at the table, a frown peppering his brow. 'Gabby, have you forgotten the bread?'

Gabby gasped. 'Sorry, Papa, it's just over here. Let me get it.'

His smile was pinched as he turned to Eve. 'You're looking much better. I was concerned at finding you on the road, but more so when you collapsed before my horse.'

He lifted his knife as Gabby brought him the bread, where he proceeded to lather it in butter. His movements were careful and precise. Eve stared at her own setting, where she only found a lone spoon.

'Gabby, perhaps our guest would like some butter on her bread,' he suggested, and she flushed.

'Of course, Papa.'

The words sounded polite, but there was an underlying tone Eve couldn't pick. She watched Gabby crumble into herself, her father's eyes watchful and sharp.

Eve's stomach dropped, and the food seemed less appetising.

'We don't normally welcome strangers here,' Gabby's father said in a low, rasping tone. 'But a girl on her own is worrisome. Especially one wandering private property. I hope my daughter has taken good care of you.'

Eve nodded politely as Gabby placed the buttered bread beside Eve's plate.

'The knife, Gabby,' the man warned.

Gabby picked it up and shot an apologetic look at Eve. But it wasn't Gabby that Eve was concerned about, it was the man sitting across from her.

Gabby's strange words had raised the hairs on her arms. She couldn't place it just yet, but low in her gut, there was a warning. Enough for her to think about her words: to survive.

'I apologise,' he said to Eve, the words about as sincere as a con man. 'But I've a mind to be careful in these dark times, and I don't know you.'

'Is that why my belongings are hidden?' Eve asked, already knowing the answer but wanting his confirmation.

'They are safe,' he replied. 'I couldn't know what you would do in my home when alone with my daughter. You understand?'

Eve could understand his caution; she would have done the same. However, not just her knives were missing, but her entire pack.

Her weapons. Her clothes. Her purse.

And the stone.

Gabby sat in silence, eating her stew, when Eve finally said, 'Thank you for your hospitality.'

Her tone was flat, mocking against her better judgement. Every instinct in her was urging her to flee, to find her things and run.

But she was stuck, trapped until she could convince this man to give back her belongings.

'Tomorrow is market day,' he stated. 'I expect you to help if you'll be staying here a while. Gabby will continue to tend to your wounds, but we don't give free handouts. You will work and earn your keep for the food given and the medicine used to save you.' He smiled, but it didn't reach his eyes.

Gabby looked meekly at her bowl.

'Of course, I'm not looking to exploit you or your daughter. She's been nothing but kind.'

The man laughed at that. 'Kind, yes, but she's a bit dim-witted, I'm afraid.'

Gabby flinched, and Eve gripped the handle of her spoon with white knuckles.

'Tell me,' he said. 'Where are you from?'

'Nearby,' Eve replied, taking a well-timed bite of her bread.

'Nearby as in Cawdor, or nearby as in only a few days away?'

She shrugged, choosing that moment to slowly chew on the bread. While the food tasted like ash with the tension in the room, she would need her strength. Not to mention, she refused to give this man anything he could lord over her.

His eyes narrowed at Eve's silence. 'If I am to house you, then I ought to know who I'm welcoming in, don't you think?' He turned to Gabby. 'What did she tell you?'

'Not much, Papa,' Gabby said quietly.

His eyes darkened, his hand balling into a fist upon the table.

Gabby's eyes darted to it before she met his gaze again. 'Just that she was lost, that she has a home and a huntsman.'

'A huntsman?' he asked. 'What does a huntsman have to do with things?'

Gabby swallowed. 'I think she loves him, Papa.'

Eve flinched as Gabby looked at her regretfully. Anger seared in her gut. Hansel was hers. Just as whoever Gabby's secret crush was her own.

'Well, at least one of you has marriage potential,' he said. 'Where is your *huntsman*, Gabby?'

'I—'

'Do not have one,' he said, speaking over her. 'But as your father, I'm not surprised. Your mother was the beauty. Unfortunately, that was not passed on to you.'

'Yes, Papa,' Gabby murmured, turning back to her soup.

He turned to Eve. 'You will assist Gabby tonight in bringing in the firewood. We will set you up in the barn. Once you have earned your keep at the markets tomorrow, I will return your belongings.'

Eve seethed in silence, knowing full well that if she opened her mouth, she would say something highly inappropriate.

'Gabby, my dinner is done. Clean up before you assist our guest. I'll do a stocktake on what we need replacing after her visit. Make sure not to have seconds. I won't spend money on a new dress, and that one is already too tight.'

He stood from the table, then grabbed his jacket, and paused at the door. 'I'll be back soon. I expect you'll be in bed before I return.'

Or there will be consequences, his unspoken words said.

'Yes, Papa,' Gabby murmured.

He shut the door behind him.

Eve sat in silence and watched Gabby clean up. There was a dimness to her now, as if her light had been doused by a few cruel words.

Gabby's father was the opposite of every kindness Gabby had shown. He was withered and beaten and cruel. It was so unlike the affection or love Eve had grown up with.

'Are you okay?' Gabby asked from the kitchen. 'Is my cooking that bad?'

'What?' Eve asked distractedly, lost to the simmering wrath of her thoughts.

'You haven't touched your food. And you're scowling.'

'Oh.' Eve relaxed her shoulders and looked up at Gabby – kind, chatty Gabby – and placed down her spoon. 'Does he always speak to you in that way?'

Gabby's plump cheeks flushed, and she avoided Eve's gaze. 'Papa is a good man. He doesn't always mean things the way they come out.'

Eve wasn't surprised Gabby hadn't told him about the girl at the market. If that was him being pleasant, she was cautious to see him angry.

'Gabby—' Eve started.

'I'm so sorry,' the girl said with a sniffle. 'About telling him about your huntsman. It wasn't my place. But he always knows if I'm not telling him the whole truth.'

Eve cocked her head, wondering at the true pull that Gabby's father had over her.

Gabby knelt by her side. 'Please don't tell Papa. Please don't tell him about her. Or I'll never go to the market again. I can show you who she is, but you must promise to not say anything. Promise you won't, Eveline? *Please?* The girl sobbed into Eve's trousers.

Eve inhaled. Hesitantly, she lifted her hand to the girl's hair. She would play her part, if only for the sake of the stone and her knives. Her gift had led her here, only disappearing when she'd met the farm's fence line.

She had to trust her gift. And though she had no belongings, an awful man, and a crying girl on her lap, she had been led here for a reason.

Eve cradled Gabby's tear-soaked face and lifted her chin. 'I promise to help you. But only if you introduce me to your girl tomorrow.'

Gabby agreed.

XV

The Traveler and the Wolf

The market hummed with life as Eve, Gabby, and Gabby's father rode into town. Banners with the royal insignia of Ardenbeux – a crimson bird perched behind a crown, its wings spread wide in welcome – were draped across white pillars, the dark colours stark in comparison.

It was strange and familiar at the same time. Eve had seen the Evil Queen's insignia for so long now, she'd almost forgotten that other parts of the realm had other royal families with their own crests, too.

Symbols are powerful things, my little one, her father had once said. *But often they don't represent the ruler. A dove does not always mean peace, just as flames cannot hide a cold heart.*

Back then, it had been King Arthur ruling Ardenbeux. Now, his offspring ruled, orphaned as a young boy when the King died, making him the last of the Ardenbeux line. The starlight family had a long, gory history; though, the strangest part was that the family hadn't been seen in three generations.

Eve used to indulge in stories about them. She remembered spinning tales of them turning into frogs, or worse, eaten by dragons. She could still remember her father's warm chuckle the more embellished her tales became.

Eve smiled at the memory. Despite being born near Cawdor, Eve knew of the distinct kingdoms that stretched from one corner of the realm to another. Powerful regents that commanded their own crown and people, symbols born in their own right.

Bellatorre had been ruled by the Whitmore line for generations – until Myrenna had wormed her way into being queen.

Carnell was where the twelve princes dwelled, a court of constant bickering and power plays. Eve wondered how Florian had survived that toxic kingdom for as long as he had.

Aurelia was commanded by a bachelor king that had his hands full with a troll infestation.

Ashenfell was one of her favourite kingdoms, where the tale of Brianna-Rose was a living legend, like the Great War of Thorns. It was run by three queens, equal in their gifts and in their power.

Lastly, there was Perridorm to the south. It was ruled by twins, their family killed after a massacre in the palace. They were at war with Bellatorre now, fabled to have an army of the dead at their disposal.

She could still hear the cadence of her father's voice, warm like toffee, reciting the kingdoms' histories on his fingers like treats. He'd told stories of great battles, and dragons, and princesses, of treasure buried deep beneath the watery depths of the Mermaid realms and the Floating Isles.

Gabby coughed, smiling awkwardly when Eve glanced up. Eve couldn't help admiring the twin braids that Gabby had coiled into a neat bun. Eve's hair certainly didn't behave that well, no matter how she fought her tangles with a comb.

Gabby looked pretty, her cheeks blossoming with a tinge of pink.

'Here will do,' Gabby's Papa stated as he pulled up the cart and jumped out. 'Gabby will show you what to do. I have business to tend to with some of the other merchants.' His voice hardened. 'Do not stray.'

Eve jumped out, stretching her muscles after the long ride. 'Is your father always so …'

'He's not had it easy,' Gabby said. 'Mama died when I was very young. She was with child. And it crushed him. I don't remember what he was like before.'

Eve began unhitching the ropes. 'What do you remember of your mother?'

Gabby pulled at the ropes on the opposite side, speaking softly. 'Not a lot. I don't even know where she was born, though I've asked Papa. I stopped asking questions after …' Gabby paused, twitching her shoulders as though shrugging off a dreary memory. 'All I have from Mama is her belongings, her clothes. Pretty things, but not useful, as Papa would say. My favourite piece is a ruby red cape.'

Eve grunted as she turned a heavy plank, pulling it from the cart to attach to another piece. She pressed it into the crevice, and Gabby handed her a hammer so she could nail it tight. Eve wiped at the sweat stinging her eyes. Summer wasn't far off now.

She was keen to get her belongings back. She felt naked without her knives, and she grieved the loss of her stone. What had seemed like a silly yet priceless token had become the most powerful object she held.

Destroying that mirror was no small task. Eve's spine tingled at the memory of Nona's magic gripping her in smoky whispers. Of how she'd spoken of Eve's fate. Nona had only given her snippets, pieces of a puzzle she couldn't quite connect.

Gabby laughed, pulling Eve out of her thoughts, as a woman with bold, blue braids walked towards them. She smiled eagerly, waving. Freckles dotted her cheeks, and Eve couldn't help but think of the pretty wooden dolls she'd seen painted in the shop windows of the cities she'd visited.

Gabby's blush deepened. 'Lily,' she called, tugging on Eve's sleeve. Gabby glowed, embracing the girl in a close hug. 'Eveline, come meet Lily.'

'Hello,' Eve said.

'Pleasure to meet you,' the girl said, taking Eve's hand. 'I haven't met many of Gabby's friends. Are you visiting?'

'That's one term for it,' Eve answered. 'Gabby has been nothing but a gracious host.'

Lily smiled at Gabby, like they were part of a secret.

'Let me help you,' Lily offered, picking up a crate from the cart. 'We've set up our stall, so I'm all yours, as long as you have a need for me.'

'I always have a need for you, Lily,' Gabby said. She blushed brighter than an apple and lowered her head. 'I just mean, your assistance is always welcome. You could never be limited … I mean, I appreciate your assistance of course.'

Eve grinned. It was nice to see something so simple as a crush light someone up. It reminded her of Hansel and their first days together, how he always found ways to talk to her, or pushed her to step outside of her comfort zone. She rubbed at her chest, trying to rid the ache in her heart at the thought of him.

'It's my favourite part of the day,' Lily replied, a little shy. 'Helping you, that is.'

'So, Lily,' Eve said, interrupting. 'Which stall is yours?'

'Oh, it's the cluttered one over there,' she said, pointing to a stall lined in midnight blue. A woman draped in jewellery stood at a newly made stand decorated with silver, crystals, and old books.

'That's Mama,' Lily said. 'She likes to set things out exactly right.'

'What is it you sell?' Eve asked.

'Trinkets and charms, mostly,' she said, her voice growing quieter. 'Mama's a witch. Not powerful or anything. But she dabbles in small magic – lucky charms, hair growth serums, that sort of thing.'

'Interesting,' Eve replied, assessing the witch closer. Most witches didn't advertise their skill; not in Bellatorre anyway. Most hid away and blended in in the hope of avoiding notice. Ardenbeux was different to Bellatorre in that witches weren't sent to the mines here, but they still made people uncomfortable. Magic always did.

'That's why Lily's braids are blue,' Gabby gushed. 'Her Mama did it. Isn't it pretty?'

'I'd much prefer your auburn hair,' Lily said as she brushed a loose curl from her face. Her fingers lingered a beat longer. 'It reminds me of sunrise.'

'What do you think you're doing?'

The three of them jumped back as Gabby's father appeared, his eyes nearly black.

'Apologies, Sir,' Lily said, bowing her head. 'I just thought the girls might need assistance. We're family here at the market, after all.'

'We do not associate with gypsies,' he stated flatly.

Lily flinched.

'Go back to your cart and stay there, where you belong.'

Lily's face paled. 'I didn't mean to intrude.'

He took two steps forward, his broad shoulders towering over the nervous girl. 'We don't need help from *your* kind.'

Lily's mouth was a tight line as she fled. Eve watched the droop in Lily's shoulders, noticing her mother's keen gaze. The elder woman pinched her mouth like she wanted to say something.

A *crack* echoed. Eve whirled to find Gabby hunched by the cart. Her father's arm was raised, the man towering over his daughter. Gabby cowered, an imprint of his hand already blooming on her cheek.

Eve only saw red. She stepped forward, ready to knock him on his arse, no matter his hospitality, when she halted at the look in his eyes. They were black holes, depthless and something *other.*

'What have I told you?' he growled.

Gabby's fingers twitched at the hem of her dress, tears threatening to spill. 'That we aren't to talk to them, associate with them, or even look at them.'

'Then why would you accept her help?' he growled.

Eve stood an arm's length away, her palms twitching for the knives she didn't have, watching Gabby crumple.

'She offered to help since the crates are so heavy,' Gabby said softly.

Gabby's father bared his teeth and Eve swore they were pointed. 'You're reckless, just like your mother.'

Gabby winced, her eyes wet, and peered at the ground. 'I'm sorry, Papa.'

'Sorry doesn't change your mistake. Get back to work.'

'That's a little harsh, don't you think?' Eve said, voice cold.

'I didn't ask for your opinion. Nor do I appreciate you influencing my daughter.'

'She's not a child,' Eve snapped. 'She's a grown woman, and she can certainly make her own decisions.'

He leaned in, close enough that Eve shuddered at his hot sticky breath. 'I'd keep your mouth shut if you want any of your belongings. The sooner you do your work, the sooner you can leave me and my daughter alone. Do you understand?'

'I understand perfectly.' Eve let her fist fly before she'd finished speaking, punching his jaw and nearly doubling over at the crack in her wrist, gasping at the white-hot pain that shot up her arm.

Gabby squealed beside her; a mouse caught in a trap.

Gabby's father didn't flinch, his dark eyes swirling into a mirthless black. He leaned closer, his shoulders seeming to widen in front of Eve to block out the sun. 'You filthy, ungrateful, little bitch.'

'How?' Eve mumbled, clutching her wrist. She'd seen grown men fall with a hit like that. She'd taken down a troll, for cauldron's sake! She was quick, and she'd been trained to hit where it hurt most. She may love her twin blades, but she didn't always need them. Her hands were weapons too.

But he looked untouched, whole.

He smiled cruelly. 'I'll have you arrested for this.'

Eve didn't think he'd do it until he turned towards the guards posted nearby and shouted. Gabby's father pointed squarely at Eve, his face twisted in fury. 'Thief!'

The guards stood, weapons springing free as he shouted again. 'Thief!'

'Shit,' Eve swore.

'Papa!' Gabby yelled. 'What are you doing? She meant no harm.'

'If she wants trouble,' he spat, 'then that's what she'll get.'

Shouts echoed across the market. Gabby squeaked as the guards approached, pushing through the throng of people.

She'd only needed to behave for one day, and she'd already messed up.

Gabby stepped in front of Eve. 'No, Papa.'

Eve had only seconds to decide. Her body ached from Rapunzel's assault and the wounds that were barely healed.

She cradled her sprained wrist to her chest, and made the only choice she could.

She ran.

Gabby gasped as Eve dived over the cart, cleanly landing on the other side in a crouch before bolting behind the cluttered stands. She hurtled across carts, ducking past the owners that screamed and shook their fists at her, cursing as she knocked aside trinkets like a pissed off cat on a windowsill. The guards were closing in, yelling obscenities from behind her as they bolted through the crowd. Her breath was hot, her heart loud in her ears as she ran through a tent, barely missing a half-naked man as he tried on a robe.

'Sorry!' she called. 'Excuse me, please move, thank you. OUT OF MY WAY!'

She heard metal vibrate as it was ripped from the guard's sheaths. She felt her braid unravelling, sweat plastering loose strands to her face, blinding her momentarily. Her knees creaked as she leapt, jumping for the nearest cart that smelled like a butcher's delight.

She choked as the smell of dead animal invaded her lungs. Her gaze fell on the edge of the table. There, in a neat row, lay several sharpened knives.

Perfect.

Grabbing two butcher's blades, Eve spun and whipped the blades behind her. But they were heavier than she was used to. One hit true, stabbing one guard's shoulder, making him scream and fall to his knees. The other missed her target, grazing his wrist when he pivoted, and his armguard protected him. Curse the Cauldron.

She ducked as they screamed, hissing at the pain ricocheting through her body. A man whimpered beside her, his bald head sweating, and she smiled at him apologetically. 'Ah, sorry about this.'

Picking up two more knives, she pivoted, hurling them at two more guards. Both hit their mark, impaling the guards' hands. They dropped their weapons, blood dripping from their palms.

'You little—' one yelped, as she shoved him aside, already moving.

The air rushed over her skin, the market another obstacle course as she skidded around a corner. People screamed as a sword was hurled, cleanly smacking into the wall beside her head.

The market split, some people diving for safety, others looking for a weapon, ready to defend their wares. Eve ran, her feet nearly flying past the narrow lanes, her mind clear despite the chaos surrounding her. She pivoted and ducked, careened around another corner near the outskirts of the markets when she spotted a wagon that stood out from the others. Swathed in purple and gold, its side wall was covered in weapons, gleaming iron and silver and gold. Eve's gaze caught immediately on the two blades crossed in the middle, like a handshake.

She bolted forward, jumping over the counter as she reached for them. They slid off the wall smoothly as the owner eyed her viciously.

'Very nice,' Eve whistled, the handle fitting into her palm comfortably.

'They're not for sale,' the woman grumbled.

'Think of it as an IOU,' Eve said, as the guards yelled behind her.

She sprinted from the stall, aiming for the middle of the market. Her feet beat under her, the two blades an extension of her arms, and her heart thrummed. She pushed through the crowd, her elbows meeting screams.

Eve whirled, her blade clashing against the guard who dared to grab her. She swung upwards, crossing both her blades against his sword.

They parried as a circle of onlookers surrounded them. Eve slashed back, her wrist screaming with each block and thrust. She pushed through the pain, her heels skidding as she fought to hold her ground. It was the snap in her wrist and her sharp cry that gave the guard the upper hand. He slashed down, knocking one of the blades from her hands. She lifted the other weakly, but it flew free as he swung again, his smile savage.

Run.

Eve rolled, avoiding the soldier's death blow, and scrambled to her feet. She ran in a zig zag to find a break in the crowd. She was desperate, cornered, and hurt.

She just needed a sliver of luck. A chance.

The people were a blur, distorting into one another as panic took over. Spots bloomed in front of her eyes, stars among the crowded square, when she heard a whistle. Lily waved at her wildly, her skinny arms lifting the canvas behind her stall.

Eve didn't hesitate. Dodging past a child, Eve sprinted for the woman's tent and dove inside.

Lily dropped the canvas before Eve landed, covering her in darkness.

Eve crashed to a stop. She would be covered in new bruises, and the nick on her leg was pooling blood. Eve blew the hair out her face, listening to the muted mayhem outside.

Lily entered the tent and rushed her towards a large chest. She lifted the lid and expelled the clothes in a flurry of colours and material.

'Get in,' she ordered.

Eve didn't particularly want to hide in a box, but it was that or a knife in her gut. Muffles came from outside, a clamour of armour as Lily's mother shouted, 'She fled by the east gate.'

Cursing quietly, Eve climbed into the cramped compartment, the edges squeezing her knees as she looked at the girl with the blue braids. A girl now holding Eve's life in her hands.

'This is either a good decision or a really, really bad one,' Eve mumbled.

Lily laughed as she shut the lid and locked Eve inside.

Myrenna's hands shook as she dismounted at the edge of the Dark Forest. She had galloped through the night, only stopping as day broke over the world. Her black horse panted, exhausted from the hard ride. Myrenna tied him up, fed him, and gave him water.

'Good boy,' she whispered, patting his mane.

She'd never particularly liked humans, or dwarves, or trolls, or giants. Or anyone, really. But she did like horses. Not only were they beautiful, but they were strong, loyal, and fierce. A rare combination in any creature.

The sun rose above the trees, its golden glow dripping through the branches like raindrops. She didn't have long now. Being mortal, even temporarily, was not a game she wanted to play. One petal was all it took to cease all magic in any being. It was poison. Debilitating. But necessary.

Thankfully, the effects wouldn't last long, and even though she'd brought a spare, she didn't wish to prolong this tortuous ache.

She hated to admit it, but she was tired. Her mortal body not used to the strain that hard riding entailed. She stretched her legs, pain shooting through her muscles in a way she hadn't felt for years. Though she held no magic right now, she swore she could feel the magic of the grimoire seeping through the trees.

She closed her eyes and listened for the whispers of song, the melody of old magic. It wrapped around her as she peered into the darkest pocket of the forest.

'I'm coming for you,' she whispered.

A promise. And a threat.

Hansel and Viper followed the changeling through a porthole by the canal. Hansel grunted as it squeezed his broad shoulders before opening into a wide stone tunnel, the rushing water echoing off its moist walls.

Porchid perched on his shoulder, pulling his ear, huffing. He flicked his fingers at her, and she bared her teeth. Her light glowed through the darkness, changing with her uncertainty over Piccadilly.

Though it was Porchid's style to pout, her twitching had him on edge. Should he have trusted Porchid over his gut?

The changeling was light on her feet. There was a blunt beauty about her. The way she moved, hair glowing like starlight and skin that shimmered no matter what dark tunnels they walked.

Porchid's glow turned a rich green, and she yanked his ear again.

He swatted at her, and she crossed her arms.

'We're not as helpless as you think,' he said. 'You need to stop worrying.'

Porchid only huffed in response.

Viper lagged behind them, with the occasional huff herself. Her boots clicked on the floor, the black leather of her once shiny shoes now worn and dull.

The changeling halted at an intersection, her eyes flitting between the two tunnels.

Hansel approached her. 'Lost?'

'Debating,' she replied.

'Debating what?' Viper asked. 'It's cold and wet down here, and I'm starving. What are we debating? Possibly whether to die in this underground hole? Or maybe we're just sticking around for the view?'

Hansel snorted.

The changeling raised her brow. 'Is she yours?'

'Hardly,' he retorted.

'I'm nobody's but my own,' Viper said, raising her chin, and scoffed. 'How do we get out of this hideous place?'

'Turning left will take us to the rebellion, straight into the heart of those fighting for Snow's right to the throne. On the other hand, going right will take us to the huntsman's old apartment.'

'And?' Viper prompted.

'And,' the changeling continued, 'I'm not entirely certain on the best course of action for the both of you. One of you is across the city on wanted posters with a very large reward, and though the Commander wants to overthrow the Queen, I'm hesitant he won't throw you to the Queen himself for the reward she offers to fund the cause.

'If we choose right, however, I could take you to your old apartment, where you would be safe to plan your next move. Or …'

'Or …?' Hansel prodded.

'Or I could turn you in myself. Reap the rewards. Dead or alive, it matters none to them.' She sighed deeply. 'It's a conundrum.'

'Well,' Hansel said drily, 'while you're making those difficult life choices, we might just sit down. Maybe pour a cup of tea. Viper can tell us all about the old days.'

The changeling laughed. It sounded musical, like the breeze on a summer day. 'Well, aren't you a cauldron of fun.'

'Only when required,' he retorted.

She smirked. 'We'll head right, then.'

Porchid gnashed her teeth in irritation.

The tunnel became dark and dank, the rotted stench of mould and decay coating the walls. Hansel didn't need to see in the dark to know Viper was holding her nose, her groans evidence enough that she disapproved of the tunnels. Light appeared before him as the changeling opened a hidden door above, the wooden sides bent and worn from use.

The familiar smell of wood filled his nose as they entered his old apartment. He hadn't stayed here much, not when Myrenna had called him throughout the night, but he'd bought it after his first paycheque, needing somewhere away from it all. Somewhere he wasn't expected.

A small chaise stood by the fireplace, and the kitchen was down the back. When he turned, he saw his old room. It was more decorated than he remembered. Artwork hung from the walls, a lush blue carpet lined the floor, and trinkets were spread upon the mantel.

The changeling shook off her cloak. 'I took the liberty to decorate.'

'You live in my apartment?' he asked, mouth open. 'Where are my things?'

'I didn't throw them away, if that's what you're asking,' she said. 'There was so little, I packed them into a box.'

'You placed my belongings in a box and took over my apartment?'

'It was vacant,' she said, turning to Lady Viper. 'Is he okay? He just keeps repeating me.'

'Well, you did take his apartment and box up his belongings,' Viper shrugged. 'Is there food here?'

'It was *my* apartment,' Hansel said, seething. 'It wasn't vacant at all.'

'Well, yes, I always expected to you to return. I just didn't know when, so I—'

'Took the liberty,' he finished for her.

Porchid whizzed to the carpet by the fireplace and curled into the plush chair nearby.

'My name is Piccadilly, by the way,' the changeling said, heading towards the kitchen. 'I'll start cooking, but keep the windows shut and the curtains closed. The guards will be on the lookout after we took out nearly a dozen of their comrades. They'll be out for blood.'

'A dozen?' Viper snorted. 'We only took out three.'

'You mean *I* took out three,' Hansel said pointedly, taking a seat near Porchid.

'Yes, and I took out the other nine whilst you dragged those three bodies at an impossibly slow pace,' Piccadilly retorted.

'Well,' Viper said, appraising Piccadilly, 'I wish I could have seen that. Maybe I need to recruit you into my circus instead.'

'No, thank you,' Piccadilly replied crisply. 'But I'm hoping to recruit you and anyone else wanting a better life into the cause.'

'The rebellion,' Hansel said.

She nodded. 'But, before we begin down that road, there's a bath down the—'

Hansel's look of contempt must have told her all she needed to know because she paused before saying, 'Of course, you already know where to find the bathroom.'

'I don't,' said Viper.

'Down the hall, first door on the right,' Hansel said, defeated.

Viper straightened her jacket, and without a word, strutted to the bathroom, slamming the door shut.

'At least she won't smell anymore,' Piccadilly said.

He groaned, running his hand through his hair. It was his space but not his space all at the same time. He wondered if it would even be familiar to him if he had still had his belongings out, or had he been gone too long, seen too many things, to consider it home? His fingers twitched as he grabbed the poker, knocking aside the ash to reveal the flaky wood beneath.

There was a soft shuffle of feet as Piccadilly stood next to him and extended her hand. 'Sorry about, you know, the apartment. I mostly live with the others, but sometimes I just need to get away, and this seemed like a good place to do it.'

He stared at her hand, willing the tightness to ease from his shoulders. He had a poker, but she still had her blades, and he was too tired to fight. For now, he would wait and see what she wanted.

Find her at the end.

'How did you even know about it?' he asked.

'Truthfully?' she replied.

He nodded.

'I'd heard talk about the Queen's pet, and I was curious. I found out where you lived, but when I heard you were on some unknown mission, I waited. Only, you never came back.'

He frowned. 'And yet you still took it?'

She shrugged. 'It's a nice apartment.' She held out her hand again. 'Let's try again. I'm Piccadilly.'

'I'm Hansel,' he said with a sigh, clasping her hand. 'That's Porchid, and down the hall is Lady Viper – or Tabitha, or whatever, really.'

Piccadilly smiled. 'Pleasure.'

'Is it?' he asked.

'I don't remember the tales saying you were this morose.'

'Tales are just stories, lies,' he replied.

'Sometimes. But there are always sprinkles of truth. Trust a fairy on that.'

Porchid twinkled from the chair, her dark blinking eyes narrowed.

Piccadilly smiled at the little fairy. 'You must be hungry.'

Hansel watched as Piccadilly went to the kitchen, wrapping a plain brown apron around her shimmering form. His body ached, exhaustion seeping into his skin. First, he'd lost his family. Then he'd given up his standing in the Royal Guard, only to fall in love with a woman that had almost killed him. He'd lost the Princess, lost Eve, and now he'd lost his apartment.

What was next? A limb?

He held hope, he always had, but the rebellion had been a dream. He'd never even met the rebellion, and now he had a high price on his head.

Perhaps Eve was right. He'd thought he'd been pushing in the right direction, but maybe, just maybe, she'd been guiding him.

He knew the Princess was awake, but did she live? Malak would protect her. So would Pip. Even Florian, in the best way he supposed the timid prince could. It was an odd group. Two royals, a troll, and an elf with a magic pipe. But as always, he held hope. Hope that they were alive and not yet captured. Hope that they would find their way to the rebellion. Hope that they would win this war and bring the kingdom back to its glory days. Hope for happiness. Hope for love.

And, against all odds, or the smell coming from his clothes, or Viper's tantrums and Porchid's moods, he held hope for Eve. That, despite being alone, she would conquer the huge task before her.

In the meantime, he would prepare for war.

XVI
The Ancient One

Eve had fallen from towers, killed men with her bare hands, lost her father, and faced monsters. But she had never been locked in a box. Eve felt her chest constrict, her breathing shallow. Her knees were tucked into her chest, with little room to move. Sweat pooled at the base of her spine. To calm herself, she tapped her finger repeatedly against her knee and counted.

One, two, three.

Time had become meaningless. She didn't know if it was daylight or night, whether she'd been locked up for an hour or a day.

A sharp rap against the top of her cramped prison was a signal to keep quiet as they took a sharp turn, jostling her aching body. Eve's nails gripped the walls to keep herself steady as muffled voices echoed through the wood. As her head bashed against the side of the box, she *really* regretted her life choices. Were they to dump her in the river, then? Perhaps toss her on the Queen's doorstep? Maybe even set her alight?

She gritted her teeth, and the box landed with a thump. She tasted blood in her mouth where she bit the inside of her cheek to keep from screaming as she felt herself being moved again. Hooves clopped down the road. The creaking turn of the wheels caused her muscles to freeze. Surely this wasn't her end. Despite her questionable decisions, she was hard to kill. It had been proven time and time again.

If Dante were here, he'd chastise her. *'You must be careful, little one. Not everyone in this realm is as they seem, and trust is a great gift to give.'*

She knew better than to trust so blindly. Yet in the moment at the market, she'd just handed it over like a medallion for a stick of candy.

Idiot.

She'd dived into a box without knowing who these people were. All because of a few hot-headed guards and a girl with blue braids she'd met for a second. What was she becoming?

Stupid. That's what she was becoming.

Perhaps even reckless. She'd been off her game for weeks. Ever since Roserock, when Hansel had hired her to save a missing princess. Her emotions tangled inside her, making her stomach clench.

She blinked back tears.

I need a distraction.

Impatient, she felt around the edges of the box. Looking for an opening, a crack. As her nails trailed the indent of a groove, she smiled to herself, and pushed. It didn't budge.

Coiling her muscles, she readied herself for another heave just as the lid flew open, and harsh morning light blinded her.

She blinked as a face hovered over her, one with bright green eyes and braids of blue.

Lily.

Eve launched herself out of the box, tackling the girl to the ground, her knees landing either side of her thrashing body, and her forearm jammed against Lily's jugular. Eve's arms trembled from being contained.

Her fear slowly dissipated as she inhaled the crisp, morning air, letting it ground her.

'If you value your life, you will unhand my daughter immediately.'

Eve tensed, but she didn't move, nor did she take her eyes off Lily. She heard the scrape of steel behind her.

'I will not ask again.'

Eve slid her gaze towards the voice. She wasn't surprised to find Lily's mother with a very large, very powerful crossbow. The woman was covered head to toe in jewellery and her brown ringlets almost reached her waist.

Eve debated the distance between her and the crossbow, assessing whether she could roll free in time. Maybe if her body wasn't so beaten and her joints weren't stiff from being stuffed in a box, she would've stood a chance.

Eve slowly stood, hands raised.

The woman didn't lower her crossbow. 'You sure have an interesting way of saying thanks for saving your sorry arse. You've got ten seconds to explain yourself before I bury this bolt in your brain.'

Lily's eyes were wide. 'Ma, no! She's a friend of Gabby's. She didn't mean it.'

The woman grunted in response.

Eve held her arms high, her eyes roving over the weapon. It was expensive, and well cared for. The bow's wood was lacquered to near perfection, the lines smooth and wire taut.

'Nice crossbow,' Eve commented, keeping her arms high.

The woman smirked. 'Compliments won't win you any favours here, girl.'

Eve licked her lips. The point of the bolt was ready to pierce through her chest if the woman even twitched.

'Ma, put it down,' Lily said, walking over to her. 'She needs our help.'

'She needs the cauldron,' the woman retorted.

'Ma,' Lily said softer. 'Please.'

The woman glanced at Lily, relaxing slightly. She lowered the crossbow slowly, and Eve dropped her arms. 'If she hands us to the cauldron, Lily, there'll be blood.'

Eve sensed it then, the familiar tingle on her skin. Her gut tugged in response as her gift flared to life. Without a second thought, she limped towards cluster of wagons and tents.

'Where in the cauldron does she think she's going?' the woman yelled.

The call of her gift felt different, somehow warped and wide awake at the same time. It had been dormant for so long it almost felt like a stranger.

Eve's steps were unsteady as she moved past the carts, weaving around vans and tents where people did ordinary things – hanging washing here, playing with a child there, setting a fire by a tent.

She ignored them all as her gift dragged her straight to an old vargo squatting on the edge of the clearing.

'Now, hang on,' the woman said.

Eve could hear the women's hurried steps, but their voices were murky, as if they were underwater. Her ears rang, the sensation of her gift vibrating right down to her toes as she stared intently at the vargo. It wasn't overly large, but it was strangely familiar. Nona had owned one of these at the circus, Viper actually coughing up the coin on something. One of the rare selfless acts the woman had ever displayed.

She reached for her stone, her hand brushing her empty pocket, making her heart spike.

Cauldron damn Gabby's father.

She'll have his blood for that.

Lily's mother spoke first. 'I just held a crossbow to your chest, and the first thing you do is walk away. You're either bold or stupid.'

Eve let the threat wash off her, though she clenched her fist at the insult. She remained focused on the vargo, her gift intensifying. She traced her fingers along the sculpted wood. Paint peeled from its sides, worn from years in the sun. The flakes coated her fingers as she grazed over the intricately carved patterns of cauldrons and fairies and trolls. She sensed magic – faint, but still there.

For the first time in a long time, Eve felt a sense of purpose. She peeled back the paint, the flakes falling to the ground like snow. But where the wood should have been worn, it was fresh and smooth.

Eve frowned. 'How old is this vargo?'

'Old,' the woman stated, frowning at her like she was some lunatic. Eve was starting to wonder this herself.

'*How* old?' Eve drawled.

The woman shrugged. 'Who knows? It was my mother's, and my mother's mother's before that. It's ancient.'

'Ancient,' Eve repeated to herself. 'Has it ever been repaired? Refurbished?'

The woman shook her head. 'No, the wood has always been pristine. Magic, my Ma used to say. It runs in our blood.'

Eve checked the wheels. Not a single scratch or dent despite the journey across rough roads. 'What wood is this? Where did it come from?'

The woman watched her warily before answering, 'I don't know.'

'I don't believe you.'

'I don't particularly care.'

'Ma,' Lily said calmly, 'we can trust her.'

'Can we?' she asked her daughter.

'She's Gabby's friend.'

Exasperated, the woman turned back turned to Eve. 'Why? Why do you want to know?'

'Ma,' Lily repeated.

'It's a family secret,' her mother hissed.

A pull spurred in Eve's gut; the sound of hooves riding in the wind, the smell of a stormy night and of fear. She whirled towards the women.

'*Please*,' Eve begged. 'It's important. I'm not sure how or why, but I *know* that your answer matters. Where did this vargo come from? Why is it here, in a gypsy camp?'

Eve never begged. It wasn't in her nature. She'd learned early on that, to survive in this realm, she couldn't yield any answers unless given freely, and she didn't owe anyone unless it was in her favour. Yet she felt it, that this moment was important – vital.

The woman twitched at Eve's question. 'First of all, don't call us gypsies. It's insulting.'

Eve paused. 'What do you call yourselves then?'

'Travellers.'

Eve flushed at the error of the term before asking again. 'Tell me about the wood.'

The woman's stroked Lily's head tenderly. 'It's a family heirloom, but one that comes with a heavy tale. Before I share this with you, you must promise never to utter this secret. We will shake on it, and seal it with magic. If it's broken, I will know. And I will come for you. Do you understand?'

Eve nodded. A promise was no small thing, but even Eve knew not to go against a witch.

'I suppose, if we're making promises, we ought to know each other's names,' she said, staring Eve down. 'I'm Iris.'

'Eveline.'

With a sharp nod, Iris stepped forward. They grasped each other's forearms, Iris' hands warm and callused. Her eyes were bright with challenge as she spoke, locking eyes with Eve as she chanted, 'At the twining of hands, a promise with breath; shouldst thou break it, a promise of death.'

Eve twitched as the promise burned into her skin, a print of the woman's hand as a red mark, just as hers did to Iris.

Satisfied with Eve's performance Iris grunted.

'Tell me about the wood,' Eve said again.

'Impatient, aren't we?'

'It's not my best quality, but a quality all the same.'

Iris brushed her hand against the vargo's side. 'As I told you, this has been in our family for generations. How long exactly'—she shrugged—'we're not certain. But it's always been with us.'

'Specifically,' Iris continued, 'it's passed through our female line. It doesn't have any particular special properties, not like a stone or bones or spells. More that its magic lies in the wood it was crafted from. Never bent, never broken, never scarred – like the women in our family, my mother used to say.'

She moved to the front of the vargo and took a seat on the steps, grasping the railing for balance. 'The story goes that my ancestor Anna-Mae was lost in the woods after running away. Treated miserably by her brothers, she would be forced to work and was called unforgivable things. One day, Anna-Mae had enough and ran.

'She went so deep into the Shadow Forest that, even if she wished to return home, she could not. Starving and alone, Anna-Mae came across a place that was lost. A place of magic. Growing grandly in the middle of the forest, was a great tree, its bark white with a hint of silver, and with roots that ran deep.

'Anna-Mae claimed it was the first tree, the beating heart of this very land. And she called it "The Ancient One".'

Lily shuffled her feet beside Eve and whispered, 'I used to love this story as a kid.'

Eve barely heard the words, her heart racing like a shooting star as Iris told her tale. The prophecy burned bright in her veins. She felt the echo of its power, heard it in the long-ago voice of Lady Nona. She could smell the familiar incense, feel the heat of the sun beating down on the vargo.

Wood from a tree that's existed an age,

And mirrors of glass in a watery cage.

Iris smiled at the vargo, proud of her heritage. 'The story goes that the tree looked after Anna-Mae. It granted her somewhere to lay her head, grew her fruit, and with time, bestowed her small gifts, but only with the promise to never use them for ill.

'Anna-Mae was humble and took this magic as a great gift. We don't know how long she stayed, but it was long enough that, after a time, she requested to return home.

'She was homesick, worrying for her brothers. The Ancient One was impressed with her kindness and granted her permission to leave. Upon her departure, the tree created this vargo to help her find her way. Crafted from the Ancient's bark, it never ages, never fades, and never wears.

'Anna-Mae took it with thanks, promising she would only use her magic for good and would bring no harm. But when Anna-Mae walked through the rickety gate of her home, all she found was death.

'In her grief, Anna-Mae turned to the road, travelling the rest of her days from town to town, sharing her gift, and then bearing a little girl. It's been in our family ever since; a male never having been born into our lineage.'

Lily sighed at the end of the tale.

Eve stepped towards Iris. 'Has the tree ever been found since Anna-Mae?'

Iris snorted. 'Absolutely not. I wouldn't even believe it existed if it weren't for the vargo being hard proof.'

'Did Anna-Mae ever go back?'

The woman shook her head. 'I believe she tried, but the Ancient One finds *you*, not the other way around. The forest rustles with secrets, but if you listen close enough, it's said that you might hear the path to the sacred tree. Most become lost and crazed, searching for something that never appears.'

'Unless you have a specific gift,' Eve mused to herself.

Iris snorted again. 'Yeah, the gift of finding an impossible thing. I don't know anyone with that kind of power.'

'Luckily,' Eve replied, her mouth curling, 'I do.'

Hansel should have felt at home but couldn't, his apartment a foreign thing. Strangely enough, it wasn't because Piccadilly had moved in, or the fact that his things were boxed away. He just didn't feel like he fit. He felt odd and out of place, as if he were a ship floating across a vast sea, the land he craved nowhere in sight.

He tried to recall the last time anything had felt like home but could only recall Eve's whiskey eyes and rare smile, her fiery gaze and messy braid. His home was passing through mountains, hunting for food, sleeping under the stars by a campfire, Eve's laugh echoing through the trees. It was the first time his heart had felt full, lulled into belonging. He'd been a guard, a huntsman, a warrior, and a brother, but he'd only ever been grounded when he had been hers.

The entrance door slammed open, and he jumped. Piccadilly came waltzing in with a pile of guard's uniforms.

'Are they from the bodies in the canal?' Hansel asked, rubbing sleep from his eyes.

'Does it matter where I got them?' she asked, dropping them onto the bench. 'They'll be useful either way.' She turned to Hansel with hands on her hips. 'On that note, I may have a plan. It's either brilliant or very, very stupid.'

Porchid floated in front of Hansel, choosing to poke his tongue mid yawn. She giggled as he nipped at her hand.

Hansel faced Piccadilly. 'Does the plan involve wearing these uniforms somewhere with a lot of guards? Perhaps with the expectation of blending in?'

She flashed a secretive smile. 'Sort of. Not really. Yes?'

'It won't work,' he said, stretching, 'I'm plastered on wanted posters all over the city. not to mention you're both fairies, which means you're too recognisable. We'd be arrested.'

'Did you not hear the part where I said it could be a brilliant idea or a very stupid one.'

Hansel snorted.

'I think, at this stage, we have limited choices,' she continued. 'We have to work with what we've got. You've met the Princess, and she's alive. We think. We hope.' She bit her bottom lip.

Hansel frowned, wondering what she was hiding.

'But that won't be enough,' she said. 'Without the Princess here, the Commander will hand you over in a heartbeat. The bounty on your head is worth more than your sword.'

He'd heard about the Commander from the pig farmer; the person running the rebellion from a chamber in the Silver City. When Hansel had broken from the Queen, he assumed the rebellion had been run by the people. Assumed he could join if there was enough of them standing to challenge Myrenna's rule. He'd never considered there would be someone running it all, and, thinking back, he realised how naive that was.

'You said you already had someone inside,' Hansel said. 'So why are we taking a further risk?'

'The person we have inside doesn't have the same *qualifications*,' she replied carefully. 'Whilst he's part of the guard, he doesn't have access to the inner circle.'

Hansel raised his brow. 'And you think I do?'

Piccadilly shifted on her heels, resting her hands on the hilt of her curved blades like they brought her comfort. 'Our informant is not part of the typical guard. He's tough and he's wily, though. Traits necessary to our cause. He's close enough to the Queen that what he can give is invaluable, but he's not an officer.'

Hansel's jaw tensed. 'Placing value on people now, Piccadilly? That's a dangerous game.'

'That's not what I mean, and you know it,' she snapped.

The air in the room tightened. Hansel racked his brain for another topic, coming up short when the memory of last night surfaced.

How long has the Commander been in charge? Hansel had asked.

A few years now. Used to work in the castle, knew the Princess personally, she'd replied.

Hansel frowned. The thing about knowing Snow personally was that nobody did. The Queen saw to it she remained isolated. Which left the possibilities for the Commander minimal.

Snow and Hansel had used the library as a safe place, escaping to a hidden alcove behind an old bookcase. They'd plucked pillows from rooms all over the castle and spread it out to make it theirs. Their own little secret.

Besides himself, he only knew of three others. Malak, who had worked as a stable hand on the grounds, completing odd jobs others did not want to do. Sometimes he'd picked Snow fruits from the orchid, and planted roses by her tower.

The other two people that were close to the Princess were her private tutor and the cook, leaving Hansel to ask as much. Piccadilly had only answered that she didn't know.

Hansel's sleep had been broken since then, his time in the castle playing on repeat until he'd finally dozed off.

'What is it you do in the rebellion?' Hansel asked.

She shrugged. 'Mostly recruitment. But I get given other tasks, too.'

'Directly from the Commander?' he asked.

Piccadilly eyed him curiously. 'Yes.'

Before he could ask more, she threw him a uniform. 'Speaking of the Commander, he's given me some information. I need to find out if it's accurate. With your help, we could confirm the rumour, and the Commander will see that you're more valuable than the reward the Queen is handing out.'

'The plan that you tried to sell as either brilliant or really stupid?'

Piccadilly preened. 'The exact one.'

Viper walked in, her usually perfect hair sticking out at odd ends. Piccadilly threw her a brown bag. Viper smiled shrewdly as she pulled out a glazed pastry. 'I knew I liked you.'

'Have you had that the whole time?' Hansel asked.

Piccadilly shrugged, a smile playing on her lips. 'Be a good huntsman and you'll get one, too.'

Porchid glowered at Piccadilly's tone, puffing her chest out in Hansel's defence. But it was short lived as Piccadilly laughed, pulling a bellberry from her pocket. A berry that was only produced in certain fairy colonies.

The betrayal hit Hansel like a blow as Porchid left his shoulder and dived for the food, glowing gold as she smacked her face into the fruit.

'Really?' he said. 'You leave me for a berry?'

Porchid smiled, red juice dripping down her chin.

'There's been information about a prisoner under the keep who could prove valuable.' Piccadilly said, holding Hansel's food hostage. 'It's someone I suspect you're familiar with.'

Hansel rested his arms on his knees, stomach growling. 'Who?'

'A certain creature with a magical wooden spindle.'

'Rumpelstiltskin? Why would he be under the castle?'

She pursed her lips. 'They're only rumours. For now.'

'And if they're true?'

'Then we free him,' she replied.

'Why?'

'Because the spindle in Myrenna's hands is dangerous.'

'And it's not dangerous in his?' he drawled.

Piccadilly stared at him pointedly. 'Rumple's had it for years. He's a safer bet with the spindle than the Evil Queen.'

Though he wanted to, Hansel didn't argue her point. 'If we succeed,' he said, 'where does he go after that? To the Commander?'

Piccadilly raised her brow. 'Where else would he go?'

'I'm just not sure handing over something as powerful as the spindle to a man who won't even show his face is a good idea,' Hansel grumbled.

'I don't see how someone who's never met the Commander or the rebellion can make judgement calls. Weren't you the one to steal it in the first place?'

'That was different,' Hansel said. 'That had a purpose.'

'A purpose that involved a pretty young woman with a talent for knives?' she asked.

'If you're referring to Eveline,' Viper said, mouth full of pastry, '*pretty* is not a word I'd use to describe her.'

'She's a very handsome woman,' Piccadilly replied. 'I met her in Roserock when I was undercover as a barmaid.'

'Does it matter?' Hansel snapped. 'She was hired to find the Princess, and she did exactly that.'

'Before promptly disappearing, which is a habit of hers,' Viper drawled.

'Okay, enough.' Piccadilly replied. 'Let's get back to my idea.'

'The stupid one?' Hansel said.

'The brilliant one,' she corrected. 'I've asked a few questions here and there, and I know that the guards are rotated three times a day inside the prison.'

'Then they go to the Tinder Box,' Hansel said. He'd been with the guard long enough to at least know that.

'Exactly,' Piccadilly said. 'Most of them go to the Tinder Box after their shift. I've been following them for a few nights now, which is how I came across you pulling along those bodies last night. That drunk act you performed was …'

'Disturbing to behold?' Hansel asked.

'Tear jerking and brilliant to witness?' Viper piped up.

'*Interesting,*' Piccadilly replied, diplomatically. 'But it won't work again. You can only get so much information from sitting and watching from the outside. With the two of you, we have a real shot at getting inside.'

'I'll be recognisable,' Hansel said flatly.

'Yes, but I'm hoping on the cauldron you are. You held a respectable rank in the guard.'

'I betrayed and left them. They'll kill me on the spot.'

'I don't think they will,' she said confidently. 'You haven't been gone long, and most don't know you left. You never actually joined the rebellion. Most only know you were sent away on a mission for Myrenna, and that's the last of it. They'll assume you've just returned from wherever it is you were.'

'That's a very big assumption, considering the posters in the city.'

She waved him off. 'We'll deal with the posters.'

'I haven't been to the Tinder Box in years,' he said.

'Minor details,' she said. 'I think this will work. We can use it as a way to announce your return – there's no better place than where people drink and let off steam. Loose lips and all that.

'Porchid will sneak in with you after the watch has finished. She can go through the barkeep and watch from a distance as you get access to the pits beneath. The guards behind those doors are the ones with the real knowledge.'

'You were right about your idea,' Hansel drawled.

'Brilliant?' she asked.

'Undoubtedly stupid.'

'But you'll do it?' Piccadilly prompted. Her eyes were wide, dark as black tar, but sincere. He chastised himself, wondering at how he managed to get dimmer with age, instead of wiser.

'I'll do it,' he sighed. 'But on one condition.'

'And that is?'

'That you'll introduce me directly to this Commander once it's done. If I'm working for another monster, I want to look him straight in the eye.'

She tossed him the brown bag and Hansel caught it swiftly. He smelled custard and glazed butter before he'd even opened it.

'Deal,' Piccadilly said, 'We'll begin tonight.'

Eve hid behind the barn as Gabby's father left the cottage on horseback. She waited until the trotting of the horse was a distant echo before she crept across the dry grass and peered through the window.

Gabby sat by the hearth, her head in her hands. Eve rapped on the window gently, hesitant.

Gabby's eyes met hers, her cheeks wet with tears as she hauled open the window. 'Eveline,' she whispered, 'by the cauldron, you're safe.'

The relief in her voice warmed Eve's heart in a way she didn't care to admit. 'Thanks to Lily. Can you let me in?'

Gabby hesitated, then nodded. She clasped Eve's arm and helped her to manoeuvre through the narrow window, bracing her arm when Eve grasped the windowsill, still a bit dizzy from days of healing.

Gabby embraced her before she could fully stand, her bosom squashing against Eve's face until she coughed and stepped back enough for Gabby to hug her properly.

'I'm so sorry,' Gabby sniffled. 'What Papa did to you was awful.'

Gabby wiped her eyes, giving Eve a proper view of her in the light. One of her eyes was swollen, and a ring of bruises coated her forehead and temple.

'It's not as bad as it looks,' Gabby said, touching Eve's arm lightly.

All Eve could do was swallow, her fists curled at her sides. Gabby's father was lucky he was gone, because she wasn't sure she'd be able to control herself if he dared burst through the door then.

Gabby grabbed Eve's hand as if she could read her thoughts. 'He means well.'

Eve breathed deep, a clock ticking in the background. She pulled a twig from Gabby's hair. 'As you say.'

'He loves me,' she said softly.

But whatever had happened to her face wasn't love. It was power – a trait Eve had experienced far too often in the realm.

Eve couldn't help herself as she said, 'Lily loves you.'

Gabby's face flushed pink, eyes solemn. 'How is she?'

Eve tried for a comforting smile, but it probably just made her look constipated. 'She's safe, just worried about you.'

Gabby's eyes welled again.

Before she could respond, Eve continued, 'I didn't just come here to pass on messages. I need your help. It's very important I collect my belongings. I can't leave without them. Do you know where they are?'

Gabby bit her lip. 'I think so, but I could be wrong.'

'That's okay,' Eve said. 'I just need somewhere to start.'

Gabby walked to the door and grabbed a rusty shovel, then handed it to Eve. 'Papa likes to bury things of value. Considering your gem and your knives looked expensive, I'd say they're buried.'

It was a start, but it would be like finding a star amongst a thunderstorm.

'Buried where?'

Gabby swallowed, her voice barely a whisper. 'My mother's grave.'

Eve frowned. What widower would dig up his dead wife's grave to hide a stranger's belongings? Then again, what father would bully and beat his only daughter?

Eve accepted the shovel and stalled by the window. 'I know it isn't my place, but I've never been good at staying in my lane, so I'll say this once.' She looked at Gabby's bright eyes. 'I can't tell you what love is, but I can tell you what it isn't. Love isn't hurting the other person. It is not belittling them, or excluding them, or pushing them around. It is not locking them inside a cottage.

'Out there is a girl with a very large, very kind heart. One she is willing to give, if you let her.'

Gabby's eyes welled again, tears streaming down her face.

'I know it's scary,' Eve said, her chest hurting. 'Trust me, it's terrifying. But only you have the power to change your fate. You deserve love and a happily ever after, and you're not going to find it here.'

Embracing her again they stood in silence, the hug saying nothing and everything all at once.

'Thank you,' Gabby whispered. When she looked up, she licked her lips. 'Be gentle when you dig.'

Eve held back a snort, the clock's tick echoing through the cottage.

Gabby gave her a sad smile. 'I hope the fairy godmother guides you, Eveline.'

'May she guide you too,' Eve replied. Then she crawled through the window, dragging the shovel out after her.

XVII

The Soldier and the Beast

Hansel scowled at his reflection in the mirror. Viper snorted from the kitchen. The uniform wasn't a perfect fit, but considering his size, the likelihood of finding one that was had been slim.

'You look radiant,' Piccadilly said, clasping her hands.

Now it was Hansel's time to snort. This was the third uniform he'd tried on, a small hope lingering in his heart

249

that none would fit. He didn't like this mission, nor the way his chest constricted every time he thought about entering the Tinder Box.

'You'll just need to comb your hair, and then you'll be perfect,' Piccadilly said, her smile a little too bright.

Hansel ran his hand through his hair as Porchid settled on his shoulder and took in his outfit. The tilt of her head told him she was unsure, but her lingering smirk meant he'd also passed some test he didn't know was happening.

They had to wait for nightfall before he could walk into the Tinder Box. The tavern would be at its fullest – and drunkest – when darkness came. The whole day had been a waiting game. Hansel's palms hadn't stopped sweating in anticipation as the sun dropped further into the horizon. Each hour too fast and too slow for what he was about to do.

They'd gone over the plan several times and Hansel was still unsatisfied with the gaps open for failure. Piccadilly was adamant it would work, but Hansel had his trepidations. What if someone knew he was a deserter and recognised him? What if his influence wasn't enough and he couldn't get into the back den? What if Porchid was seen?

'So, your contact will be inside?' Hansel asked, stretching his shoulders in the jacket.

'His name is Flynn,' she replied.

'What's his station again?'

'He's in the street watch.'

'How long has he been in the rebellion?'

'Long enough,' she replied, coolly.

Hansel had never been cynical; he'd always chosen to believe in the best in others. And if it had been a year ago, he would have gone into this mission with the best intentions hoping for its success rather than expecting its inevitable failure. Eve had influenced him more than he'd realised. He felt her sceptical presence like an echo, a wild thing pressing against his chest.

Hansel closed the last button on his right sleeve and smiled softly at Porchid in reassurance. She twinkled back at him.

He faced Viper and Piccadilly. 'What will you be doing during my welcome back party?'

'I'll be nearby,' Piccadilly said. 'Should anything go awry, Porchid will report, and I'll be at the ready.'

'And I'll be here, with the instructions on how to contact the rebellion should you both die a horrible and bloody death,' Viper said, pouring herself a large glass of wine.

Comforting.

'Not to mention, I'll be ridding the city of a few wanted posters,' she said, eyeing him over her glass.

The Silver City reflected in the mirror behind her, the alleyways and cobbled streets reminding him of times he'd tried to forget.

When he'd first arrived, he'd only been a boy. He remembered huddling inside a small alleyway, starving, his hands having awkwardly outgrown his lanky form. Without food, malnutrition had kicked in. Where he'd learnt to run with Gretel, he'd learnt to remain hidden from the world on his own. But in those black moments he'd also seen the beauty. The kindness of a couple that would bring him an apple. The smile of a soldier who didn't report him but gave him his water skin. If it hadn't been for the old king's guard taking a chance on a boy from the street, Hansel might have been dead by now.

The day he was handed a sword was a day of promise. A promise to build a better life, to protect those who couldn't protect themselves. And then Myrenna had come, waltzing into the barracks like smoke and shadow. When she'd pinned those amethyst eyes on him, he'd known his life would change.

Myrenna during the nights. Snow and Malak during the day.

He'd become lost in a cycle.

But whilst he'd broken that cycle, the stakes were higher than ever. It wasn't just the Queen anymore, it was the Grimms, and Eve, and the dwarves, and the realm. It was bigger than Bellatorre now.

It involved everyone.

He'd felt the change before he'd taken the job to find the Princess. He had sensed the anticipation of the people, the electricity in the air as uproars began in the mines.

War was inevitable.

Events had been set in motion long before he'd crossed paths with the Seeker, determined to rescue the Princess, all of it unravelling at the tips of Myrenna's manicured nails.

'You look pale,' Piccadilly said. 'Are you okay?'

'I'll be better once this is all done.'

'I'd say another hour and we're good to go.' She paused. 'Are you ready?'

Hansel swallowed, his muscle memory kicking in as he stood tall, the uniform bringing out the lonely soldier in him. He winked at Porchid, welcoming her slight form and comforting glow as she flew to his shoulder. 'Let's get charming.'

Sweat poured from Eve's brow as she dug her shovel into the ground, heaving more dirt to the growing pile next to the unnamed grave. Her arms ached from ploughing the earth, but it was the itching along her skin that set her teeth on edge. The urge to scream at the man who'd buried stolen things in his dead wife's grave.

Rage coiled in her gut the further she dug, blinding her so much she had to stop for a breath. She was angry at Gabby's Papa for hurting those he loved. Angry at herself for not throwing her knife at his head instead of her fist. She was angry at Nona for leaving her. She was angry enough to punch the Fairy Godmother in the face should they cross paths. She was tired and aching and irritated, sick of being commanded by the strings of fate.

Her gift flared the deeper she dug. She was close, expecting to hit the coffin at any moment, when something glinted under the dirt and muck. Eve knelt, the mud burrowing under her fingernails as she uncovered a wooden box.

Eve frowned as she picked it up, feeling the thrum of power vibrating from inside. Using a rock from nearby, she cracked open the lock. The lid creaked as she revealed its contents. Her stone was there, glowing alongside her twin blades. Her rucksack sat at the bottom, her water skin intact. She hugged them and smiled, then grabbed her knives and placed them comfortably in their holsters.

Before she could leave, she paused. The grave was shallow, but there'd been nothing to indicate that anything but the box was buried here. Curious, Eve prodded the dirt for a coffin, only to find the grave bare.

'What in the cauldron?' she said, frowning.

In the distance, a lit candle sat in the window from Gabby, the shadows flickering in the night. Eve climbed out of the grave and sat at its ledge questioning how to tell Gabby she visited an empty grave each day. The girl would be heartbroken.

A twig snapped nearby, causing Eve to jump to her feet. She eyed the growing dark, her hand clammy against her blade. Goosebumps trailed her skin as the wind picked up, reminding her of the wraiths in Parador. She peered into the night, wondering if she'd imagined it, when hot breath caressed her neck.

She hadn't had time to reach for her blade before she was seized from behind, a calloused hand smothering her mouth.

'I knew you were trouble the moment you stepped into my home,' a voice growled deeply in her ear.

Eve bit down hard, eliciting a howl from her attacker. She burst from the grip, knives in hand as she spun, weapons poised. 'To be fair, you carried me in passed out.'

Gabby's father gripped his hand and hissed. 'You shouldn't have come here. Shouldn't have dug out this grave.'

'Is an empty grave still a grave?' Eve demanded, gripping her knives tight. She couldn't help the tilt of her lip at the sight of his bleeding hand. She could still taste his blood.

'Only one day and you've managed to sway my daughter and steer her towards an early grave of sin and deceit,' he spat. 'Did you think I didn't know about the gypsy girl?'

'Travellers,' she corrected, but it went over his head.

'Liars and vagrants, all of them,' he growled.

'Liars?' Eve responded. 'Coming from a man who isn't even a widower? Is she alive? Or did she just leave you after realising how awful you are?'

His eyes were dark, melting into black. Claws sprung from his hands as his teeth grew into sharp fangs.

Eve's heart quickened, her knuckles going white as Gabby's father shifted before her. Hair sprouted from skin, his nose elongating and his shoulders grew large enough to resemble a bear. Eve stepped back, her weapons feeling far too small.

When a giant wolf stood before her, he licked his lips. 'There doesn't have to be a body to be a widower.'

Bile crawled up her throat as he grinned, meat still hanging from his teeth from his last meal. Surely, he hadn't *eaten* her.

But as he stalked forward, more wolf than man, Eve stumbled. 'That's disgusting.'

'Says someone who's never tried it.'

'Does your daughter know?'

He laughed, whiskers protruding from his face. A crack rang out as his neck twisted, thickening under his chin.

And then a scream rippled through the night.

Eve tensed as Gabby froze a few feet away, eyes wide at the sight of her father. 'Oh Papa, what have you done?'

Eve dared not take her eyes away from the monster before her.

'What big eyes you have,' Gabby said, and gasped.

Eve could smell Gabby's perfume now, a floral scent of daisies.

'What big ears.'

Gabby's Papa twitched, his eyes piercing the girls like the prey they had become. Eve could see it in the tension of his muscles, the way drool spilled from his mouth.

'Get away from here,' Eve warned.

Gabby shook, her voice hoarse as she stared at her father. 'What big teeth you have.'

A slow, methodical grin stretched his lips. 'All the better to eat you with.'

He dived. Eve didn't have to time to think. She spun, grasped Gabby's arm, and shoved her to the ground. The beast leapt over them, his claws snagging Eve's hair as he landed on all fours.

Eve was up in an instant, knees bent, twirling her knives. Her wrist still stung, but she'd dealt with worse.

Gabby squealed, briefly distracting Eve, and the beast took his chance.

Pain rippled down Eve's arms as his claws tore skin. She spun, letting her blade slash his side as she rolled out of his grasp. She ignored the pain as he came again, the stench from his breath blinding as she managed to stab his leg.

Eve could hear screaming, but whether it was from herself or Gabby she couldn't tell. Every muscle in her body was too wired, her survival instincts taking over as she dodged and parried and cut with everything she had.

The beast lashed out, his back legs throwing her halfway across the grass, the breath knocked out of her.

Eve clasped her empty hand, her knife still lodged in the beast's leg. 'Are you hungry, old man?' she taunted.

He snarled and charged, his claws slicing through the dirt like butter. Eve pounced, dodging claws or teeth by a hair. One wrong move, one wrong pause, and she'd be sliced bacon.

Eve ducked, and thrust her knife above her, managing to cut the beast's left eye. His howl rose towards the moon. She rolled but wasn't fast enough. Pain rippled down her jaw as his claws connected with skin.

Eve tried to catch her breath. The wolf's eye dripped blood into the upturned earth, and his snarl was somehow more vicious than before.

Blood painted the grass, slippery and rotten against the darkness of the night.

Her chest thumped as she flicked her knife and raised her finger, beckoning him in challenge.

The wolf came for her again, slower this time. Like Eve, he was covered in blood. His panting heavy in the dark, his legs unsteady as he approached.

For one breathless moment, they took each other in. Eve gripped her slick blade, then ran. The wolf echoed her speed and opened his great maw, drool slipping from his misshapen teeth.

Eve jumped. She floated mid-air, hanging by a thread, before the wolf appeared below her.

And swallowed her whole.

The insides of his body slicked across her skin. The stench of rotted meat and sulphur choked her. Before she could think about the rotted cage of his body, Eve positioned her blade and started cutting through his stomach from the inside.

The body shuddered as she hacked at every organ, sawing the thin blade through thick muscle and tendons, retching from the blood that flooded her face, her lungs.

Then cool air was on her face, the scent of fresh grass tingling through her nose. She slid out from his stomach onto the dirt, his insides falling in a sloppy mess on top of her.

She heaved up blood and bile.

Gabby screamed, but it sounded muted. Eve shook, unable to stare at anything but her hands. From the corner of her eye, lanterns appeared in the distance. There was an echo of voices, the shuffle of running feet. Then Eve saw those damn familiar blue braids.

Lily ran straight for Gabby, wrapping both arms around her. Eve wiped the blood from her eyes as Lily's mother came to stand before her.

'Impressive,' Iris said, staring at the wolf. 'Not many people can bring down a shifter.'

Eve coughed a small laugh and tried to sit, only to find her legs pinned.

She dug her nails into the dirt, a prayer on her lips. She tried to still her hands. Her heart felt like it would break through her chest. The heat from the wolf's insides made her sick, the weight trapping her to the point of panic.

Iris whistled, calling over the other Travellers. There were footsteps, grunted voices, and then a weight was released. Eve scrambled away, panting as she took in the ropes from the Travellers pulling the corpse away.

She dropped on the grass, arms spread wide, the sting on her jaw burning like a raging fire. It was over. He was dead.

She counted her breaths, feeling her heart finally slow.

Iris stood over her. The light from her lantern caused Eve to blink. She lifted Eve's chin and clicked her tongue. 'It's not too deep. I can help it heal, but it will leave a scar.'

Eve didn't care, her body already held years of scars, of memories, of pain. What was one more?

'Eat this,' the woman urged. She held a brown, wrinkled prune in her palm.

Eve looked up at her like she was crazy.

The woman rolled her eyes. 'You want my help or not, stubborn girl?'

Eve caved, the pain too overwhelming. She opened her mouth. Juice squeezed out of the halopod's crunchy exterior, the sour liquid dropping down her throat. Her pain receded almost immediately.

Iris rifled through her bags and pulled out a stitch kit. She handed Eve a piece of leather, and Eve locked her jaw around it.

Iris poured liquor onto Eve's cheek before pulling through the stitches in succinct movements.

Eve fought against the scream that kept building. It clawed through her chest, each stitch worse than the one before. Until she set it free, shaking the air.

'I'm almost done,' Iris murmured, but it didn't lessen the pain.

With the snip of a pair of scissors, Iris eased Eve into a sitting position. Her body shook with exhaustion. The pain was muted but still there from the bruises that would no doubt appear. She turned to find Gabby holding her father's wolfen head, tears streaking her cheeks. Pain shot through Eve's heart, rivalling the pain of her wounds.

'You did the right thing,' Iris said.

It didn't feel like she'd done the right thing. He might have been a beast, but was he not Gabby's father as well? Eve quieted the thoughts and turned to meet Iris's gaze. But there was no judgement behind her eyes, no malice.

Iris gripped Eve's shoulder. 'She would be dead if it weren't for you. You did what few others would do.'

Eve tightened her jaw. 'I killed her father.'

'You also rid her of a demon and a cage.'

Eve could only watch as Iris packed the medical kit, her hands steady. 'We've been tracking the shifter for weeks. We followed his trail here and found you instead.'

Eve blinked at her. 'You knew he was a beast?'

'No, we knew there was a beast. It being Gabby's father was just a sad plot twist.'

Gabby wailed, clutching the grass, her body shuddering. It cut through Eve's chest. Eve would never forget that sound.

'We'll look after her,' Iris said. 'You have a greater purpose. I feel the magic on you. It's beating in anticipation.'

As if awakening, her gift flared again. Eve shoved it down. Prophecy or not, all she ever did was bring death. Gabby's father. The grotto. Her own family.

As if reading her thoughts, Iris leaned down. Her voice was sombre, but there was understanding there, too. 'In time, the pain will dull. You'll never lose it, but it will get easier.' She turned towards Gabby and Lily. 'If Lily loves Gabby, then so do I. She'll be cared for. For now, you must go. Here, take these'—Iris dropped more of the prune-looking balls into Eve's hands and urged her to put them into her rucksack—'These are halopods, they have numbing and healing properties. The inside is a silver liquid. Considering the trouble you get yourself into, you'll need them more than I do.'

She ruffled through her bag again and pulled out a small tin. 'Take this, too. It's ointment for your cuts whilst they heal.'

Eve's eyes watered with exhaustion and with pain. She accepted Iris's hand and stood.

Iris inspected Eve's stitches and grimaced. 'You know you must go. You won't make it through the forest, but I believe you already know a shortcut?'

Eve nodded. She'd had a hunch since hearing the tale of Anna-Mae and knew she needed to follow it.

Iris squeezed Eve's hands reassuringly. 'You have more challenges to come. Be brave, Eveline, and remember … have hope.'

Hope. Eve scoffed.

Hansel came to mind. His warm smile embracing her despite her pain. His tender hands and his scent of wood as he reached for her.

'Thank you,' Eve whispered.

Iris nodded. 'One more thing.' She tore Eve's knife free from the beast's leg and used it to slice off a claw. She placed it into Eve's bloody hand. 'You'll need this.'

She called over another man, who carried something wrapped in cloth. Handing it to Eve, she said, 'The claw may come in handy. They hold and expel magic. The other pouch is food.'

Saying her thanks again, Eve bid them farewell. Gabby was silent in the darkness.

Lily gave Eve a firm hug. 'May the stars watch over you.'

The halopod had done wonders, numbing her and giving her strength as she looked towards the curve at the edge of the farm. The familiar tree line was only a short distance away.

She wouldn't need to travel through the forest to find the Ancient One. For inside that same grotto lived another old tree, one with a burrow that she'd climbed into during her father's death.

XVIII
The Pit and the Burrow

Hansel hid in the shadows, the alley ripe with the scent of mould and decay. The square was dark, the only illumination coming from two fairy lanterns near the main street. A rat scuttled across the stones by his feet, causing him to shrink back and Porchid to squirm in his pocket. Music echoed across the square from the Tinder Box, reminding Hansel of days he wanted to forget. He flexed his hands to alleviate his nerves, but he still sensed the tingle along his skin.

It was hard to forget sometimes how Myrenna's dark hair curtained her face, or the flash of her amethyst eyes in the night. Even harder to forget her demands for blood. For him.

He wanted to hate those memories, wanted to hide them away. But a part of him also missed the structure of his days. The surety of his purpose. He missed sneaking away with the Princess and Malak where they stole moments in time under the stars or in the library.

His hand grazed the stone wall, cutting his index finger. He peered towards the broken lamp in the square. It hung silently above the rotting doorway of the tavern.

You can do this.

This world had saved him, shaped him, given him the building blocks to be a man.

But it had also forsaken him.

It was a world of hidden whispers, of power plays and competition. Where authority and secrets ran as currency, and everyone was a piece in a much larger game. If it hadn't been for Princess Snow, he wasn't entirely sure that he'd have ever survived, let alone remained there long enough to mean anything to anyone.

Wouldn't Eve laugh at him now? The brave huntsman, the soldier, the saviour of a realm, hiding within the shadows of a wall, questioning himself.

A hero complex, she'd accused.

She was wrong.

Deep down he knew what he was. He'd known it the moment he'd run from the woods, abandoning his sister's corpse in a witch's cottage. He'd known it the moment he'd defended the Queen for using him as a puppet.

Hansel wasn't a hero.

He was a coward.

Porchid rustled in his pocket, impatient. He grunted at her. He could take a hint.

He calmed his breathing to centre himself and entered the square. He'd been a soldier in the Queen's Guard before and he'd survived. He could wear the uniform once more.

His ill-fitting boots clicked against cobblestone, his shadow passing beneath the flickering streetlamp. He timed his steps in his head, chin high and shoulders straight, then pushed his way inside.

A violin resounded as he entered, the chatter of voices a cacophony of noise. Warmth permeated from the open fire, urging him to strip off his coat. A barmaid nodded in welcome, balancing a stack of empty glasses.

Hansel ran his fingers through his hair as he pushed through the throng of patrons. The music was sweet, jolly. So out of place with his jumbling thoughts.

The beat hit a heavier rhythm, and a group of soldiers raised their cups in a loud cheer, spilling brew.

Slowly, Hansel made his way to the bar and pulled out a stool, careful not to interrupt the two soldiers beside him. He tapped his pocket twice, warning Porchid to remain hidden.

He undid his top button, and nodded to the bartender, whose eyes skimmed him up and down. 'I'll take the brew,' Hansel said.

Cup in hand, he took a sip, the drink watery and weak – the cheap, sticky kind you only found in back-alley places. Marcellus, the owner of the Skinny Piglet, was probably their supplier, too. Hansel grunted at the memory of the slimy barkeep.

'It's not the best brew,' a deep voice said, 'It's the whisky that keeps us coming back.'

Hansel turned to the stranger. He was young, and his black hair was slicked back and shiny. His eyes were a deep shade of green, bright but cunning.

There was something about him Hansel couldn't pin.

The stranger pulled out the stool beside him and held out his hand. 'I'm Flynn,'

'Hansel,' he replied, shaking Flynn's hand.

Flynn gave Hansel a wide grin and winked, reminding him of a shark. 'I hear we have a mutual friend, Captain.'

'Major,' Hansel corrected. Hansel wasn't sure why he said it – he'd never been one to flash his titles, even when he'd been in the castle, but the word just came out.

Flynn's eyes glittered in dark recognition before he lowered his chin and smirked. 'My apologies, *Major*. I hadn't realised your rank. She failed to mention it to me, but I had been curious.'

Piccadilly mentioned her companion could be overzealous, maybe even a little sly. But she'd assured Hansel of his loyalty. It still didn't settle the tightness in his muscles or the ringing bells in his ears. He eyed the door, assessing how quickly he could escape if he needed to.

'Looking to leave already?' Flynn asked, taking a sip of his whisky. 'She said you'd be a great asset when the time came. I can only hope that proves true. Your reputation precedes you.'

Hansel stared at his watery brew, focusing on the drops sliding down the outside of the glass. 'There isn't much of a reputation.'

'I doubt that,' replied Flynn. 'You were once in the Queen's inner circle, her little puppet. Parading you around the court, from what I hear.'

Hansel clenched his fist.

Flynn leaned in closer. 'Tell me, *Major*, did you enjoy being the Queen's plaything? Rumour has it that you put in some long hours in the Queen's bedchamber. You certainly are the committed soldier.'

Hansel jumped to his feet, fists clenched, his stool scraping the floor. 'If you'd like to keep all your teeth, I'd suggest shutting your mouth. You know nothing about me.'

Flynn shrugged. 'I'm just curious. Call it a sin of mine.'

Hansel swallowed his brew in one gulp.

Flynn winked as he finished his own. He waved to the barkeep to order more, then leant in. 'Our friend informs me that you have a few contacts in here that I may be … lacking.'

Hansel watched the bartender pour their drinks to distract himself from punching out Flynn's lights.

Flynn tapped his fingers on the bar, but Hansel didn't react. 'This is woefully boring. I thought you'd be interesting. She seemed enamoured by you.'

Hansel snorted. 'Careful, your jealousy is showing.'

Hansel swore the Corporal flinched, but it was gone with the shrug of his shoulders. 'Not the term I'd use per se, but nonetheless true. I suppose you'd know better, considering your history with the female specimen.'

Hansel remained still despite the wiggling fairy in his pocket.

Flynn leaned back grinning. 'I even hear you've got the elusive Seeker wrapped around your finger.'

'You don't talk about her,' Hansel growled, snatching his drink from the bartender.

Flynn raised his hands in surrender. 'It seems my small talk is rusty.'

'More fossilised than rusty,' Hansel replied.

Flynn chuckled. 'At least we agree on something.'

Flynn straightened a crease in his shirt. His fingers were long, and pale. Catching Hansel staring, Flynn's eyes roved over Hansel's uniform, noting the lack of badges or insignia. 'Not easy to get a Major's uniform, I see.'

'Not easy to get the rank, but it's still legitimate.' Hansel spoke flatly, ignoring the nagging fact that his title was in name only, if that. His face was plastered on wanted posters, after all.

Flynn laughed again, the sound fraying Hansel's last wisp of patience. 'I didn't say it wasn't.'

'Then what are you implying?' Hansel said stiffly.

Flynn bit his bottom lip but kept his smirk firmly placed. 'I was informed you had a sense of humour.'

'Funny,' Hansel drawled, 'I wasn't informed much about you at all.'

The smirk on Flynn's face dropped. He'd clearly hit a sore spot.

'*Funny* is the epitome of this whole situation, it seems.' Flynn leaned in closer, his cologne smelt of cinnamon and vanilla. 'How about I buy you another drink?'

Hansel narrowed his eyes. Piccadilly had said to wait for the line. The code. Flynn had been baiting him, wasting his time. The longer he stayed here, the higher the chance of being discovered and matched with the posters of him around the city.

Porchid shifted in his pocket, agitated. Flynn caught the flash of blue hair and narrowed his eyes. 'Tell your fairy to hide better, lest she become a new pair of winged earrings.'

Hansel showed no sign of surprise, though inside he boiled. 'Do you have a reason for sitting here, or are we just having a catch up?' Hansel snatched his whisky from the bartender.

Flynn raised his brow. 'Maybe it's because I don't trust you. Maybe it's because I question your sudden appearance and assistance. Particularly when you seem to have such close proximity to our mutual friend.'

Hansel slammed his drink down on the bar. 'Let's get one thing straight: I don't answer to you, and we both have our roles to perform.'

'Be careful, *huntsman*,' Flynn warned. 'Your chance at getting to the Commander rests solely on my assistance with this mission. One word about your little winged friend and I'll—'

'What?' Hansel said. 'Have me outed?'

Flynn's face twisted in contempt. 'Be careful, comrade. Our friend's not as honest as she seems. She may look like starlight, but she knows darkness all too well. She may not lie outright, but that doesn't mean she speaks the whole truth, either.' Flynn clenched his jaw like he wanted to say more but held back. Instead, he replied, 'I'd like to say this has been fun, but why lie?'

When Flynn spoke next, he made sure his voice was raised, clear for the tavern to hear. 'I'd rather report to a dog than call you "Sir".'

Hansel's eyes darkened with ire, gritting his teeth at Flynn's answering smirk. The smug prick had been taunting him on purpose, only giving up the line that was needed now.

He crowded Flynn, raising his voice enough for the nearby soldiers to hear him. 'Get him out of here before his head appears on a spike.'

Flynn licked his lips and dived. Despite Hansel expecting it, he could admit that the cocky soldier was quick. Flynn swung at Hansel, the drink is his hand forgotten as it smashed to the floor. Hansel stumbled back, ears ringing from the blow as Flynn smiled triumphantly. Hansel shook off the pain in his jaw and charged.

Somewhere, there was a shout and a stool collapsing as the men went for each other. Hansel dodged an elbow, and Flynn swung. Hansel blocked, but Flynn was stronger than he looked. With a grunt, Hansel managed to dodge the next blow and grab Flynn by the throat. Flynn whimpered as Hansel's fist smacked into his nose, blood blooming down his face.

Hansel growled about to strike again when a sharp pain lashed his right arm.

Flynn had a knife.

The bartender yelled obscenities as soldiers intervened, trying to break up the fight. Hansel smashed Flynn's head into the bar, relishing the crack of his stubborn skull against wood, Flynn's knife clattering to the ground. He held Flynn down, not minding at all that he was choking on the stale brew and his own blood that spread across the counter. Hansel's knuckles ached from his grip. He was breathing heavy when two soldiers grabbed Flynn and hauled him away.

Hansel ran his bloodied fingers through his hair as he looked up. Flynn shot him a wink just as they threw him out the door.

Hansel heaved in a shaky breath. He had only meant to pretend, to play his part. He knew he would fight with Piccadilly's contact, but Flynn's baiting and taunting had dug under his skin far more than he should've allowed.

The bartender grunted, waving at the violinist to start playing. When the music filled the tavern once more, the room returning to their drinks, the bartender tapped Hansel on the shoulder. 'If you're looking for some privacy and quality drink, Major, there's an area reserved at the back for officers.'

'Show me,' Hansel replied.

The bartender led him through a dimly lit hallway, the wood stained from years of misuse and neglect. Hansel tried to keep his hands steady as he made his way through.

They entered a doorway and were led down wooden steps. Here, the walls were shinier, and the candelabras were lit up without dust or rot. Intimate alcoves were carved into the edges as secret havens for those who wished to remain present but unseen. Shouts and clapping echoed along the air as he descended, the walls vibrating with loud cheering.

He checked behind him before tapping his pocket once. Porchid's head popped out, her blue hair sticking out at odd ends. She shook herself. Her pale skin was a stream of moonlight against the flickering candles.

'It's time,' Hansel whispered.

Part of the plan hinged on Porchid's ability to remain unseen. Her size made her the perfect spy, far more valuable than any fashion statement. She could fit into the tiniest of spaces and stay perfectly quiet. She could hear things in a way that humans couldn't, and should she need to run, she could *fly*.

However, where she excelled in her size and stealth, the shining colours of her moods were her downfall.

Hansel had been reluctant to bring Porchid with him, not wanting to risk her safety, but Piccadilly had been insistent, and in doing so, had wrapped the little fairy around her finger. He watched as she disappeared into the dimness, and straightened his jacket.

The noise became rowdier as he reached a large underground room. It was packed, nobody lower in rank than a lieutenant judging from the insignias displayed on their uniforms. The walls were lush with lounges and cushions. Scantily clad women of all species squeezed through the crowd, expertly dodging grabbing hands or welcoming them, serving top shelf liquor.

Despite the luxury, it wasn't the women or the soldiers or the lounges Hansel noticed.

It was the giant gaping pit.

Soldiers pressed close around it, shouting and cheering at what lay below. But before he could take two steps, an arm halted him.

'The only weapons allowed here are your hands, Major.'

Hansel turned to find a lanky, towering man beside him. His mouth hung down as if he'd eaten something sour, his eyes beady and small. He wore all black, the shirt clean of any insignia. Hansel could only assume he wasn't a patron but an employee.

'Where will they be kept?' Hansel asked, loathe to let any of his weapons go.

The man assessed him from head to toe. 'In the vault, as always. Until you've completed your stay.'

Hansel carefully unhitched his knives and placed them into the man's outstretched hands.

'And the boots, Sir,' he said.

Hansel looked at his feet. 'My boots?

'The weapons in your shoes, Sir.'

Hansel sighed, taking out the small knife hidden there.

'You've done this before,' Hansel joked as he put it on top of the others.

The man grunted. 'First-timers. All the same.'

'Did I hear "first-timer"?' another man asked, stretching out his arms. 'Welcome to the pit, the most fun you'll have in the Silver City!'

The man embraced him, and Hansel went stiff. He was roughly the same build as Hansel, stocky with a broad chest. His hair was cropped close to his skull, and when he smiled, Hansel noted a few teeth of gold.

'Not often we have newcomers in the Pit. Especially a higher-ranking officer. Most are initiated here as part of their regiment.' The man looked Hansel up and down, noting his uniform. His eyes hovered over the missing insignia and Hansel braced himself. 'Take a seat with me and Druscilla, yeah?' he asked instead, pointing to a couch nearby. 'Tell me about yourself.'

Hansel followed him towards a set of lounges, his eyes tracking the rowdy crowd as they booed at the cavern below. 'I'm Major—'

The man clicked his tongue. 'No names here, Major. Unless you're one of the consorts. Otherwise, it makes for a very dangerous environment.'

Hansel blinked at him before answering. 'I'm in the immediate Queen's Guard. Personal protection.'

The man chuckled. 'I hear that post can be *very* personal.'

Hansel flinched but his eyes remained steady as they met his new companions'.

'Of course, everything inside the pits stays in the pits,' the man stated, grabbing at a woman in a sheer purple dress. 'May the Queen reign forever.'

Hansel took in the woman. Her eyes were silver, cunning under the surface despite her cool playfulness. 'I'm Druscilla,' she purred.

'I'm a Colonel,' the man replied, his eyes roving over Druscilla's lush curves and soft skin. 'The Pit can be overwhelming on your first time. Let's get you a drink, shall we?' He patted Druscilla's leg. 'Please be a diamond and get our new friend a whisky.'

Her smile was sultry as she glided off his lap to collect their drinks. Hansel's eyes followed her as she disappeared into the crowd, but not before she turned and winked at him.

'It's a cauldron of fun,' the Colonel began, lighting a cigar, 'but there are rules, of course. We're military and can't have ranks running amok. You seem like a solid soldier. A good man, I suspect.'

The Colonel clasped Hansel's shoulder, his eyes navy with a touch of gold. Knowing. He spoke with clarity that belayed his tipsy manner. 'Good men rarely do well here. The pits were made for our inner beasts to unleash themselves. Set free the wolf clawing inside most. Do you have a wolf inside that heart of yours, Major?'

Hansel thought of his heart. The same one he'd given to Eve when they'd kissed under the stars. He may not have a wolf inside his heart, but he understood darkness. Something even he couldn't quite pin down.

'I'm not sure I even have a heart anymore,' he said gruffly.

The Colonel chuckled. 'Praise the Fairy Godmother for that. Now,' the Colonel continued, leaning back. 'There are only three rules of the pit. Rule one: above ground is for morals, respect, and loyalty. Anything that happens here stays here.

'Rule two: everyone here is an officer – no exceptions or outsiders. The dregs don't get what they haven't worked for. And lastly …' He paused, smiling at Hansel as he clapped him on the shoulder. 'No killing another soldier, despite any unsavoury happenings outside of this establishment. Understood?'

Hansel hid his grimace, accepting the drink Druscilla served him. Hansel tried not to look, as Druscilla sat on the other man's lap, eager to win the Colonel's attention.

It was clear that coin mattered here. Medallions meant drink, which meant attention and likely safety for the girls that served beneath the Tinder Box. He didn't like it and he knew he couldn't change it. He averted his eyes, focusing on the Queen's banners that hung from dim corners.

Hansel sipped his whisky, glancing to every corner for Porchid. The liquor was sweet and husky, like molten honey dipped in something spicy. It wasn't like anything he'd tasted on his travels.

Hansel finished off his drink, pardoned himself, and made his way towards the howling crowd. He was glad to get away. Blood, he could do. Battle, he could do. Death, he could do. And yet he struggled with politics and a scantily clad woman on a lap.

He imagined Eve laughing at his awkwardness, and shut the thought down. If he focused too long on her he would remember she was alone, fighting and clawing against a destiny set long before her birth.

Hansel shoved through the crowd. Some tried to push back, but most moved aside due to his sheer bulk and determined expression. Wild cries pierced his ears, and medallions were plentiful, tossed like rice into the blood-soaked pit below. Hansel was jostled from either side as the crowd grew feral, their excited savagery suffocating the air.

When he'd finally pushed his way through, Hansel froze at the top of the pit, unable to look away.

He knew it was a fighting pit. He'd scented the blood and violence the moment he had stepped into this underground debauchery. What he didn't expect was to see a dwarf fighting for every inch of his life against a feral troll.

But that wasn't the worst of it.

Because standing in the sandy dunes of the fighting pit was Bjorn.

Eve kept running, the crisp night air rushing over her skin as she bolted through the bones of her old home.

The humble cottage lay in shambles, the edges of the wooden palings coated in black. Hollow and broken, like the space in her heart left for her father.

She sprinted under a stormy sky, her feet slipping, yet her gait never faltering as she finally reached the hidden burrow that her father had showed her.

His voice was an echo in her mind.

'Just as we practiced.'

The memory was as crystal clear as if it'd happened yesterday. She could still smell him, leather and smoke and tobacco. Even now, he whispered to her of wrath and warning. His strong hands leaving marks on her skin as he'd let her go. His sad smile, as he'd closed the entrance and whispered goodbye.

She blinked through the rain, the urgency in her blood stilled to silence as she squashed the memories of the past.

She was thankful to the Travellers. They'd saved her life, and the halopods had given her the energy boost she needed to keep her going. But whilst they worked wonders, they didn't last long.

Her face throbbed, blending with the beat of her heart as she raised her fingers to the brutal wound on her face. The cut ran down her jaw, a jagged and bloody souvenir left by Gabby's father. The scar would never fully heal, despite all the magic in the realm. She tried to make peace with that and accept another scar in her fight.

Eve stalled at a gnarled tree and leaned down to catch her breath. She pulled back a moss door. It cracked under her fingers, weather and time cruel to the natural materials. Water ran into her eyes, dropping from her lashes and blinding her in the dark.

She stripped off her knives and threw them down into the burrow first. The drop was far lower than she remembered. The earth beneath her was cool, soft to the touch but drenched.

She lowered her legs first, eased her body in, and dropped. She landed in a crouch, her ankles barking in protest.

At the bottom she picked up her knives and wiped the rain from her eyes. The burrow was neatly curved. Hanging vines and roots dropped from the ceiling, creating a natural maze in the dark. The vine was soft as she pulled it back and recognised the opening that lay beyond.

Eve's gift pressed in urgency as she followed the same path she'd walked years ago, that time in a dress, this time covered in blood and dirt and torn leather.

Her hair yanked on a sharp root, making her wince. She gently untangled it, grabbed a ribbon that Gabby had given her, and tied her hair back. She was anxious, her palms sweating at what lay on the other end.

This place had been her nightmare, a reoccurring tragedy in her head for over a decade. Now it seemed to be her only hope.

She veered around another curve under a root and met the intersection of two small tunnels. The left had led her to Rapunzel once upon a time. A pink tower hiding a nightmare. Eve's memories echoed with hurt, and the throbbing stone in her pocket urged her to go right.

Eve bit her bottom lip, gripped her knives, and followed her gift to the right. The opening was slightly larger than the left, but still cramped enough that she would need to crawl. She gave herself a quick pep talk before she lowered onto her hands and knees.

Her mind whirled in a thousand colours, a thousand moments—

A truth for a truth—

You'll know it when you feel it—

Just as we promised—

Come with me—

The tunnel weaved as Eve went further into the earth. The air grew thinner, colder. Her breath caught when she saw ice coating the walls. She thought of the wraiths, the ice following their footsteps through Parador. She envisioned the great, dark dragon that had shot from the sky as the thorns fell around her in Hasleholme; the giants yelling bloody vengeance as the doorway closed to their realm; and the Chomping Changers that grew and grew and grew.

She saw the onyx bridge and its gate made of black stone.

Hansel grasping her hand over a cliff.

A kiss by starlight.

Nona's tent.

Dante's death.

She choked on a sob.

Her hands sunk into mud as she pushed onwards, grimacing at the damp darkness that pressed in. The cold reached its peak, biting at her skin, turning her numb. Her throat burned. Her body shivered. She had no idea what she was doing.

The Queen was powerful. Snow was awake. Hansel was far away. Porchid was gone, too. She had three mirrors to find. And from what she knew, the rebellion was a sad excuse for an army. She'd lost her father, and Dante, and now Nona.

Was she to die next? Or was she simply waiting in a line for the noose that death held patiently whilst she watched those she loved perish before her.

A tear snuck down her face as her body revolted, her muscles locking against the cold. It seized her as if the hands of the Fairy Godmother were pulling her into the Ever After.

The stone began to burn into her side. She held onto its warmth and fought against the itch to crumble, to fold into the earth and stay there forever.

Eventually, the tunnel opened, and tiny stars shimmered against the dank walls. Light filtered through the gloom; a torch leading her out.

Eve moved more fervently now. The need to get out of this small, dark place as strong as hunger or thirst. The light roared around her, and the tunnel broke into another burrow.

Eve gasped in the fresh air, her heart thundering. She pulled out a halopod with shaking fingers and swallowed, stilling for a moment to let it kick in.

When Eve finally calmed, she took in her surroundings. The roots were thicker here, and older; more withered and twisted and gnarled. She smelt metal and thunder. It was a smell she knew well.

Magic.

A flap of wings caught her attention: a fire fairy, landing on a branch nearby. Her eyes were white as opposed to Porchid's black. Her wings were larger too, burning like coals.

More came, a swarm of curious eyes and fire-bright wings, as she carefully stepped over the thick, gnarled roots.

They began to sing, the ethereal tones echoing along the air and raising goosebumps on Eve's skin. She breathed it in. Breathed in the wonder and magic and hope.

She could do this. She could help Hansel and the realm and earn her right to the Grimms.

But just as she smiled at the array of feathered wings, they all went dark.

XIX
The Little Lamb

Hansel steadied himself as he stared down at the dwarf. He felt as if he stood on the precipice, one step wrong, one slip of the tongue, and the troll would be the least of their problems. He was surrounded by enemies: the Queen's army. Her little puppets ready to cut, and kill, and damn themselves for 'glory'.

Bjorn winked at Hansel before the crowd roared in unison. Nausea rolled in Hansel's stomach.

Bjorn stood at the ready, fists raised. The troll spat blood. The dwarf's clothing was torn, ratty at the edges and covered in blood and dirt. His dark beard had grown out, making him look older. His gold earring was still visible, but gone was the neat, rugged leader of the Seven that Hansel had met in the grotto.

Bjorn's teeth were ringed in blood as he smiled at his challenger. The troll stood over twice his height, his toothy smile big like the muscles that rippled under his mottled, green skin.

Whilst Bjorn looked like an infant next to the troll, he didn't look weak. He turned in a circle, raising his arms towards the crowd, and roared. He was fierce. Brave. Unafraid and defiant.

The crowd bellowed, medallions falling into the pit like metallic rain.

'I put my money on the troll, but I think I may have underestimated the dwarf,' the Colonel said, coming to stand beside Hansel and offering him a drink.

Hansel clenched his fists. He knew Bjorn was tough, but it was hard to imagine his victory when the troll's chest was bigger than his entire body.

'I'm not a big gambler,' Hansel said, not trusting himself to jump down into the pit and help his companion.

The Colonel chuckled. 'Need some coin to get you started?'

Before Hansel could answer, the crowd screamed, drowning out his reply. Bjorn was rabid, spitting blood into the sand as the troll laughed.

Bjorn made the first move and ran towards the bulk of his opponent with speed and agility, narrowly avoiding the troll's massive swing but falling over his own two feet.

He didn't falter, just became more animalistic – if that was possible – and jeered at the troll.

Hansel shook his head and swore under his breath.

'Not gambling and still betting on the dwarf?' the Colonel said, clapping Hansel on the back. 'How about, instead of coin, we bet on a drink? Got to believe in something. Why not the dwarf's victory, eh?'

Hansel watched as Bjorn jabbed then rolled, slicing the troll's thighs. Hansel may not like gambling, but he'd previously bet on Snow. He'd also bet on Eve the day she came crashing into his life, in the back of the Skinny Piglet. He'd bet on the dwarves to protect his friends, and he'd bet on his own life on more than one occasion when he joined the Queen's Guard.

'Fine, a drink,' Hansel agreed.

The troll swung hard and fast. Bjorn wasn't so lucky this time; even amongst the uproar of the crowd, the loud *crunch* echoed along the arena.

'It's a deal,' the Colonel replied, eyes sparkling. 'The undefeated versus the underdog. How entertaining.'

Hansel ground his teeth and looked for Porchid. Having one friend in trouble was bad enough, but another? He'd peel off Piccadilly's skin for this.

Inside the pit, Bjorn lay on his side, panting. The blow from the troll should have been debilitating, but he was conscious, at least. Blood covered his face as he struggled to get back up.

The troll was on his knees, the backs of his legs bleeding into the brown and red sand.

They were at an impasse.

'Do these happen often?' Hansel asked the Colonel.

The Colonel shrugged. 'Usually. The fights are weekly, but finding a good opponent is always tricky. Especially with our undefeated champion. You've brought us some luck.'

He raised his drink to Hansel's, cheersing him and laughing. He stumbled a bit in the crowd, and Hansel gripped his shirt to make him steady. The Colonel laughed it off as Hansel sipped at his drink, seeing the opportunity in front of him.

Some luck indeed.

If Bjorn managed to survive the pit and Hansel could keep himself steady, the Colonel's drink wouldn't be the only thing they were spilling tonight.

'Like a little lamb served up for the slaughter,' said a silky voice from the shadows.

Eve blinked against the exhaustion in her body, still startled from the silence of the fairies. Despite the halopod, her eyes were heavy and groggy, her view hazy.

Dirt lined her mouth as she rolled over, a sharp pain in her back receding as she dislodged herself from a root of the tree. When had she fallen?

'Like the prey of the lion before it's killed.'

Eve groaned as she felt inside her pocket and pulled out another halopod. She chewed on its rough surface, the juice coating her tongue, and surveyed her surroundings. She sat within a copse of trees, thick within the Dark Forest. The branches created an ivy roof above her, coating the sky in a tangle of leaves. To her left, ancient, pale roots stretched along the ground like an entangled web among the soft grass.

She touched the silver bark, the wood smooth beneath her palm. But it was the thrum of a beating heart beneath it that jolted her.

The Ancient One.

She scrambled back.

'A hurt little lamb.'

Eve swallowed, gauging whether the tree was speaking to her or someone else. The breadth of it alone was the size of twenty full grown trolls, filling the space like its own world. Its branches reached far into the sky, stretching for the space between time.

Eve had never been here, had never touched this soil, and yet in her heart she felt … recognition. Her head was heavy, her memories a jumble of shadows and colours and cold. She remembered leaving the tunnel and breaking free into an array of fairy light. But the light she had found earlier was gone, the flowers no longer glowed under the pale moon, and the silence was heavy without the song.

There was only the *voice.*

'I thought I'd only receive one present today; it seems the cauldron has granted me two.'

The accent ran along Eve's skin like a soft touch, its smooth, lilting tone familiar and foreign. Eve bit her bottom lip, eyeing the shadows as a cold sweat broke over her skin.

As if she'd coaxed them, the shadows broke like a splintered web, revealing two amethyst eyes piercing the veil of darkness.

Eve only had to blink, and they were gone.

She scanned the forest for her knives, scowling when she only found one. She leapt for it, clenching it to the point of pain, her mouth bone dry. One blade would have to do, especially if she were facing the enemy she suspected.

Eve only knew one person in the entire realm with such eyes: one who ruled behind the gates of the Silver City with her murder of crows, high on a golden throne. The muscles in Eve's back retracted, her body bracing for battle.

This wasn't a wolf like Gabby's father, or the blight infecting the land. This was a monster. *She* was the thing of nightmares, dipped in jewels and velvet, with poison in her blood.

The Evil Queen.

Myrenna's voice drifted through the trees, barely a whisper but as clear as glass. 'And here I thought I was the only one that knew about the knowledge hidden here.'

Surely this was a dream. A delusion, or a trick of her imagination. Eve steadied herself, and pinched her arm to ensure this was real, that the Queen was *here*.

Though she might die, Eve stood tall; she would die no other way, the steel in her stronger than the Queen.

'Pity about the face,' Myrenna taunted. Her eyes flashed, then became smoke. 'I wonder if the huntsman will find you as alluring after he sees what you've done with it.'

Eve gritted her teeth, willing the words away. If the Queen lowered herself to taunt her about Hansel, then it meant he was alive. Not safe – never safe. But at least alive.

Eve swivelled her head, grasping her blade like a lifeline.

'I suppose the bigger pity is that I didn't give it to you,' Myrenna cooed.

Nobody knew of this place. Even Eve hadn't. Not really. It had been her gift that had led her here, the knowledge that Nona would have left something precious, something so powerful that even she couldn't destroy it. So how did Myrenna know? How was she here?

Eve spun to the left, her eyes tracking the cold voice through the shadows.

'What did you do, I wonder?' Myrenna said. 'Did the little lamb take from the wrong person? Or did you steal the wrong heart? Perhaps you learnt a secret? Tell me, Seeker.'

Eve spoke with a calmness she didn't feel. 'Hello, Myrenna.'

A dark chuckle coated the shadows. 'We are not familiar enough for that.'

Shadows shifted through the night. Eve twisted at every sound.

'Tell me, Seeker,' Myrenna continued. 'Was it coin, or secrets?'

'We both know that secrets are a far more valuable currency than coins,' Eve replied.

'And hearts more valuable still,' said the Queen, her voice humorous.

Eve wondered, why wasn't she dead yet? What game was the Queen playing?

'Hearts will always be the greatest gift, but they are to be kept safe, not stolen,' Eve replied.

Eve heard the dark Queen's laugh before she slashed through the night. Light pierced the shadows, blazing to life in the Queen's palm. It was a lantern, Myrenna's pale hand clutching the handle. Myrenna's sharp chin and porcelain skin glowed under its golden light. 'You were always far cleverer than people gave you credit for.'

Eve stood firm despite the pain in her back and the cold sweat that pebbled her spine. 'Should I be flattered?'

The Queen clicked her tongue and stepped forward, the light now coating them both. They were each a beacon in the night: one made of shadows and ice, the other of fire and gold.

Myrenna wore riding leathers, with soft, worn boots. Her hair remained loose, tangled around her face in disarray. Eve's mind whirled, gears clicking into place. The woman before her had the capacity to kill with the flick of a wrist, but under the blanket of stars and soft light, she looked almost … human.

Where the Queen would normally don rubies, her hands remained naked, her fingernails plain; she even had dirt on her cheek. If Eve didn't know better, she'd suspect Myrenna as nothing but an unassuming village girl.

Eve fought against the urge to stagger back as Myrenna moved closer. From here, Eve could see the strain of Myrenna's muscles, the way her steps faltered as if she'd been riding too hard for too long.

Why would the Queen ride when she could fly?

'Can the clever girl guess why I'm here?' Myrenna asked, lifting the lantern higher, casting them both in moving shadows.

Eve didn't need to speak. They both knew why she was here.

Nona's grimoire.

'You're here because you followed the herd,' Eve said.

Myrenna grinned at the use of her metaphor. 'I am not naïve, little lamb. I observe what others do not, predict what others do not see, and when I look at you, I see a spirit that echoes my own.'

Eve was stunned, her own voice failing her. She was alive by sheer luck, it seemed.

Myrenna had been a baker once. Eve envisioned the Queen coated in flour, her hands kneading dough on a bench with care, and mixing colours to create instead of destroy.

Hansel had known her. Had touched her. Had *pleased* her.

Jealousy lurched in her stomach.

As if reading her thoughts, the Queen hummed. 'Enjoy him while you can, Seeker. I have no use for him. Let him die for his traitorous little *princess.*'

'You would give him up so easily?' Eve asked, shifting the grip on her knife.

The Queen watched her curiously as she replied. 'I didn't say I would give him up. Merely that he is yours for the time being. I have other … priorities. In time, he will return. He, too, shall receive his rightful punishment.'

'Punishment,' Eve repeated under her breath. Rapunzel's voice echoed from somewhere far away.

'He will die slowly. Of that I am certain.'

A wave of protectiveness rushed over Eve, almost bringing her to her knees.

Slowly, she faced the Queen. She'd had some wonderful gut feelings in her life, ones that had led her to very important contacts and jobs. Ones that had led to her arrest and losing a bed for the night. This time, it urged her to be brave.

Surely, now wasn't the time to bargain her life, but if her destiny was as sealed as Nona had supposed, then perhaps, she was meant to be here, meant to play house with the monster.

Eve met the Queen's eyes, her bravado far more fragile than it seemed. She swallowed back the little voice. The one inside, telling her, *this is a very bad idea.*

'Do you ever listen to yourself when you talk?' Eve asked, 'Do you practice it in that mirror of yours, or does the piety come naturally?'

The Queen's eyes flashed with anger before her face smoothed into her familiar political smile. 'You realise,' the Queen warned, 'I've killed others for far less disrespect.'

'Which begs the question, why haven't you slaughtered me yet?' Eve's heart felt as if it would explode from her chest. She clenched her hands into fists to hide her shaking. 'What is it you want, exactly? The grimoire? Because you already know it's here. I can only think that it's something else you want. Something else you seek. Something that maybe only I can give you?'

Instead, Myrenna tilted her head. 'It would be easier to kill you, snap you like one of the branches in the clearing. But perhaps even my curiosity is piqued.'

She stepped closer, the light harsh as she raised it in front of Eve's face. Myrenna's breath was warm from this distance, her scent of blood and lavender pungent.

'I have a question for you, Seeker. What is it, exactly, that you need with a grimoire, when the only magic you possess is controlled by a whim and not by any skill on your part? It would be worthless to you.'

Priceless, Eve thought, *not worthless.*

That's the word Eve would have used, but it was best not to correct royalty when her life hung in the balance. 'Would you believe me if I said I've been hired to find it?'

'No,' Myrenna replied.

'What if I told you it would be a *really* great paperweight?'

The Queen hissed, and Eve gripped the knife firmer in her palm. 'What is your secret, you scarred, little lamb?'

Eve took a step back, the sharp eyes of the Queen following her every move like a snake. Where Eve moved, the Queen copied. Two pythons let out of their baskets.

Eve's eyes had adjusted now as she moved with care over the roots. Her body had adapted to the new terrain.

'Have you ever hunted?' Eve asked as the Queen followed her. The ancient tree pulsed around them, aware of its uninvited visitors. 'Have you ever slain a rabbit or a deer and then invited it to tea?'

'I don't like riddles,' Myrenna seethed.

'Allow me to speak plainly, then, so you understand,' Eve said. 'Didn't anyone tell you not to play with your dinner?'

Eve kept note of her steady movements, her gut guiding her to the grimoire.

The Queen watched her with slitted eyes. 'I've decided I don't want to play anymore.'

'But this is your game, isn't it? We're all just pawns in your happily ever after.' Eve moved closer to the trunk, the pull in her stomach becoming more of a humming pulse. The grimoire was near her feet, but she didn't dare look down.

'Indeed, it is, but the time for your move has passed. That little knife won't save you.'

'Oh, I know that,' Eve replied, inching closer to the trunk. 'But I'm curious as to why you're giving me time.'

The Queen was burning with hatred now, it poured from her like liquid fire. 'Enough!'

With the political facade now erased, the Queen lunged for Eve. She was quick, but Eve was quicker, twisting round the trunk and using the barrier and roots to her advantage.

'There she is,' Eve whispered.

'Why purposely piss me off?' Myrenna seethed, hunting her through the roots. 'I can offer you anything, give you *everything*.'

'What about your heart?' Eve asked.

Eve leaned into the shadows, the roots crawling along the ground. She carefully avoided one as it slid across another, silent and slick.

Who are you? the tree seemed to whisper.

'You seem to have no concept of what is *actually* happening here,' Myrenna said.

The Queen's footsteps were muffled, but Eve heard the grunt, the misstep. The roots provided a cover, one Eve was grateful for. She kept moving, using the stirring limbs to her advantage. The lantern bled through the night, just out of reach.

'This isn't about your silly little rebellion,' Myrenna snarled into the dark, 'or your lovesick eyes for the huntsman. It's bigger than that. So much bigger.'

Eve leaned into the roots, feeling for the pulse of the tree. It reminded her a little of Nona, of incense and fires under the stars. Of smoke and shadow and grey eyes.

Who are you? the tree sang through her fingertips.

I'm a friend, Eve whispered back.

'This isn't about you or me,' the Queen continued, the light peeking through the roots as she came closer.

'Isn't it always about you?' Eve chimed back, ducking as the light almost reached her.

Her heart sped as she twisted around the trunk, keeping her hand attached to feel her gift. There was a throb in her belly, a warmth with each step. She was close.

I'm a friend, she whispered again.

It was then her hand sunk into the once hard surface of the bark. She bit back a yelp as her hand disappeared, only to find something solid on the other side. Eve pressed herself against the tree as Myrenna passed and pulled out the object inside. She blinked back tears as a book followed her, its worn pages familiar and old.

But her smile died when Myrenna's hand grasped her neck, the Queen's hot breath inches from her nose. 'Stupid, *stupid* girl. This is about the sisters Grimm.'

Eve choked. 'What?'

'You know *nothing* about what is at stake. You think you know the realm and me, but how could you when you don't even know what's inside of you?' The Queen seethed as her other hand pushed against Eve's chest. Her nails were scraping where the Seeker's heart was.

Eve waited for it. The searing pain of flesh being torn as the Queen readied herself to tear out Eve's heart and devour it.

But it never came.

The Queen's face contorted in frustration, then panic. Then she recoiled.

Eve held herself steady, blinking, as Myrenna stared at her hands as if they'd betrayed her. It was almost as if … Eve choked out a laugh.

Myrenna has no magic.

Eve laughed louder as she realised it was the only reason she was alive. She hadn't been the only one playing a game, it seemed. The Queen had also been fooling her.

Sisters Grimm, indeed.

Eve's hand twitched as she lifted her knife. One flick through the air and it pierced the Queen's shoulder.

Myrenna screamed and tore the blade from her body, but the blood didn't stop. Her eyes narrowed on Eve and the grimoire, her voice melting into something dark and dangerous. *'I will kill you.'*

Myrenna's eyes turned fierce, fire igniting behind them. Eve stepped back. Myrenna was living death, layered with blood and vengeance.

She snarled, then dived.

Eve couldn't move. Her energy was almost depleted, her fighting skills useless amongst the roots. Even without her power, the Queen was a terrifying monster. The kind parents warned their children about at bedtime.

Eve closed her eyes and held the grimoire tight, Nona's magic pouring over her. One heartbeat. Two.

Eve waited for the final strike. The final breath. But when she opened her eyes, the roots shifted. They flicked over her wrists, her torso, her arms, and pried her off the ground. She held still, her eyes piercing the dark as Myrenna screamed.

Roots tore from the soil, covering Myrenna's body. They seared her skin, crushed her bones, and dragged her into the dirt, burying her deep.

The only remnants of the Queen were her weathered riding boots protruding from the ground.

XX
The Soldier and the Brew

Porchid monitored the crowd from behind a pillar, keeping a watchful eye on Hansel as he spoke to another man. Despite his hesitancy about this mission, Hansel blended in well.

Porchid slid closer, minding her light as music played from a stage near the bar. Whilst she normally loved her glow, her light was a hindrance in these dark chambers.

At least she wasn't the only non-human in the room. The space was filled with creatures – pixies, fairies, dwarves – each one dressed more fanciful than the other. All wore colour, something vibrant and bold. Some showed skin, with sheer fabric and belts to hold it up. Others went for a modest look, with long skirts and high neck pieces.

The commonality, Porchid noticed, lay in their roles. Each one seemed to gravitate to the men, laughing at things that weren't funny, or batting their eyelashes to the point of blindness.

Porchid's gaze tracked the sultry touch of a knee, her gaze flicking between the loud laughter at the tables and a soldier with a nymph as they stumbled past a thick curtain at the back. Some girls were lined by the walls, standing like pretty dolls ready to be plucked by the raucous soldiers. Porchid glowed a deep ruby hue but she stamped it down, focusing on a dwarf leaning against the back corner.

The dwarf's scowl was deep, as was the mouthful of brew she drank. Her dress shimmered like the sun, the silky material brushing against the shadows like stardust. She wore her blonde hair tied back, with pearls weaved through the cascade of curly ringlets that reached the middle of her back.

Despite the lush room, there were secrets here. Probably too many for Hansel and Porchid to uncover in one night. But that wasn't the mission anyway. His job was to find out what prisoners were kept here, and hers was to keep a lookout for danger. But wherever she flew, there was always something hindering her view. She'd need to get closer to the pit.

Porchid was already moving when the crowd bellowed, coins raining down as the fight continued in the pit. She flew past the ceiling beams, making sure to stay hidden, whilst keeping a lookout for any threats or discovery. The den looked different from this angle, more open. Porchid spotted a nook with barrels of brew and aimed for the narrow space.

She squeezed through the gaps between the barrels until she was perched above the females. At first all she could hear was snippets of gossip, their painted faces plastered with fake smiles, or grimaces when no one was looking.

'The Colonel's with Druscilla *again*,' one of them whined. 'She always pockets *loads* of medallions.'

'The Colonel smells like fish,' sniped another. 'I'd much rather know about the treat of a man he's speaking with. The gorgeous, bronzed one.'

'He already rejected two girls,' snapped a third.

'Probably swings for humans only.'

Porchid rolled her eyes, though she couldn't disagree – Hansel was *very* pretty.

But he was Eve's, and Porchid wasn't about to let these urchins talk nonsense. The colouring of the wall dimmed in red as her emotions took control. She chastised herself and looked down, and met the eyes of the golden dwarf, who frowned at her. Before her wings could take flight, the dwarf reached out and smothered her in darkness.

Porchid struggled inside her tiny cage. Her wings bent the more she fought, but the grip never faltered. She sucked in a breath, the seconds ticking by, when light suddenly blinded her. Air rushed into her lungs, and she shot from her prison, only to crash into a mirror. Porchid rolled across a table, tipping over brushes and makeup.

When she looked up, the blonde dwarf was staring at her. 'Who, exactly, are *you?*'

Porchid started trembling, scanning wildly for an exit. She couldn't be caught. Not now, not with Hansel outside waiting for her.

She was the backup. The eyes. The messenger.

Porchid eyed the velvet curtains and launched herself from the table, aiming for the exit. She'd barely made it the length of a pixie before she was promptly swatted into the nearest mirror. Bells rang in her ears and stars crossed her vision.

Porchid blinked past her hazy vision and took in the golden-haired dwarf looming above her in swirling hues of gold and grey.

Porchid glowed crimson, and her vision cleared. She shot forward, grabbing the dwarf's locks, and yanked as hard as she could. The dwarf screeched, her hand flinging out. Porchid dodged, and was almost near the door when she was grabbed again.

She squealed.

'Hush now,' the dwarf hissed, as she trapped Porchid on the table. Porchid winced at the pain in her wings.

'You don't belong here,' the dwarf said, a loose ringlet falling over her bronzed eyes.

Tell me something I don't know.

'Where did you come from?' she prodded.

Porchid looked around frantically for an escape, growing desperate and frustrated at her strange surroundings.

The dwarf tightened her grip, snapping, 'Answer me, fairy. Why are you here? Are you from outside?'

Porchid was trapped. A fly in a spider's nest. But she kept her chin high. Hansel was out there; she had to get to him, had to warn him she'd been compromised.

'Answer me now, fairy!'

Porchid looked into the dwarf's eyes. They were rimmed in brown and gold, with a touch of kohl on the eyelids. They were determined, but there was also a vulnerability there, a sorrow Porchid couldn't place.

Pinned, Porchid couldn't do much else, and if she lied her light would give her away. Reluctantly, she nodded.

The dwarf sighed in relief, her grip loosening slightly. 'So, you're from the outside? Are you with the resistance? Or are you a spy from another kingdom?'

Porchid widened her black eyes and twinkled at her in frustration.

'Okay, okay. Yes or no questions. I don't speak fairy. Answer the first one. Are you from outside?'

Porchid nodded.

'The resistance?' she asked.

Porchid nodded again and the dwarf laughed. 'Thank the Fairy Godmother.'

Porchid frowned in confusion.

'As reckless as it is that you're in here, I'm thankful. I'm going to release you now, but please don't fly away. I won't hurt you – I swear on the cauldron.'

Porchid met her eyes and gave her one stern nod. When the weight released off her wings she tested them, stretched them, relieved there was no lingering effects besides a mild ache.

'Are you with someone?' she asked.

Porchid nodded again.

The dwarf furrowed her brows. 'We don't have much time, but I can help your friend and you, if you get a message out for me. Do we have a deal?'

They both froze as voices sounded behind the curtain. The dwarf covered Porchid in a handkerchief as a tipsy sea nymph entered. She bumped into a table before grabbing her compact mirror and disappeared into the back.

The dwarf swore under her breath, then grasped a quill and paper. She looked down at Porchid. 'Do we have a deal, fairy? Time isn't on our side.'

Porchid, seeing no other alternative, nodded.

'Good,' the dwarf breathed. 'Then get in my pocket and deliver this message to Zacariah.'

Piccadilly sat within the confines of the Sanctuary, watching those below build makeshift homes beneath the stone walls of the underground. Some were talking by bedrolls, others cooking a meal. A few were dancing by the back near a couple sneaking kisses in the corner.

They were all safe.

For now.

It was borrowed time. It always was, until the Queen's guard found them. They were already doing raids, pulling people from their homes, killing those in hiding or taking them to the mines.

The Queen was restless. Whatever she was looking for hadn't been found. And though she was away visiting those horrible twelve princes, the guards still swarmed the city, wielding the Queen's power eagerly.

How long did they have until they were discovered?

The ruse of the Commander was wearing thin. Several creatures had already asked where he was, why he wasn't around. Despite it all, she kept playing the game.

If only for a little longer, she told herself.

The tasks she had set for Hansel and Flynn, and for Bjorn, would prove invaluable if they succeeded in their mission. She needed to know if Rumpelstiltskin was in the castle and, more importantly, if he possessed the spindle.

It was a long shot, but perhaps he held the key to what the Queen was hiding and what it was she was searching for. Why the colony? Why the mines? Why seek power solely within one kingdom when she could take them all?

Why Bellatorre?

A headache built behind her eyes. She rubbed her temples, the scent of vanilla and cinnamon nearby.

Flynn.

'How did it go?' she asked, checking her knives were secure.

'A resounding success,' he said from behind her. 'Though I can't say I approve of your choice in companions.'

She held back her eye roll as she turned to meet him. 'And why should I care for your approval? You were given a task to complete, preferably without the commentary. I'm your superior, after all.'

'Depends what army I'm in, I suppose,' he said with a smirk.

Piccadilly sighed, turning back to the onlookers below.

Flynn rested his arms on the railing beside her, as he always did.

'What happened?' she asked.

'He got in,' Flynn sneered, his feelings about Hansel clear.

'He's a Major. We needed him. His rank alone should prove invaluable.'

His eyes were hard as he asked, 'Did we need him? You already had someone inside the pits, and I can name a few females that would gladly volunteer to help our cause.'

'The less who know, the better,' she replied. 'We've had this conversation before, Flynn.'

He huffed and inched closer, his arm brushing against hers. 'I don't suppose you'll tell me what it is we're looking for?'

She remained silent, closing her eyes in silent prayer. 'You know I can't.'

'Alright then, don't tell me. But I'm not the only one asking questions. People are becoming restless, and while you stand here watching from above and inviting outsiders with secret plans, we all wait down there.' He nodded towards the crowd. 'Waiting for answers, waiting for safety. I can't keep them quiet much longer, Piccadilly. A decision must be made, and steps have to be taken.'

Piccadilly rubbed her chest at the reminder and turned towards him. Her gaze travelled over his features, noting the bruise forming on his cheek and the swollen lip. Seems the huntsman did a little too well with his task.

His cold fingers found hers. 'If the Commander cannot make a decision, then you must.'

She swallowed, feeling as if her secrets were unravelling, leaving her exposed. 'That's treason,' she warned.

'Not when he isn't a royal,' he replied, his fingers rubbing over her palm. 'He's not shown his face. We all know it's been you. So, continue to lead. Otherwise, someone else will take that power from you.'

'I sincerely hope that isn't a threat.'

His other hand strayed to her locks of silver. 'It's a reminder from a friend of what's at stake.'

'I know what's at stake,' she snapped, batting his hand away. 'I'm a changeling, not a child.'

His eyes went cold, and he took a step back. 'All I'm saying is that we're losing this war before it's even begun. Do you know where the Princess is? How do you even know she's alive?'

'She's alive,' Piccadilly hissed. 'You said you'd seen her.'

'I said I saw someone who *could* be her,' he corrected, flicking invisible lint off his uniform. 'We can't place all our hope on one person.'

'Do not presume to know what I know, or what my plans are,' she hissed.

His green eyes darkened but he remained calm. 'So, you've heard from your new recruits, then? Even Zacariah seemed distrusting of them, and aren't they kin? How do you know Bjorn will succeed in the pits?'

'First threats, and now you doubt me, Flynn? If I didn't know better, I would wonder if the huntsman hasn't ruffled your feathers more than I thought.'

Flynn's lips thinned. 'Doubt is a seed easily grown in times like this. I'm only repeating what I know to be true and asking questions that must be asked.'

'Well then, ask them elsewhere and get me something useful.'

He grimaced, looking down into the Sanctuary. 'There's been no news from my contact in the mines.'

'That's two days overdue now.'

'I'm aware,' he replied coolly. 'I've just sent another message, hopefully we should hear within the week.'

Piccadilly's stomach flipped at his words. Her hands gripped the railing, and she took a deep breath. 'I'd strongly suggest you look after your own mess before you go judging mine. Make sure your contact hasn't been killed, or worse, captured.'

'I live to serve,' he drawled. He dropped his arm from the railing and gave her a mock bow.

Piccadilly could hear the click of his boots on the stone floor as he left, but it wasn't until he had turned the corner that she dropped her shoulders.

They had nothing.

Minimal funding, a missing commander, and more refugees pouring in every day. Those who weren't already on missions ached to do more, but without information she had no way of determining the next steps. How did they defeat a dark queen with unlimited resources and a hidden agenda? Never mind Myrenna's wicked gifts and the kingdom's power at her fingertips. Whatever was in that castle was the key.

She only had Hansel and Bjorn now. And she prayed to the Fairy Godmother they'd achieve what others could not.

Hansel watered down his whisky whenever Druscilla or the Colonel weren't looking. Despite his best efforts, he could still feel the expensive liquor's effects. He was moving slower, laughing at things when he normally wouldn't.

'Tell me, Colonel,' Hansel said. 'Where did you find a troll to fight in the pit?'

The fight had ended hours ago, with Bjorn becoming the unexpected winner. Surprisingly enough, the dwarf had sliced the trolls throat open with one of the spikes from the troll's club. The crowd had raged, and Hansel had won his bet. He'd asked at the time where the champions went, but all he'd gotten was a chuckle with a vague description of food and a bed.

Now, the Colonel swigged his drink, spilling it halfway down his chin. 'On a royal visit to Maelstrom,' he slurred. 'Would you believe? He tried to hijack the Queen's carriage. Could you imagine? Hijacking the Queen! He's lucky she didn't melt his bones with a snap of her fingers.

'She's a terrifying beauty, that one. She wanted to kill them all, but I convinced her otherwise. I said, "My Queen! Surely, they are of more value to the cause? Send them to the mines, let them find what you seek most. Let them sacrifice for you and atone!"'

Hansel leaned back, hiding the rise of his brow as the Colonel bellowed his story. Druscilla had left at some point, for a drink or whatever it was the girls did between.

'The Queen was in awe of me,' the Colonel continued. 'She said, "Yes, Colonel, you are right. Let them live and go to the mines."'

Hansel bit his lip, his vision blurring as the Colonel fell into the cushions behind him.

'You see, Major,' he said, wobbling his finger in front of his mouth to keep a secret. 'Not all go to the mines. Some we take for the pits. Gotta keep some to ensure a worthy fight, eh.'

'And where are they kept before the fights?' Hansel asked, keeping his tone neutral.

The Colonel laughed. 'Locked up, of course.'

'But where? Surely not in the castle?'

'Don't be daft, boy.' The Colonel chuckled. 'Only the rarest of prisoners go there. Our prisoners are lucky. They practically live in luxury compared to the mines. No, no, Major, our prisoners are locked up here.' He banged his feet on the carpet and laughed in glee, leaning right into Hansel. His wet breath reeked of whisky. 'Right below our very feet.'

Hansel laughed with him, his own feet echoing the motion but with no feeling.

He swallowed the dread building in his throat, the way his mind fumbled through the haze of whisky for a plan and came up with nothing. The only thing he knew with absolutely certainty was that he couldn't leave without Bjorn.

The Colonel soured at the empty glass in his hand, pursing his lips as he stared into the crowd. 'Where is that girl? I'm empty of a glass.'

Hansel promptly handed over his own, and the Colonel clapped him on the shoulder. 'Ah, my boy! I knew you were worth my attention. I'm very important, you know.'

Hansel laughed with him again, but the charade was wearing thin. Hansel wasn't sure how much more whiskey he could take. He hadn't seen Porchid, and despite the heat of his blood, he was still cold. A cold that hadn't left him since Eve's absence.

'You said only the rarest of prisoners go to the castle,' Hansel commented.

'What of it?' the Colonel replied, sipping at his half empty glass.

Suddenly, the couch felt like a cliff, Hansel about to drop right off. 'I can't think of any so rare.'

The Colonel eyes shone in suspicion. 'There are many rare creatures in the realm.'

'None as rare as our beautiful queen,' Hansel said with a slight slur. 'And she wouldn't be locked away in her own prison.'

'Indeed,' the Colonel mused, his eyes sharpening for a moment. 'Tell me, Major, how is it that you're at such a rank, yet are so unaware of the prisoners kept by our queen? Somehow, you're new here and yet I swear I recognise you. You have the uniform, but it has no rank on it, nor do you seem to know the inner workings of the Queen when you're in the Queen's Guard.' He tilted his head. 'If I didn't know any better, I'd smell a rat.'

Hansel's throat went dry and a drop of cold sweat pooled down his neck. He wouldn't escape this with a lie. The Colonel would see through it like the haze from the whisky.

But perhaps he could twist the truth. A part truth for a whole truth.

'I'm not just in the guard,' Hansel said, keeping his voice steady. 'I'm in her majesty's personal guard now, but I did have some time out west, in the hills.'

'Not many postings, then?'

'No, Colonel, mostly my career has been inside the walls of the western compounds or the castle. I haven't been out much.'

The Colonel grunted. 'Not much experience with war then, or the locals.'

Hansel shook his head, trying not to move his hands for fear the shake in them would give him away.

'Disgusting, filthy things,' the Colonel gruffed, distracted from his previous question. 'Tainting our fair queen and princess in the name of, what? Freedom? What have they done for us? The trolls rob us blind in the north. The fairies play their little tricks and spike our food and wine. The nymphs are vicious hoarders with more blood on their hands than mine. And the dwarves … *The dwarves,*' he spat, 'belong back under the ground, hidden away like the greedy vermin they are.

'They should all be thankful. We've given them purpose. A job. A role to play. Instead, they run that silly little rebellion and trick humans with magic into their cause. Trust me when I tell you, Major, that there is a lot you need to learn. Ignorance is not bliss, and there is far more happening behind the curtains than it seems.'

He swallowed the remainder of his drink before he turned to Hansel. 'Have you ever heard of Rumpelstiltskin?'

Hansel's blood froze. Piccadilly's suspicions were confirmed.

'Rumpelstiltskin is the rare creature I speak of,' the Colonel continued. 'Whatever dark magic built that absurd *thing* has now been contained by the Queen.'

'What would her Majesty want with Rumpelstiltskin?' Hansel asked, working to keep his voice even.

The Colonel leaned in and grabbed Hansel's jacket. His mouth stunk of whiskey, and he reeked of unwashed skin. The Colonel smiled but it didn't reach his eyes. 'It's not him she needs. It's the spindle.'

'The spindle?'

'He is the Dream Weaver, my boy!' the Colonel said, his lips curling into something nasty. 'And the Queen intends to weave those dreams herself.'

XXI

The Golden Deceit

Eve clawed free of the darkness, covered in dirt and blood, and opened her eyes to sunlight. The roots laid her gently on the grass before retreating into the forest, slithering back into the soil. Birds chirped nearby, obnoxiously cheerful, as she clutched the grimoire to her chest, her knife and her pack laid beside her. Eve squeezed her eyes shut against the blinding headache that felt like a dozen fairies were smacking her skull with tiny, persistent hammers. Her right knee ached, and she was pretty sure some of her wounds from the wolf had reopened.

She swiped at blood crusted on her chin, then took a moment to breathe and to process what in the cauldron had just happened. Fighting back the pain gripping her body, Eve remembered the Queen sinking into the ground, only her riding boots peeking up through the soil. She shuddered, still trembling from her own dark travel here. It was her worst nightmare to be trapped underground with no light and no way out, buried alive.

Even she didn't wish that upon anyone.

Except maybe the Grimms.

Eve moved, and her arm jolted, searing pain shooting through her muscles. A wooden spike had pierced her skin, leaving a tear in her shirt along with a bloodstain she suspected would never wash out. The roots may have saved her life, but they certainly left their mark. She swore as she yanked her shirt free, the squelch of her skin an unfriendly sound. Blood trickled down her arm as she inspected the wound. She would need to clean it.

She smelt smoke before she saw it. She didn't know where she was, but in her condition, she had little choice but to follow. Eve winced as she put her full weight on her right leg and picked up a fallen branch to use as a crutch.

She needed help.

Time seemed to press on her, ticking like an ancient clock. She desperately wanted to find Hansel and Porchid. Desperately wanted a familiar face.

But she was alone.

Groaning, Eve stumbled through the high-reaching trees towards the smell of fire.

Bryn hadn't heard from Bjorn in days. His mission was so secretive that even Piccadilly had given him nothing. Bryn had huffed at her when she'd come that night, calling upon them both in the light of an almost melted candle. Gone had been the warrior from the night when she'd smuggled them all here, instead replaced with the smell of desperation. Since then, he'd only seen her watch from the balcony above, patiently waiting.

Bryn hadn't been in the Sanctuary long, but he could already tell something wasn't right. The crowd seemed unsettled somehow, some groups returning from their excursions with a hunch in their shoulders, laced with uncertainty when others didn't return.

The dwarves recognised him now, nodding when he walked past, thanking him when he dropped off parcels from the sparse deliveries from outside. He visited Doc and Rabbit regularly, checking on the dwarf's condition that hadn't seemed to have improved despite his constant care.

'Soon,' Doc would say. 'The s-scouting party will be b-back in no time.'

Though Bryn doubted it.

From the reaction of the refugees, it seemed that only a few groups came back. Most vanished, probably caught by the Queen's guard or sent to the mines.

Bryn's main concern laid with little Rabbit. He didn't have long, and Bryn's patience was slowly running out.

Piccadilly – when she did visit – would always leave him with more questions than answers. And Doc – whenever he wasn't consumed with a project or patient – hid away behind his vials in his private quarters.

In a strange twist of fate, Bryn found himself for the first time in his life without purpose and, well, alone. Since before he could even remember, it had always been the Seven. All of them together, working as a team. Clinging to the hope of rebuilding a home, saving the Princess, and bringing Parador back to life.

The Queen had merely been a story then, a tale of warning to those who dared cross her.

He jumped as a hand tapped his shoulder, turning to find Doc standing on tiptoes.

Doc removed his hand to rub his glasses. 'I m-must talk to you urgently.'

'Is Rabbit alright?' Bryn asked, aware of listening ears.

'It is a d-delicate matter.'

Bryn nodded quickly and followed Doc towards his quarters, one of the only locked doors in the entire underground complex. Doc's fingers unlocked the chamber smoothly, unlike his shaky speech.

Surgeon's hands, Bryn thought.

The dark room smelt of coal and ash and spices. The clashing scents swirled in the air as Doc lit his lantern, revealing a makeshift lab.

Plants hung from the ceiling, and dust smeared every surface. Bottles filled with coloured brews lined rows of shelves, some simmering, some boiling over, others frosted over with icy coolness. In the corner lay a small cot with several trays of moulding food. The only other object adorning it was a large jug full of what Bryn assumed was water.

In the centre was a large table, surrounded by books and ingredients he'd never seen before. Doc shuffled around, opening drawers and sighing to himself. He waved at Bryn to come in further.

Uncertain, Bryn trailed his finger along the large table coated in a fine white powder. He sniffed it, his lungs heaving in sharp pain.

'I w-wouldn't do that,' warned Doc, as he continued rifling through drawers. 'It's a highly p-potent poison. Eats at the lungs like acid.'

Bryn flinched and clapped his hands together to remove the powder, then dived for the water jug. He gulped it down and used the last drops to wash his hands. 'Why do you have that?'

'It's a very useful drug,' said Doc, finding a blank sheet of paper. He found a quill, dipped it in ink, and scrawled across the top of the page.

'Why am I here?' asked Bryn, wheezing a little. 'You said the matter was delicate?'

'I need you to d-do s-something for me.'

'Do what?' Bryn repeated, baffled. 'Surely you have people who do that already.'

'Not ones I can t-trust.'

'You barely know me,' Bryn pointed out, still rubbing at his hands. He was sure that the powder itched beneath his skin.

'T-true, but I know your intentions, and whilst your little f-friend remains in my c-care, I know you won't do anything s-stupid.'

Bryn couldn't fault his logic. Rabbit was still sick and the only hope he had was from the little elf before him.

'When is the scouting party due back?' Bryn asked. 'When will they bring the cure to the vox leaf poison?'

'C-cure?' Doc asked, looking over the rim of his glasses.

Bryn frowned. 'You said there was a cure, but you were low on stock. You said you'd keep Rabbit alive until your search party brought back a cure.'

'Ahh,' he said evasively, still scribbling on his parchment.

The silence was heavy.

When Doc didn't elaborate, Bryn stepped forward. 'There is no cure, is there? You lied to us. To me and Bjorn.'

'I d-did not lie, young dwarf,' Doc insisted. 'The s-scouting party never returned. The only c-cure for your friend is weaning him off the vox leaf.'

'You mean to tell me that you haven't been feeding him medicine?' He couldn't hold back the hysteria in his voice. 'You've been giving him more of that leaf this whole time?'

'N-Not more. Less. Bit by bit. W-whilst it's still in his system, this is what he needs. If he s-s-survives the weaning process, we can give him the medicine. For now, his body is consumed.'

Bryn went cold, his voice barely a whisper. 'You're poisoning him.'

'I'm s-saving him.'

'By killing him?' Bryn accused. 'Do you have this so-called medicine? Or is that another lie? What did the scouting party have? More of this … this plant?'

Doc nodded. 'We're almost out.'

'Good,' Bryn said. 'Get it out of his system like you should have in the first place.'

'That is not how this w-works,' stated Doc. 'Vox leaf is a h-highly addictive substance. It c-coats the blood and attacks the nervous system. It releases c-chemicals in the brain, endorphins so that you enjoy being p-poisoned. Rabbit's body is ac-c-customed to it. Should you s-simply cease it, his body will go into shock. His heart will f-fail. We must wean him off bit by bit and pray to the Godmother he s-survives.'

Bryn clenched his fists, fighting the urge to smash every stupid vial into smithereens.

Rabbit was going to die. Because of a cauldron-forsaken plant.

'How much vox leaf do you have left?' Bryn asked, his voice low.

'Very little.'

'Will he die, then?' Bryn asked.

Doc paused, considering. 'W-without it? Yes.'

'What do you need me to do? What's more urgent than Rabbit's care?'

Doc pushed up his glasses, warily watching Bryn's hands as he clenched them open and shut.

Bryn strode around the table and stood over the elf to read his scribbling. He was surprised when he saw two drawings: one of a small flower with round bulbs and pale petals, the other of a pointed leaf, stark lines of black against pale parchment.

'This is for Rabbit's c-care,' Doc stammered. 'If you are to s-save your friend, you must f-find these plants.'

'Where?' Bryn asked.

'The vox leaf c-can be f-found on the outskirts of the S-silver C-city, near the hills. The starkiss f-flower is harder. It only grows near the Queen's m-mines.'

The mines.

Bryn swallowed as Doc's swift fingers finished the illustrations and wrote down his notes.

'The mines are swarming with the Queen's Guard,' Bryn said. 'Does it not grow anywhere else?'

'It's rare,' Doc replied. 'It only grows in p-places with p-potent magic. The m-mines are a breeding ground for it.'

'Anywhere with that amount of magic is unstable,' Bryn frowned.

'Y-yes,' Doc replied. 'That is why you m-must go alone. Unseen. The others are likely to have been c-captured. I told P-P-Piccadilly, but she was so s-stubborn, making decisions without the C-commander and p-playing a dangerous game.'

Doc folded the paper twice and placed it in Bryn's hand. 'Your f-friend is still alive. But he c-cannot be saved. P-perhaps Rabbit c-can.'

Bjorn had left Bryn the night they'd spoken with Zacariah, taking on the dwarf's heartfelt plea to free his people. Bjorn had always been one to show his high emotions and Bryn had always kept his in check. But recently he'd found himself moving closer to the gruff dwarf's habits.

Bjorn had left them. The Seven was separated, shattered apart, and Bryn wondered if they'd ever be whole again. Rabbit was deathly sick; he'd looked so pale the last time Bryn had seen him and now Bryn had a real opportunity to do something.

He had purpose.

Bryn wouldn't leave him. Not when the little dwarf had nobody else. These dwarves inside the Sanctuary didn't know him. They didn't care.

But Bryn did.

He turned to Doc. 'Tell me what I need to do.'

Doc beamed at him and picked up the parchment. 'F-first, we start with this.'

The scroll was awkward in Porchid's grip as she was hushed through the back curtains near the bar. Not one to say no to freedom, Porchid flung herself towards the shelves full of bottles and hid. She gave no second thought to the golden dwarf as she disappeared back into the crowd.

The soldiers laughed through the music. Porchid wrinkled her nose at the rotting smell of human sweat.

She spotted Hansel upon a lush couch with another gentleman, both laughing. He sat with ease, one glass in his hand, the other shaking his companion's hand. She moved with care, flying from one dark place to another. First the bar, then the pocket of a soldier, then on the back of one of the girls. Sweat rolled down her neck between her wings, adrenaline and fear coursing with her struggled movements.

She heard his voice and that smooth, honeyed laugh. Hansel commented on the gentleman's wisdom.

Porchid darted to the floor. Feet stomped around her, making the ground vibrate. She dodged the boots of drunken, swaying soldiers, finally tucking herself under Hansel's table. She hugged herself, struggling to douse her light against the dark shadows of the room.

Porchid pulled at Hansel's trousers and got his attention. His foot shuffled to cover her between the lounge and his shoe. He ushered her into his pocket as he laughed at one of the man's silly jokes to cover her.

She hated travelling in pockets, but at this moment, being back with Hansel was a relief and she curled in towards him. His body rumbled against her as he spoke.

A hush fell in the room.

The den's lights blacked out, darkness enveloping them. Porchid peeked out of Hansel's pocket as all eyes fell to a spotlight on an elevated podium. The golden dwarf stood before the single light, a fierce shimmer in the dusty atmosphere. The beam turned her dress into a cascade of sunlight. Her skin sparkled, and her smile was brilliant and fierce as she winked at the men, the band striking a bold chord, welcoming her performance with a sultry melody. The violin began as a solo, matching the movement of the golden dwarf's hips as she lowered her long lashes.

Porchid was mesmerised, her mouth slightly ajar. Hansel shuffled uncomfortably. The tempo picked up, the song luring the crowd like a forgotten dream. The golden dwarf lifted her skirts, baring a hint of skin before raising a hidden knife. The men laughed as she smiled serenely, subtly slicing at the golden material of her dress. They all cheered, whistling as more of her bare legs were revealed. She giggled as the crowd surged closer, enthralled.

She moved from the podium, sweeping through the crowd in a graceful dance. A touch here, a stroke there. Using the knife not as a weapon but as a plaything.

'By the Godmother,' Hansel's companion whispered, nearly tipping out of his chair.

On the Colonel's lap, Druscilla's face turned sour as she watched the golden dwarf dance through the men, the crowd parting like curtains before a show. Porchid grimaced as the dwarf's eyes locked onto the Colonel's jacket, his badges and markings the only indication of his rank.

A slice here, a step there.

The Colonel was enamoured, his gaze locked on the dwarf with such dark desire that Porchid couldn't hold back her blush. He shoved Druscilla off his lap, the woman yelping as she fell to the floor. He reached out his hands, pulling the dwarf into his lap with hunger.

The den went silent as she splayed over his legs, her skirts pooling along the floor. The Colonel giggled like a child, his eyes drinking her in. She played with the knife, seductively cutting off one of his buttons and gave him a sultry smile. He chuckled.

Hansel's muscles went rigid, his hand automatically reaching for a weapon that was not there. Porchid pulled on his shirt, but he didn't respond.

That's when it all went wrong.

The Colonel's eyes widened as he noticed Porchid's glow.

'What is that *thing* doing in here?' he bellowed. And the knife of the golden dwarf slid with a wet crunch into his throat.

Mayhem erupted as the crowd surged forward and Hansel grabbed Porchid. He dived as the soldiers shot towards their Colonel, and the scream of the girls echoed throughout the den. Hansel shuffled back, barely missing the corner of the couch as he looked for an exit.

Porchid watched with horror as the soldiers grabbed the golden dwarf's hair and threw her to the ground. She didn't scream as they ripped her hair from its roots, or when they kicked her. She didn't make a noise when they spat on her and dragged her across the den, screaming for revenge.

They pulled her through the exit, stones tearing her skin as they hauled her into the square outside, all piling in together in a crowd of anger and hatred.

Porchid could only scream silently as Hansel stood, shocked, weaponless, and outnumbered while they tied a noose around her neck, hitching the other end to the statue in the centre of the fountain.

'Find Piccadilly,' Hansel whispered urgently.

Piccadilly waited in the shadows surrounding the Tinder Box.

Since Flynn's visit, she'd known that Hansel had made it safely into the back den of the tavern. She'd originally stopped to pick up Lady Viper, but the woman had swiftly waved her away, sniping at her about being perfectly capable of removing a few posters.

Piccadilly assessed each drunken soldier that left the tavern, waiting for the glow of a small fairy or the confident stride of the huntsman. The hours ticked by slowly and her nerves set her pacing across the rooftop. She hadn't heard from Bjorn, but she knew his time was limited. Had the huntsman also failed?

Her life revolved around so many moving parts, so many what ifs. The rebellion was growing desperate, and her entire mission, the entire war, sat in the hands of strangers. What would her commander think? What would he say if he were here now?

She chastised herself. It had been stupid to let them go on that scouting trip. Yet, she'd done it anyway.

And now they were nowhere to be seen.

She could only control so much, do so much. But she felt every decision she made, every play, as if they slipped through her fingers down into the very canal below her.

She heard the bell and creak of the tavern door before she saw them. A collective of soldiers spilling out into the square, smelling of blood and brew. They screamed in anger, demanding justice, moving like a viscous disease behind a burly man dragging along a golden dwarf. She was covered with blood, her gilded dress in tatters. Her face already swelled from a beating. Piccadilly ducked into the shadows, a snarl on her lips. But then the rope came, one end tied to the fountain and the other in a noose.

The dwarf remained silent. Stoic. Even as they jeered and kicked her.

Piccadilly's grip tightened on her curved blades. She was good, but she wasn't good enough to take on this many soldiers.

A white light flared from below, and Piccadilly spotted Porchid. She whistled into the dark, calling the fairy towards her hiding spot. 'Over here.'

As soon as the fairy arrived, Piccadilly pushed her behind the barrier, hiding them both.

Below, the crowd cheered, spilling their drinks upon the stones. Piccadilly flinched as the rope went taut. The sound of the dwarf's snapping neck echoed violently across the stones.

'May the ever after hold you close,' Piccadilly whispered.

She peered over the edge and raked her eyes over the crowd. 'Where is Hansel?'

The fairy swallowed, silent.

Piccadilly peered down at her, already voicing the answer before Porchid could. 'He's gone after Bjorn, hasn't he?'

Porchid nodded, her light paling.

Piccadilly swore. 'Show me the way.'

Hansel left the destruction of the square behind him and raced through the decrepit door of the tavern. He was met with chaos.

So much for a unified, organised army, he thought.

Men ran everywhere in a disarray of blurred fists and shouts. They screamed profanities, placing blame on the feral creatures and the unruly, the unworthy.

The girls from the den were in trouble. They had transformed from fun playthings to terrorists in the blink of an eye. Hansel hoped Porchid had safely found Piccadilly. She would protect the small fairy.

Hansel wound his way through the wooden corridors and found a spiral staircase near the back of the den. He followed it down, leaving the pandemonium upstairs and making his way into the damp quiet of the prison below. The stench of faeces burned his nostrils, and his boots slid through slick mud. Most cells were empty, only containing a bench, a bucket, and a tap.

He remembered the Colonel's words: *They practically live in luxury compared to the mines.* Hansel shuddered to think of the conditions in the mines if this was luxury. But now the Colonel lay upstairs, with a blood bib from the knife the dwarf girl had driven into his throat.

A whimper echoed from ahead, and Hansel ran.

Whilst most of the cells were empty, some held broken creatures. An elf sat on the cold ground, heavy-lidded and silent; another was a sea nymph, covered in silver scars as though she'd walked through a shredder and survived. Hansel moved with caution, squashing his guilt down as he searched for Bjorn.

Eventually, Hansel found the bloodied and bruised dwarf in a cell near the back. The dwarf wheezed, but upon seeing Hansel, he choked on a laugh. 'Hello, huntsman. Have they run out of maidens, or are you looking to save a dwarf in distress?'

Hansel sighed with relief. 'Nice to see you haven't lost your sense of humour.'

Bjorn snorted.

Hansel peered into the dark, his fingers fumbling across the locks and coming up short for a way to open the door. 'I didn't see a guard, or a key rack.'

'As always, huntsman, ever prepared,' Bjorn replied, sitting himself up shakily.

'I'm serious, Bjorn. We don't have much time.'

Bjorn coughed, wincing a little as he grabbed his ribs. 'I've been locked in here. How would I know where the keys are? Try that axe of yours.'

'I don't have it.'

'Any weapon,' Bjorn said, exasperated. 'I don't care, just get me out of here.'

'I don't have a weapon.'

Bjorn blinked at him in irritation. 'Who's the joker now?'

Hansel swore under his breath.

The nymph in a cell behind him spoke. She had long, red hair, her sleek, blue body lined in scars, some old and some newly carved. 'The pocket of the Colonel.'

'The now-dead Colonel, thanks to that stupid little dwarf,' said a cold voice from behind them.

Hansel turned, meeting the vengeful eyes of the Colonel's favoured girl. Druscilla stood in the same purple dress, the keys in her outstretched hand, glaring at them. Guards flanked her sides, their swords gleaming in the torchlight.

'You're a dead man,' she said, seething.

XXII
The Fires of Purgatory

Piccadilly raced down a side alley, following Porchid's light. She skidded to a halt in front of the old delivery entryway to the Tinder Box and yanked off the wooden slats. They rushed down the stairs, following Porchid through decaying corridors until they reached the den.

It was absolute mayhem.

Blood stained every surface, the torn curtains hiding little of the bloodshed. Soldiers were wielding their weapons as if in battle. Screams rang out in place of music. A girl ran past, wearing nothing but her knickers.

Piccadilly cursed.

This was far worse than anything she had imagined, and yet so predictable when it came to the Queen's men.

Porchid squealed as a soldier ran towards them, his sword raised.

Piccadilly released her blades. 'Get behind me!'

He attacked. Piccadilly parried the soldier's blow with a cold anger. He swung again, using his size to press towards her. But this wasn't her first time in a sword fight. There was no finesse to his movements, no dance like the one she used.

It was almost insulting.

Piccadilly shoved him back with a foot. She used one blade to disarm him, and the other to slice his throat. There was a gurgle, then a shout. She spun to find another soldier raising his weapon. With an ease that should frighten her, Piccadilly loosed her blades on him. Two hits and he was weaponless. Another and he was dead.

He hadn't struck the floor yet when several gazes snapped her way. As if the room had only just noticed she was the biggest threat here.

A group of soldiers readied themselves, swords shining as they raised them to attack.

Piccadilly flipped her curved blades in challenge. 'Do your best.'

Then she unleashed herself.

Hansel's hands went to reach for his weapons and clenched into fists instead. He faced a small army with no keys, no weapons, and no hope. It was almost as if this were a preconceived trap, but nobody had seen the golden dwarf coming.

Druscilla sneered at him from the shadows, the only sound coming from the clink of the keys she held.

'To think I pitied you for being groped by the Colonel and laughing at his poor jokes,' Hansel said.

Druscilla's gaze turned lethal at the mention of the Colonel. 'I don't need your pity,' she spat. 'I reaped the benefits of his deep pockets. I was more than one of those *creatures*. I was a prized possession. And now I'm without a benefactor, thanks to you.'

For such a small woman, Druscilla possessed so much hate.

Prisoners pressed against the bars, their breaths heavy in the dark. Hansel could feel the eyes on him, the way the air thickened with fear.

The guards stepped towards him, hungry for a fight.

Hansel glanced at Bjorn, hoping for some sage advice, but the dwarf only shook his head. He was alone, then.

'So, what's it to be?' Hansel asked, his voice low. 'A fight, or a massacre?'

Druscilla rolled her eyes. 'And it's said women are dramatic.' She turned to the guards. 'Kill him.'

All at once, the guards surged forward, crowding the hall with shimmering steel.

Hansel evaded the swipe of a sword but was punched in the jaw. He stumbled back. Fists and swords swung, crowding the small space. Between all the bodies, it was hard to tell who came from where.

Hansel dodged a soldier swinging his blade in a wide arc. Steel rang against the cell bars. Another fist swung out, but he managed to pivot at the last second. The soldier who'd missed only grinned.

Druscilla cackled as Hansel's skin tore open from a blade. His breath was sharp as he ducked below a swinging sword and managed a hit to a soldier's chin. Warm blood trickled down his arm, but he couldn't recall receiving the wound.

'If we're under the pits,' Hansel screamed, dodging another blade, 'then let's fight like it.'

Hansel's knuckle broke open as his fists struck a waiting soldier. The soldier's blade clattered to the ground, forgotten as Hansel tackled him to the floor. They thrashed with blood and teeth and sweat until the soldier blacked out.

Hansel stumbled back as the cells went silent, bracing himself for the next attack.

When he looked up, one of the guards with a gap in his teeth grinned. 'Suits me just fine.'

Collectively, the soldiers dropped their weapons. Hansel should have been relieved, but it only provided more room for them to attack and to corner him.

Hansel smashed his elbow into the first guard that ran at him, relishing the crunch of his jaw. He ducked below the guard's wild swing and kicked his knees out beneath him, enjoying the breath of air as the guard collapsed. He didn't pause when another guard crumpled, didn't stop as he took on the next, blocking their fist and slamming his own into their face. It was the one advantage Hansel had fighting in such a cramped space: he could take them on one or two at a time.

The prisoners were riotous now, screaming and chanting so loudly that it echoed in his veins.

Hansel tore and punched and dodged and parried. He ignored the wound on his arm, the way his body protested. He lost himself to it, blinded by the urge to survive, to win. Then a fist slammed into his stomach.

Pain rippled down his body, sharp enough to pull the breath from his lungs. Then his ribs cracked. Hansel tumbled over, clutching his stomach, and another blow came, blackening his vision.

Druscilla's cackle echoed off the damp walls as the ground wobbled, and Hansel finally collapsed.

Hansel spat blood onto the stone floor as one of the last soldiers picked up his sword. Bjorn yelled, but Hansel couldn't hear the words. The cold point of the blade was held against his neck. His throat bobbed against the sharpness.

A scream broke out before Hansel could speak. Blood splattered his face, as a curved blade sliced through the guard's stomach, ripping his innards out in a single swipe.

The ringing in Hanel's ears intensified as the man dropped in a pile of blood and bone. Piccadilly stood over him, her curved blades crimson from her kills. She snarled at the cages and the remaining guards, her twin blades singing a song of death as she charged. Druscilla whimpered from the corner as Piccadilly dispatched the men with ease.

She looked like death incarnate.

'I didn't—' Druscilla stammered. Then her head was severed.

Hansel flinched at the wet crunch of it colliding with the ground and held back the bile in his throat.

Piccadilly said nothing as she took the keys from Druscilla's corpse and threw Hansel one of the dead guard's swords. He didn't miss the way her eyes looked like pools of oil. The hard stare was unrecognisable compared to the warm one she'd worn in his apartment.

This was what Myrenna had meant when she called other species 'monsters'.

'Nice timing,' Hansel choked out, wiping blood from his borrowed sword.

Piccadilly blinked, seeming to come back into herself as she lifted the largest key. 'Porchid's been a busy and very resourceful fairy. She took me straight to the den.'

Porchid fluttered around him, fussing over the blood. 'I'm okay,' he reassured her.

Piccadilly unlocked the cells.

'Changeling,' Bjorn greeted.

'Not even a thank you?' Piccadilly mused before pausing at the next cell. She leaned in close, a gasp escaping as she said, 'Cyrene? What in the cauldron are you doing here?'

The blue skinned sea nymph waved away her question. 'Not now, Piccadilly. I'd love to get out of this pit, but I can't walk. Someone will need to carry me.'

'Hansel,' Piccadilly said, 'can you carry her, or do you need carrying yourself?'

He grimaced in pain, but he could move. 'I can carry her,' he confirmed, before Piccadilly unlocked the next cell.

Eve ached all over. She was weak and her footsteps were sloppy. Her body fought against every movement, screaming at her to stop. To lie down. To die.

She felt as if she was somehow on the outside looking in. Hovering above herself as she made her way through the thick forest. She was dirty, her hair matted and coated in blood. Her face was almost immovable from the swelling, her wrist stiff and sore. She trembled with each jerky movement, gulping in air.

She would have new scars. Ones to match the large gash on her cheek, but also ones on her soul.

Sweat beaded her brow, and her skin was pale. She was already dead. A walking ghost amongst the thriving forest, pulsing with life.

Eve dragged her feet over the pebble and stone bridge, the slight arch more like a mountain from the burning in her legs. She gripped the grimoire in her left arm, her nails pressed painfully against the worn leather, like a talisman that might somehow protect her.

From here, she could see the cottage, smoke billowing from the stone chimney. The burning scent leading her towards it.

Eve couldn't tell whether the path was moving or if she was. When she eventually fell against the door, she choked back a sob. It took effort to knock, so when she heard no movement from within, her heart caved a little.

Was this it, then? The end? Had she failed Nona so completely?

She was broken after all. Had been since her father was ripped away. She thought that the years had toughened her up, made her strong. But with a deep sob, all she felt was weak. After everything, she'd never outgrown the little girl crying in the rain in her blue dress.

All she'd ever done was borrow strength from others. She'd borrowed it from Porchid, whose tiny stature never obstructed her love of life or the pretty things she found even in the darkest of places. Borrowed it from Hansel, who found hope in the shadows even though he'd been hurt. He'd even opened his heart and given it to her. She'd just been too weak to take it.

The door dug into her shoulder as tears pooled in her eyes. She'd failed. She'd faced the Evil Queen as a *mortal* and still had barely survived. She finally had the grimoire, but she wasn't a witch. Eve didn't even know if she could do magic.

She still didn't understand the prophecy. Or where she was supposed to go. No matter how hard she fought, what deals she made, the adventures and hardships she'd survived, she was still here. Alone.

What was hope against this war? What was love against the Queen? What was one girl's worth against the history of the realm?

Her fingers groped the inside of her pocket for the wolf's claw she'd won from Gabby's papa.

The claw may come in handy. Iris's voice echoed in her mind. *They hold and expel magic.*

Tightening her grip, she jammed it into the lock, working the sharp claw delicately until it clicked. She summoned her dregs of strength and pushed against the door.

A great white light flared. Then the door heaved open.

'Hello?' she croaked, entering. 'Please help me.'

Nobody answered.

Eve blinked, letting her eyes adjust before she took in the cottage. The hearth burned bright with a freshly lit fire, and the scent of a hearty stew hit her watering mouth. In the centre was a table filled with papers and books and dirty plates. On her right was a kitchen with shelves upon shelves of odd knick-knacks and plants. Vials and mortars and pestles stood ready on the counter, with knives designed for specific purposes.

Eve stumbled towards the table and reached for the jars. She didn't know who lived here but she could respect their extensive collection, though it was certainly creepy. There were jars of pixie ears, and midnight flowers, and the teeth of children and human tongues – every ingredient you could think of was stacked here, waiting.

Eve rushed painfully through the books on the table. She needed a recipe, a book for medicinal brews. She couldn't do it on her own. Her father had always made the brews for her mother when she'd been sick. Had always done it with care. She remembered the smells of spice and the sound of the pestle crushing fragrant herbs into a fine powder.

Her eyes blurred and she blinked the memory away. She just had to hold on a little longer, push through the pain. Then she could rest and heal.

Despair bit into her belly when she flipped through the pages. She couldn't understand the words. This was an old language. One she didn't know. She kept going, her fingers hurried and heart beating hard. The pages she could read covered mostly everything, from history, to dreams, to magic.

The War of Thorns. By R.S.

The enchanted forest and its hidden gems. By N.G.

Dreams and understanding them. By R.S.

Nothing on medicine. Eve screamed before shoving them off the table. Her energy was waning, slipping away from her with every breath. She stood so close to the ingredients that would save her, but she didn't know how to use them.

She tugged at her matted hair. If only she'd watched her father more and listened when he'd insisted it was a useful skill to have.

'Not all strength lies in swords and action, my little princess.'

She'd scoffed at him then, playing with her doll and singing to mama. But he'd been right. He'd always been right.

Eve squeezed her eyes shut, trying to remember his instructions. Sometimes he would tell her the recipe. What each herb did. But every memory was a jumble, a hazy mess. She cursed at herself before her eyes fell upon the leather of the grimoire.

Nona had been a potions master. Could she be so lucky?

Eve heaved herself off the table. She grasped the grimoire and unwrapped the leather tie sealing it shut. It smelt of incense and of the rose oil Nona would dab on her wrists. Eve closed her eyes and breathed it in. She sensed Nona's presence like a ghost watching from afar. She was not alone whilst she held this piece of her.

Eve turned the pages, her fingers tingling as she landed on a page with illustrations of ginger, feverfew, and honey.

For pain, the first page read. Eve choked a laugh as she flipped through the pages. *For infection. For sleep. For lust.*

She'd held her own cure this whole time.

Using the last of her remaining energy, Eve collected what she needed. They were simple potions, even for someone as inexperienced as her. If she managed to hold herself together long enough, she may just survive this after all.

Bells blared through the city as the Tinder Box went into lockdown. Soldiers commanded the streets like a wall of steel. Sharp. Organised. Hansel, Piccadilly, Bjorn, Porchid, and Cyrene pressed into the shadows of an alley, watching as the streets of the city transformed into chaos.

Getting back to the Sanctuary unnoticed was going to be a challenge. Hansel had never been trained for this. He had always been the one expected to be in formation with the others, ready and willing to fight for their Queen.

Piccadilly scoped the area. 'I have an idea.'

Cyrene leaned her head against Hansel's chest, pale from blood loss.

When Hansel had asked about her injuries, she'd only laughed. 'I won. I survived. And that is all there is to it.'

Piccadilly ushered them through the rows of houses, silent as a wraith. Each direction was sharp, each threat assessed as they trailed after her. She had a familiarity with the hidden alleys and back routes, leaving Hansel to wonder how little he knew about the city he'd lived in for years.

How vastly different they were.

Her dark eyes warily monitored the soldier's movements and those of the citizens. She shuffled them between buildings, behind carts and through darkened stalls of markets.

They'd managed to cross five blocks before fire lit the sky. The street ahead of them glowed orange and yellow from the burning torch lights of soldiers. Piccadilly swore and pushed them back.

Hansel stood taller, using his height to assess the street. Shadows stretched along the cobblestone streets, the scent of ash and smoke thick in the air. A large man with dreadlocks shouted orders, his deep voice commanding. In groups they kicked down doors and searched houses. Cries came from the distance, the shouts and grunts of people struggling testing Hansel's patience.

I have to do something.

Cyrene breathed heavily in his arms, her energy fading fast. 'There's no point being a hero when we can barely save ourselves.'

Hansel's jaw twitched as he looked down at her. She was pale, a cold sweat sticking to her skin. She was getting heavier in his arms and Hansel's body ached from his earlier beating. He shuffled on his feet to ease the weight, but it was mostly to distract himself from the guilt.

Piccadilly scouted ahead. She scaled the wall, nimbly climbing the wood as if she'd done this a thousand times.

Bjorn wasn't as nimble, and Hansel could see the tired muscles in the dwarf's shoulders. Porchid gripped Hansel's shirt, her tiny fingers tearing a small hole.

Hansel was weary. His life had been consumed by violence despite his calm nature. Snow's safety and the civil war had been paramount to him for so long that he couldn't remember anything else. He was a soldier. A huntsman. He had planned and fought and prayed for so long on a single dream: for a happy kingdom with its rightful heir, a fair and just ruler. Equality. Peace. Safety.

It had always been the bigger picture, his goal and purpose something greater than him, something worth the sacrifice and the blood and questionable decisions. But it felt empty now. He wanted it, still, of course. He couldn't stand the death or the poverty or the hunger any longer. The fires burning the city reminded him of that.

But somewhere along the way he'd found a new dream, too. One that involved a girl whose smile lit him up inside. A dream that pierced his soul with soft eyes and an uncanny ability to push his buttons and drive him to insanity, but it was that insanity he craved. The way Eve challenged him, prodded him, questioned him. What was the sacrifice worth when, in the end, if he couldn't share it with her?

It was as he watched another flame light up a townhouse, that he knew. Myrenna could not be saved. But maybe Eve could.

'Who is she?' Cyrene asked.

Hansel shook his head, bringing himself back to the alleyway. 'She's not important.'

Liar.

Cyrene scoffed. 'Love is always important.'

Hansel watched her carefully as she coughed, her blue skin almost white. Porchid whimpered.

Piccadilly landed back on the ground, Bjorn grumbling as she used him to steady herself.

'What are we up against?' Hansel asked.

More screams lit up the night as creatures were torn from their houses. The guards pulled them across the pavement and locked them in the cages of horse-drawn carts. Hansel winced at the sight of another changeling being torn from her mother.

Piccadilly flinched, too, as she turned to him. 'It's not looking good.'

Bjorn grunted. 'What? You thought they'd pave a path for us? Welcome us through with cheers and smiles? This isn't a bedtime story. There's no happy ending for the route we've chosen.'

'Your negativity should no longer astound me, but somehow it always does,' Piccadilly drawled.

Cyrene went limp in Hansel's arms.

'We need to move,' he said. 'Tell me you saw a way out. Something. *Anything.*'

Piccadilly looked at the sea nymph in his arms and sighed. 'There is one path, but I don't know if she'll survive it.'

Hansel gripped Cyrene tighter. 'It's better than no chance of survival at all.'

'With the riots, there are no eyes on the canal,' Piccadilly replied. 'Two blocks from here is a gondola that a friend of mine uses to scope the water. It should be free for the taking.'

'You're friends with a reaper?' Hansel asked.

She glared at him. 'I hate it when people call them that. They don't kill. They ferry bodies where they need to go. Much like when we bury or burn our dead.'

Bjorn snorted. 'Except they rob the corpses first.'

'Enough,' Piccadilly retorted. 'It's the canal or a city of soldiers.'

Hansel took one last look at Cyrene, her wheezing filling the space between them, and steeled himself. 'Lead the way.'

XXIII

The One-Way Journey

Bryn galloped down the moonstruck streets, keeping to the shadows, draped in a dark green cloak. The crumpled paper in his pocket felt like a weight. Rabbit's imminent death loomed heavy on his heart as he rode for the one place that few dared to tread: the Queen's mines.

He'd already found the vox leaf in sparse shrubs scattered around the rocky hills outside the city. Bryn was surprised he'd found them on his first day, wondering if it was dumb luck or fate that guided him, not asking questions as he'd plucked the deadly leaves and folded them into the pouch Doc had spared.

Bryn wasn't familiar with this part of the country, and he'd been sorely underprepared. His departure from the Sanctuary had been quick, Doc shoving him out the door before anyone objected. Left with only a small pack of food, his own two feet, and the paper with illustrations on what he needed to collect, Bryn had left the city.

So far, the roads had been relatively empty. He'd avoided checkpoints, but eventually his luck would run out. Some dwarves still traded, and if he was lucky, he'd be able to lie his way through.

Bryn had stumbled upon a farmhouse the night before. He hadn't seen the family as they'd been asleep, but he'd promptly saddled a shaggy, brown horse and found a cloak hanging on the outside of their front doors. He'd seen a smaller cloak next to it, and as thanks had made a simple doll of straw, leaving it where the young one would see it. He knew it was trivial, nothing at all compared to the cost of the horse – or of some of the other pieces he'd made – but it soothed his guilt all the same; took the edge off his already aching heart.

He rode on the main road now, his steed carrying wares – though the packs were filled with straw – watching as carts passed him by, the onlookers wary.

Bryn wondered if Bjorn had returned from his mission, and whether he was panicking at Bryn's departure. He shivered at the thought of one of Bjorn's lectures, his breath stale from brew.

Hooves stomped in the distance and Bryn slowed his horse. But when a group of soldiers lined the horizon, he realised he should have run.

Bryn gripped the reins as the soldiers spurred their mounts. He closed his eyes, hoping they'd pass him by. But whilst he'd been lucky with the vox leaf, it seemed his luck had run out. Before he could think, they'd surrounded him with sharp steel and cold stares.

One, with a garish helmet, rode forward, his toothy grin unnerving. He took in Bryn on his tired horse. 'You're on a one-way journey to the mines, dwarf, for theft and possession of stolen goods.'

He gulped before they yanked him off his horse, crushing his legs beneath him.

His straw doll hadn't been enough payment after all.

Hansel's breath was ragged as they emerged from a side street lining the canals. The gondola lay hidden beneath a sheet of mouldy cloth, reeking with the stench of decaying bodies. Inside, narrow containers lined the sides, used as storage and seating. White cloths were strewn amongst the rot, as if whoever had used it last had left in a hurry.

Holding Cyrene carefully, Hansel inched into the slender boat, placing her under the flimsy fabric to hide her. Hansel checked she was safe before holding the vessel steady for the others to climb in.

Screams wrenched the night, the firelight straight from the early tales of the cauldron. It reminded him of how fire had spat from its belly during the Battle of Thorns. If the guards kept this up, there would be no city to defend by sunrise.

In the distance, lights lit Myrenna's tower, showcasing she was back from Maelstrom. Why wasn't she intercepting? Yes, she was cruel; certainly heartless. But she wasn't reckless. None of this made sense.

Hansel turned back to the gondola as Piccadilly grumbled something. As she clambered in, more torchlight filtered from above.

Hansel ducked. Porchid flew to Piccadilly's side, hiding her light beneath the changeling's body, and Hansel lifted a cloak lying by the stern and draped it over them, nearly gagging at the awful smell. The only irritation from Piccadilly was a slight wrinkle of her nose before they disappeared under its cover.

Hansel took his place at the helm and picked up the oar. With the cover of darkness, he hoped the blood coating him wouldn't be too noticeable.

The canals were starkly different to the city they traipsed through, it's lowered position cold and eery against the screams and shouts above. Hansel listened intently as they sailed through the water, his heart beating fiercely in his chest. Whoever owned this boat would have many corpses to rob after the guards had let loose on the city.

Crows cawed in the sky and his breath hitched. The Queen's eyes were everywhere.

He kept calm, his movements precise against the dark, silty water, as if he was meant to be here. They went under one of the main bridges connecting two areas of the city. This water flowed from the Crystal Lake and rose with each passing year.

A soldier stopped above them and called out. 'Who's there?'

Hansel sucked in his breath and kept silent, praying to the Godmother they wouldn't come down.

Another soldier stopped. 'It's just a reaper.'

Hansel exhaled as he heard the rap of Piccadilly's fingers on the wood. He steered towards a curve in the canal, parting the water in front of them, and stopped in front of a set of stairs in the slums of the city.

Hansel checked the coast was clear, then set the others free and picked up Cyrene. Her breaths were shallow.

Piccadilly was weary as she ushered them all forward to a grate in the wall. Bjorn groaned, and she warned him to be quiet before they moved underground. Piccadilly lowered herself in first, then reached for Cyrene. Hansel carefully placed her in Piccadilly's arms, and she grunted at the weight. Hansel came through last, behind Bjorn, and found himself knee deep in thick sluggish water.

'By the cauldron,' Bjorn choked. 'What is that *smell?*'

'The sewers,' Piccadilly whispered, handing Cyrene back to Hansel.

Hansel was careful to not let Cyrene's head near the water and lifted her higher. Clumps of cauldron-knows-what trailed along his legs, and he shuddered.

'Lovely,' Bjorn said sarcastically.

'Always the best for you, dwarf,' Piccadilly echoed back.

Hansel snorted.

They moved through the sewers for a while, pausing at the openings above them as soldiers ran back and forth. The only light emanated from Porchid, who glowed a pale white in the darkness. They treaded with caution, avoiding any missteps to not fall. Hansel tried to ignore the clumps tickling his legs, the way the muck stuck to his skin and sunk into his pores.

'We're here,' Piccadilly said, pulling herself onto a platform. She ushered Porchid forward, and she illuminated a hole in the wall where a ladder disappeared into darkness below.

Hansel cradled Cyrene over his shoulder and made sure the sea nymph was secure before he grabbed the rung with one arm and slowly made his way down. The darkness engulfed them, the smell of sewerage and dampness coating them from head to toe.

Before long, they reached an opening with blazing light. Hansel gripped Cyrene tightly as he made his way into a giant underground cavern made of pillars of white. Creature after creature sat in groups and turned silent as they entered, each one watching with care as Piccadilly led the group deeper into the room. They nodded as he followed her through the crowd, some wrinkling their nose as they passed.

He felt exposed, as if each gaze was peeling off his skin and peering at what lay beneath. He hurried his steps.

When they reached the end, Piccadilly pulled back a curtain and Hansel was faced with a small elf. His age was unknown; he was wrinkly but with smooth, lean fingers.

'Doc,' Piccadilly said sternly. 'We need your help.'

'Why am I not s-surprised,' he stammered.

Piccadilly motioned Hansel towards a cot, where he laid Cyrene down. Porchid took a seat beside the sea nymph, running her hand through Cyrene's vibrant hair.

'Another p-patient?' Doc said behind him.

Piccadilly replied, but Hansel's ears rang as he turned towards the entrance and took in the high crested ceiling, the rows of balconies and the number of creatures in one space.

His heart filled with something he couldn't pin down. Relief. Awe. Confusion. Hope.

He jolted at Piccadilly's touch as she grasped his shoulder, her fingers firm but comforting.

'Welcome to the rebellion,' she said.

Bryn wasn't ashamed of the single tear that crept down his cheek, watching the world from behind caged bars. He sat on the rotted wooden floor and wiped at his eyes, finding only dirt and dust.

His hands were wrung in iron chains and his packs had been taken from him. But the piece of paper in his pocket remained tucked away, hidden from the roaming hands of the soldiers.

He'd not been so lucky with the velvet pouch. The guards had laughed when they'd smelt the contents and crushed them into the dirt.

'Nothing new from a dwarf,' one had said. 'Filthy scum.'

To them he was nothing but an addict, a dwarf clutching to a high as the world moved on without him. They'd beaten him and clamped him in chains, but whilst Bryn yearned for the cure for Rabbit, he also whispered to himself that it was okay. He could always find more.

So, as the cart travelled along the main road, the haunting whistles of the Queen's Guard around him, he realised one thing: he wouldn't have to sneak around the mines when the cart would take him straight into the heart of it.

The only problem was getting out.

XXIV

The Silver Commander

Bryn stared from the bars of his cage as a cart carried him through the high, wrought iron gates of the Queen's Mines. The air stank of ash and old blood. The land spread outwards like a vast desert, the high, black walls looming like shadows in the distance. Smoke drifted from cavernous holes in the ground, bleeding into the air like a heavy fog.

Prisoners huddled together, their bones protruding through their flimsy shifts. Their eyes were hollow as guards lined them up. A whip cracked on the ground, making them shudder. Even from here, Bryn could feel the despair, the way a sense of despondency lingered.

The driver grunted as his feet hit the ground. The clatter of keys sliding into the lock. The doors opened, and Bryn found himself hurled from the cart and pushed towards a dark building.

As he stumbled, Bryn thought back to his conversation with Bjorn in the tavern upon entering the city. Grand were their claims of freeing their cousins, of killing the Queen and saving the realm. It had been so easy to think of themselves as heroes. He realised his mistake as he took in the vastness of space before him. They'd been fools. Fools to think they could go up against *this*.

His eyes swept over the towers where guards roamed in sync with ghastly creatures. Some with claws and teeth and twisted limbs, as if they had crawled out of the darkness itself. Giant sweeping crossbows and cannons lined the ramparts keeping out trespassers.

Or keeping prisoners in.

In the centre of it all, beyond the dark building in front of him, lay the largest, gaping pit Bryn had ever seen. It stretched like a wound in the earth. Smoke and ash and fire poured from its depths. Amongst the drilling and clanging, Bryn could hear screams.

Where Parador had been a work of art, crafted with love, the walls etched in beauty and the stories of his people, this place reeked of death.

The guards kicked him from behind, pushing him forward. His chains clattered with his steps. Bryn trembled, his hopes dashed away with each step closer to his new future.

Gone was the bravery of three small dwarves with big dreams. Replaced by the dawning realisation there was no way out of this.

Hansel hadn't been with the rebellion for an hour before Lady Viper found him.

'I was worried sick,' she snapped. Her voice was like screeching steel, causing Hansel to rub his temples. 'I waited *hours* for you to contact me, but I heard nothing. Instead, I was left alone to pick up your mess. Do you know how many posters of you there are in the city? I had to tear them down and hide in the shadows. I'm not made for the shadows, Hansel. I'm made for the stage!'

Hansel held back his groan. Supposedly, Piccadilly had collected her from the apartment after they'd entered the Sanctuary and brought her here, meaning he now had to deal with her.

'This was a disaster,' she said, ignoring the way Hansel rubbed his temples. 'I knew I shouldn't have come. I should have left after Nona died. Should have taken what little I owned and started new.'

Hansel nodded wearily, the words fading into the background as he considered his position. Whilst he'd finally found the rebellion, his closest companions were scattered to the far reaches of the realm. He had no idea where Snow or Malak was. Had no idea if Eve was even alive. If it weren't for Porchid, he'd be utterly alone.

Bjorn had remained silent on how he'd arrived in the city, much less about the pit or his brethren, beelining for the whisky upon their return. Not that it mattered; Hansel's priorities were not with whatever schemes they were doing, but with Nona's dying wish.

Find her at the end.

Viper abruptly stopped talking as Bjorn's scream rang across the Sanctuary's walls, startling Hansel from his thoughts. He turned to see Piccadilly harshly whispering to the elf they called Doc.

Hansel excused himself, Viper's scowl enough to know he'd have to apologise later.

'Where in the cauldron is he?' Bjorn said, seething at the twitching doctor. 'What did you do? He was to stay here with Rabbit. He was supposed to be *protected*. Are you not a sanctuary, or did your ninny brain forget that?' He poked Doc's chest.

The elf grimaced in response.

'How about we find somewhere private for this conversation,' Piccadilly urged, her gaze raking over the hovering crowd.

'I'll do what I cauldron please,' Bjorn yelled.

Hansel pushed between them with his hands raised. 'What's happened?'

Bjorn glared at the doctor before turning to Hansel. 'The elf has taken it upon himself to send people on missions and not tell anybody. Bryn is gone – sent off to find some stupid leaf that Rabbit's got himself hooked on.'

Hansel blinked, trying to put together what was happening but finding too many pieces of the puzzle still missing. 'What do you—'

He was cut off as Bjorn lunged for the elf, his hand nearly throttling Doc's throat before Piccadilly shoved him back, one hand on her blade. 'Enough! I will not have you brawling here. You want answers? So, do I. Doc can't tell us about Bryn if he's not breathing.'

Piccadilly didn't budge until Bjorn stood down, his slight nod his only agreement. Hansel breathed a quiet sigh of relief. He watched Bjorn carefully, ready to restrain the dwarf or fight alongside him, when a voice spoke up.

'I call for Council.'

'Zacariah,' Piccadilly groaned.

Zacariah strode towards them, eyes narrowed. Hansel noticed he was older than Bjorn, his brown beard streaked with grey. His shoulders were thicker, as if he was used to wielding a weapon more than words.

'If we are to discuss matters of unapproved *missions*,' Zacariah said, shooting an unapproving look at Doc, 'or any matters of my kin, I will be present to discuss and pass judgement.'

Piccadilly took a deep breath, staring at Zacariah in consideration. 'I'll get the preparations sorted and I'll see you all in the back chamber in thirty minutes.'

They all nodded in agreement, and she took that as her cue to leave. Hansel watched her as she weaved through the crowd and disappeared.

Bjorn crossed his arms and huffed at Hansel. 'There better be brew.'

'With you around, there probably won't be any left,' Hansel said, clasping his friend's shoulder.

Food and sleep were what they really needed. But Hansel couldn't deny that it fell down the ladder of priorities when it came to their predicament. What he needed more than anything right now, was answers.

The meeting room was more of a study or makeshift library compared to what Hansel was used to from the castle. Mismatched sets of tables and chairs had been placed together. Some sat higher than others, creating a stitched-together mock-up of a larger table, oddly reminding Hansel of the mixed species all working together in the rebellion.

Piccadilly had come through on her promise. She'd laid out food rations, mostly bread and cheese with a bowl of apples, and some knives. Though it wasn't much, it would still fill their bellies and, with any luck, help the mood.

Piccadilly gave Hansel a weary nod as he entered. So far, they were the first to arrive.

Hansel pulled out the chair closest to him and sat at a chipped, red table, the paint flaking off like dried blood.

'How many are we expecting?' he asked as he reached for some food. His knees hit the underside of the table.

'Eight,' she replied, taking her own seat at the table. 'With Cyrene awake, she can stand for the Sea Nymphs.'

'Is she well enough?' he asked, placing a bit of cheese carefully on a cracker.

'We'll soon find out.'

As he took his first bite, Zacariah entered, followed by Bjorn. Two dwarves and kin, but carved from two very different stones. Bjorn was still beaten and, despite his earlier disagreement with Doc, the elf seemed to have patched him up nicely. The only visible scars were covered in a wet, green sludge.

Porchid came soon after, with Viper in tow. They sat in silence as they waited for the others to arrive.

Doc entered with Cyrene; she held a crutch in one hand, and a dark-haired soldier helped her on the other.

Hansel spat out his water.

Flynn.

He scowled.

Flynn helped the sea nymph to her seat and winked at Hansel. His other eye was swollen and black. The swagger of him poisoned whatever good mood Hansel had been in.

Piccadilly began without fanfare. 'There has been some … tension. This is the time to air out your grievances.'

Bjorn at least had the decency to look sheepish at her glare.

'It's apparent the Queen is looking for something,' Piccadilly continued. 'Her guard grows more out of control, especially her crows. And things inside the forest are moving. Things that should be asleep. Anyone who isn't human is taken, killed, or tortured.

'I want to remind everyone before we begin that while we might be at war, we are not just here to shed blood. We are here for equality and freedom. We are here to see the rightful heir on the throne. To show mercy and justice, and lead in peace.'

'You're talking about Snow,' Bjorn interjected.

'Yes,' replied Piccadilly. 'She is currently our first choice to take over the throne.'

'Who's the second?' asked Bjorn.

Piccadilly paused. 'The Commander.'

Flynn, beside her, was cleaning his nails. 'You mean our missing commander?'

'Missing?' Zacariah sputtered, 'Who in the cauldron is in charge?'

'We all know who's in charge,' Flynn said, grinning as if he'd won a fight. 'Don't we, Piccadilly?'

She blinked at him as the room erupted. Hansel enjoyed watching the smirk on Flynn's face die at Piccadilly's glare, making him look like a petulant child.

'How long?' Hansel asked, his jaw twitching.

'What does it matter now?' she asked.

'You've *lied* to us,' Zacariah hissed.

'Not lied,' Flynn corrected. 'She just omitted the truth.'

'It's the same thing,' Hansel said, meeting her gaze. 'I had a suspicion at the apartment when you wouldn't elaborate about him.'

'Are you going to yell at me, too?' she sniped.

'Would it be useful if I did?'

'No,' she replied, rubbing her temples.

'For what it's worth,' Hansel said, noting the way Flynn glared at him. 'I'm impressed.'

'Impressions aside,' Zacariah snapped, 'how do you expect to continue this charade? We've come here for safety, and you've only given us falsehood. We haven't yet chosen to aid your little war.'

'I haven't given you only falsehood, Zacariah,' Piccadilly said firmly. 'I've given you somewhere to hide, somewhere to eat and sleep and heal. And in repayment I've not even asked for a single medallion.'

'Though we need it,' said Flynn.

'Yes,' she replied, slightly defeated. 'Though we need it.'

'I'll ask again,' Hansel said, more out of curiosity than anything else. 'How long has the Commander been gone?'

The group fell silent.

Piccadilly took a deep breath. 'Almost four months now.'

Hansel sat up straighter. 'Four months? You've been holding this place together for that long? With no experience in running a rebellion, let alone leading a war, and you've been bleeding money ever since?'

'This is insanity,' Zacariah muttered.

'I agree,' Hansel replied, leaning back in his chair. 'It is insane. Whilst I'm impressed you've kept it together, how do you expect to take an army into battle when they don't know you're in charge. There's no trust there.'

She nodded. 'My priority was recruiting and saving as many lives as I could. I organised a few scouting missions here and there, but nothing really eventuated besides little trickles of whispers and rumours. It's how I managed to organise safety for the dwarfs, and how we found out about the pits under the tavern.

'It's been slow moving, but it hasn't been a total loss. With the trust of the people, I thought they might join our cause as I talked with them, dealt with them directly. I came up with the lie, but a good story only goes so far before the cracks begin to show.'

'So, what now?' Hansel asked.

'I don't want to lie to them. It will only give Myrenna the upper hand she needs to divide us more.'

'You need to let the people choose,' Cyrene said from where she sat, her ruby hair limp. 'Trust them, and they, in turn, will trust you. You've protected them this long. Why not longer?'

'I'll have no choice now,' Piccadilly conceded, falling back into her chair. Flynn went to reach for her, and she pulled back, her eyes never leaving the group.

Cyrene leaned forward. 'I'm the heir to Nysa. I know what it's like to bear the weight of another's rule. From one ruler to another, I'm also impressed.'

'How broke are you?' Bjorn asked, veering the conversation back.

'Very,' replied Flynn. 'I looked at the books yesterday and we're almost out of food and water. Add to that clothing, bedding, and weapons.'

'Funding is no longer a problem,' Bjorn said flatly.

'No?' Flynn asked sceptically. 'And why is that, little hairy man?'

Bjorn reached for a slice of bread. 'We have gems.'

A frown peppered Flynn's brow. Before he could speak, Zacariah slammed his fist into the table. 'You can't just offer our gems!'

Bjorn scoffed. 'I can when they're from *my* mines and I'm paying for my own kin. But I also won't just hand them over. I'll need something in return.'

The changeling watched the dwarf carefully. 'What is it, exactly, you ask in return? That's no small sum of money.'

'No, it isn't,' Bjorn said, a smile curving his lips. He lathered the butter on his bread. 'I want the Seven reunited. I want Snow's safety as a priority, and I want to be directly involved in Myrenna's downfall.'

Flynn laughed and hit the hard-wooden table with his palm. 'You don't honestly believe you can take on the Queen yourself, do you?'

'No,' said Bjorn with a mouthful of food. 'But I'd still like to swing my axe at her.'

Hansel smirked, though his vision of how that would play out would only end with Bjorn's neck snapped.

'Consider it a deal,' Piccadilly said. 'We'll make sure to find the remainder of the Seven, and then you can have at the Queen. With conditions, of course.'

Bjorn nodded in agreement.

Piccadilly sighed, then smiled at him gratefully. 'Those gems will go a long way for food and water.'

'And weapons,' Bjorn mumbled through his next bite. 'We'll need more weapons.'

At least everyone agreed on that.

Bryn's eyes stung as he swung the blunt pickaxe repeatedly against the solid rock and dirt. The handle was wonky and splinter-ridden from the many hands that had wielded it before him. It was nothing like the beautiful tools they used in Parador.

The dwarves prided themselves on not just making their weapons sharp, but also appealing. Each weapon was sturdy but also a piece of art, with handles decorated in gems and carvings. Everything held a song or some heart, from the pictures of old or the quotes engraved into the metals.

He looked down at his worn and bloody hands. He'd only been here a few days and already blisters had formed then broken and formed again. His normally tough skin stung.

Time was beginning to blur like the silt of a river churning to the shore. His days began at dawn, the first rays of light peeking over the great, black wall before he was ushered into the dark again, only to exit at dusk when the same rays dimmed the sky into purple and disappeared again.

He was used to working beneath the earth, but nothing like this slow torture. He'd never cared for the sun – and why should he, when his blood was born for the underground. But now, as the sun etched below the surface of the wall, Bryn found himself longing for it.

These tunnels were cold, severe. There was no history etched into stone or marble. They didn't have the sparkle of a thousand stars creating its own living sky underneath the soil.

This was darkness and silence.

He remained quiet for the most part. Watching, observing. The main guardians of this dreadful place weren't the Royal Guard; those men merely stood above the high gates, watching the towers, pacing the above balconies in shadows against the sun's dying light.

The true owners of this place were the gnarled, cruel creatures he'd seen upon entering. Dark hounds with thick hides and sharp teeth. Shaiths, who reminded him of ghouls, their black wings and screeches piercing every nook and corner. Not to mention the warped, elvish beasts with knifelike claws, who watched over everything with their beady, fathomless eyes.

Bryn had monitored locations of buildings, watched the changing of the guards in the hopes for a set pattern. He'd squeezed between places to see the main hub, the burning middle of what was being collected, what was being dug. But all he'd found were bones.

So far, there had been no sign of the starkiss flower; no sign of any flowers at all.

A shout echoed along the tunnels, and Bryn curled into himself with the other prisoners as a guard strode past.

His kin hadn't been the only ones sent to this place. Bryn had found fairies with shredded backs, their wings torn in brutality. He'd seen changelings, not like the silver of Piccadilly but some with scales of green or eyes of gold; variations on the mix of species that were swapped with human children. There were humans branded as traitors, some trolls – though, they were rare – even elves, most of them used as caretakers for the guards.

As the mines' horn rang out, Bryn placed down his axe and shuffled into formation with the other recruits. When they broke through the darkness of the tunnels, Bryn's eyes locked onto the sky, and for one blessed moment he caught a glimpse of the orange and violet sunset as it faded behind the blackened walls of the fortress.

XXV
The Missing Queen

Eve smelt wood and dust. Her eyes snapped open to the harsh scratching of a bird outside the window matching the dull ache at the back of her head.

She moaned as she sat up, blinking at the grey light streaming into the kitchen. The grimoire remained open on the table, expectant. Rain fell outside, the pitter patters the only sound against the crackling fire. The hearth looked newly lit, stoked by an invisible hand.

A faded red shawl lay on the lounge and Eve pulled it over her shoulders, then peered out the nearest window and gasped. Her tight grip on the bench was the only thing keeping her standing when she caught her first glimpse of outside.

Gone was the forest she'd trekked through, the pebbled bridge a memory. It was now replaced by sweeping cliffs and a churning sea that stretched to the sky. Lightning lit up the gaps between the bulging clouds, promising the storm to come.

Where am I?

Eve jumped as a *thud* came from behind her, her blade free before she'd even turned around. But the room remained quiet, empty. She blinked as lightning flashed against the walls, the white light breaking through the orange glow of the hearth.

She shook her head, blaming delirium and sickness. The scar on her face itched and with it came hunger. Still holding the knife, Eve checked on the fire where a stew boiled in an iron pot. She cautiously sniffed the simmering soup, inhaling the rich herbs and spinning around to find the table set for one, with a pale blue bowl, a serving spoon, and a pot of tea that smelled of roses and mint.

That had not been there before. She swore it hadn't been.

'Who's here?' Eve demanded, gripping one of her knives and moving slowly around the cottage. 'I'm in no mood for games or trickery. Show yourself!'

But when no one answered, she was only left with her own drowning thoughts.

'*Something evil is coming, Seeker,*' Cyrene had warned her at the Skinny Piglet, so long ago it felt like another lifetime. *'And I fear we may all be doomed unless we can find a solution.'*

The memory brought a shiver with it.

Eve served herself dinner, her knife set beside her on the table should someone show themselves. But whilst the soup warmed her belly, it did not warm her soul. Weariness pressed a hand on her shoulder, weighing her down.

Eve pulled the blue stone from her pocket and turned it over, assessing the strands of silver inside. They reminded her of veins.

Her fingers shook when she recalled the silver mirror shattering into a rain of glass, cuts turning to scars. Memories, carved into her skin for a lifetime that would always be a reminder of the life leaving Rapunzel's eyes.

She heard the grimoire's pages flipping behind her, though the windows were shut tight, stopping any wind. Eve placed her bowl down and slowly walked to the large counter. She ignored the crushed powders, the shattered vials, and stains she'd left on the wood, to stare at the grimoire's pages.

The book fluttered and settled on a page with a sketch of a young girl, her round face flushed as a man hurried her towards the burrow of an oak tree. Eve's finger trailed the sketched man, a tear snaking down her chin.

Nona had known her as a child, had stroked her hair and told her stories around the firelight as Dante played the mandolin. The pages kept turning, revealing the smiling face of a young man, his dark hair tied in a bun. The lines were beautiful, the shadowing realistic enough that her mouth went dry. Her fingers moved without thought, tracing the lines of his jaw, the sharp cheekbones. Dante had been beautiful.

A tear dropped onto the parchment, smudging a bit of his shoulder.

And though she didn't want to look away, the following page on the right was different. No longer a sketch, but words, inked in Nona's cursive writing, still precise despite the age of the paper.

Eve traced the first and second line of the prophecy. That day in the tower, the silver mirror had shattered but it had still moved. Somehow it had liquified and transformed, drawn to the odd little stone Hansel had found within Parador.

Eve flipped through the pages, notes upon notes of spells and questions and possibilities, the calligraphy messy and erratic. She found sketches of herself and Myrenna and the sisters Grimm. There were the mirrors and gems and the Ancient One.

Lines were scrawled next to the drawings – predictions, or memories? Eve kept reading, recognising the words of the prophecy.

Wood from a tree that existed an age. The
Ancient One? Dragon Fire?

She flicked to the previous page with sketches of bold and elaborate mirrors. Including the distinctive frame of the silver one that shattered in Rapunzel's tower

Mirrors four, of black and bone,

Of silver and gold, and night blue stone.

Eve read Nona's jotted-down thoughts, her curiosity, her need for answers, and halted at the bottom of the page.

From the creation of the mirrors came forth great power, but also great weakness. To create and to destroy, one in the same. The girl is the key.

The stone pulsed in Eve's palm, aching like another scar where the silver veins of the mirror glinted. If this stone could contain one mirror, could it hold the others?

And, somehow, if Eve could miraculously find them all and meld them together … Would it be enough?

Hansel began to lose track of time.

The candles' wicks burned lower as the council sat around the jumble of tables discussing the future of Bellatorre.

Cyrene had just updated them on how she'd been caught without papers on the road back to Nysa and, despite her royal blood, had been taken to the pits. Savage, they'd called her, locking her up and only setting her free when it was time to fight. She had spat the words like poison, her vengeance palpable as she spoke of the blood she'd spilt for entertainment.

'I'm royalty,' she hissed. 'Not some prized possession for show.'

Piccadilly leaned closer, studying Cyrene intently. 'Are there more establishments like the Tinder Box?'

Cyrene dug her nails into the table, nearly vibrating with rage. 'I can guarantee it. The Tinder Box isn't the only soldier's establishment in the realm. There's another fighting pit in Roserock. But that's the only other one I've heard of.'

Roserock was the same village in which Hansel had bargained with Eve. Where the trees lined the road in a lovers' embrace and Eve had thrown her knives as a good morning.

One didn't forget when a woman threw a knife at one's face.

'Roserock has its own pocket of freedom fighters,' Piccadilly said. 'I'll get a message to my contact there and see if they can do anything from their end. Our eyes must remain here, in the Silver City. With the raids and uproar, I expect little to no travel in or out of the city. It's only a matter of time before Myrenna descends from her castle and flushes us out.'

'Will she condone the raids?' Zacariah asked.

Hansel ran a hand through his hair. 'It's hard to say. Myrenna gives her men a little freedom so they feel powerful, but when something has gone too far without her direct approval, she'll quickly remind them who's in charge. Just because they're her men doesn't mean they aren't on a leash.'

'Like well-kept pets,' Bjorn gruffed.

'Even Myrenna understands fear is not enough,' Flynn said, leaning back in his chair. 'Whilst others suffer, those who serve her remain loyal with … privileges. Such as good whisky, medallions in their pockets, and a powerful ally. Her men will remain loyal because of that *and* because they believe her to be all powerful.'

Cyrene raised her brow. 'So, why exactly are you here? You look very … well-kept.'

He gave her a lazy grin that made Hansel want to lay his fist into his nose.

'I'm here,' Flynn began, 'because I take pleasures in other things. *And* I do not believe anyone is all powerful. Myrenna is just simply harder to kill.'

'What pleasures are those?' Cyrene asked.

Flynn rested on his forearms on the table and locked eyes with the sea nymph. 'I can show you one time, but it might not be to your taste.'

Cyrene gave him a vicious smile. 'You don't know my tastes, land dweller, but I'd bet they're far too bloody for you.'

Flynn laughed in response.

'Can we please focus?' Piccadilly urged.

'Yes,' interjected Bjorn. 'Let's focus on the fact my cousin is missing because of this stupid elf.'

Doc looked down at his lap before raising his eyes to Piccadilly, who sighed. 'I spoke with Doc just before the meeting and I've decided to approve the mission.'

Bjorn almost spat out his drink. 'You approve? Bryn isn't a warrior. None of you had the right to send him *anywhere* without talking to our kin. He has no clue about medicine, or war, or being on his own.'

'Your *kin* are dying,' she replied. 'I'll admit, I was uncertain at first. We have lost so many to the cause. To lose another for the life of one was … questionable. But he's also part of the Seven. You as a group have your own sort of fame, which is valuable. Especially to the cause.'

'We are not something you can just place on a recruitment poster,' Bjorn retorted.

'But you are,' she replied. 'If we can reunite the Seven, we can unite a larger force to fight for the Princess.'

'What if he doesn't succeed?' asked Zacariah. 'What if Bryn is captured and tortured, taken to the mines?'

Piccadilly looked pained as she said, 'Considering that's exactly where he needs to go then so be it.'

Bjorn slammed his fist against the table, his drink spilling over. 'HOW DARE YOU.'

'I understand your frustration.' she started, 'However, in our current predicament we have more pressing matters. Bryn is a capable young dwarf. He will save your friend.'

Bjorn stared at her darkly, but she stood firm. Hansel noted the strain in her shoulders, the dark circles around her eyes, and the way she rubbed her temples when she was stressed.

She looked up at him. 'Hansel, what in the cauldron happened at the Tinder Box?'

Hansel relayed his story, Porchid twinkling at certain intervals, leaving out none of the details, including the conditions of the pits, his surprise at seeing Bjorn, and the Colonel's arrogant claims.

'The Colonel was always an idiot,' Flynn said from across the table. 'Somehow, I'm not surprised he chose you.'

Hansel glared at Flynn, 'He may have been careless, but he was still a high-ranking officer and not some low-strung soldier looking for praise.'

Hansel could feel Flynn's irritation even from across the room, and couldn't help smiling in satisfaction. The sweet spot which he could hit without fists. Hansel didn't know him well, but his instincts hadn't been wrong before, and he wasn't going to question them now.

Piccadilly cleared her throat, reminding Hansel this wasn't the time.

Hansel ignored Flynn's glare. 'You were right. Rumple is the one locked inside the dungeons. The Colonel insinuated that the Queen is somehow learning to manipulate the spindle. To weave dreams.'

'That can't happen,' interjected Cyrene. 'Do you know the kind of power that holds?'

Bjorn gruffed, 'The spindle is completely interconnected with him. Surely even she can't hope to understand how to use it.'

'Her Tinker might,' said Hansel. 'The creature has always had a way of breaking things, of twisting them.'

'What happens if she gets that power?' Viper asked. 'Surely weaving dreams isn't a very useful skill when ruling a kingdom?'

Porchid pulled at Hansel's sleeve, and he shook her away.

'Ah,' replied Doc, speaking for the first time since the meeting started, 'that is where you're w-wrong.'

He straightened his glasses and stood on his chair. His long nose was bent ever so slightly on the ridge, and Hansel wondered whether it was an indent from years of wearing his goggle-like specs.

'The s-spindle is old magic. It does not j-just take dreams but c-can also c-control them. It d-does not matter who owns them.'

'Control them?' asked Piccadilly. 'How?'

Porchid flew to Hansel's shoulder and pulled his ear.

'Ouch.' he hissed, shooing her away.

'When one is unc-c-conscious, their mind is p-pliable. Easily manipulated,' Doc stuttered. 'With the s-spindle, you can warp one's d-desires. Mould one's memories into anything the owner w-wishes. They will see and believe w-whatever they d-dream.'

'Anything from a kiss to a nightmare,' Piccadilly stated.

'Y-yes.'

'So,' Hansel started, 'what you're saying is that if Myrenna can somehow control the spindle, she can also manipulate dreams? Control them to do whatever she likes?'

'That would mean she could make anybody do her bidding. Twist memories. Sow mistrust. Or even torture,' Zacariah responded.

Cyrene stood from her chair, Doc supporting her arm as she waivered from her injuries. 'She cannot be allowed to reap such power. In the wrong hands, that spindle could shape history and everything in it.'

'This is bigger than we realised,' Hansel said, sounding calmer than he felt.

His heart thrummed in his chest at the thought of Eve. If Myrenna found her, and if she wielded this kind of power, Eve would be a target. One of the first on her hit list.

Myrenna did not forgive, did not forget. He knew that firsthand from the burned crisp of land that used to be the bakery in her old village.

'We need a plan,' he said. 'Something to stop or distract her.'

Porchid grew a shade of tomato and flew at his face, flapping agitatedly. Hands on hips, she squealed in a high pitch tone.

'*What?*' he asked, exasperated.

Porchid scowled and flew to his pocket, pulling out a small scroll.

'We need to break Rumpelstiltskin out of prison,' said Piccadilly. 'Steal the spindle back.'

Bjorn snorted. 'Surely, it's not that easy. You saw what happened when we tried to break people out of a tavern cell. The castle is a whole other beast.'

Porchid gripped a corner of the scroll and heaved it across the table to Zacariah, practically shoving it in his face. When he ignored her, she glowed hot crimson.

'Myrenna will take pleasure in killing us,' Flynn said.

Cyrene ticked off her fingers. 'We have an untrained army. A missing princess. And no plans. We have no way to stop her.'

In a huff, Porchid pushed the scroll towards Zacariah again and stamped her foot down, silencing the table.

'I think she wants you to read the scroll,' Hansel said, just as confused as everybody else.

Zacariah's eyes lingered on the tiny scroll. It was minuscule in his thick fingers as he unravelled it.

Porchid's light dimmed as she sat down and exhaled.

Zacariah sucked in a breath, tension lining his shoulders. 'It's from my niece. Where did you get this?'

The fairy looked towards Hansel in a plea, her dark eyes wide.

'She was carrying it in the Tinder Box,' Hansel said slowly, unsure how to continue. 'She put it in my pocket for safe keeping. I didn't know it was for you.'

Zacariah paused, his eyes brimming with red. 'What did she look like? The female from the tavern?' His voice cracked on the last word.

'She was golden,' Hansel replied. He swallowed roughly. 'Like a walking sun. She killed the Colonel before they dragged her out. Before they—'

Zacariah held up his hand. 'I don't need to know more. Only that it was her.'

'May the Ever After hold her close,' said Hansel. The group repeated after him.

'What does it say?' Piccadilly asked softly, her hand squeezing Zacariah's shoulder.

Hansel held his breath, waiting for the dwarf to break. To rage. To scream. But he simply sat in silence.

The worst kind of grief.

'It says,' he began, 'the black carriage is a lie. Myrenna isn't in the city.'

'The black carriage returned from Maelstrom days ago,' Flynn pointed out. 'The flame is lit to signify she's home.'

Hansel leaned forward. 'Myrenna usually timed the carriage's comings and goings with her trips. It would have to be truly strange circumstances for her to say she's here when she's not.'

'Like she doesn't want anyone to know where she's going,' Piccadilly said.

'Where would she be going?' Flynn asked. 'She's never been one to hide.'

'Perhaps,' Piccadilly mused. 'But what if she's afraid?'

'Who would the Evil Queen be scared of?' Cyrene asked.

'The sisters Grimm,' Hansel finished.

All eyes fell on the huntsman.

He shuffled in his seat. 'They are the only beings powerful enough to stop her. She's always been terrified of them.'

'So, if she's hiding from the sisters Grimm, then where did she go?' Piccadilly asked.

'It doesn't matter where she went,' Zacariah said. 'What matters now, is that if she isn't in the castle. We have an opportunity.'

Hansel thought it did matter. Myrenna always timed her trips to match her departures and arrivals like clockwork. If the carriage returned, then she should have too. But it was something to consider later.

He leaned forward. 'Let's say she's gone, and nobody is inside that castle. Let's say we attempt to break into its walls and free Rumpelstiltskin. What's to stop the magic that protects it? Or the constant watch of guards? Or the unknown location of the prisoner and the spindle? Whilst this all sounds perfect tucked away underground, we're still taking a big chance on a what-if.'

'True,' Piccadilly replied. 'But this chance has someone who knows the walls of the castle inside and out.'

Hansel's hope crept further into the darkness the more he found himself in this war. With Snow, it had burned brightly, shining the way towards a future of peace and prosperity. Even when he'd journeyed with Eve, he'd believed his path had been chosen, carved out for him by fate.

But as his companions had slowly dwindled, his hope dimmed with it.

He met Piccadilly's dark eyes, her gaze reflecting what he thought had once glimmered in his: faith, triumph, and courage. She had true belief in what she was doing. They would call out her name as they hauled Myrenna to the stocks, lighting the flame beneath her feet and watching her turn to smoke.

He'd wanted that once.

But when he thought about it now, he'd only ever wanted the Princess's safety. Only ever wanted a home for Malak.

A hero complex, Eve had said.

A coward, he had believed.

But he was neither a hero nor a coward. He was a man. And he would do the right thing. For the safety he craved. For the home they could create. For peace.

Where Malak and Snow and Eve could be happy.

Even with Myrenna away, it was a long shot. The castle was a fortress, and a heavily guarded one at that. But it was their best chance. *He* was their best chance. He knew those castle walls inside and out, its secret little tunnels, its hidden little nooks, which tapestries ran into one another in the maze that stood proudly above the city. Besides Snow, he knew that castle better than anyone.

And so, as all eyes stared at him around the table, he steeled himself. 'I'll need some ink and paper, and potentially more brew. We're in for a long night.'

XXVI

The Cottage of Convenience

'Mirrors three. Mirrors four. Will the seeker find them all?'

Eve huffed the tune to the point of insanity, moving through the kitchen, still sceptical of the cottage as it magically poured tea, washed dishes, and fed her. She'd been mixing concoctions from the grimoire, utilising the materials on the shelves.

The cottage had moved again overnight, leaving them in a field of verdant grass with bright pink lilies – a distinct change from the stormy shores of the ocean. In a short span of time, she'd seen snowy mountains, flat, packed earth, a desert stretching towards the sun, and an island in the sky.

The lily-filled meadow had appeared when she'd awoken, leaving the house smelling of fresh flowers.

She tended to her cuts and bruises. Despite how careful she'd been, she couldn't help the wince of pain. The scar on her face was the worst. She'd found a small mirror in one of the chests and gazed towards the thick, jagged line running down her jaw. The wound had only just missed her eye, but it covered half her face ending, near her neck.

Each time the cottage travelled, the windows would blanket in thick green smoke which would curl into itself as the house warped. Eve wasn't entirely sure how it did it, or why. But she'd accepted it. In her boredom, she'd scrawled *The Cottage of Convenience* onto a ripped piece of parchment, finding ink in a nearby drawer, and pinned it to the kitchen wall.

She named it for having exactly what she needed in a life-saving emergency; for having food, and a hot hearth, and medicine. Sometimes, she would hear a *thump*, and things would fall or reappear. It unnerved her, but the things left were usually helpful.

She also didn't mind the fact it had the extra perk of hiding her far, far away from a queen who wanted her dead.

So, she kept thanking the cottage, and she kept on healing.

'Mirrors black and mirrors blue, why must it always be black stew?' she sang as another potion turned a hideous coal ink and made a *pop* sound.

She swore. It had failed again.

Jars and bottles littered the countertop after perfecting the pain killer she needed. In her confidence, she'd aimed a little higher on the next. She'd found a recipe for light, and whilst it would light up in need, if the bottle were to smash, it would explode in blinding light. Handy for all the dark places she found herself in, and even handier should she find herself fighting an enemy … again.

This particular batch was her seventh attempt, and each time she added the shaved scarat nail, it went *pop*.

According to Nona's book, she was looking for more of a *poof*.

'Mirrors new and mirrors old, why can't this potion just do what it's told!'

When her mother had been ill, her father had been the one to mix her medicine. His fingers had been smooth, deft, and determined. Eve tried with him but could never get it quite right.

Her father used to laugh. *'Slow down, little princess. Potions are practice and patience. Two disciplines you haven't yet mastered.'*

Eve scoffed. Patience and practice weren't skills she'd learnt as an adult, either. If only she'd listened, *truly* listened when he'd given her his time.

Time she would never get back.

Eve poured out the black sludge with a growl. 'I need a distraction.'

She had begun to move again; the healing in her body was faster with the potions. She'd fidgeted her way around the house, slowly sorting through its contents and its owner's belongings in the hope of finding something helpful. So far, she'd managed to find a map, create some medicinal potions, and feed herself. Otherwise, she'd mostly slept and dreamt.

Each dream had a been a mixture of hope and nightmares. Amethyst eyes in the dark, then Hansel as he smiled in the sunlight of the forest.

During her waking hours, she focused on the grimoire. Sifting through the pages as if she could reach out to Nona and smell the incense of her tent. But like Dante, Nona was also gone, merely another dream to add to the pile.

She wiped her palms on the loose, white shirt she'd found upstairs, dragging black gunk all over it. After her ordeal, the teal tunic and black pants from Gabby's mother were ruined – torn and stained like her own in her rucksack. With a heavy heart, she'd set them by the couch ready to burn and went to find a clean pair of clothes. She'd gotten lucky when she found a trunk of men's clothes in the upstairs rooms, but when she'd gone back to the fire, her old outfit had gone missing.

Strange things happened in this cottage.

Eve had deciphered from Nona's works that the mirrors and the stone were somehow connected. Still, she didn't even know where to begin.

Her gift had been silent, slumbering away in the dark. Over the years she'd learnt to urge it towards the small things – a lost watch, missing coins, or a set of keys. But she'd never mastered its control for bigger things, other things. It had never driven her to her father when she went back to find him. Never driven her to riches when she needed money for leisure or comfort.

But it had driven her to Hansel. And the grotto. And the bloodkiss flower for her father.

It had also driven her to the silver mirror in Rapunzel's castle. *Twice.*

She huffed. Her hair had come out from her braid, and she untwisted it, letting it fall down her back. She'd managed to wash it but had come up short on finding a hairbrush, so she made do with her fingers.

She padded across the wooden floor to the back room lined with mismatched rugs. It was filled to the brim with piles of boxes and items covered in sheets and dust. She made her way to the window, and pushed her shoulder into the frame, trying to open it as the wood creaked. Eve sneezed, then heaved against the grinding wood until the latch clicked and it groaned open, washing the room in the scent from the lilies outside.

Satisfied, she pulled off the first sheet, unveiling a stack of briefcases and carry bags. She found one with a gold buckle, the satchel's leather peeling across its surface from use, and unclipped it. Inside held some stale biscuits, an old, blunt knife, and travelling papers. She peeled another box open and found a picture of a short, young man.

Kedden Baltmore, 23, Blacksmith, Aurelian Born

This hadn't been the first set she'd found. It seemed that, whoever the owner of the cottage was, they enjoyed keeping other people's things. People she'd never seen or known.

Just as she'd done with the others, Eve placed it in the pile she'd made, right on top of a Roslyn Lester and the map she had found that belonged to a Sarah Hatter.

Nothing of value lay amongst any of the belongings, probably taken by the owner long before she'd set foot here. Eve didn't know why she kept the travelling papers, or why she tried to recount the names. She didn't know them. But, somehow, it seemed like she should. Possibly because nobody else would.

The second sheet she whipped away uncovered a cot made of hay and feather. She coughed as dust flew into her eyes. She wiped down her grimy shirt before moving onto the next covering. This was by far the largest one in the room. It was wide, stretching across the side wall, with a small curve at the top. Eve reached above her, stood on her toes, and pulled – hard.

Light gleamed across the floor, mesmerising in the way it moved with swirling colours. Almost like the reflection of water.

Curious, Eve kicked the sheet away and turned to find a tapestry loom, the weaving half-complete with colours of pearl and indigo and silver. It shifted like its own universe, glittering like tiny little stars. By its side was a large spindle, the thread half-woven. The yarn or whatever it was rippled, lucid and alive.

Magic like this only belonged to one person: Rumpelstiltskin.

Eve stepped back. Was he the thief, or had he again been robbed? She remembered expecting a spindle this size when she pulled open the crate in the Skinny Piglet. Instead, she'd found the tiny spindle he'd caressed and paid her for. The Dream Weaver's gift and weapon and curse.

Her gift woke from its slumber, itching for her to touch.

Run, her mind echoed, but her hand lifted on its own, reaching towards the moving light. There was a pull she couldn't explain, a *need* she couldn't resist.

Her mouth went dry with anticipation and curiosity. Her gift pulsing and writhing under her skin.

Run.

Her finger hovered for a moment over the spindle, as if that little voice held her back. Taking a breath, Eve let her gift guide her and pricked her finger.

Run.

But it was too late. Deep crimson blood pooled on her finger. She stumbled, her head woozy as she took in the spindle. Her heart was loud in her chest. The colours too bright.

Run.

Eve swore. 'Oh, for cauldron's sake. Not again.'

And she fell to the floor.

They didn't have the luxury of days. They only had now.

Hansel had drawn the layout of the grounds to the best of his ability. He knew how to handle an axe, after all, not the smooth lines of ink to page. But it had sufficed.

He'd talked through the rotations of guards, the locations of standing points, specific enchantments on certain areas and explained – roughly – where the dungeons would be located. The question now was, even if they could save Rumpelstiltskin, how were they to find the spindle? Hansel had a hunch on where it would be, but with the size of the castle, it was, again, another long shot.

Cyrene was unavoidably excluded from the plans, to her dismay. She cursed at them for leaving her to wait. Piccadilly had to intervene, explaining that, with her blood and injuries, she would most likely need to head south back to her own kingdom of Nysa. If the Evil Queen was planning domination, then the Queen of Nysa needed to be warned. As a neighbouring kingdom, they, too, were at risk.

She'd grumbled, but eventually agreed.

Doc would remain with his patients, waiting for Bryn to return with what they needed for Rabbit's recovery. And Zacariah was left to mourn his niece.

After long discussions, the dwarves would be there should the rebellion go to war. Piccadilly had been relieved to no end, but it came with conditions: Zacariah had agreed that, if it was an army she needed, then the mines should be their next target. It had been an ongoing argument for them.

Piccadilly stated that the current loss of people did not outweigh the overwhelming risk such a mission would be. But Zacariah had convinced her, his gruff nature turning her thoughts to what if they did succeed. There were hundreds upon hundreds of creatures down there, a lot of them trained and motivated. She hadn't liked it, but she'd agreed, whispering to Hansel that it was a future problem to solve.

That left Hansel, Flynn, Porchid, Bjorn, and Piccadilly for the prison break. Theoretically speaking, if they did have an army and enough magic at their side, Hansel would have better planned a siege, but as the realm would have it, he'd be planning for a small, quiet team. It had its benefits, but it still posed the problem of being outnumbered against a fortress protected by magic.

If they were caught, they were dead. This was Myrenna's place of power, the heart of her kingdom, and they were going to sneak into it like cockroaches and steal from her.

It had been his home once; Snow's and Malak's, too. How very different it was now, almost like a lost shadow of himself, standing upon the tall hill of the city, watching them from above.

Piccadilly's dark eyes roamed Hansel's map again, learning the layout and taking down her own notes. She asked questions about certain tunnels, clarified with him on occasional logistics, and, after it all, she did it again. She was thorough, to say the least, and Hansel respected it. Piccadilly was a warrior, a fighter, a leader. If it did come to war, Hansel was happy to be on the same side as her.

That's how, a few hours later, he found himself and the others following her through the lower levels of the Sanctuary. She'd taken them deep underground. The stairs and walls narrowed the further they went. When they'd finally reached the lowest floor, he'd had to inch through sideways to fit his shoulders.

'Were these made for children?' he complained, ducking again under the low-hanging entryway.

Piccadilly laughed. 'The doorways are old, built for a time where people didn't grow as large. Someone your size would have been accused of having giant's blood.'

The corridor had been filled with alcoves, the ceiling low against the damp stone walls. Piccadilly lit several candles, illuminating the space. Built into the walls were cages made of iron – thick, flat lines crossing over one another like a chess board. She revealed a set of keys as they veered right through a small hallway, stopping halfway.

'I've been saving this for when the war came,' Piccadilly said, eyeing Flynn in the darkness. 'Very few know this exists, and I'd like to keep it that way.'

Hansel could feel Flynn's unease as Piccadilly used the ring of keys to work the hidden locks.

'The contents were not easy to obtain,' said Flynn. 'If we use it all, we have no way of getting more.'

'What is it?' asked Bjorn.

'You'll see in a moment,' Piccadilly said, opening the gate wide.

Porchid zipped past Hansel's ear, her light shining on several shelves. The door led into another dark hallway, with a curved roof higher and walls wider than the ones they'd just walked through.

Piccadilly lowered her candle to an inlet. The fire caught a line in the wall and flared up lighting the whole room.

'I guess I stand mistaken,' Bjorn said, following the hallway as he smiled in glee. 'We are not without hope.'

Rows upon rows of weapons flickered in the firelight and Hansel's breath caught in his chest. He hadn't seen a collection like this since the armoury at the training camp. Long swords, short swords, cannons, bows, armour, crossbows, maces, spears, and everything in between.

Hansel reached out for a cannonball and stroked its hard, cold surface. 'How?' he breathed.

Flynn was the one to answer. 'You wanted to know what I did for the rebellion? What I still do? Well, this is what I do, *huntsman*.' His eyes flickered an olive green in the firelight. 'I do it in the dark; unseen and unknown. And I've spilt a lot of blood to obtain it. So, if you even breathe a word of this to anyone. I'll have you killed so fast you'll never even know it happened.'

Hansel's hand halted at the threat, but he merely smiled at the soldier. He didn't like Flynn, but he did admit he was impressed. He now understood why Flynn sat near the head of the table, why Piccadilly trusted him and let him in on every movement of the rebellion. He may, after all, be the person to have saved them.

'Understood,' Hansel replied, trying to contain his smile.

'How far does this go?' Bjorn called from up ahead.

'You better go help him,' Piccadilly whispered to Flynn. 'He might blow himself up without supervision.'

Flynn's eyes widened, leaving the three of them near the crossbows as he jogged away. Porchid fluttered across the shelf, eyeing the weapons like new toys. She reached out towards a crossbow latch, and Hansel yelled before grabbing her, accidentally squashing her wings as he pulled her away.

'I wouldn't do that,' he warned. 'It'll shoot you straight into that wall and squash you like a bug.'

Porchid only tapped his nose and giggled in response.

'I want to show you something,' Piccadilly said, calling Hansel forward.

Hansel eyed the shelves as he followed her, pausing briefly at a shelf with bowls of powder. He frowned. 'Is this what I think it is?'

'It's stardust,' she replied.

He dipped his fingers in one of the bowls, the fine powder coating his finger and thumb as he rubbed it together. 'You realise you have these sitting in the open and use fire to light up this place? Are you insane? You could blow up the Sanctuary and a big chunk of the city cauldron high.'

'Over there we have jars and vials. We'd started trying to protect it from the elements, but between Flynn and I only knowing about this, it proved difficult to get it all done with everything else going on.'

He shook his head in horror at the thought.

'How did you get this?' he asked. 'Even in the guard it was hard to obtain. Most of the stock goes to the mines.'

Piccadilly laughed. 'This *is* the stock for the mines.'

His eyebrows rose. 'I now understand why they kept demanding so much. Considering they weren't getting any, I'm surprised they haven't rioted.'

'Come on,' she said, smiling. 'I still haven't shown you what I wanted you to see.'

Leaving the powder behind, he followed her further down, the echoing voices of Bjorn and Flynn still far down the corridor. Flynn looked exasperated as Bjorn carried a pile of weapons in glee.

'Here,' she said, stopping in front of a large wall.

Hansel laughed. On the wall, an array of battle axes of all shapes and sizes curved around each other like a piece of art. His hand twitched to reach out; each axe was more beautiful than the one before it. He smiled at Piccadilly, his fingers twitching to hold the familiar weapon in his hands again.

'I'll leave you two alone,' Piccadilly joked, and wandered towards Flynn and Bjorn.

Hansel stroked the handle of a large, cerulean, metal axe, hanging high over some smaller throwing ones. He held it firmly in his grasp. It was heavier than what he was used to.

'She's a beauty,' he said to Porchid.

The fairy looked at it, unimpressed.

'It's not the right one though, is it?'

She shook her head.

Whilst the axes were lovely, crafted for killing, they were nothing compared to the one he'd found in the market that day, the one with the red leather and the engraving on the handle.

After three or four, he found a plainly decorated one with unblemished steel, the blade's edge rinsed in black.

The metal was cool, but it was light, easily manipulated, and balanced.

The others made their way over. Bjorn was carrying a mace, a sword, and a hammer.

'You going to be okay with all that?' Hansel asked.

The dwarf shot him a sour look. 'I'll be just fine, thank you.'

'He's just upset he couldn't carry the whole armoury,' Flynn scoffed.

'Does everyone have what they need?' Piccadilly asked.

Hansel gripped his new axe and eyed the stardust ahead. He turned to her and nodded with the others.

'Good,' she replied. 'Because we do this tonight.'

Eve floated through nothing and everything at once. She shielded her eyes against the vivid colours and blinding light, then hit a hard surface. Rocks dug into her arms, the breath knocked out of her. She looked up and gasped.

Eve scrambled back, halting when she hit the sharp edges of brush. Before her, four cloaked figures stood over a boiling cauldron. Their chanting was a thrum, a chorus of odd music.

She sat frozen, half expecting them to see her, when one of the figures went silent. With a heavy sigh, they removed the hood of their cloak, revealing a woman.

It was Nona. And it wasn't.

She was younger, her hair long and honeyed blonde. Her lips were pink, and her cheeks full. Mid-thirties, maybe. But it wasn't the hair, or mouth, or youthful features of the woman before her that gave her away.

It was her eyes.

The familiar smoky grey that had watched her as a girl, who had seen her future. Eyes that had seen many fates and that now pierced through Eve. Nona frowned at her.

'What are you doing, Nona?' one of the cloaked figures on her left hissed. 'We're almost there.'

Nona broke her stare, her concentration returning to the cauldron as she lifted her hands above its swirling black smoke.

Eve watched from the ground, her heart beating like a million drums. She tasted magic, something akin to ash and stale meat. The leaves beside her shifted, the forest closing in with the magic's weight and the Grimms' chanting voices.

The cauldron boiled and broiled, shaking with the earth. Its *pops* and *crackles* breaking the silence as one of the women reached into the cauldron's belly and pulled from it a mirror of gold.

One by one, the other Grimms did the same. Each mirror unique, yet no less powerful.

Nona's eyes locked onto Eve, twinkling in curiosity, but she did not say a word, did not give Eve away as her sister pulled out a mirror of onyx. The third a mirror of bone and, lastly, as Nona drew her gaze away, a mirror of silver.

The cauldron shook, and Eve felt her body warp, pulled along by a phantom wind as she was sucked through a storm of moments in time. Her head spun. She landed by the sea, the sunset dropping low over the horizon. A young

Nona waited on the sand, her cloak billowing in the wind. The waves crashed in front of her.

Eve's hair whipped her face, and the sand dug into her knees. Nona nodded as the Queen of Nysa and the King of Teal Cove broke through the ocean's waves. Neither were the royalty Eve recognised from today, but upon their brows remained the crowns of each kingdom – one etched in sea glass, the other in pearl.

Removing her cloak, Nona looked back at Eve once, then faced her companions.

Eve couldn't hear them, could only watch from the rocks as Nona handed the sea nymph and mermaid a small mirror of black glass, then watched as the royals disappeared behind the waves.

The beach melted. Eve was yanked again into whirling colour. She reached out to grasp onto something but failed. It twisted around her.

This time, when she fell, she was in a cell, the wet stone seeping into her skin through her loose shirt. Inside was a younger girl in a plain brown dress, just like her features. Tears streaked down her cheeks, cutting through dirt and grime.

She looked familiar, though Eve didn't know from where.

The girl knelt as if in prayer, her dark hair wild and loose around her shoulders. A needle dripped with blood in her hand, and a hunched figure with cruel eyes leaned over her. The figure hissed at the young girl, its nails digging into the girl's shoulders, drawing blood. But the girl said something that made the witch halt, her old eyes intrigued.

The scene changed to a forest, the girl's hands dripping in blood as she handed the crone a chest. Eve couldn't see what was inside, couldn't move or breathe as the Grimm twisted her lips into a cruel smile. From the depths of her cloak, she produced a gilded mirror and handed it to the girl.

This time, when Eve was torn away, she landed in a field of half-dead grass. It ran red and black, bodies strewn across the ground. Another cloaked figure raised its arms and lightning shot down from the sky. Eve crawled towards a corpse as the terrain shook, taking cover.

A chasm sliced through the battlefield like a jagged wound. Eve gagged at the smell of burnt flesh and death as the witch stood at the chasm's edge. From her cloak she pulled out a bone, spikes of glass spearing from it like blades of thorns. The figure turned, smoky grey eyes twinkling, before she threw the bone into the chasm's depths.

Bile filled Eve's throat as she was thrown again, landing hard on stone. She spluttered and puked, her limbs shaking. Then she heaved in a breath. She wasn't sure how much she could take, how much more her body could flip inside out before she broke.

Eve turned to find the cloaked figure hovering over a small babe in a cot. Hung on the far wall was the silver mirror Eve had already destroyed.

The baby cooed, her golden curls and porcelain skin smooth against the gnarled fingers that held her. Shadows crawled along the floor, grazing the mirror and the babe.

Eve choked out a sob as she was hauled back through space and time, plummeting and floating and falling again. She whirled past visions of the Princess Snow, her eyes pitch black, her hands sharpening into claws. She floated past a slumbering baby dragon, hidden deep within the mountains. She flew through the clouds next to a large, scarred crow. Past a campfire with a dozen trolls and a beaten pixie. Past an old dwarf dying in a dark cell. And a castle shrouded in thorns.

She blinked as one vision morphed into another. Her stomach roiled; her head pounding with each fracture in time, each memory and dream and scene until, finally, Eve landed once again in front of the onyx cauldron.

Breathing heavily, Eve met Nona's familiar eyes. The woman showed no surprise, only curiosity. Slowly, she leaned down. 'I knew you would come, as you have come for every moment before.'

Eve was dizzy. Her stomach churned and her heart clenched. Nona was familiar and unfamiliar all at once.

Nona clasped Eve's hand, pricking the top of her finger in the same place as the spindle had. Eve flinched, though the pain barely registered.

The young witch dropped Eve's arm, revealed a small blue stone, and dropped it into the cauldron. The stone in Eve's pocket thrummed, her hand twitching to reach for it.

Nona dropped Eve's blood into the cauldron. 'Pray the Fairy Godmother forgives me and that the stars guide me.'

Eve shuddered as the sticky feeling of powerful magic coated her skin. It was as if she was too big for her body. As if she'd been squeezed into a box too tight.

'This is what you will need,' Nona said, though Eve wasn't sure if she was speaking to her or the cauldron, 'what you must use, to unite them. The only magic that will make them mortal again – *us* mortal. We must act in haste. They will be back shortly.'

Nona's gaze trailed over Eve's pocket, as if she too sensed the beating heart of the stone.

'Mirrors four, of black and bone, of silver and gold, and night blue stone. At the dawn of light with powers three, a soul will tear, and hearts will see.'

Eve's eyes widened as Nona repeated the words that had put her on this path. The same words that had set the course for her entire life, driven her to this very moment.

But instead of running from it, Eve let it build in her. Old, living magic flared to life, and without meaning to, without a thought, Eve began to chant with her.

'A gift for giving at the aftermath, or a land in ruin of pain and wrath. When one will stray, another shall gain, and in blood and loss they will be slain.

'When betrayal and love finally mix, hearts will shatter as seven become six. Wood from a tree that's existed an age, and mirrors of glass in a watery cage.

'The theft of a gem and its keeper's revenge. An obsidian cauldron and the price to avenge. Shadows of memory, death will reap, but an act of love will wake her from sleep.'

Again, they repeated it. Their voices entwining like the summer wind calling through the trees.

Nona smiled as the cauldron sputtered fog in sapphire and coal and crimson.

Again, they repeated the prophecy as the cauldron and the stone thrummed as one.

Again, as the stars came out and the smoke swirled.

They repeated it until the cauldron shattered. Taking Eve with it.

XXVII

The Tinker Torturer

'This was a terrible idea,' Flynn murmured towards Hansel under his breath.

Hansel tensed his shoulders against the tight uniform, arms aching as both men dragged a chained Piccadilly through the streets of the Silver City.

'You're still on a wanted poster, if you haven't forgotten,' Flynn whispered. 'If we're caught it's all for nothing.'

Hansel held firm, grasping his hands around Piccadilly's arms as she hunched. Despite her tough demeanour, he still remembered the crunch as he hit her jaw and she fell with a thump to the floor. She now dragged her feet, wincing every now and then.

She played her role well.

Flynn sighed. 'We're all dead. Maybe we should just accept it now.'

'With that attitude, we are,' Piccadilly huffed under her breath.

They followed the long winding path up the hill towards the castle's main entry gates. The sun paused above the mountains in the distance, casting an orange glow across the city. The castle grew larger as they neared, each step bringing them closer to their doom.

Bjorn and Porchid had taken the hidden path Hansel had drawn out for them. If all went to plan, Flynn and Hansel would be within the dungeon with their 'prisoner' in tow, and Bjorn and Porchid would use the tunnels to locate the spindle.

Piccadilly winced again as Hansel dragged her forward towards the gates. He, too, had a part to play.

'What is this?' asked the main guard stationed at the gate.

Hansel lifted Piccadilly with a sneer. 'We have something her Majesty has been seeking for a long time.'

The guard looked hesitant, his roving gaze lingering over the two of them before stopping harshly on Piccadilly. 'The prisoners from the raids have been rounded up in the square. Why isn't she lined up for hanging? The Queen's crow said nobody is to come through.'

'She's too important for the square,' Hansel said in a low voice.

The guard swallowed, his eyes peering towards the city. 'The Queen is currently occupied. She has no need for a changeling.'

'Not just a changeling,' replied Flynn. 'The Commander.'

The guard's eyes widened before narrowing in suspicion. 'That cannot be true,' he said. 'Does her majesty know?'

'Her majesty will know as soon as you let us through those gates,' Hansel retorted, yanking her forward. 'Look at her. She is everywhere and nowhere. How many of your men have seen her?'

The lieutenant frowned, uncertainty gaining the upper hand as he swallowed. 'I've had reports,' he agreed. 'A silver ghost with twin blades.'

Hansel smirked and dropped Piccadilly's arm. The guard eyed his uniform before standing with a salute.

'Do not waste my time, Lieutenant,' Hansel said darkly. 'Or will you be the one to advise the Queen that you had the Commander at your fingertips?'

His eyes locked with Hansel. 'No, Sir.'

'Tell your men to open the gates,' Hansel ordered, picking up Piccadilly's elbow again. She curled in on herself as Hansel barked at her to get up. The guard waved to his companions and gave them an order. In seconds, the grinding gears of the gates began to move, raising it upwards.

Hansel nodded at the soldier who stood to the side and let them through.

'Mack will guide you to the prison,' said the lieutenant.

'I know my way,' replied Hansel.

'As that may be, Sir,' he replied, 'it's protocol.'

With a curt nod, the guard left them.

Mack was a young boy, lean and lanky, not yet grown into his skin like most teenagers. 'This way, please.'

Hansel met Flynn's eyes, both of them already regretting what they had to do next. Cutting across the square, they followed the young boy towards the dungeons.

Why was it that, whenever Bjorn went out in this city, he always ended up in literal faeces?

Porchid grimaced as she clutched his hair to the point of pain, pulling hard whenever the smell overwhelmed her.

'Stop it,' he snapped. Her light flickered crimson, but she released her hold, easing the strain on his neck. Bjorn grumbled under his breath as he lifted Hansel's map towards her light. 'The entrance should be somewhere on our left.'

Porchid flew forward, her light scattering the rats, to illuminate the wall. According to Hansel's drawing, there should be a tunnel, but Bjorn could only see solid stone. He heaved himself onto the ledge trailing the side of the brown sludge, his blade scraping across the stone.

Porchid zipped back and forth, assessing the gritty wall. Bjorn studied the stone's edges. The castle was known for its undisclosed tunnels, the way it hid more secrets than rooms. Theoretically, if Bjorn and Porchid could gain access from this entrance, it would place them near the throne room and the Queen's quarters.

Bjorn tapped his foot. The wall glared back.

There was a plan B if they couldn't access the tunnel. And if Piccadilly had her way, there would have been a plan C, D, and E. The only problem was that plan B lay directly on the other side of the castle and, with the urgency of the mission, Bjorn didn't have the time or, frankly, the patience to go the other way.

The castle is well protected, but there are tunnels underneath we can use to gain access, Hansel had said. *Each entrance is different from the last. Some open with a latch, some with a spell, and others with a kiss.*

Bjorn had faltered at that, and Hansel had laughed. *When Snow and I lived in the castle, we made a game of it. Each door opens to a different command or action. The trick is to figure out the key.*

Following the huntsman's advice, Bjorn investigated the left wall, leaving Porchid the section to the right. He slid his fingers across the indents of the stone. Maybe if he could find a latch or a handle, they could open this hidden door.

Porchid twinkled, calling him over, her light shining bright against the grey stone. She brushed her tiny hand against a rock lower down the wall, almost at the ground. Bjorn leaned down, his nose stinging with the scent of excrement. He refused to open his mouth for fear of tasting it.

Engraved into the rock was a symbol of a droplet.

'Water?' he asked. 'Or blood?'

Porchid wrinkled her nose at the suggestion of blood.

Bjorn sighed. 'Let's hope water.'

He took out his container of water, careful as he dribbled it onto the stone. Nothing happened.

'Of course, it's blood,' Bjorn gruffed. 'It's never a flower, or a good brew, or a nice meal.'

As he yanked free his knife Porchid whizzed back so fast that he was drowned in darkness.

He scowled at her. 'Not your blood, you ninny. Now, come back here so I can see what I'm doing.'

Porchid inched closer and peered at him as he calmly sliced the tip of his finger, placing it onto the droplet mark.

One heartbeat. Two.

Nothing.

Of course, it wasn't that easy – it never was. Bjorn smacked his fist against the stone, and his hand throbbed.

Porchid's light dimmed to a pale white at his outburst. Her twinkle of disapproval gnawed at his bones. She flew towards the engraving, back facing him, and traced the drop etched in stone.

Bjorn slumped down on the ledge, resigned, and glared hopelessly at the unmoving, unfaltering walls. They'd been here a thousand years, and after he was gone, they would stand for a thousand more. It reminded him of Parador, the ancient archways and diamond-encrusted halls. Where the forges blew fire and music had played before turning to cold tunnels and whispering wraiths.

Parador was its own kind of graveyard now, silent and lonely.

How had everything gone so out of control?

Bjorn had always held the Seven together, had always prioritised their wellbeing. Recently, though, it felt like they were falling apart.

His heart ached at the memories of the grotto and laughing around the fire. Bonyx's tales of ghosts and magic and heroes. Rabbit's cooking as he smacked his lips then ran around the forest to find the hidden ingredient. He missed the grumbles of Brufell, and the sound of Bronson's voice as he sang along to Beetle's violin. He missed Bryn's constant fidgeting, the way he built something from nothing and created works of art.

Bjorn was no stranger to war or to heartache. But once had been enough. As much as he boasted, he loved them. His family.

His eyes burned. Porchid flit closer and reached out, her eyes watering with him.

'It's the smell,' he grunted.

But Porchid called fairyshit. Her smile was understanding as she nestled in his beard.

Bjorn closed his eyes for a moment to grieve. He didn't open them until the soft touch of the fairy's fingers laced his cheek. Blinking, Bjorn looked down to find Porchid clutching a tear, her dark eyes wide. Bjorn watched in fascination as she glided to the engraving, carefully placing the tear upon the drop made in stone.

Something inside the wall clicked, a hiss of air escaping as a doorway opened.

Bjorn let out a laugh. 'I take it back, Porchid. You're not a ninny. You're a genius.'

Porchid glowed brightly as though saying, *I know.*

Hansel's palms were sweaty as the young boy led the three of them through the back entrances of the castle. Piccadilly's feet dragged across the marbled floor as both men carried her. Flynn met Hansel's worried gaze as they veered down cramped hallways, descending a tight staircase into darkness.

Eventually, the boy stopped at a round door at the bottom and knocked thrice.

The hairs on the back of Hansel's neck stood as he assessed the corridor, recognition flickering.

'What's wrong?' Piccadilly whispered. 'Is this not the dungeon?'

They had a taken a different route, but Hansel knew the castle well enough to know they were in the east wing. The dungeons were in the west wing.

Hansel's jaw stiffened as he assessed the stairs, figuring out if they could run.

'We need to act now,' Hansel warned under his breath.

Flynn frowned. 'It's too early.'

The young boy's foot tapped impatiently as he knocked again. Hansel held his breath. Movement echoed from the other side, locks unclicking one by one as the occupant went to open the door.

Hansel dropped Piccadilly's arm and stepped towards the boy, releasing his axe in one swift motion. The boy didn't even turn as the door swung wide, leaving Hansel stunned.

Dark, conniving eyes narrowed on the visitors: the Tinker, dressed in his purple finery. 'I know you,' he said.

Hansel swung his axe.

XXVIII
The Bottle of Stardust

Eve vomited onto the wooden floor of the cottage as the spindle spat her out. She heaved in breaths as her eyes refocused on the familiar room. The sky through the window was dark, the once picturesque fields now a beach, the waves lapping in a swirling riot.

She wiped the sweat from her brow and stared up at the tapestry. She had dream walked. This was what Rumple's power contained, what he lived and thrived in.

It terrified her.

When she'd met him that day near Roserock to return his spindle, she'd had no inkling of the power the object held. He'd whispered to it soothingly as if it was alive, as if they shared spirits. And now she understood why.

Nona had died for this. Sacrificed the trust of her sisters and had run for this. For this stone, for Eve, for the mirrors.

Eve didn't know how much time had passed while she'd been in the dreamscape, how much time she had lost while discovering Nona's secrets. She scrambled to her feet, and began gathering her belongings, planning.

She had to destroy the mirrors.

The fireplace burned low, but there, neatly patched up and clean, were her leathers and the teal tunic from Gabby. She frowned as she picked them up, the cloth soft and stain-free. She whirled around at the sound of bright giggling drifting down from the rafters.

Another *thump* and her boots were by the door, cleaned and repaired.

Eve still wasn't used to the magic in this cottage. With a small, 'Thank you,' Eve changed back into her leathers and packed her potions, food and water. She tucked her map in her corset, opened the cottage door, and stepped out into the cool air.

She knew this place.

Eve knew it from the dream of a woman in a cloak and two royals leaving the tides.

She was on the edge of the kingdom of Nysa. The kingdom of the sea nymphs and the merpeople.

'Mirrors four, of black and bone, of silver and gold, and night blue stone,' Eve whispered to herself.

The cottage sat on a cliff, overlooking the sea, and Eve made her way down with care. When her boots sunk into the cold sand, she stared at the horizon where black islands lay scattered in the distance.

The waves lapped over one another as if warning her to stay away. The sea nymphs were not kind people, but they were her only hope. Eve stepped towards the water and let it coat her boots. The cold seeped into her bones as she moved in deeper.

She took a breath and whispered Nona's words.

A prophecy, a story, a promise.

'… mirrors of glass in a watery cage.'

Then she dived.

Bjorn raced down the twists and turns of the tunnels deep beneath the castle, Porchid by his side. He muttered Hansel's instructions quietly: left at the chalk star, a turn at the arrow, and a right when he'd reached the cross.

Bjorn wondered what it had been like for the huntsman to play house with the Queen, sneaking around with the Princess, all while killing those who fought for the same cause he did. Did it make him wonder if he'd made the right choice?

Hansel was a great warrior, Bjorn knew that, but the boy's affinity for the three women would destroy him when this was all over.

The Queen. Snow. Eveline. None like the other, but still the same.

Porchid became Bjorn's eyes, her glow leading the way. He would have never guessed a tear, had never even thought about it. Not until the little fairy in front of him had taken charge.

Porchid waved, urging him towards a grate. Careful to not let any sound give them away, Bjorn peered through the gaps to find a hallway.

Bjorn heard voices. There was a grunt, and the shuffle of feet. Bjorn's eyes widened when he saw Hansel and Piccadilly being dragged through the halls of the castle by a short man in purple robes. His nose was crooked, his skin almost translucent. His cloak trailed along the floor, too long for his body.

His eyes made Bjorn pause; they were so black they reminded him of pits, his sneer almost kind in comparison. And in his hand was a small wooden spindle.

Piccadilly and Hansel were bound by a leather strap, gagging Hansel tight enough to leave a mark. His uniform was smeared in blood, and his hair was mussed. Piccadilly's face was a bloodied mess. Bjorn leaned forward, but he couldn't spot Flynn.

Porchid's light changed colour with her worry. Bjorn's mind raced. At least the spindle was in sight, which meant Rumple must be near also. He needed to save his friends and get the spindle, find Rumple, and get out of the castle before they were spotted, or worse – captured.

Piece of cake.

Bjorn took a healthy gulp of whisky from his flask, then offered some to Porchid.

She scrunched up her nose.

'Suit yourself.' he replied, tucking it away and reaching for his sword.

Bjorn rolled his shoulders and peered through the grate again. This was either fortuitous, or a trap. Either way, Bjorn couldn't let them die.

'Follow them,' Bjorn whispered to the fairy.

Hansel's axe never hit the target. He'd swung, diving for the boy, only for his fingers to slide through him like a ghost.

The Tinker's laugh pierced his ears, and he lifted the spindle. Green magic poured from it, hitting Hansel like a hammer. He was thrown to the ground, his shoulder screaming on impact.

His eyes were droopy, lulled into a dreamlike state. He remembered being shoved to his feet, hands bound, walking sloppily when he could barely stay upright. He remembered muffled voices, one heavy and commanding, another slick and cold.

Hansel had barely opened his eyes when they crossed the threshold of the throne room. His knees hit the familiar tiled floor, his vision focusing in and out like a drunken blur.

The Tinker yanked Hansel's head back and the gilded mirror shimmered, a face of shadows filling its frame.

'Mirror, mirror, on the wall. For the Queen, shall I kill them all?'

A silky voice filled the hall. *'In the Queen's absence, lock them underground. Their lives have more value to be found.'*

The Tinker's pitted eyes bulged. 'Why do I even bother? Should we not kill them? The Queen would wish them dead. A problem gone.'

The mirror watched him calmly, smoke coating its edges. *'Do you assume to know what the Queen would wish? Have you the arrogance, when you're an insect she could squish?'*

The Tinker jolted back, pulling at Hansel's skull. 'When will she return?'

The mirror smiled, though it was cold. *'The Queen will return when she is ready. When the darkness has consumed her, and she is once again steady.'*

The Tinker snarled and, with his free hand, waved the guards forward. Hansel was lifted, his feet stumbling across the floor as he was dragged.

Piccadilly winced nearby, her body shaking. She was bloody, her hair tangled, and her clothes half torn. What had they done to her?

Hansel struggled, but failed, against the guards tugging him through hallways and doors. He was groggy, but his nose was clear, the ripe smell of stale air wrapping around his senses. It smelt of mould and urine, of blood and stone.

The dungeons.

It was silent here except for the shuffling of feet. A door creaked open, and he was shoved into a dark room. He stumbled, falling, the pain in shoulder from earlier rippling down his side. The iron slammed behind him, sealing him into the dark.

Blood seeped from his nose, wet and hot. He shouted, but it rang weak even to his own ears. Hansel crawled to the bars of his cage, the Tinker stroking the spindle. Hansel glared at the creature, a threat in his eyes. But the Tinker only grinned.

Bonyx halted at the grinding sound of the locks. The soldiers' footfalls drowned out the silence of the dripping water. He opened his eyes to find fairylight, and shadows pulling along prisoners.

Chains clattered with a harsh, rhythmic clang, and a groan punctuated the dark. It had been so long since somebody new had been brought in. Would his new neighbours be forthcoming? Or were they already as broken as the other one?

He shuffled towards the door and tried to speak but it came out as a dry rasp. He needed water. Needed to stay alive. To hold onto life. But he could feel it dripping out of him like a broken tap. Just like the one he heard down the hall. Each time it dripped, he sensed a little of himself leaving with it. Like a call.

Bonyx reached out to hail the guards, but he only heard rage as a prisoner screamed out a warning of death.

The tunnel ran into an intersection that Bjorn was unfamiliar with. One path was marked with a rectangle,

while the other was indicated by a line over a moon —
symbols he didn't recognise, leaving him torn between
which direction to choose.

He'd followed as far as the doors, Porchid zooming
ahead in haste and coming back to urge him forward. She
moved faster than him, and more silently.

If Bjorn was aiming for the dungeons, down was the
logical way, but something called to him. He pointed to
the right path and told Porchid to follow the left. He didn't
want to separate if he didn't need to, but his gut had saved
his life in battle. He'd learnt to trust it.

Porchid grabbed his cheek and gave him a quick kiss
before she flew away.

'Stay safe, my friend,' he whispered after her.

Bjorn followed the stairs upwards. The hallway began to
curve, the walls slowly shrinking as he took careful steps.
Ahead, light protruded through a tiny hole cut into a
wooden surface. Bjorn propped his hands against the wall
and peeked through.

On the other side was a room draped in red velvet, with
cushions of gold. The lush carpet had patterns of stars
leading towards a vanity mirror piled with jewellery. Small
tables were placed between chairs and lounges, and there
was a portable bar by the wall. A breeze lifted a set of dark
curtains open, exposing a room beyond with black and
white chequered tiles.

The throne room.

Moving quickly, Bjorn followed the hallway further
along, finding another hole in the wall where he glimpsed
the throne room. The worn, chequered tiles clashed with
the golden throne, shining against the dusk as the sun set.
His eyes fell onto the rug at the edge of the dais, stained in

black, and he shuddered. How many had been slain in that very spot? How many had experienced their life trickle out of them as they faced the Evil Queen?

His eyes roamed to the stairs where he spotted the spindle, its thin frame locked in the spindly fingers of the Tinker. The withered creature muttered to himself, alone.

Bjorn held tightly to his sword. He turned away and braced himself against the wall. This was his opportunity, his only chance to get the spindle. Perhaps this was his destiny: to face the very thing that fed Myrenna's black heart. If he couldn't have the Queen, he would certainly take one of her closest allies.

He swallowed his fear and followed the wall back towards the room with the cushions. His fingers trailed along the indents, seeking another symbol or button, when they landed firmly on a latch. With a click, the doorway opened behind an old portrait.

Bjorn made his way across the rug and took a deep breath. He kept himself steady and opened the curtains on the other side of the room.

The Tinker placed the spindle on the carpet beside him as Bjorn took another step. The open air made him feel vulnerable. He stood on the podium overlooking the hall.

Bjorn's heart thrummed. He would do this for the Princess. For the Seven. For Rabbit.

As Bjorn lifted his sword, his eyes flicked to the spindle close by.

'Not all heroes stand tall; sometimes they are small.'

Bjorn whirled around to find the mirror grinning. He hadn't seen it on his way in.

'How did you get in here?' the Tinker shouted as Bjorn twisted around and eyed the forgotten spindle.

The Tinker saw it, his eyes widening. Then they both dived for the small, wooden trinket.

XXIX
The Fairies in Shadow

Piccadilly's eyes adjusted to the dark better than humans' did. The fog of the spell had worn off, but her eye still stung from the wounds to her face. She sat on the floor of the cell and rubbed her temples. This was exactly what she needed: the head of the rebellion rotting in the same dungeons as the Dream Weaver. So much for her backup plans.

She called out, 'Hello?'

The drip of a nearby tap echoed.

Across from her came a croaked voice, dry and soft. 'Are you another dream?'

Piccadilly crawled towards the iron bars and peered into the darkness. 'I'm real.' When they didn't reply, she licked her lips, her head throbbing from pain. 'I'm looking for a friend.'

A pause. 'There are no friends here. Only shadows.'

She swallowed. Of course, she'd been locked up with the crazies. 'Are you Rumpelstiltskin?'

'I'm only a storyteller. I'm not who you seek.'

She slumped against the bars, letting the cold metal seep into her bones. She tried to peer through the bars towards the dark corridors when a floating light pierced the darkness. It moved like a small orb, darting from one cell to another.

'Porchid?' Piccadilly asked.

Despite it having been a whisper, the orb zoomed towards her. Piccadilly flinched back as the light blazed her cell, and Porchid flung herself into the changeling's chest.

'It's so good to see you,' Piccadilly choked. 'Where's Bjorn? They've taken Hansel.'

The fairy twinkled and Piccadilly interpreted as best she could.

Bjorn had followed the spindle, and Porchid had followed them.

Piccadilly nodded. 'Hansel is here, too. There's a man across the way, but he's not the Dream Weaver. Can you get us out?'

The fairy bit her bottom lip. She flew towards the cell doors, showing the cell held no lock.

Piccadilly stood at the bars, her voice carrying as she called out again. 'How do the doors unlock? How do we get out?'

Porchid moved closer to her, wary of the stranger as he choked out a dry laugh. 'Only two can open them, and you do not wish for them to come.'

'Who?' she urged.

Silence.

'We can get you out,' Piccadilly pressed, desperate. 'We can set you free.'

Silence.

Piccadilly swallowed, unsure on where to go next.

'The Tinker or the Queen,' the prisoner replied. 'All they need to do is touch. But only them.'

It didn't leave her with much. The Queen was away, meaning the Tinker was their only option for a way out of here. Piccadilly turned to Porchid. 'I need you to do something. Be brave, Porchid.'

The fairy nodded, her light flashing, face determined.

'Find Hansel,' Piccadilly said. 'Then find Bjorn. If he is with the Tinker, then we need him, too.'

Porchid nodded, then flew from the cell, her light whizzing between the prisons and disappearing.

'Thank you,' Piccadilly said into the dark.

She received nothing but silence in return.

Bjorn's hands clasped around the spindle as the Tinker dived into him. Their bodies rolled across the floor, snatching at each other like wolves over a fresh carcass.

The Tinker howled as Bjorn smashed a fist into his face.

Despite the Tinker's thin frame, he was as strong as stone. His limbs were quick, and his nails sharp. They tumbled along the ground. Bjorn used his knee to push the creature away, scrambling back just in time to avoid the Tinker's next blow.

'Stupid little dwarf,' the Tinker growled. 'Thinking you can take what is not yours. I'll peel the skin from your bones and enjoy eating it.'

Bjorn grimaced. The Tinker's teeth were encrusted with blood, and his gums blackened from years of misuse.

Bjorn's fingers twitched at his sides, used to going for his sword or axe, but this time he had neither. A clink from Bjorn's pocket reminded him of the vials of stardust he'd taken from the Sanctuary.

The Tinker licked his lips. 'You'll make a good roast.'

Bjorn felt like he was in the pits again, fighting against an undefeated opponent. But without the raining coins, or the chants of a drunken crowd.

And without a weapon.

They moved like cats around one another. The Tinker's deep purple robe followed his footsteps smoothly behind him. His eyes darted from Bjorn to the spindle, and back again, burning with revulsion.

Bjorn considered his options. The dwarf had already used the element of surprise. His left boot held a small knife. If he could reach it in time or use it effectively, he may just win. One hand on the spindle, the other with a blade.

He'd dealt with worse odds.

The Tinker twitched, barely registering as Bjorn dived. The Tinker swerved, but stumbled as Bjorn grasped his velvet cape and pulled. With a choking sound, the Tinker dropped, and Bjorn grabbed his knife. There was a screech, and blood spattered along the tiles as Bjorn severed the Tinker's hand. The creature screamed, thrashing, and his boot collided with Bjorn's jaw.

Stars smeared Bjorn's vision as his elbows hit the cold floor and he rolled.

The Tinker hissed, clutching his knobby arm. 'I'll enjoy breaking you.'

The dwarf tried to stand, but the ground was slick. There was a growl to his left, and the Tinker broke into a run.

Bjorn winced as they collided, tumbling along the floor. The cold surface bit into Bjorn's skin and they scrambled, fists flying. The Tinker clawed at Bjorn's face, broken sharp nails raking down his cheek, and pain surged through Bjorn's leg as he rolled away. He panted, noticing the blood leaking through his pants.

The Tinker laughed again, clasping a knife.

Bjorn's knife.

This wasn't how he had envisioned his day. Nor how he had envisioned his death. Bjorn had battled beasts, had been in the great War of Thorns and fought for his people. He remembered Rabbit's sickly form, and Bryn's wary eyes as he'd said goodnight. Bjorn thought of the grotto, of the fairies that danced in colour, and of the great, wandering halls of Parador.

No. It was not his time to die. The Seven needed him. His kin needed him. The Princess needed him. And if he didn't protect his legacy, who would?

Bjorn backed away as the Tinker strode towards him, the thirst for death bright in his eyes. His leg throbbed, the gash deep and hot. The Tinker threw himself forward, swiping as Bjorn dodged left, barely avoiding the blade.

With some space between them, the Tinker laughed again and wiped his face, smearing blood across his cheek. 'Tired, little dwarf?'

Bjorn stood to face his enemy. 'I've fought foxes bigger than you.'

The Tinker licked the blood off his lips, turning his teeth a sharp red. 'Prove it.'

He thought of Porchid, waiting for him in the tunnels, and his friends down below.

Bjorn took his shot when the Tinker's gaze flickered towards the spindle on the floor. He skidded across the blood-soaked tiles, the world blurred. The Tinker looked up, surprise in his eyes, as Bjorn grabbed his legs and pulled.

The Tinker's skull cracked on the tiles, the knife clattering along the floor.

Bjorn dove onto the Tinker, grabbing for his throat.

The Tinker thrashed under him, eyes filled with panic. 'You. Will. Die,' the Tinker choked.

Now it was Bjorn's turn to laugh. The Tinker struggled underneath his weight, his burly body the wall of a fortress. The intimacy of this kind of murder was not lost on Bjorn. He'd always been more prone to using a weapon – a way to separate the kill. But with his hands on warm skin, it was personal, close. The realisation made his fingers twitch, loosening his grip.

The Tinker didn't hesitate.

Bjorn was flipped and the Tinker dived on top of him, pressing his hand into Bjorn's throat. Bjorn thrashed, his enemy heavier than expected. His eyes stung, and his chest heaved. The dark eyes of the Tinker glistened, a sick smile playing on his lips as he watched Bjorn struggle.

Bjorn smelt the blood on his breath as the Tinker gripped harder, pushed harder. 'You will not be my last kill,' the Tinker rasped, 'but you may become my favourite.'

Bjorn choked, gasping for air as he threw out his fists. He tried to swallow but the white-hot fire of the Godmother burned in his throat. He saw stars, and the Tinker's grin coming in and out of focus like the shadows from a candle's flame.

Bjorn saw nothing and everything. He saw Snow buried under crystal glass. Bronson laughing at Bryn as he cried over the onions. He saw the little ones – Rabbit and Beetle – running towards Bonyx in embrace. And finally, he saw Brufell, sitting by the fire with his pipe and weapons, his old, bushy eyebrows watching in amusement as the others played.

The Tinker pushed down, leaning into Bjorn's throat with voracity. Bjorn's energy etched away, his arms dropping as his consciousness began to slip. His eyes rolled back, saw the hazy shining light of the gilded mirror, and the spindle mere feet away.

So close.

With shaking arms, Bjorn reached for the spindle. His fingers grazed it. The pressure too much. He tried again, somehow pulling the spindle towards him. He clutched it tight, his throat constricting. In one last attempt, Bjorn turned it in his palm.

And lodged the spindle's sharpened point straight into the Tinker's eye.

Bjorn heaved in a breath as blood ran down the Tinker's skull.

'I …' the Tinker stammered, 'I can't see!'

Bjorn pulled forth one of the vials in his pocket and popped open the lid. 'But you can feel.'

Bjorn aimed for the dark velvet cape and hurled the vial.

The room exploded. Bjorn was thrown backwards. He held his arms in front of him but the heat from the blast still singed his body. The carpet erupted in flames, spreading throughout the throne room like wildfire.

The Tinker screamed, and clawed his face with his intact hand, his nails digging and scratching into his own skin.

Bjorn tore his eyes away and looked for an exit. He didn't have much time before the fire would consume the entirety of the room. He coughed into his elbow, clutching the spindle tightly as the air grew thick. Flames crawled up the walls, grasping at the tapestries and curtains greedily. Bjorn heaved another cough and ran towards the double doors. As he bolted down the corridor, servants and guards shouted orders, trying to contain the fire.

'Intruder!' someone called.

His leg throbbed and he swore as he veered around the corner into a corridor he didn't recognise. The guards were yelling behind him, hot on his trail.

'This would be a good time, Fairy Godmother,' Bjorn prayed as he limped past the portraits. His vision blurred, and he paused at an old tapestry with a garden and cauldron.

Hansel had mentioned this one.

'There's a dwarf in the castle!'

Footsteps rumbled down the hall just as Bjorn pushed himself behind the tapestry. 'Pickle juice,' he said under his breath. 'Or was it pineapple juice?'

Orders were called and swords drawn. The footsteps approached, growing louder.

'Pear juice?' Bjorn guessed desperately. 'Stupid saying. Stupid password. Stupid huntsman.'

Bjorn smacked his hand against the wall, desperation clawing under his skin. 'The password may as well be peanut juice.'

The door clicked open, and cool air rushed across his face. He breathed a sigh of relief as he threw himself inside and closed the door behind him.

Guards rushed past, screaming out as Bjorn peered through the eyehole beside the door. 'Peanut juice?' he whispered. 'Why peanut juice?'

Bright light blinded him as Porchid shot forward, her wet eyes glowing in the dark. She beat her fists on her chest, frantic and wild.

Bjorn had no time to catch up, to process. His legs wobbled under him, his wound still bleeding. He sagged as the fairy came close, and lowered himself to the ground, his leg a dead weight as he stretched it out.

He just needed a moment, a quick rest. But Porchid was beside herself.

'Did you find the others?' he asked, assessing his wound.

Porchid twinkled, her answers too fast for him to catch. He didn't understand, couldn't follow as she sprinted in the air. She eyed the corridors and turned back to him with thinned lips.

He shook his head, not following. 'Porchid, we don't have time for this. I've just stabbed the Tinker in the throne room and set it on fire. Not to mention I have a knife wound in my leg.'

Porchid glowed a burning crimson before she pointed to the floor. A command.

'Wait here?' Bjorn asked, more than a little confused.

He wasn't going to say no. He was tired, his body beaten and ravaged. With a resigned sigh, he agreed, and Porchid zoomed down the hallway, leaving him in the dark.

The Tinker was gone, but it wasn't over yet. Piccadilly and Hansel were still locked away. He checked his pocket and released a sigh. He had the spindle and three bottles of stardust left.

Three was his lucky number.

Porchid zoomed through the hidden tunnels, her breath ragged as she tried to remember the way. All the symbols blurred together. She had always known she was fickle, her moods and brain changing whenever her interest waned. It wasn't her best trait, but she accepted it.

The others were still locked away, hidden underneath the old stone of the castle. She was the only one able to save them now. She and her fitful little brain.

Porchid slowed as she reached a corner, pausing at the symbols scrawled on the brick. Had Hansel said the moon, or the bird?

She banged her fists against her skull, trying to remember, to *think.*

Guards' voices rang out, and she shot to the nearest wall, her heart thrumming so hard she thought it might leave her chest. She peered through the hole as a group of them ran past the gilded furniture. More shouts lined the hall, and she felt along the stone.

Her fear came back. She would be caught. They would all be caught.

And then her wings would be torn.

A shiver traced the skin down her spine. She tried to forget when she'd been caught by a fairy hunter, his jagged knife ready to cut. Tried to forget the net she was caught in, the sweat that had laced her skin. If it hadn't been for Eve, she wouldn't be alive, wouldn't be able to fly.

The fairy owed the Seeker more than she knew.

Porchid pushed herself forward and aimed for the moon symbol, following it towards the smell of smoke. Bjorn had smelt like smoke and blood. He'd mentioned setting a fire.

She wrinkled her nose and pushed the hair out of her face. She hated fire. The uncontrolled element had almost scarred her in the past.

But she had little time. She urged herself forward, pushing through a curtain and entering the throne room. Flames leaped up the walls, melting the paint and carpet. She choked as smoke filled the room, her eyes watering in the acrid air.

The Tinker lay in a heap on the ground, his robe in flames. She saw his charcoaled arm, his melted face. Bile crept up her throat at his burnt husk. But she had to be brave, had to help Hansel and Piccadilly.

Be brave, Porchid.

Swallowing back her fear, Porchid zipped around the body, her eyes trying to pierce through the haze when they landed on a hand lying by the dais.

Relief only lasted for a second as she reached it and smacked out a tiny flame from the withered skin. She coughed as she gripped the detached limb, her arms and wings burning as she pulled it across the floor. It was heavier than expected, the skin leathery and wrinkled. She choked on smoke as the doors flung open and guards stormed the room. One screamed for water.

With sweat-soaked skin, Porchid heaved the hand painfully up the dais steps and scrambled towards the wall. The hand was too heavy to fly with, so she'd have to drag it all the way back to the dwarf. She twinkled expletives as she entered the tunnels.

If Bjorn was a good dwarf, he'd take the hand from her.

Because it was already staining her dress.

Bjorn was carrying a severed hand.

He hadn't asked questions when Porchid had given to him, just readied himself for whatever came next despite the pain in his leg. Battered and bloody and bruised, Bjorn now ran along the corridors, following Porchid. His pockets clinked, the stardust, spindle, and Tinker's hand filling them to the brim.

Taking two steps at a time down the stairs, they stumbled into the darkness and Bjorn lit a torchlight. He swung out at a guard, who appeared with a grunt. Bjorn's knife hit the soft spot of his throat and he fell.

Porchid flew ahead as Bjorn did the familiar dance of battle. The pain dulled as his arms reached out in a wide arch, slashing through stomachs like fodder. A step to the left, stab. A duck to the right, another stab.

The guards' shouts were white noise as he forged through them like iron. Two more came for him when the heavy steps of reinforcement echoed in the stairwell. He slashed at the guards in front of him, metal clashing against metal, then dived again and drove the knife upwards, hearing the sick, wet crunch of their bones.

Bjorn grasped the stardust in his pocket, lobbed it through the air, and ran around the curve. He covered his ears as the explosion hit, the floor vibrating underneath him. Screams echoed from above, shouts and warnings, then silence.

Bjorn breathed heavily; his vision blurred. The blood loss was draining him. Despite the adrenaline that came with battle, he knew he couldn't hold on for much longer.

He stumbled as he followed Porchid into the dungeon, a wall of broken stone behind him. Porchid twinkled urgently at the hand, pointing to the fingers then the cell bars lining the prison. Bjorn frowned but followed her directions. Using the knife, he cut off one of the Tinker's fingers and handed it to the fairy. She gagged, then flew towards a cell and touched the fingertip to the iron bars. When it unlocked, he understood.

Bjorn took another finger for himself and followed. Each lock whirled as he touched the Tinker's severed finger to the bars, releasing the hinges in a beautiful wail. Bjorn found Piccadilly first, and the relief and grin on her face were contagious despite the circumstances.

Porchid moved ahead, unlocking cells with a precision and haste even Bjorn found impressive.

Hansel was found next, his body still weak, but he was conscious at least.

'Can you walk?' Piccadilly asked.

Hansel nodded. 'I can walk.'

'Come on, let's find Rumple,' Bjorn said, grimacing at the finger he held. He had no love for the Tinker, but even he found holding severed limbs a little disturbing.

'May as well unlock them all while we're here,' Hansel replied, standing on unsteady feet.

Bjorn unlocked another cell, cautious as he entered. A shadow sat against the far wall and Bjorn whistled at Porchid. The fairy illuminated the room, the finger she'd held long gone.

Shaking his head, Bjorn inched closer. The prisoner lay still in the shadows, a small white cloth covering their body in blood and dust. There was warmth at Bjorn's side as Piccadilly stepped forward.

'Hello?' Bjorn asked, his voice gruff. 'We're here to free you.'

Porchid's light shone against a hollowed face, his eyes blank, his mouth open. He was a husk of a body, as if his lifeforce had been sucked dry.

Piccadilly rushed forward before Bjorn could stop her. 'Commander? Commander, it's – it's Piccadilly. We're here to save you.'

But there was nothing left to save. Whoever the Commander had been, he wasn't the same anymore. Bjorn assessed the condition of the body, the bruised, stiff skin. The scent of rot and decay was rife in the air.

'Leave him,' Bjorn said. 'May the Ever After hold him close.'

'We can't leave him,' she whispered, clutching the stiff hand. 'He's the Commander.'

'No,' Bjorn said, tugging her back. 'He *was* the Commander.'

'I—' she croaked, her eyes watering.

'He is *gone*,' Bjorn said. 'We must move.'

Piccadilly took a deep breath before tearing her gaze away from the body. Bjorn moved with fervour, his body screaming. He hoped that Rumple had come out the other side far better than the Commander.

Bjorn continued to unlock the cells, inspecting every crevice before moving onto the next. Most were empty, but some held the dead, bodies long forgotten, just like the Commander. In one, the prisoner was still alive. His cloak was torn but had clearly been expensive. Bjorn assumed he was a noble, or royalty, but when he'd tried to coax him, the crippled man hadn't moved, his eyes lost to whatever horror he saw inside his head.

In the next cell they came across a hunched body, his ribs clearly visible beneath the skin under ragged, torn clothes. Piccadilly leant down, lifted the prisoner's chin, and turned to Hansel and Bjorn.

'Is this him?' she asked.

Hansel moved slowly, sluggish from the spell. His eyes narrowed and Porchid lit up the prisoner's face. He was beaten and bloody, the swelling shaping him into a beast. Hansel nodded grimly.

'Thank the Godmother,' she said as she picked him up. Voices rang out above, echoing down the stairwell as she clutched Rumple to her chest. Though, the creature didn't move. The stone wall caused from Bjorn's explosion began to shift, rocks falling, as the voices on the other side became clearer.

'Kill on sight.'

Piccadilly swore as she ran, and Bjorn followed close behind. The dungeons were on the lower level, but not entirely underground; windows were etched into the walls, but they were too small to climb through.

Piccadilly halted at a cell. 'Porchid,' she yelled. 'This one.'

'There is no time!' Bjorn hollered, yanking her backwards as guards piled in.

The fairy flew forward and stole the finger Bjorn held, unlocked the cell, and dropped the finger in disgust.

Before Bjorn could move, the dungeons filled with guards, their swords held high. Bjorn shoved the group into the cell.

'Any great ideas left?' Hansel asked in the dark.

'Just one,' said Bjorn.

He had two bottles of stardust left. He took out one vial, popped open the lid, and prayed to the Fairy Godmother before he threw out his arm and let go.

The explosion rocked the ground beneath them as the ceiling fell. Stone collapsed into the corridor in an avalanche, creating another barrier between them and the soldiers.

'Move back,' Bjorn yelled as he popped off the lid of the last bottle. He aimed for the back wall of the cell. If Hansel's map was accurate, this was a way out.

He threw the last bottle with all his might. The wall blew outwards, stone and rock and mortar crumbling like a waterfall. The fairy lanterns from outside broke through the darkness, blinding them momentarily as they shoved themselves towards the exit.

They climbed out of the hole and barely made it twenty steps before Piccadilly stopped. 'I have to free him.'

'Run,' Bjorn hissed, sick of pointing out the obvious.

'I can't,' she urged. 'I promised I'd set him free if he helped.'

'Who?'

'The other prisoner. The one who told me the Tinker was key. It's how Porchid knew to get the hand.'

Bjorn swore and shoved the spindle into her hand. 'I'll do it.'

'Go,' Hansel implored to Piccadilly.

Porchid was unlatching the lanterns and letting the fire fairies go, and the night became darker, Piccadilly gave them a curt nod before running into the dark, starlight blending into the sky.

Hansel and Bjorn turned back to the mess they'd made. Coughing, the two of them made their way back and clambered down, scraping their hands on the slick stone. Bjorn's eyes adjusted to the dark as Hansel followed. The guards were barely audible through the destruction.

Bjorn blinked, dust floating around him like snow. In the corner of the cell, on the hay bales, lay a small body, their pale skin bone-white, on the brink of death.

Their voice was so soft, almost a whisper on the wind. 'By the Godmother.'

Bjorn halted. He'd know that voice anywhere.

The prisoner blinked, familiar eyes meeting Bjorn's gaze.

'Bonyx?' Bjorn gasped.

Bonyx thought he'd imagined the gaping hole that consumed the back wall of his cell. It opened straight onto the castle gardens, the fresh air cold against his skin. He blinked, his old eyes adjusting as the brightness of the lamps seared through him like the Fairy Godmother.

He wasn't sure if he choked or laughed.

If it was delusion, it was one he would gladly stay in. But if it was real …

Shadows crawled across the broken stone. Dust melted in the air, clogging his lungs as he turned towards the strangers. They looked like dark fairies, coming down through the light only to smite him. But he was ready. Ready to stand with death, to take its hand gracefully and whisper his goodbyes.

The dark fairies came upon him, and in the murky light, Bonyx embraced them.

'By the Godmother,' Bonyx whispered.

A familiar voice broke through his haze.

'Bonyx?'

Epilogue

Myrenna had been in darkness her whole life. Now was no different.

The roots strangled her, pulled her deep underground, and leashed her like a wild dog. But Myrenna had never been good at being caged.

She screamed into the dark, the fire within her burning cold as she sunk into the never-ending darkness. She would not be confined. Not again. Never again.

Her magic coiled, ready to strike, the nightkiss already filtering out of her system. It slithered and surged, pressing under her skin like bottled blood. Myrenna grasped it like a buoy thrown out to sea and held tight. She was a huntress. A queen. A monster.

Magic seared her veins, spiralling as she opened her eyes, amethyst blazing into the dark abyss. She was no mere mortal. She was a sorceress. A goddess.

She was stardust. A weapon. A thing to be feared.

The magic blackened inside her, and just as it scorched her skin, she let go.

The ancient tree screamed as she shattered the wooden chains around her, laughing as she released herself from its grip. Roots and soil and wood crashed around her, and she clawed her way out of the earth. Moonlight shone through the open gaps of the covering branches, where the sky sparkled with stars and the moon hung low.

Myrenna cackled as the roots slithered back from her, black poison seeping into them like a disease.

'What are you?' it murmured.

Myrenna tasted its fear and rolled it on her tongue. Coated in blood and dirt, she sneered at the Ancient One's white branches, flashing her white teeth.

'I am death.'

End of book two.

The Cauldron and the Baker's Girl

A SHORT STORY

Once long ago, the kingdom of Aurelia glittered in gold and thrived in trade, its very heart a beating, living thing. Each year, to celebrate their good fortune, the king would throw a grand celebration, full of lights, feasts, and dancing. The kingdom flourished, and with it, its people flourished, too.

Every twelve moons, kings from other lands would come to witness this great affair, trading in riches and gold. The event was the jewel of the kingdom, and it was dubbed the Coronation of Cakes. But the real reason people flocked, was that at the end of the faire, the good king would judge the baking competition and choose a winner who would be draped in wealth and granted one single wish.

Not far away, in the little village of Butterpond, there lived a baker's girl who dreamed as dreamers do and sat near the hearth of a blazing fire. She was not beautiful like the others in her village. Her hair was a dull brown, matching that of her worn dress, forever covered in flour.

She dared not go outside often, for the villagers could be cruel, and beauty held a high price. But they did not see the beauty that she did. Did not see the dreams she held of one day attending the Coronation of Cakes and winning a wish.

She dreamed as dreamers do, with a song in her heart and a vision in her head.

The girl's father was cruel, never recovered from her mother's death. Quick to blame and quicker to judge, he would punish the girl. His fist became his weapon, and his words a cut. He would shout and scream, leaving the girl to weep.

'Plain girls account for plain dreams, for the world is harsh and darker than it seems,' he would say.

Though his words carved the baker's girl like a knife, she still did as dreamers do: she sat by her hearth, with a song in her heart and a vision in her head.

Three more winters passed, and whilst the other girls in the village grew tall in grace and beauty, the baker's girl stayed, obedient to her father's commands. Her skin was more worn than in years passed, her dress more torn, and her family outcast.

She would hear the laughter as the celebration came and went. And as dreamers do, she sat by her hearth, with a song in her heart and a vision in her head.

One winter, a spark ignited within the girl and grew in her heart – for that day, Tomas of Locke had tasted her baked goods and exclaimed, 'My! What a fine taste this has! And what a dear maiden to bake it so!'

The baker's girl was giddy with glee. She travelled home with a kick in her step, but when her father saw her happiness he said, 'Plain girls amount to plain lives; your happiness will die like the stab of ten knives. Obey, you must, and stop being silly. Or I'll throw you away to be dragged by a filly.'

Obedient she was, so obey she did. But, as dreamers do, she sat by her hearth, with a song in her heart and a vision in her head.

Days later, as the baker's girl carried her goods through the village, she saw fair Annabel with Tomas of Locke. Annabel's glowing hair of gold and porcelain skin was a heavy contrast to the baker's girl's freckles and worn hands. But, though Annabel was beautiful, her words were cruel.

'Dull, little girl. Plain little duck. A no-good father without any luck. Dirty little girl. Ugly and alone, get out, get out, this isn't your home.'

When the baker's girl reached her house and all her goods fell from her basket, she stopped to weep. The song had been sung, its sting on her skin. Her dreams seemed a faraway thing.

Tomas of Locke came forth, reached out his hand, and helped the poor baker's girl to her feet. 'I promise you this, you talented girl. Keep on baking, and you'll marry an earl. That apple pie was magic, to not taste a bite would be tragic.'

Relieved by his words, the baker's girl packed up her things. That night, as dreamers do, she sat by her hearth with a song in her heart and a vision in her head.

Her first crushed dream came at noon, when her drunken father found her and crooned, 'Tomas of Locke is a bridegroom to be, Annabel his betrothed, to wed in days three.'

The baker's girl wept by her hearth. And though she had known it an impossible thing, all hope for Tomas of Locke's heart was dashed.

Upon the morning of the wedding, the baker's girl donned her loveliest dress. With a freshly baked cake, the young woman urged her courage to rise. She attended the ceremony, wearing her best. The whole village had come, and it was a grand affair, the bride in white, with flowers embedded into her hair.

But when Annabel found the baker's girl there, she said, 'I will not eat that cake, for she will poison me as Tomas's namesake!'

Tomas stood in stupor, and he turned to the girl, 'You would my poison my love, after everything I have done? Cruel, plain girl, your evil will be undone.'

As the baker's girl wept, her father's words played on her fears, 'Plain little girls do not deserve kings. You will never be loved or amount to a thing.'

That night, whilst her father lay asleep, her heart in shatters, the baker's girl saw the snow melt. Spring had sprung, and with it, the Coronation of Cakes.

It was then the baker's girl no longer wished to obey. Despite her father's words, she packed up her belongings, her dreams a whisper and an echo of longing. The Coronation of Cakes would be her glory, she would live in wealth and have her wish granted. So, during the dark, whilst her father lay snoring, the baker's girl left without any warning.

Upon her arrival in the capital city, she found work to keep her busy. A local baker took her in and worked her to the bone. Though the days and nights were long, the baker's girl smiled to the beat of her own song.

When the celebrations had finally begun, the baker glowed at the taste of her apple pie. And that night, as dreamers do, she sat by her hearth, with a song in her heart and a vision in her head.

But in her happiness, she did not see the baker's jealousy turn dark green, and when the girl slept, the baker poisoned her pie.

The cruelty of her employer unbeknownst, the baker's girl entered the Coronation of Cakes, only for the king to taste her pastry and die.

The crowd hurled curses at her.

'King Killer!'

'Witch!'

'Murderer!'

That day, her heart snapped in two, her dreams broken and shattered. And for the first time, the dreamer no longer did what dreamers do. The song in her heart lay silent, and the vision turned black. And throughout the winter, within the dungeon under the keep, her heart shrivelled each passing day. The baker's girl whispered sweet nothings, the voices of old – her father, and Annabel, and the crowd – a dull ringing inside her head. 'Plain little girls with plain little hearts, with plain little dreams and plain little starts.'

She was due to be hung the following day.

As the sun set, the baker's girl found a needle. In her desperation, she pricked her finger thrice and let three drops fall as she offered a heavy price. 'Sisters Grimm, I call to thee, my blackened heart a raging sea. Power I seek, to avenge my soul; bringing death my dying goal. Plain no more, but with beauty and power, I offer a bargain to avenge my last hour.'

At the drop of her blood, a Grimm appeared, her fingers made of bone and decay.

The Grimm smiled at her cruelly, her teeth almost black. *'Hello, King Killer, your blood has called. Revenge you seek, but my price is tall.'*

Her voice hissed and echoed. The baker's girl wiped her tears, temptation and power and revenge heavy on her tongue.

'For the power and beauty you desperately seek, I require your soul for us to keep. This is an immortal contract of debt, of pain and murder – a prison you'll never forget.'

The crone looked down upon her as she brought the needle to her palm. 'What must I do to bind my soul and gain what I desire most?' the baker's girl asked.

The crone smiled broadly and held out her hands. *'Three hearts my dear, then you'll have all you desire. Blood and pain and all the world's ire.'*

Upon that white-covered night, the baker's girl took the hands of the Grimm and set out to collect her hearts, much to the Grimm's glee.

The first one taken was from her father's chair, a task that could not be undone.

The second heart from Tomas of Locke: a widow, from the birth of his son.

Upon the third she heard its cry and walked to its white-laced cot. Its tiny heart a beating thing. Tomas of Locke's and Annabel's child could grow into beauty and kindness, but in her hate, the baker's girl tore its chest, her rage pulling her into blindness. The song in her heart was silent and the vision turning black.

The Grimm cackled as they watched the baker's girl's soul turn dark, hefty the bounty she was to receive, the girl too far gone to turn back.

The Grimm gave her a looking glass rimmed in gold, as part of the deal. Carved in blood, it sung to the girl, the bargain's final seal.

'Magic breeds magic,' the sister warned. *'Sacrifice is a wound not easily healed. If you continue down this path, your fate will be sealed.'*

But the baker's girl took away her prize and taught herself to wield magic. 'Plain little girls do plain little tasks, but beauty and power is all that I ask.'

With the mirror's power, the girl's eyes turned amethyst, and her hair tumbled down in rich ebony. The girl's skin smoothed out, as milky white as snow, and her blood filled with power.

'Plain little girls have plain little talents, but beauty and power are truly gallant. First comes revenge, then a kingdom and king, then my story will truly begin.'

And so it happened, that under the starlit winter sky, the baker's girl twisted into a great beauty indeed. Filled with revenge and pain and jealousy, she whispered to the mirror, 'A queen of beauty, I will be. No more will I obey another, for my story begins with the name Queen Myrenna.'

In that darkness, as dreamers do, Myrenna sat by her hearth, with a song in her heart and a vision in her head.

The End

Acknowledgements

Where do I even begin?

Writing is a slog for the most part where you wade through sludge only to fight your way to the other side. (Much like our heroes). But writing is also magic.

There's something wondrous about imagining something and having it come alive before your eyes. It fills you with joy and heartache. It pushes your boundaries and dares you to fly.

Most of all, it's an acceptable way for me share all my imaginary friends.

While the drafting process of a book is solo, publishing it is not. So, to start, thank you to everyone who contributed behind the scenes for These Grimm Fates and to those who have been with me since the beginning. Without you, I wouldn't be where I am today or have this version of the book.

Thank you to my brothers Davis and Trent who always helped me believe in magic. Though, Trent is no longer with us, it's him I think of when I write.

Thank you to my sister from another mister, Jess. If you ever wonder how I choose my quotes for the naked hardcover, you have her to thank.

Thank you to my friends who have never put down my writing. You've championed me, supported me and encouraged me when I wanted to give up.

Thank you to my parents, for never saying no to any of my dreams. For saving the newspaper clippings of my poetry as a child and reading to me at night. My love of books is all because of you. Thank you for the stories, for the bookstore visits and for teaching me the value of words.

Thank you to the other parents in the world too who gave this book to their teens and friends and supported a small author. To those who recommended the book and bought it as gifts.

Thank you to my friends and colleagues, who smiled when they saw what I had done and have encouraged me to pursue this dream. Especially, when I broke out on my own and faced the terrifying reality of independent publishing.

Thank you to my partner Jared, who doesn't get as much attention as he deserves when I'm lost in my words. Thank you for always being there to talk it out with me and push me to finish the manuscript. You're my person and I cannot imagine doing this life without you. However, I can't kill everybody though, so we need to veer away from that… I'm not sure the readers would ever forgive me.

Thank you to my incredible beta readers, who are muses in their own right. Who are magic lovers and readers and writers. Mikayla, for being with me in the early days. Jenna, who believed in this series and talked through the ending with me.

To Brianna, for talking books, plot points and sharing all the loves and hates in this series. I'm so privileged we met and though we aren't in the same city, I miss you every day. I wish you the happiest book birthdays with this release!

To Candi, for being the very best person I could have ever met at a London pub. Who knew that more than ten years later we'd be here together? Thank you for doing book swaps, talking reviews and spending every waking hour helping me improve this manuscript to be the best it could be. You've been my soundboard, my crying place and my inspiration.

Thank you Rae and Braidee and Ingrid, for being the author friends I never knew I needed. For gossiping with me, and for teaching me things about publishing I never knew. I cannot thank you enough for the guidance and love.

Thank you to my editor Daniel, for agreeing to stick with me on this journey and for loving this story just as much as I do. You're an absolute gem and I'm lucky to have you.

Thank you to Kathy, for formatting this book into the beautiful thing it is. You're amazing at what you do, not to mention how incredibly patient with me you are.

Thank you to my cat Coco (yes I'm thanking my little lion) for being my writing buddy. There's nothing better than having a thirty second break to pat your fluff and avoid a bite before I get back into the manuscript.

And lastly (but the most important), thank you to my readers. For the reviews, for the liked posts, for the recommendations, for the purchases, for the messages and the championing of this series. Eve's story is nothing without you and I'm excited to follow your journey through the pages of this series.

There's more people I could thank, but if I don't stop now it'll be a whole other book.

So, for now, take my hand, and let's go tear out some hearts.

About the Author

K E Barden is an independent author based in Brisbane. Her first book, The Gilded Mirror was written entirely on a mobile phone and the dent in her pinkie finger proves it. When she isn't writing, you can usually find her spoiling her high maintenance cat, building fairy castles, or comparing her real boyfriend with her book boyfriends.

Her books are a combination of fiction, romance and fantasy with the express intent of stealing you away from reality and creating characters that will become your entire personality.

You can find Kim on social media @ KEBardenAuthor

Authors Note

Thank you for making it this far. I hope you enjoyed These Grimm Fates.

Reviews are the lifeblood of indie authors. Without them, there's a very high chance our books fade into obscurity. If you are enjoying the Finding Ever After series please take the time to leave a review on GoodReads, Amazon, Social Media, or anywhere you want to share.

Thank you, *Kim xx*